THE MARRIAGE CONTRACT

BY
KAT CANTRELL

MILLS & BOON

First Published in Great Britain 2017
By Mills & Boon, an imprint of HarperCollins*Publishers*
1 London Bridge Street, London, SE1 9GF

© 2017 Kat Cantrell

ISBN: 978-0-263-92818-1

51-0517

McKenna pulled back.

But Desmond still had her trapped between his body and the table. Her pulse thundered in her ears as they stared at each other.

"That was…"

"Amazing?" he supplied, his gaze hot. "Yeah. But I'm sensing we're going to stop now."

"See, we communicate just fine." She gulped. "I'm just… not sure this is a good idea."

They were not two people who had the luxury of an uncomplicated fling. They were married with a divorce agreement already hammered out. That was not a recipe for experimentation, and she wasn't much of an experimenter anyway.

Where could this possibly go?

"Oh, it's a good idea." His piercing gaze tore her open inside as he promised her exactly how good it would be without saying a word. "But we both have to think so."

With that, he stepped back, releasing her.

She took a deep breath and nodded. He was being gentlemanly about it, putting all the balls in her court. "I agree. And I don't think that right now."

Her mind didn't, at least. Even if her body did.

* * *

The Marriage Contract
is part of Mills & Boon Desire's No. 1 bestselling series, Billionaires and Babies: Powerful men… wrapped around their babies' little fingers.

USA TODAY bestselling author **Kat Cantrell** read her first Mills & Boon novel in third grade and has been scribbling in notebooks since she learned to spell. She's a Mills & Boon So You Think You Can Write winner and a Romance Writers of America Golden Heart® Award finalist. Kat, her husband and their two boys live in north Texas.

One

Despite never having believed in miracles, Desmond Pierce witnessed one at 7:23 p.m. on an otherwise non-descript Tuesday as he glimpsed his son for the first time.

A nurse in navy blue scrubs carried the mewling infant into the small room off the main hospital corridor where Desmond had been instructed to wait. The moment his gaze lit on the baby, he felt a zap of recognition in his gut.

My son.

Awed into speechlessness, Des reached out to touch the future.

Warmth and something totally foreign clogged his throat. Tears. Joy. Vindication.

Amazing. Who knew money really *could* buy happiness?

The kid's face screwed up in a wail of epic proportions as if the nurse had poked him with a pin. Des felt his son's distress with deeper empathy than he'd ever experienced before—and that was saying something. It winnowed through his pores, sensitizing his muscles almost to the point of pain as he held himself back from snatching the boy from the nurse's arms.

Was this terrible combination of wonder, reverence and absolute terror what it was like for all parents? Or had he been gifted with a special bond because his son wouldn't have a mother?

"How are you this evening, Mr. Pierce?" the nurse inquired pleasantly.

"Regretting the sizable donation I made to this establishment," he growled and immediately bemoaned not taking a moment to search for a more acceptable way to communicate. This, after he'd *vowed* not to be his usual gruff self. "Why is my son crying?"

Better. More in the vein of how he'd practiced in the mirror. But the hard cross of his arms over his chest didn't quell the feeling that something was wrong. The baby hadn't been real these last forty weeks, or rather Des hadn't let himself believe that this pregnancy would end differently than Lacey's.

Now that he'd seen the baby, all the stars aligned. And there was no way in hell he'd let anything happen to his son.

"He's hungry," the nurse returned with a cautious half smile. "Would you like to feed him?"

Yes. He would. But he had to nod as emotion gripped his vocal cords.

An explosion of teddy bears climbed the walls behind the rocking chair the nurse guided him to. A vinyl-sided cabinet with a sink occupied the back corner and the counter was strewed with plastic bottles.

Des had done a lot of research into bottle-feeding, as well as all other aspects of parenting: philosophies of child rearing, behavioral books by renowned specialists, websites with tips for new parents. He'd committed a lot of it to memory easily, largely owing to his excitement and interest in the subject, but then, he held two doctorates from Harvard. There were not many academics that he hadn't mastered. He was pretty sure he could handle a small task like sticking the nipple into the baby's mouth.

Carefully she settled the baby into his arms with a gentle smile. "Here you go, Dad. It's important that you hold him as much as possible."

Des zeroed in on the pink wrinkled face and the entire world fell away. His son weighed nothing at all. Less than a ten-pound barbell. Wonder tore a hole through Desmond's chest as he held his son for the first time. Instantly he cataloged everything his senses could soak in. Dark eyes. Dark hair peeking from under the knit cap.

Conner Clark Pierce. His son.

Whatever it took, he'd move heaven and earth to give this new person everything. Private tutors, trips to educational sites like the pyramids at Giza and Machu Picchu, a workshop that rivaled his father's if he wanted to invent things like Des did. The baby would have every advantage and would never want for anything, let alone a mother.

The nurse pulled the hat down more firmly on the baby's head. That's when Conner started yowling again. The baby's anguish bled through Desmond's skin, and he did not like it.

The nurse turned to the back counter. "Let me make you a bottle."

She measured out the formula over the sound of the baby's cries, which grew more upsetting as the seconds ticked by.

Des had always felt other people's pain deeply, which

was one of the many reasons he avoided crowds, but his response to his son was so much worse than general empathy. This little person shared his DNA, and whether the suggestion of it sharpened the quickening under his skin or there really was a genetic bond, the urgency of the situation could not be overstated.

She finally crossed to Des, where he'd settled into the rocking chair, and handed him the bottle. Like he'd watched in countless videos, he held the nipple to the baby's bottom lip and tipped it.

His son's lower lip trembled as he wailed, but he would not take the bottle. Des would never describe himself as patient, but he tried diligently fourteen more times.

"Why is he refusing?" Des asked the nurse as the sense of something being wrong welled up in his chest again.

"I don't know." She banked the concern in her expression but not before Des saw it. "It's not unusual for babies who are taken from their mothers to have difficulty acclimating. We can try with a dropper. A bottle isn't the only way to get the formula into his body."

Desmond nodded and bit his tongue as the nurse crowded into his space.

The dropper worked. For about five minutes. Then Conner started spitting up all over everything. The nurse frowned again and her expression tingled his spine.

Thirty minutes later, all three of them were frustrated.

"It seems he might have an allergy to formula," the nurse finally announced.

"What does that mean? He's going to starve?" Des shut his eyes in pure agony and scrubbed at his beard, which could probably use trimming but, like usual, he'd forgotten. Sometimes Mrs. Elliot, his housekeeper, reminded him, but only if they crossed paths and, lately, he'd been hiding out in his workshop in preparation for today.

For no reason apparently, since none of his prep had covered this scenario.

"No, we're not going to let that happen. We've got some options…" She trailed off. "Never mind that one. I've been made aware of your wishes regarding your son's mother, so—"

"Forget my wishes and tell me your suggestion. The baby has to eat," Des insisted.

The nurse nodded. "The baby might breast-feed. I mean, this is highly unusual. Typically it's the other way around, where we have to supplement a mother's breast milk with formula until a lactation consultant can work with her, but—"

The baby's wails cut her off.

"She's still here? At the hospital?" He'd never met his son's surrogate mother, as they'd agreed, but he was desperate for a solution.

"Well, yes. Of course. Most women take a couple of days to recover from childbirth but—"

"Take me to her." His mind went to work on how he could have said that better, but distress wasn't the best state for a do-over. "Please."

Relief eased the nurse's expression and she nodded. "Just a warning. She might not be willing to breast-feed."

"I'll convince her," he countered as he stood with the baby in his arms.

His agreement with McKenna Moore, his son's surrogate mother, had loopholes for medical necessities. Plus, she was still legally his wife; they'd married by proxy to avoid any legal snarls, but their relationship was strictly professional. Despite the fact that they had never met, hopefully being married would count for something. The baby had to eat—as soon as Desmond convinced Conner's mother that she was his only hope.

Frankly, asking for her help was a last resort. Their agreement limited Ms. Moore's involvement with the baby because Des wanted a family that was all his own. But he was desperate to look after his son's welfare.

Out into the hall they went. At room 247, the nurse stopped and inclined her head. "Give me a second to see if she's accepting visitors."

Des nodded. The baby had quieted during the walk, which was a blessing. The rocking motion had soothed him most likely. Good information to have at his disposal.

Voices from inside the room drifted out into the hall.

"He wants to what?" The feminine lilt that did not belong to the nurse could only be McKenna Moore's. She was awake and likely decent by this time since the nurse was in the room.

The baby stirred, his little face lifting toward the sound. And that decided it. Conner recognized his mother's voice and, despite the absolute conviction that the best way to handle this surrogacy situation was to never be in the same room with the woman who had given birth to his son, Desmond pushed open the door with his foot and entered.

The dark-haired figure in the hospital bed drew his eye like a siren song and when their gazes met a jolt of recognition buzzed through all his senses at once. The same sort as when he'd glimpsed his son for the first time. *Their* son.

This woman was his child's mother. This woman was his *legally wedded wife*.

McKenna Moore's features were delicate and beautiful and he'd never been so ruthlessly stirred by someone in his life. He couldn't speak, couldn't think, and for a man with a genius IQ, lack of brain function was alarming indeed. As was the sudden, irrevocable conviction that he'd made a terrible mistake in the way he'd structured the surrogacy agreement.

He couldn't help but mourn the lost opportunity to woo this woman, to get to know her. To have the option to get her pregnant the old-fashioned way.

How in the hell had he developed such a visceral attraction to his wife in the space of a few moments?

Didn't matter. He hadn't met her first because he hated to navigate social scenarios. He stumbled over the kinds of relationships that seemed easy and normal for others, which was why he lived in a remote area of Oregon, far from Astoria, the nearest city.

Desmond had always been that weird kid at the corner table. Graduating from high school at fifteen hadn't helped him forge a lot of connections. Neither had becoming a billionaire. If he'd tried to have a normal relationship with McKenna Moore, it would have ended in disaster in the same fashion as the one he'd tried with Lacey.

Bonds of blood, like the one he shared with his son, were the only answer for someone like him. This baby would be his family and fulfill Desmond's craving for an heir. Maybe his son would even love him just because.

Regardless, the baby belonged to *him*. Desmond decided what would happen to his kid and there was no one on this entire planet who could trump his wishes.

Except for maybe his wife.

But he'd paid his law firm over a million dollars to ensure the prenuptial agreement protected his fortune and an already-drafted divorce decree granted him full custody. It was ironclad, or rather, would be as soon as he filed for the divorce.

She'd recover from childbirth, take Desmond's divorce settlement money and vanish. Exactly as he'd envisioned when he'd determined the only thing that could fill the gaping hole in his life was a baby to replace the one he'd lost—or rather, the one Lacey had aborted.

Never again would he allow a woman to dictate something as critical as to whether his child would live or die. And never again would he let himself care about a woman who held even a smidgen of power over his happiness. One day, his son would understand.

"Ms. Moore," he finally growled out long past the time when it would have been appropriate to start speaking. "We have a problem. Our son needs you."

Desmond Pierce stood in McKenna's hospital room. With a crying baby.

Her baby.

The one she'd been trying really hard to forget she'd just pushed out of her body in what had to be the world's record for painful, difficult labors…and then given away.

McKenna's eyes widened as she registered what he'd just said and her eye sockets were so dry, even that hurt. Everything hurt. She wanted codeine and to sleep for three days, not a continual spike through her heart with each new cry of the baby. The muscles in her arms tensed to reach for her son so she could touch him.

She wasn't supposed to see the baby. Or hold him. The nurse had told her that when they'd taken him away, even though McKenna had begged for the chance to say goodbye. The cruel people in the delivery room had ignored her. What did they know about sacrifice? About big, gaping holes inside that nothing would ever fill?

For a second she'd thought her son's father had figured that out. That he'd come strictly to grant her wish. The look on his face as he'd come through the door—it had floored her. Their gazes connected and it was as if he could see all her angst and last-minute indecision. And understood.

I've come to fix everything, he seemed to say without a word.

But that was not the reality of why Mr. Pierce was here with the baby. Instead he was here to rip her heart to shreds. Again.

They should leave. Right now. Before she started crying.

"He's not my son," she rasped, her vocal cords still strained from the trauma of birth.

She shouldn't have said that. The phrase—both true and brutal—unfolded inside her with sharp teeth, tearing at her just as deeply as the baby's cries.

He *was* her son. The one she'd signed away because it ticked all the boxes in her head that her parents had lined up. *You should find a man, have lots of babies*, they'd said. *There's no greater joy than children.*

Except she didn't want kids. She wanted to be a doctor, to help people in pain and in need. Desmond had yearned for a baby; she could give him one and experience pregnancy without caving in to her parent's pressure. They didn't approve of western medicine. It was a huge source of conflict, especially after Grandfather had died when homeopathic remedies had failed to cure his cancer.

Being Desmond Pierce's surrogate allowed her a creative way to satisfy her parents and still contribute to society according to what made sense to *her*. That's what she'd repeated to herself over and over for the last hour and she'd almost believed it—until a man had burst into her hospital room with a crying baby in his arms.

And he was looking at her so strangely that she felt compelled to prompt him. "What do you want, Desmond?"

They'd never been formally introduced, but the baby was a dead giveaway. Desmond Pierce didn't look anything like the pictures she'd searched on the internet. Of course she'd had a better-than-average dose of curiosity about the man with such strict ideas about the surrogacy arrangement, the man who would marry her without meeting her.

But this man—he made tall, dark and handsome seem banal. He was *fascinating*, with a scruff of a beard that gave him a dangerous edge, deep brown hair swept back from his face and a wiry build.

Desmond Pierce was the perfect man to be a father or she wouldn't have agreed to his proposal. What she hadn't realized was that he was a perfect man, *period*. Coupled with the baby in his arms, he might well be the most devastatingly handsome male on the planet.

And then she realized. He wasn't just a man. They were married. He was *her husband*. Whom she was never supposed to meet.

"The baby won't eat," he said over the yowls. "You need to try to breast-feed him."

She blinked. Twice. "I need to do what?"

"The nurse said he's allergic to formula. We've tried for an hour." He moved closer to the bed with a purposeful stride that brooked no nonsense and held out the wailing bundle. "He needs you. This is the one thing I cannot give him."

She stared at the wrinkled face of her child, refusing to reach out, refusing to let the wash of emotions beating through her chest take hold. The baby needed her and she was the sole person who could help. But how could she? Breast-feeding was far too nurturing of a thing to do with a baby she wasn't allowed to keep.

How dare Desmond come in here and layer on more impossible emotional turmoil in the middle of her already-chaotic heart?

She'd done her part according to their agreement. The baby was born, healthy and the child was set for life with a billionaire father who wanted him badly enough to seek out an unusual surrogacy agreement and who had the means to take care of him. What more could Desmond Pierce possibly expect from her? Did he want to slice off a piece of her soul when he took her baby away for the second time?

"That's too much to ask," she whispered even as her breasts tingled at the suggestion. They'd grown hard and heavy the moment the baby had entered the room crying. It was simple physiology and she'd known she'd have to let her milk dry up. Had been prepared for it.

What she had not been prepared for was the request to use it to feed her son.

Desmond's brows came together. "You're concerned about your figure?"

That shouldn't have been so funny. "Yeah, I'm entering the Miss USA pageant next week and how I'll look in a bikini is definitely my biggest objection."

"That's sarcasm, right?"

The fact that he had to ask struck her oddly, but before she could comment, he stuck the baby right into her arms. Against her will, her muscles shifted, cradling the baby to her bosom, and she was lost. As he must have known. As the nurse had known.

She shouldn't be holding the baby, but she was, and it

was too late to stop the thunder of her pulse as it pumped awe and love and duty and shock straight to her heart.

My son.

He still cried, his face rooting against her breast, and it was clear what he wanted. She just hadn't realized how deeply her desire to give it to him would ultimately go.

"There's a clause in the custody agreement about the baby's medical needs," Desmond reminded her. "You're on the hook for eighteen years if he needs you for medical reasons."

"Yeah, but I thought that would only be invoked if he needed a kidney or something," she blurted as the baby's little fingers worked blindly against her chest. "Not breast-feeding."

She *couldn't*. Judging by how badly she wanted to, if she did this, it would be so much harder to walk away. It wasn't fair of Desmond to ask. She was supposed to go back to Portland, register for school. Become a doctor like she'd dreamed about for over a decade. That's how she'd help people. This evisceration Desmond Pierce wanted to perform wasn't part of the plan.

"He might still need a kidney, too." Desmond shrugged. "Such is the nature of sharing DNA with another human."

Did he really not get the emotional quandary she was in? All of this must be so easy for him. After all, he was man, and rich besides—all he had to do was snap his fingers to make the world do his bidding. "You know breast-feeding isn't a one-time thing, right? You have to repeat it."

In the tight-knit community her parents belonged to, they raised babies as a village. She'd watched mothers commit to being a baby's sole food source twenty-four hours a day for months. Some women had trouble with breast-feeding. He acted like she could just pop out a breast and everything would be peachy.

"Yes, but once we find an alternative, you can walk away. Until then, our agreement means you have a commitment to his medical needs." He crossed his arms. "There is literally nothing I would not do to help my child. He needs you. Three months, at least. You can live with me, have your own room. Use a breast pump if you like. You want extra compensation added to the settlement? Name your price."

As if she could put a price on the maternal instincts that warred with her conviction that whatever decision she made here would have lasting impacts that neither of them could foresee. "I don't want extra compensation! I want—"

Nothing except what he'd already promised her. A divorce settlement that would pay for medical school and the knowledge that she'd helped him create the family he wanted. It felt so cold all at once. But what was she supposed to do instead? She rarely dated, not after three years with a ho-hum high school boyfriend and a pregnancy scare at nineteen, which was why she refused to go out with one of the men her parents were constantly throwing at her. Dating wasn't worth the possibility of an accidental pregnancy.

She couldn't be a mom and a doctor. Both required commitment, an exhaustive number of hours. So she'd chosen long ago which path worked for her. Because she was selfish, according to her mother, throwing away her parents' teaching about natural remedies as if their beliefs didn't matter.

So here was her chance to be unselfish for once. She could breast-feed for three months, wean the baby as he grew out of his formula allergy and go back to Portland for the spring semester. It was only a small addition to what had already been a year-long delay.

She'd wanted to experience pregnancy to better empathize with her patients. Why not experience breast-feeding for the same reason? She could use a pump if the baby had trouble latching on, just like any new mother. No one had to know that it was going to kill her to give up the baby a second time after she'd fallen the rest of the way in love with him.

She glanced up at Desmond, who was watching her hold the baby with an expression she couldn't interpret. "I'll do it. But you can't stay in the room."

His expression didn't change. "I beg to differ. He's my son."

Great, so now he was going to watch. But she could still dictate her own terms. "Can you at least call the nurse back so I can make sure I'm doing it right?"

Instead of forcing her to push the call button, he nodded and disappeared into the hall, giving her a blessed few moments alone. The hospital gown had slits for exactly this purpose so it was easy to maneuver the baby's face to her aching breast. His cries had quieted to heartbreaking mewls, and his eyes were closed, but his mouth worked the closer she guided him toward her nipple. And then all at once, he popped on like a champ and started sucking.

She was doing it. *He* was doing it.

Entranced, she watched her son take his first meal on this planet and it was almost holy. Her body flooded with a sense of rightness and awe. An eternity passed and a small sound caused her to glance up. Desmond had returned with the nurse, but he was just watching her quietly with far more tenderness than she would have expected.

"Looks like you're a natural, hon," the nurse said encouragingly and smiled. "In a few minutes, you can switch sides. Do you want me to stay?"

"I think I'm okay."

Really, fetching the nurse had been an excuse to get Desmond out of the room. Women had been doing this for centuries, including those of her parents' community who were strong advocates for removing the stigma of public breast-feeding. She wasn't a frail fraidy-cat.

The nurse left. Now that the baby was quiet, she felt Desmond's presence a whole lot more than she had before, like an extra weight had settled around her shoulders. He was so…everything. Intense. Focused. Gorgeous. Unsettling. Every time she glanced at him, it did something funny to her stomach and she'd had enough new sensations for the day, thanks.

Instead she watched the baby eat in silence until she couldn't stand it any longer.

"What did you name him?" Her voice was husky and drew Desmond's attention.

He cocked his head, his gaze traveling over her in a way that made her twitchy. "Conner. His middle name is Clark, after your father."

That speared her right through the heart. She'd had no idea he'd do something to honor his son's maternal heritage, and it struck her as personal in a way that dug under her skin. If all had gone according to plan, she'd never have met Desmond, never have known what he'd called the baby. She wouldn't have looked them up or contacted either of them. Also according to their agreement.

Now it was all backward and upside-down because this was their son. And Desmond Pierce was her husband. She'd just agreed to go home with him. How was that going to work? Would he expect to exercise his husbandly duties?

That thought flittered through her stomach in a way that wasn't difficult to interpret at all. Dear God. She was *attracted* to her husband. And she'd take that secret to the grave.

Mortified, she switched breasts under Desmond's watchful eye, figuring that if she would be living with him, he'd see her feeding the baby plenty of times. Besides, there was nothing shameful about a woman's body in the act of providing nourishment for her son. Somehow, though, Desmond made the whole thing seem intimate and heavy with implication, as if they were a real family and he was there to support his child's mother.

Desmond pursed his lips, still surveying her as if trying to figure something out. "Have we met before?"

Her pulse leaped. "No. Of course not. You wanted everything done through your agent."

Mr. Lively had been anything but. He was about a hundred and twenty years old and spoke slower than a tortoise on Valium. Anytime he'd contacted her about paperwork or medical records, she'd mentally blocked off four hours because that's generally how long the session lasted. Except for when she'd gone with him to the courthouse to complete the marriage by proxy, which had taken all day.

Suddenly she wished they'd done this surrogacy arrangement a different way. But marriage had been the easiest way to avoid legal issues. The divorce settlement, which she'd use to pay for school, was a normal agreement between couples with Desmond's kind of wealth. Otherwise someone could argue Desmond had paid for a baby and no one wanted that legal hassle.

She hadn't minded being technically married when it

was just a piece of paper. Meeting Desmond, being near enough to hear him breathe, changed everything. It felt bigger than a signature on an official document.

"You seem familiar." He shook his head as if clearing it. "It's been a long day."

"You don't say," she said, letting the irony drip from her tone. "I've been here since 3:00 a.m."

"Really?" This seemed to intrigue him.

"Yeah, it's not a drive-through. I was in labor for something like fifteen hours."

"Is that normal?"

She sighed and tried to shift her position without disturbing the baby. "I don't know. This is my first rodeo."

"I'm being insensitive."

Nothing like calling a spade a spade, which McKenna appreciated enough to give him a break. "I'm sure we'll get to know each other soon enough."

Somehow she'd managed to startle him. "Will we?"

"Well, sure, if we're living in the same house."

And she could secretly admit to a curiosity about him that she'd have every right to satisfy if they were in close quarters. There was a certain amount of protection in the fact that her time with him had predefined boundaries. The last thing she needed was additional entanglements that kept her from fulfilling her dreams. "But only for three months, right?"

"We'll do our best to keep it to three months," he said with a sharp nod, but she had the distinct impression he hadn't considered that inviting her to live in his house meant they'd be around each other. What exactly had she signed up for?

It didn't matter. All that mattered was that he'd given her three months with her son that she was pathetically grateful for. It was like a gift, a chance to know him before he grew old enough to remember her, to miss her. A chance to revel in all these newfound maternal instincts and then leave before they grew too strong. She was going to be a doctor, thanks to Desmond Pierce, and she couldn't let his monkey wrench change that.

Two

The house Desmond had lived in for the last ten years was not big enough. Twenty thousand square feet shouldn't feel so closed in. But with McKenna Moore inside his walls, everything shrank.

He'd never brought a woman home to live. Sure, Lacey had stayed over occasionally when they were dating, but her exit was always prearranged. And then she'd forever snuffed out his ability to trust a woman as easily as she'd snuffed out the life of their "accident," as she'd termed it. The baby had been unplanned, definitely, since their relationship hadn't been all that serious, but he'd had no idea how much he'd want the baby until it was too late. He'd always made sure there was a light at the end of the tunnel when it came to his interaction with women after that.

There was no light where his baby's mother was concerned. She'd brought her feminine scent and shiny dark hair into his house and put a stamp of permanence all over everything.

Did she know that he'd made a huge concession when he'd asked her to stay with him? This was his domain, his sanctuary, and he'd let her invade it, sucking up all the space while she was at it. Only for Conner would he have done this.

This, of course, looked an awful lot like he was hiding in his workshop. But he couldn't be in the main part of the house and walk around with the semi-erection McKenna gave him by simply laughing. Or looking at him. Or breathing. It was absurd. He'd been around women before. Gorgeous women who liked his money enough to put up with his idiosyncrasies. None of them had ever invoked such a driving need.

He tried to pretend he was simply working. After all, he often holed up in his workshop for days until Mrs. Elliot reminded him that he couldn't live on the Red Bull and Snickers that he kept in the corner refrigerator.

But there was a difference between hiding and holing up and he wasn't confused about which one he was doing. Apparently he was the only one who was clear on it, though, because the next time he glanced up from the robot hand he was rewiring, there *she* stood.

"Busy?" she called in her husky voice that hit with a solid *thwang* he felt in his gut.

"Ms. Moore," he muttered in acknowledgment. "This is my workshop."

"I know." Her brows quirked as she glanced around with unveiled curiosity. "Mrs. Elliot told me this was where I could find you. Also, we share a child. I think it's okay if you call me McKenna."

But she clearly didn't know "workshop" equaled off-limits, private, no girls allowed. He should post a sign.

"McKenna, then." He shouldn't be talking to her. Encouraging her. But he couldn't stop looking at her. She was gorgeous in a fierce, elemental way that coursed through him every time he got anywhere near her.

And when he stumbled over her breast-feeding? God, that was the worst. Or the best, depending on your viewpoint.

She was at her sexiest when she was nurturing their child. If he'd known he'd suddenly be ten times more drawn to her when she exuded all that maternal radiance, he'd never have invited her to live here.

Of course, he hadn't really had much of a choice there, had he?

Obviously hiding out wasn't the answer. Like always, raw need welled up as he watched her explore his workshop, peering into bins and tracing the lines of the hand-drawn gears posted to a light board near the south wall.

"This is a very impressive setup," she commented as she finished a round of his cavernous workspace.

Her gaze zipped to the two generators housed at the back and then lit on him as he stood behind the enormous workstation spread out over a mobile desk on wheels where he did all of his computation. He'd built the computer himself from components and there wasn't another like it in the world.

"It's where I make stuff," he told her simply because there was no way to explain that this was where he brought to life the contents of his brain. He saw something in his head then he built it. He'd been doing that since he was four. Now he got paid millions and millions of dollars for each and every design, which he only cared about because it enabled him to keep doing it.

"I can see that. It's kind of sexy. Very Dr. Frankenstein."

Had she just called him sexy? In the same breath as comparing him to *Frankenstein*? "Uh...I've always thought of myself as more like Iron Man."

She laughed. "Except Tony Stark is a lot more personable and dresses better."

Desmond glanced down at his slacks. "What's wrong with the way I dress?"

Certainly that was the only part of her assessment he could disagree with—he was by no stretch personable and Iron Man did have a certain flair that Desmond could never claim.

"Nothing," she shot back with a grin. "You just don't look like a billionaire playboy who does weapons deals with shady Middle Eastern figures. Frankenstein, on the other hand, was a doctor like you and all he wanted to do was build something meaningful out of the pieces he had available."

She picked up the robot hand he'd been about to solder for emphasis.

Speechless, he stared at her slender fingers wrapped around his creation-in-progress and tried like hell to figure out how she'd tapped into his psyche so easily. Fascinating. So few people thought of him as a doctor. He didn't even see himself as one, despite the fact that he could stick *PhD* after his name all day long if he wanted to.

What else did she see when she looked at him? That same recognition he'd felt, as if they'd met in a former life and their connection had been so strong it transcended flesh and bone?

Or would that sound as crazy to her as it did in his head?

"I wasn't aware I was so transparent," he said gruffly, a little shocked that he didn't totally hate it. "Did you want something?"

Her dark eyes were so expressive he could practically read her like a book. He rarely bothered to study people anymore. Once, that had been the only way he could connect with others, by surreptitiously observing them until everything was properly cataloged.

All it had ever gotten him was an acute sense of isolation and an understanding that people stayed away from him because they didn't like how his brain worked.

She shrugged. "I was bored. Larissa is putting Conner to bed and it turns out that having a nanny around means that once I feed him, I'm pretty much done. I haven't seen you in, like, a week."

McKenna, apparently, had no such aversion to Desmond. She'd sought him out. So he could entertain her. That was a first.

"I had no idea you'd mark my absence in such a way."

Lame. He was out of practice talking to people, let alone one who tied his brain in a Gordian knot of puzzling reactions.

But he wanted to untangle that knot. Very badly.

"Are you always so formal?" McKenna came around the long table to his side and peered over his shoulder at the monitor where he had a drawing of the robot hand spinning in 3-D. "Wow. That's pretty cool."

"It's just a… No, I'm not—" He sucked in a breath as her torso grazed his back. His pulse roared into overdrive and he experienced a purely primal reaction to her that had no place between two people who shared a son and nothing else. "Formal."

"Hmm? Oh, yeah, you are. You remind me of my statistics professor."

"You took a statistics class?" Okay, they shared that, too. But that was it. They had nothing else in common and he had no reason to be imagining her reaction if he kissed her.

"Have to. It's a requirement for premeds."

"Can you not stand there?"

Her scent was bleeding through his senses and it was thoroughly disrupting his brain waves. Of course the real problem was that he liked her exactly where she was.

"Where? Behind you?" She punched him on the shoulder like they were drinking buddies and she'd just told him a joke. "I can't be in front of you. There's a whole lot of electronic equipment in my way."

"You talk a lot."

She laughed. "Only because you're talking back. Isn't that how it works?"

For the second time she'd rendered him speechless. Yeah. He *was* talking back. The two conversations he'd had with her to date, the one at the hospital and this one, marked the longest he'd had with anyone in a while. Probably since Lacey.

He needed someone to draw him out, or he stayed stuck in his head, designing, building, imagining, dreaming. It was a lot safer for everyone that way, so of course that was his default.

McKenna seemed unacquainted with the term *boundaries*. And he didn't hate that.

He should. He should be escorting her out of his workshop and back to the main part of the house. There was an indoor pool that stayed precisely the same temperature year-round. A recreational room that he'd had built the moment Mr. Lively called to say McKenna had conceived during the first round of insemination. Desmond had filled the room with a pool table, darts, video game consoles and whatever else the decorator had recommended. Surely his child's mother could find some amusement there.

"Tell me what you're building," she commanded with a fair enough amount of curiosity that he told her.

"It's a prototype for a robotic humanoid."

"A robot?" Clearly intrigued, she leaned over the hand, oblivious to the way her hair fell in a long, dark sheet over her shoulder. It was so beautiful that he almost reached out to touch it.

He didn't. That would invite intimacies he absolutely wanted with a bone-deep desire but hadn't fully yet analyzed. Until he understood this visceral need, he couldn't act on it. Too dangerous. It gave her too much power.

"No." He cleared his throat and scrubbed at his beard, which he still hadn't trimmed. "A robot is anything mechanical that can be programmed. A robotic humanoid resembles a person both in appearance and function but with a mechanical skeleton and artificial intelligence."

It was a common misconception that he corrected often, especially when he had to give a presentation about his designs to the manufacturers who bought his patents.

"You *are* Dr. Frankenstein," she said with raised eyebrows. "When you get it to work, do you shout 'It's alive!' or just do a little victory dance?"

"I, um…"

She'd turned to face him, crossing her arms under her breasts that he logically knew were engorged from childbirth, though that didn't seem to stop his imagination from calling up what they looked like: expanses of beautiful flesh topped by hard, dusky nipples. McKenna had miles of skin that Des wanted to put his hands on.

What was it about her that called to him so deeply?

"I'm just teasing you." Her eyes twinkled. "I actually couldn't imagine you doing either one."

A smile spread across his face before he could stop it. "I can dance."

"Ha, you're totally lying."

"I can dance," he repeated. "Just not to music."

He fell into her rich, dark eyes and he reached out to snag a lock of her hair, fingering the silky softness before he fully realized that he'd given in to the impulse. The moment grew tense. Aware. So thick, he couldn't have cut it with a laser.

"I should…go," she murmured and blinked, unwinding the spell. "I didn't mean to interrupt."

The lock of hair fell from his fingers as the mood shattered. Fortunately her exodus was quick enough that she didn't get to witness how well she'd bobbled his composure.

He'd have sworn there was an answering echo of attraction and heat in her gaze.

He wasn't any closer to unraveling the mysteries lurking inside her, but he did know one thing. McKenna Moore had taken his seed into her womb and created a miracle through artificial insemination.

What had once felt practical now felt like a mistake. One he couldn't rectify.

But how could he have known he'd take one look at her and wish he'd impregnated her by making love over and over and over until she'd conceived?

Madness. *Build something and forget all of this fatalistic nonsense.*

Women were treacherous under the best of circumstances and McKenna Moore was no different. She just had a unique wrapper that rendered Des stupid, apparently.

Of course the most expedient way to nip this attraction in the bud would be to tell her how badly he'd wanted to thread all of his fingers through her hair and kiss her until her clothes melted off. She'd be mortified and finally figure out that she should be running away from Desmond Pierce. That would be that.

McKenna fled Desmond's workshop, her pulse still pounding in her throat.

What the hell had just happened? One minute she was trying to forge a friendship with the world's most reclusive billionaire and the next he had her hair draped across his hand.

She could still feel the tug as his fingers lifted the strands. The look on his face had been enthralled, as if he'd unexpectedly found gold. She hadn't been around the block very many times, a testament to how long she'd been with James, her high school boyfriend, not to mention the years of difficult undergraduate course work that hadn't allowed for much time to date. But she knew when a man was thinking about kissing her, and that's exactly what had been on Desmond's mind.

That would be a huge mistake.

She needed to walk out of this house in three months unencumbered, emotionally and physically, and Desmond was dangerous. He held all the cards in this scenario and if she wanted to dedicate her life to medicine, she had to be careful. What would happen if she accidentally got pregnant again? More delays. More agonizing decisions and, frankly, she didn't have enough willpower left to deal with those kinds of consequences.

And what made her near mistake even worse was that she'd almost forgotten why she was there. She'd fallen into borderline flirting that was nothing like how she usually was with men. But Desmond was darkly mysterious and intriguing in a way she found sexy, totally against her will. They shared an almost mystical connection, one she'd never felt before, and it was as scary as it was fascinating.

Okay. Seeking him out had been an error in judgment. Obviously. But they never crossed paths and she was starting to wonder if she'd imagined that she'd come home from the hospital with a man. It only made sense that she should be on friendly terms with her baby's father.

Why that made sense, she couldn't remember all at once. Desmond didn't want a mother for his son. Just a chuck wagon. Once she helped Conner wean, she'd finally be on track to get her medical degree after six arduous years as an undergrad and one grueling year spent prepping her body to get pregnant, being pregnant and then giving birth.

In a house this size, there was literally no reason she ever had to see Desmond again. She'd managed to settle in and live here for over a week without so much as a glimpse until she'd sought him out in his workshop.

Her days fell into a rhythm that didn't suck. Mrs. Elliot fed her and provided companionable but neutral conversation when McKenna prompted her. Clothes magically appeared cleaned and pressed in McKenna's closet. Twice a week, her beautifully decorated bedroom and the adjoining bathroom were unobtrusively cleaned. All in all, she was drowning in luxury. And she wouldn't apologize for enjoying it.

To shed the baby weight that had settled around her hips and stomach, she'd started swimming in the pool a couple of hours a day. Before she'd gotten pregnant, she'd jogged. But there were no trails through the heavy forest of hemlocks and maples that surrounded this gothic mansion perched at the edge of the Columbia River. Even if she found a place to run, her enormous breasts hurt when she did something overly taxing, like breathing and thinking. She could only imagine how painful it would be to jog three miles.

The pool was amazing, huge and landscaped with all sorts of indoor plants that made her feel like she was at a tropical oasis on another continent instead of in northwest Oregon where she'd spent the whole of her life. A glass ceiling let in light but there were no windows to break the illusion. She could swim uninterrupted for as long as she liked. It was heavenly.

Until she emerged from the water one day and wiped her face to see Desmond sitting on one of the lounge chairs, quietly watching her. She hadn't seen him since the workshop incident a week ago that might have been an almost kiss.

"Hey," she called, mystified why her pulse leaped into overdrive the second her senses registered his presence. "Been here long?"

"Long enough," he said cryptically, his smooth voice echoing in the cavernous pool area. "Am I disturbing you?"

He'd sought her out, clearly, since he wasn't dressed for swimming and wore an expectant expression.

So she lied. "Of course not."

In reality he did disturb her. A lot. His eyes matched his name, piercing her to the bone when he looked at her, and she didn't like how shivery and goose-pimply he turned her mostly bare skin. There was something about him she couldn't put her finger on, but the man had more shadows than a graveyard. She could see them flitting around in his expression, in his demeanor, as if they weighed him down.

Until he smiled. And thank God he didn't do that more

often, because he went from sexy in an abstract way to holy-crap hot.

So she'd do everything in her power to not make him smile for however long he planned to grace her with his presence. Hopefully that would only be a few minutes. If she'd known he was going to make an appearance, she'd have brought something to cover her wet swimsuit, like a full suit of armor made of inch-thick chain mail.

The way he was looking at her made her feel exposed.

She settled for a towel, draping it around her torso like a makeshift toga, which at least covered her pointy nipples, and sat on the next lounge chair, facing him.

Desmond was wearing a white button-down shirt today, with the sleeves rolled to his forearms and, despite teasing him the other day about his fashion sense, he had such a strange, magnetic aura that she scarcely noticed anything extraneous like clothes. All she saw was him.

"Are you settling in okay?" he asked.

She had the sense the question wasn't small talk. "Sure. What's not to like?"

His eyebrows quirked. "The fact that you're here in the first place."

"You're making it worth my while, remember?"

That shouldn't have come out so sarcastically. After all, she'd been the one to shake her head at monetary compensation, which he'd likely have readily ponied up.

But he was making her twitchy with his shadowy gaze. After visiting his workshop, she'd looked up the things he'd invented and his mind was definitely not like other people's. Innovation after innovation in the areas of robotics and machinery had spilled onto her screen along with published papers full of his endless theoretical ideas.

She was not a stupid person by any stretch, having graduated with a bachelor's degree in biology and a 3.5

grade point average, but Desmond Pierce existed on another plane. And that made him thoroughly out of reach to mere mortals like her.

But he was still oh, so intriguing. And they were married. Funny how that had become front and center in her mind all at once.

He nodded. "I'm sorry my request has delayed your own plans."

Clearly he didn't get offended by her jokes that weren't funny. That was a good thing.

"I have my whole life to be a doctor. Conner will only be a newborn for this small stretch of time."

It was a huge concession, and she had her own reasons for being there, none of which she planned to share with Conner's father. But her pathetic gratefulness for this time with her son wouldn't go away, no matter how hard she tried to think of breast-feeding as a task instead of the bonding experience it was proving to be.

Conner would not be her son legally once Desmond filed the divorce decree that spelled out the custody arrangement—she'd give up all rights. Period. End of story. She hated how often she had to remind herself of that. She was already dreading the inevitable goodbye that would be here long before she wished.

"That's true. I do appreciate your willingness, regardless."

"Is that the only reason you popped in here? To thank me?" She flashed a grin before thinking better of it. They weren't friends hanging out, even though it seemed too easy to forget that. "I would have taken a text message."

"I despise text messages."

"Really?" Curiously, she eyed him. "Electronic communication seems like it would be right up your alley."

He shifted uncomfortably, breaking eye contact. "Why, because I'm not as verbally equipped as others?"

"Please." She snorted before realizing he was serious. "There's nothing about you that's ill equipped. I meant because you're the Frankenstein of electronics."

Thoughtfully, he absorbed that comment and she could see it pinging around in his brain, looking for a place to land. Then he shrugged. "I don't like text messages because they're intrusive and distracting, forcing me to respond."

"You can ignore them if you want," she advised and bit back another smile. Sometimes he was so cute. "There's no rule."

"There is. It's like a social contract I have to fulfill. The message sits there and blinks and blinks until I read it. And then I know exactly who is sitting on the other end waiting on me to complete the transaction. I can't just let that go." His brows came together. "That's why I don't give people my cell phone number."

"I have your cell phone number."

"You're not people."

She couldn't help it. She laughed. And that apparently gave him permission to smile, which was so gorgeous she had a purely physical reaction to it. Somehow he must have picked up on the sharp tug through her insides because the vibe between them got very heavy, very fast.

Mesmerized, she stared at him as the smiles slipped off both their faces.

Why was she so attracted to him? He wasn't her type. Actually she didn't have a type because she'd spent the last six years working her ass off to earn a four-year degree, putting herself through college with as many flexible retail and restaurant jobs as she could score. She couldn't do the same for medical school, not unless she wanted to be fifty when she graduated.

She had to remember that this man held the keys to her future and to keep her wits about her.

Desmond cleared his throat and the moment faded. "I didn't seek you out to talk about text messages. I wanted to let you know that Larissa has resigned her position. Effective immediately."

"The nanny quit?" That sucked. She'd liked Larissa and had thoroughly approved of Desmond's choice. "And with no notice? Nice. Did she at least give you a reason?"

"Her mother had a stroke. She felt compelled to be the one managing her mother's care."

"Well, okay. That gets a pass."

Unexpectedly, McKenna's eyelids pricked in sympathy as she imagined her own mother in a similar circumstance, lifeless and hooked up to machines as the doctors performed analysis to determine the extent of the brain damage the stroke had caused. Of course, her mother would have refused to be cared for in a real hospital, stubborn to the end, even if it led to her own grave. Like it had for Grandfather, who had shared the beliefs of their community.

McKenna was the outcast who put her faith in science and technology.

"She did the right thing," McKenna said. "Have you started the process of hiring a replacement?"

"I have. I contacted the service I used to find Larissa and they're sending me the résumés of some candidates. I'd hoped you'd review them with me."

"Me?" Oh, God. He wanted her to help him pick the woman who would essentially raise her child? How could she do that?

A thousand emotions flew through her at once as Desmond nodded.

"It would be helpful if you would, yes," he said, oblivious to her shock and disquiet.

"You did fine the first time without me," she squawked and cleared her throat. "You don't need my help."

"The first time I had nine months to select the right person for the job," he countered. "I have one day this time. And I trust your judgment."

"You do?" That set her back so much that she sagged against the weave of the lounge chair.

"Of course. You're intelligent, or you wouldn't have been accepted into medical school, and you have a unique ability to understand people."

She frowned. "I do not. Mostly I piss people off."

Her mouth was far too fast to express exactly what was on her mind, and she did not suffer fools easily. Neither made her very popular with men, which was fine by her. Men were just roadblocks she did not have time for.

Desmond cocked his head in the way she'd come to realize meant he was processing what she'd just said. "You don't make me mad."

"That's because I like you," she muttered before thinking through how that might come across. Case in point. Her mouth often operated independently of her brain.

His expression closed in, dropping shadows between them again. "That will change soon enough. I'm not easy to get along with, nor should you try. There's a reason I asked you to be my son's surrogate."

She should let it go. The shadows weren't her business and he'd pretty much just told her to back off. But the mystery of Desmond Pierce had caught her by the throat and she couldn't stop herself from asking since he'd brought up the subject.

"Why *did* you ask me?"

Surely a rich, good-looking guy could have women crawling out of the woodwork to be his baby mama with the snap of his fingers. Obviously that wasn't what he'd wanted.

Coolly, he surveyed her. "Because I dislike not having control. Our agreement means you have no rights and no ability to affect what happens to Conner."

"But I do," she countered quietly. "You put me in exactly that position by asking me to breast-feed him. I could walk away tomorrow and it would be devastating for you both."

"Yes. It is an unfortunate paradox. But it should give you an idea how greatly I care about my son that I am willing to make such a concession. I didn't do it lightly."

Geez. His jaw was like granite and she had an inkling why he considered himself difficult to get along with. Desmond didn't want a mother for his son because he wasn't much of a sharer.

Good to know. Domineering geniuses weren't her cup of tea. "Well, we have no problems, then. I'm not interested in pulling the parental rug out from under you. I'm helping you out because I'm the only one who can, but I'm really looking forward to medical school."

This time with Conner and Desmond was just a detour. It had to be, no matter how deep her son might sink his emotional hooks.

Desmond nodded. "That is why I picked you. Mr. Lively did a thorough screening of all the potential surrogates and your drive to help people put you head and shoulders above the rest. Your principles are your most attractive quality."

Um...what? She blinked, but the sincerity in his expression didn't change. Had he just called her attractive because of her stubborn need to do things her own way? That was a first. And it warmed her dangerously fast.

Her parents had lambasted those same principles for as long as she could recall, begging her to date one of the men who lived in their community and have a lot of babies, never mind that she had less than no interest in either concept. The men bored her to tears, not to mention they embraced her parents' love of alternative medicine, which meant she had nothing in common with them.

How great was it that the man she'd ultimately married appreciated her desire to become a medical doctor instead of a homeopathic healer?

And how terrible to realize that Desmond Pierce had chosen her strictly because he expected she'd easily leave her child without a backward glance.

He was right—she would do it because she'd given her word. But there wasn't going to be anything easy about it.

Three

Since the nanny had left him high and dry, Desmond was the one stuck sorting out his son's 3:00 a.m. meltdown. Conner woke yowling for God knew what reason. Larissa had always taken care of that in the past, leaving Des blessedly ignorant to his son's needs.

Unfortunately, after twenty minutes of rocking, soothing, toys and terse commands, nothing had worked to stop the crying. If he'd known Conner would pull this kind of stunt, Des would have gone to bed before 1:00 a.m. Two hours of sleep did not make this easier, that was for sure.

Desmond finally conceded that he no longer had the luxury of pretending McKenna didn't exist just to keep his growing attraction to her under wraps. Larissa's printed instructions clearly said the baby nursed at night. He'd been hoping for a miracle that would prevent him from having to disturb Conner's mother. That did not happen.

So that's how he found himself knocking on her door in the dead of night with a crying baby in his arms. Definitely not the way he'd envisioned seeing McKenna Moore in a bedroom. And he'd had more than a few fantasies about McKenna and a bed.

She answered a minute later, dressed in a conservative white robe that shouldn't have been the slightest bit alluring. It absolutely was, flashing elegant bits of leg as she leaned into the puddle of light from the hall.

"Woke up hungry, did he?" she said with more humor than Des expected at three in the morning. "Give him here," she instructed and, when he handed over the baby, cradled him to her bosom, murmuring as she floated to an overstuffed recliner in the corner of her room.

Funny. He hadn't realized until this moment that she sat in it to feed Conner. He'd envisioned her snuggling deep into the crevices to read a book or to chat on the phone with her legs draped over the sides. McKenna seemed like the type to lounge in a chair instead of sitting in it properly.

The lamp on the small end table cast a circle of warmth over the chair as she settled into it and worked open her robe to feed the baby. Instantly, Conner latched on and grew quiet.

"You can come in if you want," McKenna called to Desmond as he stood like an idiot at the door, completely extraneous and completely unable to walk away.

"I would…like to come in," he clarified and cleared his throat because his voice sounded like a hundred frogs had crawled down his windpipe. Gingerly, he sat on the bed because the love seat that matched the recliner was too close to mother and child.

Similar to the other times he'd watched McKenna breast-feed, he couldn't quite get over the initial shock of the mechanics. It was one thing to have an academic understanding of lactation, but quite another to see it in action.

Especially when he had such a strong reaction, like he was witnessing something divine.

The beauty of it filled him and he couldn't look away, even as she repositioned the baby and her dark nipple flashed. God, that shouldn't be so affecting. This woman was feeding his son in the most sacrificial of ways. But neither could he deny the purely physical reaction he had to her naked breast.

He couldn't stop being unnaturally attracted to her any more than he could stop the sun from rising. Seeing her with Conner only heightened that attraction.

Mother and child together created a package he liked.

He shouldn't have stayed. But he couldn't have left.

This quandary he was in had to stop. McKenna would be out of his life in two months and he'd insist that she not contact him again. Hell, he probably wouldn't have to insist. She was resolute in her goal of becoming a doctor, as they'd discussed at the pool yesterday.

In the meantime he'd drive himself insane if he didn't get their relationship, such as it was, on better footing. There was absolutely no reason they couldn't have a working rapport as they took care of the baby together. At least until he hired a new nanny.

"Is it okay that I brought him to you?" he asked gruffly. "I don't know what you worked out with Larissa."

He felt like he should be doing more to care for his son. But all he could do was make sure the woman who could feed him was happy.

"Perfectly fine. She's been trying a bottle at night with different types of formula to see if she can get his stomach to accept it when he's good and hungry. Hasn't worked so far." McKenna shrugged one shoulder, far too chipper for having been woken unceremoniously in the middle of the night. "So I take over when she gets frustrated."

"She didn't mention that in her instructions." Probably distracted with trying to pack and deal with travel arrangements on such short notice. So he reeled back his annoyance that he hadn't followed the routine his son was probably used to. It wasn't anyone's fault.

Clearly he needed to take a more active role in caring for Conner. This was the perfect opportunity to get clued in on whatever Larissa and McKenna had been doing thus far.

"Taking care of a baby is kind of a moving target," she said.

"Speaking from your years of experience?" He hadn't meant for that to come out sarcastically.

But she just laughed, which he appreciated far more than he should.

"I come from a very tight-knit community. We raise our babies together. I've been taking care of other people's children for as long as I can remember."

Mr. Lively had briefed him thoroughly on the cooperative community tucked into the outskirts of the Clatsop Forest where McKenna had grown up. Her unusual upbringing had been one of the reasons she'd stood out among the women he'd considered for his surrogate. "Surprising, then, that you'd be willing to give one up."

She contemplated him for a moment. "But that's why I was willing. I've seen firsthand what having a child does to a mother's time and energy. You become its everything and there's little left over for anything else, like your husband, let alone medical school, a grueling residency and then setting up a practice."

"It's not like that for you here, is it?"

"No, of course not." She flashed him a smile. "For one, we're not involved."

He couldn't resist pulling that thread. "What if we were?"

The concept hung there, writhing between them like a live thing, begging to be explored. And he wasn't going to take it back. He wanted to know more about her, what made her tick.

"What? Involved?"

The idea intrigued her. He could read it in her expressive eyes. But then she banked it.

"That's the whole point, Desmond. We never would have had a child together under any other circumstances. You wanted to be a single father for your own reasons, but whatever they are, the reality is that neither of us has room in our lives for getting *involved*."

A timely reminder, one he shouldn't have needed.

Even so, he couldn't help thinking he was going about this process wrong. Instead of hiding out in his lab until he'd fully analyzed his attraction to McKenna, he should create an environment to explore it. That was the only way he could understand it well enough to make it stop. What better conditions could he ask for than plenty of time together and an impending divorce?

"As long as you're happy while you're here," he said as his mind instantly turned that over. "That's all that matters to me."

He was nothing if not imaginative, and when he wanted something, there was little that could stop him from devising a way to get it. One of the many benefits of being a genius.

She glanced up at him after repositioning the baby. "You know what would make me happy? Finding a nanny with an expertise in weaning when the baby has formula allergies."

"Then, tomorrow, that's what we'll do," he promised her.

And if that endeavor included getting to know his child's mother in a much more intimate way, then *everyone* would be happy.

The next morning, McKenna woke to a beep that signaled an incoming text message.

She sat up and reached for her phone, instantly awake despite having rolled around restlessly for an hour after Desmond had left her room with the baby.

Definitely not the way she'd envisioned him visiting her bedroom in the middle of the night, though she shouldn't be having such vivid fantasies about her husband. Hard not to when she'd developed a weird habit of dreaming about him—especially when she was awake—and fantasies weren't so easy to shut off when she had little to occupy her time other than feeding the baby.

Desmond's name leaped out at her from the screen. He'd sent her a text message.

That shouldn't make her smile. But she couldn't help picturing him phone in hand as he fat-fingered his way through what should be simple communication.

Come to my workshop when you're free.

God, he was so adorable. Why that made her mushy inside, she had no clue. But, obviously, he didn't realize she was bored out of her mind pretty much all the time.

She was definitely free. Especially if it meant she got to visit Frankenstein's wonderland again.

She brushed her hair and washed her face. Rarely did she bother with cosmetics as she'd been blessed with really great skin that needed little to stay supple and blemish free. Why mess with it?

In less than five minutes, she was ready to go downstairs. Desmond glanced up from his computer nearly the moment she walked through the glass door of his workshop. "That was fast."

She shrugged casually, or as casually as she could when faced with a man she'd last seen in the middle of the night while she'd been half-naked. "I'm at your beck and call, right?"

Something flashed through his expression that added a few degrees to the temperature. "Are you? I thought you were here for Conner."

"That's what I meant," she corrected hastily, lest he get the wrong idea.

Though judging by the way he was looking at her, it was already too late. He was such a strange mix of personality, sometimes warm and inviting, other times prickly. But always fascinating. And she liked pushing his buttons.

She *shouldn't* be pushing any buttons.

Desmond was not her type. There were far too many complications at play here to indulge in the rising heat between them. "But apparently I can be persuaded to make myself available to his father, as well. Pending the subject of discussion, of course."

Desmond crossed his arms and leaned back in his chair, his expression decidedly warmer. "What would you like to talk about?"

She shrugged and bit back the flirtatious comment

on the tip of her tongue. She was pretty sure he hadn't summoned her to pick up where they'd left off the last time she'd made the mistake of cornering him in his workshop—when she'd been convinced he was about to kiss her.

"I figured you had something specific you wanted. Since you crawled out of the Dark Ages to send me a text."

The corners of his mouth lifted in a small smile that shouldn't have tingled her spine the way it did.

"Isn't that your preferred method of communication? I can adapt."

The ambience in the workshop was definitely different than the normal vibe between them. If she didn't know better, she'd think he was flirting with her. "You don't strike me as overly flexible. Maybe I should be adapting to you."

His gaze narrowed, sharpening, making her feel very much like a small, tasty rabbit. Never one to let a man make her feel hunted, she breached the space between them, skirting the long end of the worktable to put herself on the same side as Desmond.

Apparently she was going to let him push *her* buttons instead.

Last time she'd cornered him, he'd been guarded. Not this time. His crossed arms unknotted and fell to his sides, opening him to her perusal, and that was so interesting, she looked her fill. The man was beautifully built, with a long, lean torso and a classically handsome face made all the more dashing by a sparse beard. It was a perfect complement to his high cheekbones, allowing his gorgeous eyes to be the focal point.

"What would that look like?" he murmured. "If you adapted to me?"

"Oh, um…I don't know. How do you like to communicate?"

He jerked his head toward the back of the workshop without taking his eyes off of her. "I build things. Shape them, put the pieces where they go based on the images I have in my head. I communicate through my hands."

Oh, God. That was the sexiest thing she'd ever heard and her body didn't hesitate to flood her with the evidence of it, heating every millimeter of her skin as she imagined the things he'd say to her via his fingertips.

"That sounds very effective." They weren't talking about communication anymore and they both knew it.

He was definitely flirting with her. The question was whether or not she wanted him to stop. This heat roiling between them surely wasn't a good thing to encourage but, for the life of her, she couldn't remember why.

Oh, who was she kidding? The man intrigued the hell out of her and she should just stop pretending otherwise.

"Sometimes," he said, his voice lowering a touch, "more often than not, I'm misinterpreted."

"Maybe because whoever you're communicating with isn't listening hard enough."

She'd definitely listen, if for no other reason than to unlock some of his secrets. His mind fascinated her and… Coupled with the body? He could definitely talk to her all night long—with his hands, his mouth, whatever he wanted to use—and she'd be okay with that.

No. That was a bad idea. This mystical draw between them would not end well. She had goals. He was a controlling, difficult-to-get-along-with recluse. They had nothing between them but a son.

"Perhaps. But, generally speaking, people find me hard to understand."

"I'm not people," she murmured instead of *see you*

later. "Why don't you tell me something and I'll let you know if I'm having trouble translating."

Delicious anticipation unfolded in her abdomen, the likes of which she hadn't felt in a long time. They shouldn't get involved. There were probably a hundred reasons their agreement would be altered if they did. Loopholes she'd never considered would bind her to this house simply because she lacked the will to step back from her husband.

He was so hypnotic she couldn't tear herself away from what was happening. She wanted to be right here in this moment, as long as it lasted.

Slowly he reached out and slid his fingers through her hair, examining it. Giving her time to hear what he was saying without uttering a word. He caught her in the crosshairs of his gaze as he fingered the lock and his expression told her he liked the dark, heavy mass that fell down her back.

She watched as he looped a wider hank around his palm, winding it up until his hand was near her face.

Desmond feathered a thumb across her cheek that drove a spike of need through her that was answered in the heat radiating from his eyes.

His other hand slid to her waist, slowly drawing her closer until their bodies brushed.

Oh, yes, she liked what he was saying.

Then he released her hair in favor of cupping her jaw with both hands and guiding her lips to his. The kiss instantly caught fire and she moaned as he tilted her head to take it deeper, levering open her lips with his. His tongue worked its way into her mouth, tasting her with intent, and she liked that, too, meeting him with her own taste test.

She wanted to touch. Resting her fingertips on his

chest, she indulged herself in the sensations of the crisp cotton and strong male torso underneath. His wild heartbeat thumped under her fingers as his lips shaped hers into new heights of pleasure.

God, yes, he was a hot kisser, communicating with his hands as promised. The heat of his palms on her flesh radiated through her whole body. The worktable bit into her back as he levered her against it, his granite-hard erection digging into her pelvis deliciously.

The unnatural attraction she'd felt for him from the start exploded. If she didn't stop this madness, they'd be naked in half a heartbeat. Not a smart move for a woman who wanted to walk out the door unencumbered in a few weeks.

That thought was enough to spur her brain into functioning.

She pulled back, but not very far since he still had her trapped between his body and the table. Her pulse thundered in her ears as they stared at each other.

"That was…"

"Amazing?" he supplied, his gaze still hot and clearly interested in diving in again. But he didn't, which she appreciated. "Yeah. But I'm sensing we're going to stop now."

"See, we communicate just fine." She gulped. "I'm just…not sure this is a good idea."

They were not two people who had the luxury of an uncomplicated fling. He'd expressed in no uncertain terms exactly how much control he liked having over a situation. They were married with a divorce agreement already hammered out. That was not a recipe for experimentation, and she wasn't much of an experimenter anyway.

Where could this possibly go?

"Oh, it's a good idea." His piercing gaze tore her open inside as he promised her exactly how good it would be without saying a word. "But we both have to think so."

With that, he stepped back, releasing her.

She took the first deep breath she'd taken since he'd told her he communicated with his hands and nodded. "I agree. And I don't think that right now."

Four

The kiss experiment hadn't worked out like Des had hoped in any way, shape or form. Instead of providing data on how he could stop the unholy allure of his wife, kissing her had opened an exponential number of dimensions to his attraction.

Worse, he wanted to do it again for purely unscientific reasons.

The feel of her mouth against his haunted him. He recalled it at the most inopportune times, like when he should be focusing on the metal pieces in front of him as he attempted to solder them to the titanium skeleton he was creating. So far, he'd had to start over three times. If he kept this up, the end result would look more like a grotesque spider hybrid than a human.

The problem his mind wanted to resolve didn't involve robotic humanoids. It involved how to kiss McKenna again. She'd backed off and then backed away. As he'd fully expected. Women in his world fell into two camps:

those who didn't think he was worth the trouble and those who did solely due to their own agenda.

His wife clearly fell into the first group.

Either way, *all* women considered him difficult. And McKenna was no exception. This was just the first time in memory that he cared. How could he get her to the point where she thought kissing was a good idea if she avoided him? As she surely had been; he hadn't seen her in two days.

He turned the dilemma over in his mind, getting nowhere with it. And nowhere with his prototype, which should be at least half finished by now. Salvation came via an email from the nanny-placement service.

Excellent. The list of candidates scrolled onto the screen. There was nothing he liked better than data unless it was even more data. The only way to make a reasonable decision was to weigh variables and risks, then chart all of that into potential outcomes. What a great distraction from his unfinished work.

Better than that, the nanny candidates were an *excuse*. He'd asked McKenna for her help in weeding out the potentials for a number of reasons, not the least of which was that she had a vested interest in ensuring the nanny had lactation and weaning experience. And he did appreciate the way McKenna's mind worked. Handy that he'd have to spend time with her to discuss the résumés. Maybe at the same time, he could get closer to that next kiss. The pluses of this task were legion.

Except when he sought her out, he found her in the solarium feeding the baby. God, why did the sight of her with Conner at her breast whack him so hard every time? He should be used to it after the handful of occasions he'd been present for the event.

Nope.

"Sorry," he offered gruffly when she glanced up and caught him skulking at the entrance to the solarium at the west end of the house, positioned just so to catch the late-afternoon sun. "I can come back."

"This is your house. *You're* free to come and go at will," she reminded him as if he needed the reminder that she was here under duress.

"You should feel as if you can move about at will, as well." At a loss as to why this whole scene was making him uncomfortable, he ran a palm over his beard, but it didn't jog his rusty people skills. "Do you need something from me to solidify that for you?"

"No." She sighed and focused on Conner for a long moment. "I'm sorry, I'm being weird."

Biting back a laugh because that shouldn't be so funny, he shook his head. "That's usually my line. You are far from weird."

She made a face. "You're not weird either. And I meant since, you know…the other day happened, we're in a strange place."

The other day. When he'd kissed her. As he worked through several responses to that in his head, he contemplated her. She flushed and fiddled with the baby's placement, shifting him around until he was precisely in the same spot he had been before she'd started.

Interesting. She was as uncomfortable as he was. Why?

Fascinated, he crossed his arms, instantly more interested in staying than in fleeing for the safety of his lab where everything worked the way he willed it to. "Not so strange of a place. We're still married, the baby still needs breast milk and I still need a nanny. What's weird about that?"

"You know what I mean," she muttered.

"Maybe I don't." Social norms escaped him on a regular basis. But he was starting to enjoy the rush of endorphins his body produced when around her. As long as he kept a tight rein on it.

"Then never mind," she said with a frown. "Obviously the weirdness is all on my side. I guess you just go around kissing people randomly whenever you feel like it and it never costs you a wink of sleep."

Well, now that *was* interesting information. "You're having trouble sleeping? Because I kissed you? Why?"

He definitely would not have guessed they'd have that in common. And now he was curious if she'd lain awake fantasizing about what might have happened. He sure the hell had.

A blush stained her cheeks. "Shut up and stop reading into everything I'm saying."

"Is that what I'm doing?"

The concept shouldn't have made him smile, but she seemed so flustered. He liked knowing that she'd been affected by what had happened in his workshop, especially since he'd have sworn she'd backed off because she had little interest in exploring the attraction between them.

Maybe she was more interested than he'd assumed.

She groaned. "Please tell me you didn't really seek me out to issue the third degree."

"No. My apologies if that's how it came across." He could circle back to their attraction and the potential for more kissing experiments later. "I have a list of candidates from the nanny service. I wanted to see when you might be available to discuss them."

"Now," she shot back. "No time like the present. The baby has about ten more minutes on this side and then I have to switch, so I'm stuck for the duration."

"Stuck?"

"Yeah, it's not like I can drive to the store in my current state," she explained wryly. "It's a necessary part of the job that you have to stay pretty much parked in one spot. I had to learn the hard way to always go to the bathroom first. It's not a big deal. You get used to it and, honestly, I use the downtime to kind of Zen out."

He'd never considered that she was essentially trapped while breast-feeding. But it wasn't as if she could move around, get a glass of water if she grew thirsty. The realization sat uncomfortably behind his rib cage. While he'd been obsessing over how to get her into his arms again, she'd been quietly taking care of his son without any thought to her own comfort. "What can I get for you? Some tea? A pillow?"

What else did nursing women need? He'd have to do a Google search, watch some videos.

She smiled; the first one he'd gotten out of her since he'd interrupted her Zen. "Thanks, I'm okay. I learned to get all that stuff before starting, too."

It was a conviction of his gender that he'd never even contemplated any of this. Maybe even a conviction of his parenting skills. There was no excuse for him having left her to her own devices as she did something as sacred and necessary as feeding his son. "From now on, I want to be in the room when you feed Conner."

"What? Why?" Suspiciously, she eyed him.

"I simply wish to support you in the one aspect of Conner's care I can't control. If you're stuck, then I should be, too."

"Oh. That's…unexpected."

"I'm not a beast all the time." Only when it mattered.

She actually laughed at that. "I never said you were. Thank you. It's really not necessary for you to hang out with me. It'll probably be pretty boring."

"Conner is my son. You're my wife. I'm nothing if not avidly interested in both of you."

That seemed to set her back and she stared at him for a long moment. "I'm definitely not used to a man who's so forthcoming."

What kind of men did she normally surround herself with? Discomfort ruffled the hairs on the back of his neck. That was a subject best left unexplored.

"Find better people to associate with," he advised her brusquely. *Now* it was time to move on. "I've reviewed the list of nannies. There are four that stand out. I'd like your opinion on them."

"Sure."

She casually popped Conner's mouth from her nipple with a finger and rolled him back on the nursing pillow to adjust her bra cup. Then she unhooked the other side, peeling it away from her breast without seeming to notice that a man was in the room avidly attempting to pretend she hadn't just bared herself.

Perhaps demanding to be present every time she fed Conner wasn't such a bright idea. He shifted, but there was no comfortable spot when sporting an erection that never should have happened. He hated that he couldn't control it, hated how wrong it felt and hated that he couldn't enjoy the sight of his wife's body like a normal husband.

But he couldn't, not without infringing on her insistence that getting involved was a bad idea. And neither could he take back his insistence on supporting her, especially given that he hadn't hired a nanny yet. Until then, he'd suffer in the trap of his own making.

"Why don't you read me the résumés?" she suggested.

He blinked. Yes. Good plan. "Be right back."

He dashed to his room and grabbed his tablet from

the bedside table, booting up the device on his way back to the solarium. By the time he hit the west wing of the house, he had his email client up and the list on the screen.

McKenna hadn't moved from her spot in the chair by the window. Sunlight spilled in through the glass, highlighting her dark hair like a corona. With Conner tucked in close, she was absolutely the most beautiful woman he'd ever seen.

There came the *thwack* to his chest, true to form.

He had to fix that. It was a problem he couldn't deconstruct and then rebuild. All he could think about was kissing her again and not stopping. He liked this attraction between them. When had he lost all his brain cells?

"I, um, have the list," he announced unnecessarily, but she just nodded and didn't call him on his idiocy.

Clearing his throat, he read through the credentials of the four candidates he'd selected from the list of twenty. She interrupted every so often to clarify a point, ask him to repeat a section or remind her of a detail from a previous candidate. When he finished, he lowered the tablet and cocked his head. "What do you think?"

"I like number three the best," she announced immediately. "Shelly. Her phrasing gave me a comfort level that she wasn't trying to pad her experience with a lot of flowery words. She's the only one who's cared for two different infants with formula allergies. And I'll admit an age prejudice. She's two years older than the others. When it comes to caring for my—your—son, that's no small thing."

The slip hung in the air, daring him to comment on it. He should. Conner was her son in only one sense of the word. Des had ironclad documents stating such. The odds were good she hadn't forgotten that, not when Des was holding back the divorce as a guarantee she'd stay.

McKenna wasn't confused about her role here. Not at all. She'd been the one to back off in his workshop, citing her belief that getting involved wasn't a good plan.

Maybe *Desmond* needed the reminder about her role.

He chose to let the slip go by without comment and she didn't miss it. Her brows drew together. "I want the best for Conner, too, of course. I assume you know that or you wouldn't have asked my opinion."

Actually he hadn't considered that. At all. Wanting the best for the baby implied emotional attachment, which was the opposite of what he'd expected to happen here. She'd completely misinterpreted his request for her help and he'd completely missed that she'd developed a bond with the baby.

Taking a seat on the long leather couch facing the window, he laid the tablet to the side as he processed.

"I asked you to help select the nanny because I assumed you would want to ensure I picked someone suited to helping you wean. So you could leave with a clean slate."

Something akin to pain flashed across her face. "Yes, I have an interest in that, too. But that's the point. This woman is my replacement. I want it to be the right person to raise Connor."

"I will raise Conner," he corrected somewhat ferociously. He had a fierce need for his son and he wasn't shy about it.

"Well, of course, but he needs a female influence. Someone who can be nurturing and kiss his boo-boos when he falls down." She swept him with a once-over that she probably didn't mean to be provocative but was nonetheless. "Somehow I don't see you filling that role."

"Because I'm male?"

Sexist, definitely. But even worse, he wasn't sure she

was wrong. He didn't see himself as nurturing in the slightest. The relationship he envisioned with Conner would be of the mind as they discussed the philosophy of physics and argued theories or studied ancient history together. He'd never once thought he'd be the one sticking Band-Aids on his son's knees, though all of his research showed Conner would need that.

"No, because you're you," she countered without heat. "It has nothing to do with being male. I've seen lots of men be single fathers for one reason or another, but they were more…adaptable to the requirements. You're outsourcing the job of mom and I want to get the right person for that, so you can go back to hiding in your workshop."

"I don't—" *Hide.* Except he did and the fact that she'd clued in to that bothered him. How did she read him so well? Better still, she'd noticed a gap in Desmond's parenting experience and brought it to the forefront. "Tell me more about child rearing in your community."

"Really?" She glanced up, her confusion evident. "That doesn't seem like your cup of tea."

On that, she *was* wrong. "On the contrary. I have an interest in ensuring Conner grows into a happy, healthy adult. I have a job, too, albeit not the bandager of knees apparently."

She stuck her tongue out at him and the sight of it shouldn't have been as suggestive as it was, but instantly he recalled the feel of it, exploratory and hot, against his. She'd kissed him eagerly, as if she'd been waiting for him to breech that wall between them. He couldn't stop himself from wanting her hands on him again.

Crossing his legs, he tried to hide the worst of the tenting in his pants but he was pretty sure that was impossible when he'd just created a mountain in his lap. What was he supposed to do to tamp down this visceral reaction he always had to McKenna?

"I'm not saying you can't," she said, thankfully oblivious to Des's inability to stop reacting like a horny teenager whenever she breathed too hard. "Just that you're not going to be the first person he thinks of running to when he's bleeding and hurt. That's what I notice when thinking about how the families at home raise babies. Mothers and fathers alike read to their kids at night before bed. Get up with them when they have nightmares and soothe them back to sleep. Feeding, changing wet sheets, looking for lost stuffed animals. The person who demonstrates the most love, tolerance and patience will be who he comes to in crisis. And there are a lot of crises for children."

As she'd talked, her hand drifted over Conner's head, absently stroking his fine baby hair. Des doubted she'd even noticed that her fingers hadn't stopped moving, even after her voice stopped. McKenna was natural at nurturing, did it without thought. Did she realize that?

"And you assume the nanny will be that person." All at once, he couldn't imagine anyone other than McKenna being that person. He tried transposing one of the women on his list into his wife's spot on the chair, bottle in hand, and it refused to materialize.

That was…disturbing. And unexpected.

She shrugged. "Maybe I'm wrong. In that case, you tell me which nanny candidate you like the best and your criteria for choosing."

No. He was done with this discussion. She'd challenged a lot of his assumptions and brought up things he'd not examined. He needed time to acclimate to all of this new information.

But he couldn't leave. McKenna was still breast-feeding. And trapped. That meant he was, too, because he'd given his word. Suddenly his skin felt too tight as the first wave of what might be a panic attack stole over him. God, he hadn't had one of those in years, usually because he avoided all of his triggers.

"Desmond." McKenna's strong voice washed over him, filtering through the anxiety in a flash.

He pried open his eyelids, which he hadn't even realized he'd closed, to see her watching him with concern flitting across her expression. She'd tucked her clothes back into place and cradled Conner in her arms as he waved a hand in a circle, content after his feeding.

"Would you like to hold him?" she offered casually, as if she hadn't noticed he'd slid into his own head. But he didn't believe for a second she'd missed it. Neither did he mistake her offer as anything other than an intervention. She'd noticed he was troubled and sought to help him.

It worked. Somehow. As she set the nursing pillow aside and crossed the room, his body cooled and settled. Conner nestled into Des's arms and he definitely didn't need any more information to know that he loved his son. The emotion bled through him, a balm to his frazzled nerves.

Yes. This part wasn't in question. He'd wanted a baby because he'd needed this connection. From the first moment Lacey had announced that she was pregnant, his heart had instantly been engaged with the idea of a child. A baby wouldn't know that Des stumbled over things normal people did without question. His son would love him even after realizing his father hated crowds and preferred to be alone.

"I want you to come to me for bandages," he murmured softly, but McKenna heard him anyway. Her hand drifted to his shoulder, gentle and warm, and that felt right, too.

"Then he will," she promised. "I didn't mean to speak out of turn."

"No. You just caused me to think about aspects of being a single father that I previously hadn't." Maybe he didn't want a nanny. It wasn't like he needed to work to provide for his son. If Des took off a year, even two, who would care?

Well, he would. His brain did not stop creating, whether he wished it to or not. Putting the pieces together of what he saw was merely a defense mechanism designed to empty his mind. But he didn't have to be a full-time inventor or even sell anything he created, which meant no business trips to the manufacturer's locations. Nothing to distract him from being a father.

It could just be Des and Conner. Father and son. No nanny needed.

McKenna smiled. "I'm glad. The secret to being a great father is that there is no secret. All you have to do is love them. And there's nothing wrong with picking a nanny who's more in the background. As long as she can work with Conner's formula allergy, I think that's the most important thing."

All at once the reality of the situation crashed through his bubble of contentment. If he didn't hire a nanny, what did that mean for McKenna and weaning? Could *he* be the one who helped her through that? Would she even accept that?

He'd never failed to master a concept in his life. If he studied up on it, surely he could fare as well as a nanny. And then, as a bonus, working together would give him more of an opportunity to be around her. Feel out what was happening between them and his odd, disconcerting urge to bury himself inside her and never emerge.

Hiring a nanny would only impede that process.

But he couldn't tell McKenna. Not yet. First he had to figure out how to convince her it was the right decision.

While Des had already done a good bit of research on Conner's formula allergy, he hadn't spent any effort on how to transition from breast-feeding to something else because it hadn't mattered yet. Now it did.

From the moment he woke up the next day until well after lunch, he studied. With way too many videos starring breast-feeding women on a continual loop in his head, he let it go for the day and took a shower.

Des's bedroom resembled a small fortress. By design. When he'd bought the house, he'd cared mostly about its proximity to other people. Namely that they were as far away as they could be. The two-hundred-acre property guaranteed that, and the forest of trees and wild undergrowth surrounding the main house shielded him from unwanted trespassers. But just to make sure, he'd installed a twelve-foot concrete wall around the grounds.

He'd stopped short at a pack of Dobermans to roam the property. Overkill. And thus far McKenna had been his only guest, so he'd accomplished his goal of cutting himself off from those who didn't tolerate his eccentricities. For an additional escape, he'd created a bedroom retreat that rivaled the poshest resorts complete with a pop-up TV, a large, oval spa tub in the cavernous bathroom and a small sitting area in the garden outside a set of French doors.

Shame he rarely spent time here, often napping in his workshop on the single bed he'd eventually had delivered when he'd fallen asleep at his desk for the tenth time. The suite was a place to hold his clothes and store his shampoo, but that was it. The workshop was his home.

Maybe not so much anymore if he didn't hire a nanny.

The concept of losing his sanctuary filled him with a black soup of nerves. But, as he continually told himself, he wasn't losing his workshop. Just committing to spend less time hiding and more time with the family he was creating with his son.

To that end, he had to actually do that. Throwing on some clothes, he went in search of his son. He found both the baby and McKenna in the nursery. She held Conner upright in her lap as she read him a chunky board book.

He cleared his throat. "Thanks for watching him while I was busy."

"You're welcome." Her slightly cocked eyebrow had a saucy bent to it, like she questioned why he was being pleasant.

McKenna wore a dress today. A rarity. Usually she had on capri pants and a short-sleeved shirt or yoga pants and a tunic. The dress showed off her feminine curves in a way he fully appreciated.

Then she smiled at Conner as he waved a chubby fist in a circle, and the desire Des had no ability to keep in check roared through his chest like a freight train. Coupled with everything else, it was nearly enough to put him over the edge.

"Did you need something?" she asked before he'd regained his sanity.

"Do I have to need something to spend time with my son?"

To her credit, she didn't flinch at his less than civil tone. "Wanting to spend time with your son is a need. There's nothing wrong with claiming it as such, especially if I'm in the way."

She levered herself out of the chair and plopped Conner into his arms, then turned, clearly about to leave the room, which had not been his intent at all.

"Wait," he called out awkwardly as Conner started fussing.

McKenna glanced back over her shoulder. "You'll be fine. He just ate not too long ago, so he might be ready for a diaper change."

"I want you to stay," he ground out. This was not one of his more stellar examples of communicating with other people.

"Why?" She seemed genuinely perplexed, like she had no concept of how she made the room brighter by being in it. Why *wouldn't* he want her to stay? "I'm just the buffet."

"That's so far from the truth," he shot back and then registered that he'd meant it.

She was more than just a means to an end. McKenna was his wife. Against everything he'd expected when he'd convinced her to come home with him from the hospital, she'd begun to matter.

"I like you," he said, marking the first time he could recall saying anything resembling that out loud to anyone. Not even Lacey.

It was an event.

McKenna was no longer just his son's surrogate mother, and Des didn't have a good foundation for managing that.

"Yes, I got that impression the other day in your workshop," she replied blithely with an ironic smile. "I hope you aren't angling for a repeat."

Of the kiss? What if he was?

No better way to take control than to lay out exactly what was on his mind. Besides, she'd seemed rather impressed with his tendency to be forthcoming. Sometimes he had no filter owing to his lack of social niceties and other times because he genuinely didn't see the point in filtering. People could take him or leave him and usually he preferred the latter.

Except with McKenna.

And she was still edging toward the door.

"McKenna." She froze. He pressed the advantage. "Stay. We live in the same house and share a son. I like your company. Unless the reverse isn't true?"

"What, are you asking me if I like hanging around with you?" She leaned against the open door as she surveyed him. "I basically spend my days feeding your son. Adult conversation is high on my list of things I look forward to."

Obviously she viewed herself as the milk supply and he'd done nothing to counter that. Perhaps it was time to change their association in her mind. In both their minds. She was a person with her own interests, dreams and opinions, some of which he'd already glimpsed, but not nearly enough.

"Then there's no reason for you to leave." Satisfied that he'd navigated this small blip, he nodded to the chair she'd recently vacated. "Sit while I change Conner's diaper. Tell me something about you that I don't know."

"You want me to provide entertainment for you?" The quirk of her mouth said she found the concept amusing but she sat in the chair as he'd asked.

"No. Insight." The more he knew about her, the more information he had at his disposal to figure out how to exorcise her from his consciousness. But even that excuse was starting to fall short.

He just wanted to know her. Period.

"I like cotton candy, thunderstorms and books about dogs. That kind of thing?" At his nod, she laughed. "I feel like I'm on a date."

Instantly a dozen different scenarios sprang to his

mind, scenes where he romanced what he wanted out of McKenna, held her hand as he led her along a rain-soaked trail through the woods. Pressed her against a tree as he fed her cotton candy from his fingers, then kissed her to treat them both to the taste of sweetness mixed with the fire that laced their electric attraction.

He was going about his problem solving in the wrong way. If he wanted insight, a next kiss, to spend time with McKenna, "hanging out" wasn't going to cut it. He needed to ask her on a date.

Five

McKenna did not like the look on Desmond's face. Or rather, she liked it a whole hell of a lot and shouldn't.

The second the word *date* had come out of her stupid mouth, something heated and thoroughly intrigued popped into his gaze and hadn't fled in over a minute.

It was a long minute, too, as he watched her without apology, contemplating. She could almost see the gears turning in his head and one of Desmond's sexiest qualities was his mind. She'd gone to college with a lot of smart people, but Desmond's brain was wired so differently, evidenced by the fascinating way he presented thoughts and concepts, drew conclusions. Threw out unexpected comments such as *I like you*.

Sometimes she wondered if he did stuff like that as a test. To see what she'd do. But she had no rubric for the grading system and therefore no way of knowing if she'd passed or not. Or whether she wanted to pass.

She and Desmond weren't supposed to become friends. Or anything else.

"We never finished our nanny discussion," she blurted out lamely, but they needed to get on to an innocuous topic. Now.

She'd grown uncomfortably aware that Desmond's hair was wet, probably because he'd come straight from the shower. It was slicked back from his forehead as it always was and hung down around his collar in solid, dark chunks. Wet, it was darker, almost black, and gave his devastating looks a wicked edge she couldn't ignore. Neither could she stop thinking about Desmond wet. And naked.

"We didn't," he allowed. "I'd like to. Another time. I have another subject of importance. Have dinner with me tonight."

She nearly choked on her gasp of surprise and the sound upset Conner, who started to cry. Desmond rocked him back and forth but his gaze never left hers.

"As in a date?" she managed to ask.

Stupid mouth. Why had she even mentioned that word? Because she'd never quite gotten that kiss out of her head, of course. She fantasized about a repeat pretty much 24/7, so no wonder she'd slipped. A smart guy like him had no problem picking up on the fact that she'd *said* it wasn't a good idea to get involved, but that didn't mean she had the ability to turn off her fascination with him.

"As in dinner. I'd like to thank you for what you've done for Conner. And for me." His gentle rocking soothed Conner into a doze, his sweet face nestled against Desmond's chest. "You're a guest. I haven't welcomed you as one."

Oh. That was a different story. Slightly. It still sounded like all the trappings of a date without slapping the label on it. "Would it just be me and you? What about Conner? Right now, we're it as far as a caregiver goes."

"Mrs. Elliot will fill in for a few hours."

He had an answer to everything, didn't he? Desperately, she cast about for a plausible reason to refuse. Except, she wanted to have dinner with Desmond. Fiercely. And have it be every bit a date, with all the long, delicious glances over dessert as anticipation coiled in her belly…

Bad, bad idea.

"I don't have anything to wear."

The protest died in her throat as he swept her with a look that could have melted the habit off of a nun. "I have yet to see you in clothing that I did not think looked spectacular on you. Wear anything. Or nothing. I'm not particular."

The shiver his suggestion unleashed shouldn't have gone so deep into her skin. It was the most flirtatious thing he'd ever said. That any man had dared to say to her. She shouldn't like it so much, but all at once, the muddle he was making of her request to stay uninvolved put her in a dangerous mood.

"I'd love to see the look on your face if I took that dare."

One eyebrow cocked at a quizzical angle. "It wasn't a dare. I merely sought to make you more comfortable about the circumstances. If you want to see my expression once you grant me the privilege of seeing you naked, my calendar is completely clear for the evening."

Somehow that got a laugh out of her. Mostly because she had a feeling he wasn't kidding. There was something so affecting about knowing exactly where she stood with him. He liked her. He wanted to see her naked. No guessing.

But he also wanted to divorce her. The contradictions were dizzying.

"What if I say yes? Are you expecting sex as payback for dinner?"

"No. I'm expecting you to eat as payback for putting food in front of you. Though, again…if you want sex to be a part of the evening, my calendar is still open."

She shut her eyes for a beat. Why was she so surprised he'd be gentlemanly about it, putting all the balls in her court? "I don't."

She did.

Oh, God, did she want sex to be a part of her relationship with Desmond. The way he communicated with his hands during a simple kiss had kept her awake and feverish far longer than it should have. But she couldn't help imaging how much hotter those hands could be with no barriers between them.

What was wrong with her? She and Desmond had the most dysfunctional marriage on the planet and sex would only complicate everything. And then what would happen? She'd end up divorced and in medical school. Exactly as she'd planned.

She blinked. "I'll have dinner with you."

And maybe sex would be on the menu, after all. What did she have to lose besides this achy, vibrating tension between her and the man with the keys to her future?

McKenna pulled out her best dress from the back of the giant closet. Everything at Desmond's house was huge, including him. His presence dominated every inch of his realm. There was literally nowhere she could go to escape his effect on her, particularly not her bedroom.

He'd become a permanent fixture when she breast-fed, which she appreciated more than she'd have expected.

But the middle-of-the-night visits were hard to take, when she was semiconscious and Desmond wore drawstring lounge pants and a white T-shirt that showcased surprisingly broad shoulders.

It seemed natural for him to be in her bedroom. It was almost hard to watch him leave when she had to go back to her cold bed alone. That had never bothered her before. But she'd never experienced such a magnetic draw to a man before either.

And in ten minutes they were going to have dinner in what she definitely considered a date. As long as everyone understood that getting involved only worked for the short term. Surely that was Desmond's thought, too.

Nervous all at once, McKenna twirled in front of the oval cheval glass in the corner of her room. She'd never had a full-length mirror before and loved it. When she left, she'd miss that, plus a lot of the other luxuries strewed throughout the mansion, especially the indoor pool.

Of course she had to actually leave before she could miss them.

The mirror reflected a woman who looked the best she could. Her hair was low maintenance, wash and go as soon as it was dry, but she'd given it extra help with a blow-dryer a few minutes ago. No makeup, thank God, because who wanted to sit around with goop on their face? The dress fit her angular body well, except for her bust line. The fabric hugged her cleavage, smooshing it prominently high and out. Only her maternity clothes accommodated her enormous boobs, but without the baby bump, she might as well wear a potato sack on her date with Desmond. Not happening. Besides, he'd seen her breasts lots of times. No reason to hide them.

When she descended the main staircase to the ground

floor, Desmond was waiting for her at the bottom. His gaze locked onto her, hot and appreciative, sending little quakes through her core that put a whole new spin on the concept of long, delicious glances.

"Conner is settled with Mrs. Elliot and a bottle of breast milk," he informed her casually, as if he hadn't just undressed her with his eyes. "Shall we?"

He gestured with his hand toward the dining room, signaling her to walk with him. Nerves and a whole lot of zingy sparks shot around under her skin, making her jumpy. The dining room conformed to the rest of the house: cavernous, a little formal and thoroughly drenched with Desmond.

During the first course of garden salad, served by the invisible staff Mrs. Elliot managed, Desmond said, "Tell me about being part of a cooperative community."

"What? All of it?"

"Sure. Whatever you want to tell me. I imagine it shaped you in many invisible ways. I'm curious."

She swallowed. This was definitely not first-date material. It was far deeper, opening aspects of her soul she wasn't sure she wanted on display. "I don't know. I don't sit around and think about my upbringing."

Except she did sometimes. Being part of a closed, united community had a lot of pluses, but losing her grandfather hadn't been one of them. It *had* shaped her. And, based on his comment, Desmond had already figured that out.

"But it matters," he said quietly, and it wasn't a question.

His insight bothered her. She forked up a bite of lettuce and tomato to stall but his piercing gaze penetrated her anyway. "Well, yeah. Of course."

"Did it contribute to your decision to be my surrogate?"

"My background has everything to do with why I'm Conner's mother," she told him firmly. "I was raised to believe that we each have a purpose in life. I discovered early on that mine is to help people when they're hurting. You wanted a baby really badly and I had the power to give you the family you wished for. It was a no-brainer."

"Thank you," he said simply. "Conner means more to me than anything else I've ever created. I would not have him without you."

The sincerity in his voice choked her up. Why, she couldn't say. She shouldn't be privy to any of this.

McKenna blinked back the sudden moisture in her eyes, mystified why it meant so much to her that she shared something so deeply personal with Desmond.

He fell silent, watching her as the staff cleared the salad plates and replaced them with the main course of locally fished salmon and asparagus. But instead of picking up his fork to dig in, he cocked his head. "Perhaps you'd be interested in taking a role in Conner's life on a longer term basis."

"What?" Her own fork clattered to her plate. "What are you talking about? That's not the deal."

It couldn't be the deal. What did he mean? Like, picking Conner up from school or taking him to the zoo occasionally? She couldn't do that. Didn't Desmond know how hard it already was to contemplate leaving? It was easier to not have contact. That's what she'd been counting on.

"No, it's not." Steadily, he measured his words as he spoke. "But you care about Conner already. I can see it in your face when you hold him. There's no reason we can't discuss a different arrangement."

Still reeling, she gaped at him. Was he insane? "I can't

do that. You shouldn't want me to do that. What about when he starts asking questions about who I am? I won't lie. And then he'll wonder why I don't live with you and be a real mother."

It would be a disaster. And, of course, Conner might still have those same questions, but she'd much rather let Desmond answer them than be put on the hot seat herself. As a surrogate, none of this should have ever been presented to her and the unfairness of it hammered at her heart.

She wasn't mother material. The first criterion was wanting to be one and she didn't. Or rather, she didn't have the luxury of wanting to be one, which wasn't the same thing, as she'd only just come to realize. It was be a doctor or be a mother. Period. And she'd made her choice so long ago that she'd reconciled it in her mind.

Until now.

The salmon dried up in her mouth as she wrestled with the impossibility of Desmond's suggestion. With the fact that her decisions weren't as cut-and-dried as she'd have once claimed.

She did care for Conner. So much so that Desmond had noticed.

Well, it didn't matter. She cared about the baby for the same reasons she wanted to be a doctor; she genuinely wanted to help Conner. The soul-deep need to fix what was wrong came so naturally that she couldn't remember a time when she hadn't wanted to be a doctor.

Besides, as soon as Desmond signed the divorce papers, the custody agreement would go into effect and all of this would be a moot point. She was here to say a long goodbye, nothing more.

"There is a reason we can't discuss this," she reminded him, but her throat was so tight it was a miracle any sound came out. "You've been really clear about the fact that you don't want me involved in Conner's life."

"I didn't, no. But obviously circumstances have shifted."

"You don't like to share," she blurted, confused about the direction of the conversation. What happened to the delicious, sensual undertones she'd anticipated for their date? "Unless you've changed your mind about being the one to make all the decisions?"

"I haven't." His tone cooled considerably. "And you're right. I'm not being fair. There isn't a way to alter our agreement to permit you a role in Conner's life past the one you have currently."

A prickle walked down her spine as she watched Desmond shut down. Their date disintegrated into a long, uncomfortable silence as she grappled to understand what had just happened. They both ate but the stilted vibe turned everything unpleasant.

"I take it your calendar isn't so clear anymore," she muttered as the staff unobtrusively removed the dinner dishes. Hers was embarrassingly unfinished, with half the salmon lying forlornly near the edge of the plate, but she'd lost her appetite.

He glanced up. "My interest in you hasn't changed, if that's what you mean. But I sense the timing is not the best."

"Yeah. That."

It had seemed so easy to imagine that they'd have some hot sex and then she'd get her divorce at some point in the future so she could leave.

But Desmond had just dropped a whole lot of reality in her lap. He had all the control and would never give up any. The thought of getting involved with someone who refused to allow her choices didn't sit well.

Rubbing at his beard, Desmond frowned. "I've angered you."

"No." Not really. He had been completely transparent from the first and she'd ignored all the warning signs that had been screaming at her to stay far away from the father of her baby. "I...just need some air."

She excused herself and went to her room to get some sleep before the sole source of her uneasiness visited her room for Conner's midnight feeding. The sooner he hired a nanny, the better.

Once again, McKenna had run away from him. Desmond stared out the window in Conner's nursery as he sat in the rocking chair holding his son later that night.

It was far from the first time a woman had edged for the door while in the midst of a date. But this marked a rarity in that it still bothered him hours later. How had things disintegrated so quickly? First they'd been talking about McKenna's upbringing and the conversation had shifted to Conner. Why not? The baby was one of the things they had in common.

But then she'd grown upset when he'd mentioned that she might extend her role, maybe spending time with their son on a regular basis. It seemed a simple enough concept, but clearly McKenna wished to keep their agreement as it was. Nor did she want to explore their attraction.

Which was the root of the problem—he did and apparently she'd clued in far too fast that he didn't have a charming personality at his disposal to woo a woman into his bed. So he'd have to be a little more inventive than the average Joe, clearly.

He dissected their dialogue, trying to pinpoint where he'd messed up.

This had been a problem his whole life. Nothing ever unfolded the way he'd constructed it in his mind, not when people were involved. Metal parts and computer programs always came together exactly as he intended. The final creation resembled the one he'd imagined. Always. His relationship with McKenna? Not even close.

Conner circled his fist and whacked Desmond in the chest. All at once, Des had the unsettling realization that his son was a person. Unless he figured out how to relate to people, he might very well have the same issues with his child once Conner grew old enough to talk. Of course, Desmond had envisioned that the baby would love him. But years of evidence indicated otherwise.

A wash of emotion tightened his chest as he captured Conner's little fist and held it in his. When McKenna had said his son wouldn't come to him with a scraped knee, she'd meant because Desmond was difficult to relate to. Conner wouldn't naturally seek out his father.

Des had to fix his people skills if he ever hoped to forge the connections he craved.

Once Conner fell asleep, Des settled him into his crib with a silent vow that he'd never give his son a reason to run away from him. That meant he had to figure out how to entice his mother to stay, since they likely shared similarities. The problem wheeled through his mind constantly, keeping Des from fully relaxing.

The hour of sleep he got before Conner woke him for his midnight feeding didn't put him in any better frame of mind. McKenna was always so much more beautiful in the semidarkness, too.

She answered her door wearing her virginal white robe that left everything to the imagination and an expression that could have frozen lava.

Usually her naturally friendly personality was in place

no matter the time or circumstance. Was she still upset about dinner? She'd said she wasn't angry. Had that been one of those times when a woman was less than forthcoming and Des should have figured out that she meant the opposite of what she'd said?

He hated being forced to read between the lines. "Conner is ready for you."

That could have come out with less of a growl. But when uncertain, he tended to retreat behind his walls. He couldn't afford to do so tonight, and cursed himself for being such a brute.

"I assumed so."

She reached out and took the baby from his arms, brushing her fingers across Desmond's chest. The T-shirt he wore provided little barrier from the thrill of her touch, which seemed constant regardless of whether things were prickly between them.

The familiar rush of awareness didn't diminish just because McKenna wasn't speaking to him. His conscience poked at him. If he wanted to change the status quo, this was a great opportunity for him to take the initiative.

"I'm, uh, sorry about earlier," he offered cautiously as she settled into the recliner with Conner. "I did not intend for dinner to end on such a bad note."

"I know." The barest hint of a smile turned up the edges of her mouth. It wasn't much, but it felt like a lot.

Instead of letting her handle her own logistics, he picked up the nursing pillow from the floor and arranged it in her lap the way he'd seen her do a dozen times. Then he helped her get Conner situated, a trick and a half since the baby already knew what was coming and had squirmed into place against McKenna's covered bosom. There wasn't enough room for two sets of hands, a baby and the enormous sensual pull that seemed constantly coiled between Desmond and McKenna. But he stuck it out and ignored the ache that sprang up at the sight of his son and wife together in the most elemental scene a man could have the privilege to witness.

And therein lay part of his confusion and consternation. His attraction to McKenna had a thread running through it that was inexorably due to the fact that she was Conner's mother. It was unexpected. Powerful. Impossible to mistake. What was he supposed to do with that?

"I'm sorry, too," she said after the longest pause.

His gaze flew to hers. "For what? I'm the one who overstepped at dinner."

"No, you didn't. It was very generous of you to offer to reexamine the agreement. I know your heart was in the right place. I...freaked out and made it weird."

That set him back for a moment. Emotional decisions weren't in his wheelhouse. Or were they? "Only because I suggested something that had no logical possibility. It was a mistake."

One borne out of his visceral need to connect and he'd bungled it.

"On that we agree." She tipped her head back against the recliner, letting her eyes flutter closed. "It would be too hard, Desmond. I hope you understand that."

All at once, he had an inkling of what she meant. McKenna cared for Conner. He hadn't gotten that part wrong, though he'd questioned what he'd seen after their discussion, assuming he'd completely misinterpreted the expression that always stole over her face when she held him. "Hard because you're giving up a relationship with your son?"

Her misty smile was a little wider this time. "It shouldn't be. I never would have thought twice about it if you hadn't asked me to breast-feed. Or, at least, I don't think I would have. Who can say at this point?"

Her pain convicted him, winnowing through his pores as easily as if he'd poured it down his throat. He'd changed the dynamic and forced her to help, with no thought to the resulting emotional turmoil he'd be causing her. Or himself.

The empathy he'd always felt for other people's strongest emotions amplified under his own unease. *Why* did he have to experience feelings so strongly? It was exactly why he stayed away from people. But he couldn't have stayed away from McKenna short of being chained in the basement.

"I didn't realize," he finally ground out through clenched teeth as he battled to get the clash of emotion gripping his chest to ease. She hurt. Therefore, he did, too. "I'm sorry."

"I made the choice." She shrugged. "And it was the right one. What would have happened to Conner if I wasn't here to feed him? It's ghastly to even consider. So it's a done deal. The only thing we can do at this point is move forward. Hire a nanny who can help us figure out the options so I can leave."

If he hadn't been paying such close attention to her, he might have missed the desolate note in her voice. But all at once he had the distinct impression she wasn't in such a hurry to leave as she had been.

Also a benefit of being so closely tuned in to one another. He could tell what she was feeling as clearly as if she'd hung a sign around her neck.

And he had to admit that he wasn't in such a hurry for her to go either. He should be. She stirred him in ways that made him uncomfortable. But she stirred him in ways that thrilled him, too. The wonder of that kept him engaged. If he was this attuned to her now, he could only image how much more strongly they might connect in the throes of pleasure.

"I've been doing some research into formula allergies," he said casually. "It's very difficult to say how Conner will stack up against the data. He may not wean for six months."

"I know." She glanced up at Des, her expression indecipherable. "I've looked into it, as well. I may be here until he's on solid food."

"Would that be so bad?" It was a bold question and, judging by the long, heavy silence, she didn't miss the significance of it. They were talking about further alterations to the agreement.

She heaved a deep breath. "Only because it puts my goals on hold even longer."

Not because she'd be stuck here with him. Not because she didn't like taking care of Conner. More had changed than just the circumstances. But how much? Enough that she might reevaluate the complications standing between them?

He couldn't barrel ahead as he'd half planned. As his body screamed for him to. If he didn't want to ruin things between them, he had to take his time. Romance her until she was hot and breathless.

He chewed on the idea until the next morning. During Conner's midmorning nap, Des considered how to court his wife. The techniques felt fake and disingenuous, like he'd have to become someone else to simply hold a conversation with a normal person.

But his wife and son weren't normal people. He loved Conner, and McKenna… Well, he couldn't say for sure how he felt about her, but it wasn't lukewarm by any stretch. She did matter, as he'd told her. The only piece of advice that he'd gleaned from all of his research on talking to people was to engage McKenna at her level of interest.

McKenna wanted to go to medical school and he'd held her back thus far. It was time to rectify that to the best of his ability.

Six

When McKenna had too much rattling around in her brain, she liked to swim. Lately she'd been spending several hours a day at the pool as she tried to get her mind off the constant turmoil under her skin.

Not only had she let herself start to care about Conner, Desmond had noticed. Noticed and commented. That made it real.

She hated the quandary. Conner couldn't be her son and she'd walked into this agreement willingly. Sure she'd known it would be difficult to give up the baby at the hospital, but she'd done it, even though it had been harder than she'd ever imagined. She'd reconciled the loss by envisioning the family Desmond would create for himself, believing that as time went on, the regret would fade.

None of that had happened. Desmond had taken her life over by storm and, instead of moving on, she'd chosen to be in the position of caring for her son day in, day out…only to have to eventually give him up again. Each additional day she stayed in this house meant one more chink in her heart. And she'd known for a while that Desmond would eventually bring up the fact that his original three-month proposal was likely dead in the water.

Being stuck in this nebulous role of mother and not mother was killing her.

How was she going to manage the mess she was making of this?

Swimming helped. But not much. Especially when she broke the surface of the water to see Desmond sitting on one of the lounge chairs, gorgeous and intense and untouchable. Her pulse stumbled and the perfect temperature of the pool rose a few degrees.

She hadn't seen him since last night. Conner had thankfully dropped one of the nighttime feedings, but showed no signs of forgetting about the remaining one, which meant a tension-filled encounter with Desmond lay in store for her like clockwork. She wished she could say she'd shut down his advances and then dismissed him from her mind.

Not so much. As if the thought of leaving Conner behind wasn't difficult enough, she couldn't get his father out from under her skin either. Late at night there were fewer barriers somehow. The dark created an oasis where anything was possible and nothing bad could touch the three of them.

Then when the sun rose she remembered all the reasons she couldn't indulge in the sizzle that sprang up anytime Desmond entered a room.

The echoing pool area amplified the undercurrents between them in spades.

"Conner is down for his nap," he announced—unnecessarily since McKenna knew the baby's schedule well.

"And that seemed like a good opportunity to tell me you hired a nanny?" she suggested hopefully.

"Not yet."

Of course not. What fun would that be? His highness liked to have control and wield his power as he saw fit.

And now she felt petulant and ungrateful. The man was treating *her* like royalty, not acting like he expected everyone to kowtow to his bidding. Desmond wished to keep an iron fist around all of the decisions regarding his son. It wasn't a crime and it was certainly his right. Some people might simply call it being protective.

"You could have flagged me down if you needed to talk," she murmured.

Like the last time he'd cornered her here, he wasn't dressed for swimming. In fact, she'd never seen him in anything but pants and a shirt.

The long look he shot her shouldn't have put so much heat in her blood. She was suddenly very aware that the swimsuit she wore might have been considered modest on most women, but on the body of one who was breast-feeding, it became more of a boob showcase starring pointy, chilled nipples.

Some of that might be the fault of Desmond and his hot-eyed gaze that never failed to make her feel both sexy and appreciated.

"I didn't want to bother you," he said with a shake of his head far past the time when it would have been appropriate to respond.

Too late for that. "But now that I know you're here, it's okay?"

He blinked. "I can come back."

God, sometimes he was so adorable. Why was that such a thing? She'd never met anyone quite like Desmond Pierce and she was pretty sure that was the reason she couldn't stop thinking about him, despite the surety that getting involved would be the worst idea ever.

"I'm just kidding." She kicked to the edge of the pool and rested her arms on the flagstone lip surrounding the water, mostly so the whole of her body was hidden from his too sharp gaze. "You should swim sometime."

"Is that an invitation?" he asked with raised eyebrows…and there came more of the heat that turned the whole exchange into a double entendre. Everything he said lately seemed centered on sex, probably because it was on both their minds constantly.

Cursing her stupid mouth, she shut her eyes for a beat. What was wrong with her that she hadn't seen that coming?

"I thought we covered that. We have too many complications to get involved."

"I am referring to swimming. Only."

Yeah, right. All sorts of non-swimming-related things that could happen in a private area when two people were already nearly undressed shimmered in the atmosphere between them.

"You and I both know you aren't. So save it," she advised.

His head cocked to the side in the way she'd come to understand meant he was about to throw her into a tailspin. "This may surprise you, but I genuinely want to spend time with you."

Yep. Tailspin. "I don't know what to do with that."

"Spend time with me," he suggested wryly. "To that end, I have a surprise for you. I registered you for a couple of online classes that will count toward your medical degree."

"You did what?"

"I thought you might enjoy having something adult

to do since you mentioned that you're bored frequently. It's a gift."

This was definitely one of those times when she couldn't remember why it was a bad idea to get involved with him. No one had ever done something like that for her and it speared her right where it counted. Dumbstruck, she stared at him.

How dare he do something so generous and kindhearted when she had nothing she could do in return to thank him? "I can't accept."

"Why not?"

Argh. Because…of some reason that she couldn't put her finger on. But it felt like she should refuse. "I can't take classes that count toward my course work online. Medical school is about hands-on experience and labs. Working toward residency."

"I am aware. I reviewed the requirements and then called the dean at Oregon Health and Science University to ensure that the courses would transfer."

God, would he just stop shocking the hell out of her for a minute? "Why would you go to all that trouble, Desmond?"

"It was no trouble. You're sacrificing so much for my son. I wished to honor your goal of becoming a doctor, which I have not done a very good job of doing so far."

He'd been listening to her. And then gone out of his way to do something special for her. As gifts went, it was the best one she'd ever received.

She blew out a breath. And then another, fighting for all she was worth not to cry. It was so unexpected, so genuinely unselfish and… "Wait a minute. What's the catch?"

"McKenna, stop. There's no catch."

The raspy note in his voice flashed down her spine

and she was suddenly very glad she'd never levered herself out of the pool. He was too close as it was, too intense, too beautiful with his gaze that missed nothing, and she was very much afraid he'd just turned the tide with his imaginative present. She didn't want to find out just how deep he could take her when he finally sucked her into his orbit.

But then he rendered that point moot by crossing the few feet separating them and kneeling on the flagstone to catch her gaze as he spoke to her.

"It's a gift," he repeated and she couldn't look away. "Because I can be...hard to take. You didn't want to put off medical school, but I gave you no choice. I'm offering you a workable solution to compensate for the difficult circumstances."

That was probably the most shocking part of all.

"I'm here because I chose to be," she corrected him. *Because I continue to choose this.* It was so critical he understand he couldn't force her to do *anything*. But the rest wasn't off base. How could she say no? She couldn't. "It's a lovely thought. Thank you."

"Does that mean you're going to take the classes?"

"Yes. Of course."

Relief rushed over his expression, tripping her radar again. What was he getting out of this? "I'm cold and I'd like to go take a shower. Did you have anything else you needed to discuss? Like hiring a nanny?"

Desmond smiled. "You'll be the first to know when the nanny situation is resolved."

In addition to registering McKenna for the classes he'd selected, Desmond had also ordered her a desk, a leather chair and a top-of-the-line laptop. When they were delivered the next day, he set up everything himself, rolling back the sleeves of his button-down shirt to the forearms and geeking out over the equipment.

Almost none of the words he used to describe what he'd bought made any sense, but the smile he wore when he talked drove it all from her consciousness anyway.

She stood back and let him do his thing because… *oh, my God*, was he sexy when he got his hands dirty in his realm of expertise. This was Desmond at his finest, building something from the ground up, and he nearly glowed with some kind of inner fire she couldn't explain and couldn't stop basking in.

Once he got the mysterious settings of the computer's brain the way he wanted, he showed her how it worked, settling her into the chair and leaning over her shoulder. Something wholly masculine wafted from him as he pointed at the something-or-other on the screen, explaining that he'd done some kind of magic mojo to hook her computer into the private network housed in his workshop.

"It'll be fast," he promised. His tone indicated this was a desirable state, so she nodded. "And I have access to all of the top academic institutions and think tanks in the world. There is literally not one scrap of information discovered in the history of mankind that is not available to you via this portal."

Not one scrap? She bit her lip before asking if his computer could explain why she wanted him to kiss her so badly that her teeth ached. It was unfathomable to her how this small act of kindness and understanding had put so much of a deeper awareness of him under her skin. But it had. And what had been there before was bad enough.

This was different. Encompassing. Inevitable in some ways.

"I installed an instant messaging client, too," he continued, tapping a little blue icon on the screen. "I'll keep mine open and if you need anything while I'm working, you can let me know."

"Isn't that the equivalent of a text message?" She couldn't help but ask because... Come on. What was she going to need to say to him that she couldn't get up and walk the two flights of stairs to his workshop? Besides, she couldn't imagine bothering him with something he viewed as an uncomfortable social contract.

Unperturbed, he shrugged. "Probably. I've never used instant messaging. But schoolwork can be lonely and isolating, especially at this level. I didn't want you to feel cut off."

That turned her heart over in a completely different way because he could only know that from personal experience. And his solution to prevent her from feeling that way? Grant her special backstage access to the genius himself. It was touching, sending little fingers of warmth into her soul.

Because she couldn't stop herself, she reached out and covered his forearm with her palm. "Thank you for this."

He glanced down at her hand and then at her, seemingly just now noticing their close proximity, which only dialed up the awareness about a billion degrees. Prickles walked across her cheeks, her neck. Across her cleavage as he stared at her. They were so close she could see dark flecks in his irises.

"You're welcome."

What did it say that she'd started loving that gruff note in his voice? That she was insane, clearly. She snatched her hand back, chastising herself for falling prey to the intimacy he'd unwittingly created. It instantly disintegrated the moment she stopped touching him. He backed away quickly, heading for the door of her bedroom.

He turned before exiting, running a hand across his beard, which was holy-cow sexy all at once. "Let me know if you're missing anything."

Like her marbles? "I can't imagine what I'd need that you haven't already thought of."

Once Desmond had taken himself and his disturbing presence out of her room, she began the long, arduous process of downloading software, updating her preferences and finally logging on to the university website to figure out how online classes worked.

As the first syllabus spilled onto her screen, she had a total moment of bliss. She didn't love the pressure of academics by any stretch, but she did like a feeling of purpose and accomplishment. This was step one toward her medical degree and she longed to immerse herself in the wonders of the human body. Biology had been her favorite subject since ninth grade when she'd dissected a frog and realized the working parts were similar to other animals but not identical. How amazing was that? She'd yearned to learn more, and had in her undergraduate classes.

Now came the really good stuff.

Thanks to the husband she'd never expected to meet let alone like, she was finally on her way.

At some point Desmond returned with Conner for his next round of feeding. Des apologized for interrupting her, but she waved it off and settled into her recliner, glad for the excuse to get up from her hunched position at the desk. Once the baby was full and happy, she started to hand him back to his father when she realized there was something she could do for Desmond to thank him for his thoughtfulness.

"You know what?" McKenna pulled a fast one, shifting the baby's trajectory, and resettled Conner in her lap. "Let me play nanny for the afternoon."

Desmond quirked a brow. "That's my job."

"I know, but even you can benefit from a break occasionally. Go build something."

His smile was far too brief. "You have class work. Conner is my responsibility."

How many men would complain about being relieved of baby duty for the afternoon? Just one in her experience. "Don't be difficult. Let me do something nice for you."

"All right." He didn't sound like it was all right. He sounded like he didn't quite know what had hit him. "If you're sure."

She hefted Conner higher against her chest, supporting his downy head with her palm. "Off you go."

Actually she looked forward to spending time with Conner. She'd tried to limit her exposure to him as much as possible and, thus far, Desmond had been pretty on board with that. But diving into medical school had brought home the fact that she would not live in this house forever with easy access to her baby. Eventually she'd have to leave and as much as she'd been telling herself she couldn't wait and moaning about how Desmond's deal was too Machiavellian for words, she'd secretly started dreading the future.

"Two hours," Desmond finally agreed with a nod. "But only because you called me difficult."

So that was a sensitive subject apparently, judging by his indignant tone. She stuck her tongue out to lighten the mood. "Is that the magic button? I'll keep that in my back pocket then."

His mouth curved and he rubbed Conner's head in farewell. Desmond faded from the room but his presence lingered, made all the more strong by virtue of the new desk standing in the corner.

She'd probably never sit at it without reliving him leaning over her with the brush of his arm against hers.

"Just you and me, sport," she murmured to Conner, who picked that moment to wail in her ear. "Oh, none of that, now. Your daddy will come running, wondering what I'm doing to torture you."

McKenna rose from the chair and paced with Conner on her shoulder. Sometimes he needed extra burping after feeding. But a few rounds of gently massaging his tummy didn't get her anywhere. Diaper change, then.

She hurried to the nursery, which was down the hall between her bedroom and Desmond's. He'd decorated the room with rocket ships and stars, with a complete solar system tethered to the ceiling with thin fishing line. It was an odd choice for a baby but she'd never questioned it because it was easy to envision the man responsible for the décor lovingly placing each item exactly where he wanted it. The theme made sense to Desmond and she appreciated that he'd taken such care with the room his son would live in.

McKenna changed Conner's diaper in no time and that did the trick. No more wailing. Smiling at her little bundle of joy, she found his favorite stuffed animal—an elephant Desmond called Peter, for God knew what reason—and played peekaboo with it while Conner kicked happily from his bouncy seat.

What an amazing little person. He was gorgeous, with dark fuzzy hair and chubby cheeks. Her allotted two hours flew by and, before she'd blinked, Desmond peeked into the room with no-nonsense purpose on his face.

"I'm done building something," he informed her, his

voice smoothed out now that he was back in control. "You can do your own thing now."

"Like biochemistry?" She frowned. That had sounded so exciting earlier, before she'd had a couple of peaceful hours with her son.

"Yes, exactly like that." Desmond swooped in and effectively kicked her out with a nonchalant wave.

With far more regret than she'd like, she left father and baby to go back to her room, but she couldn't concentrate on anything. The first lesson of her biochemistry class blurred, turning into a giant mess on the screen. Looked like a swim was in order.

But as she splashed through the water, even the normally hypnotic activity didn't help. She kept craning her neck, looking for Desmond, though he'd only sought her out in the pool room twice in the six weeks she'd been living there.

Something was wrong with her. The melancholy she'd slipped into had all the hallmarks of mild depression, but she'd never been one to mope around. Of course, she'd been busy for years. This was the first real break she'd had from life since forever. Maybe that was part of her problem; she wasn't busy enough.

What more of a distraction did she need than new graduate-level courses? Desmond had provided her with the best prescription possible for her ennui and she wasn't even taking advantage of it. Maybe she should check out the other class Desmond had registered her for.

She dried off and got dressed, then resettled at her computer to access the second class. Embryology. Huh. She had a better than average understanding of that subject. The syllabus pretty much outlined the forty weeks she'd just experienced in real life: the stages from human conception through birth, with an emphasis on cellular development as the fetus grew.

Except, in her case, it wasn't a generic fetus, as she'd told herself for the entire length of her pregnancy. Neither had it turned out to be *just* an experiment to help her understand what her pregnant patients would be going through.

She'd carried Desmond's baby. Conner. He was a sweet, darling little angel who rarely cried and made her smile whenever she gazed at his face. Conner was her son, too.

A tear splashed down on the keyboard and then another. Finally she had to admit she'd thoroughly messed up in her quest to stay removed from the maternal instincts that surged to the surface on a continual basis.

Instead of a long goodbye, she'd started loving her son.

What was she going to do?

Go back to biochemistry. What else? Maybe she was just tired and could handle the embryonic course better tomorrow, when she hadn't just spent two hours in the company of the baby.

The first lesson scrolled onto the screen again. The concepts should have been easy, a review of the things she'd learned in undergraduate chemistry classes. But she couldn't get her brain to wrap around what she was reading.

A little message popped up to inform her that Desmond H. Pierce was online.

The smile his name pulled out of her went a long way toward drying up the waterworks. How freaking adorable was that man? He had one contact in his chat program—his wife—yet he found it necessary to spell out his full name?

She couldn't help herself. She clicked on the little blue icon and opened a chat window.

McKenna: *Desmond H. Pierce? Were you worried I'd confuse you with all the other Desmonds in my contact list?* Send.

She gave it fifty-fifty odds that he'd actually respond. He might even ignore her since she was essentially being a smart aleck. But the baby was obviously taking his afternoon nap. Maybe she'd get lucky.

Wonder of wonders. A message appeared under the blank window: *Desmond H. Pierce is typing.*

Desmond H. Pierce: *It asked for my name. That's what I entered.*

She actually laughed out loud at that.

McKenna: *You're so literal.*

Desmond: *Yes.*

McKenna: *Did you change your name in your settings? Just because I said something about it?*

Desmond: *Maybe.*

For some reason that pinged around her heart. She didn't take his sensitivity into account nearly often enough when she was bulldozing through aspects of his personality she actually found really great.

McKenna: *I like that you're so literal. I never have to question what you mean when you say something.*

Desmond: *You'll be very lonely in that group of one.*

McKenna: *I didn't join so I could hang out with throngs of Desmond H. Pierce admirers. I'm your wife, not a groupie.*

The chat window stayed maddeningly blank for the longest time. So long, that she started to wonder if she should apologize for something or clarify that she'd been messing around. One bad thing about virtual communication—Desmond couldn't see her face or hear her tone, so he didn't know she was kidding.

Finally the status bar told her Desmond was typing.

Desmond: *And as my wife, you're in the position to know that I have very few admirers.*

McKenna: *Because you spend all your time building fake people instead of communicating with real ones?*

Desmond: *Because the list of those who like literal people is very short.*

McKenna: *You say stuff like that all the time. I like you. You act as if there's something wrong with me because I don't see you as difficult.*

Desmond: *You don't?*

She shook her head and typed: *Duh.*

This time the pause was longer and she waited with baited breath to see what he might come back with.

Desmond: *Then I would expect it to be easier to get you on a second date.*

Her breath gasped out in a half laugh, half exhale of shock. *That* was why he thought she'd been so adamantly resistant to his perfectly chiseled mouth?

Actually she couldn't remember why resistance had been so set in her mind as a necessity. Because she didn't like the idea of getting involved with a self-confessed control addict? Yeah, Desmond liked to keep a tight fist on his son's life and held the cards of her future, as well. But he was also kind. Full of love for his son. Beyond intelligent. And a little dorky. For some reason, she liked that about him the best.

McKenna: *I would have expected you to try harder then.*

Desmond: *Is that the magic button?*

Her eyelids fluttered closed as she laughed again. What was she supposed to do with him?

McKenna: *I have lots of magic buttons.*

Probably she shouldn't be flirting with him. But it was fun. And she definitely didn't hate the long twinge that curled through her midsection as she pictured Desmond going on an exploratory mission to see how each button worked. And how many times he could press them to get her to come.

Desmond: *Aren't you supposed to be doing school-work?*

She'd flustered him. What did it mean that she could understand him so easily despite the two floors that separated them?

McKenna: *Biochemistry is hard. It's been over a year since I was in school.*

The chat window went completely still. She waited for some kind of pep talk or maybe a condemnation for her ungratefulness. After all, he'd been the one to register her. Was he mad that she'd complained?

The atmosphere shifted and she whirled to see Desmond standing in her open doorway. Her throat went tight as she took in the look on his face. Hungry. Gorgeous. Watchful. Not safe behind a virtual chat window but here, in the flesh. In her bedroom.

"Um…hi," she blurted out as her pulse triple-timed. "I wasn't expecting you."

"Let me help you with your homework."

Oh, God. That was the sweetest thing. Almost better than what she'd assumed he'd come for. "You don't have to."

"I want to." He sauntered over to the desk, his long, lean body fluid and mouthwatering as he perched on the edge, his attention on her. Not the laptop. "Show me what you're having trouble with."

Somehow she didn't think it would be prudent to point out the real trouble was with her lungs and the whole breathing thing when he got this close. She shouldn't let him affect her this way. "The first lesson covers the kinetics of catalyzed versus uncatalyzed reactions."

He didn't as much as blink. "You're studying analytic chemistry in a biochemistry class?"

His knee brushed her hand. She should move it. But it was resting so comfortably on the arm of the chair and the zing of his touch had gone clear to her shoulder. Moving suddenly seemed impossible.

"Apparently." But given that he'd clued in on the distinction immediately, odds were good he knew both pretty well. Her genius husband was a resource she hadn't fully appreciated when embarking on a medical degree. "The reaction formulas the professor covers are a little different than how I learned it in undergrad."

He shifted to view the screen, his thigh snugging up next to her arm. Fireworks exploded in her core as his presence overwhelmed her system.

"Wow. That is a really roundabout way to demonstrate the transition. I have some diagrams that are far more useful than this garbage."

Leaning closer, he tapped on her keyboard, apparently oblivious to the fact that her shoulder was buried in his chest. She sucked in a breath and tried to ignore the way her muscles tensed, ready to reach out and touch him at a moment's notice. Because if she started, she feared she might not stop.

"See?" He pointed at the two-color graph on the screen that had materialized from his mystical gateway to the depths of human knowledge. "Quantify the energy transfer using this and tell me what you get."

No question in that statement because he didn't even stop to consider she might not be smart enough to follow him. He just believed she was. That wrung a whole hell of a lot of something out of her heart that should not be there.

He glanced at her, his expression expectant. So she indulged them both and studied his graph. The answer popped into her head instantly.

"Gibbs free energy. 20 percent." How she squeezed that out of her mouth when her tongue had gone numb, she'd never know.

Nodding, he grinned. "Told you my stuff is better than what the professor is trying to make you use. Don't hesitate to borrow my database anytime. Or me."

That had all sorts of loaded connotations she really couldn't help but consider. Her skin flushed hot as she contemplated him and his eyes darkened as he seemed to finally pick up on the less than studious energy swirling between them.

The air fairly crackled with it as they stared at each other. How was it possible that Desmond had become that much sexier just by showing off his intelligence?

But it was an inescapable fact. Her husband's brain turned her on.

She wanted Desmond H. Pierce more than she wanted to breathe and she'd spent far too much energy denying them both something that might be spectacular, solely because she didn't want to give him any more control than he already had.

There was one surefire way to deal with that—make her own choices. If she didn't like where things were going, they signed divorce papers and went on. Easy out.

"Chemistry wasn't really part of the deal," she murmured.

His body swiveled until he was facing her instead of the computer. "I don't mind helping with your homework."

That wasn't the chemistry she was concerned about at the moment. She wanted Desmond's hands on her body and his mouth following shortly behind, but she'd put up so many roadblocks it was no wonder he was practicing what she'd preached, namely that getting involved was a bad idea.

There were probably a host of things she should carefully consider before throwing caution to the wind. But right this minute, she didn't care. There was nothing separating them but her own unfounded fears.

Seven

Biochemistry. That was the chemistry Des should be focusing on, but he'd frankly lost all interest in McKenna's class work in favor of drowning in her expressive gaze. Her eyes held a whole world inside them and he couldn't stop drinking it in.

The draw between him and his wife was a whole other kind of chemistry, the kind he'd like to learn about because he had the distinct feeling there'd be a lot to absorb.

"My homework will be there later," McKenna informed him throatily. The slight rasp in her voice hooked him instantly. It meant she was as affected by his nearness as he was hers.

The desk had been an altruistic gift, solely designed to get her started on her degree. He hadn't considered that it would become a method of seduction. But the object of his affection sat within arm's length in the chair he'd selected for her. His leg had been in firm contact with her hand for the better part of five minutes but she hadn't rolled away.

"When is your first lesson due?" he asked. The last thing he wanted to do was distract her when she'd just started what looked to be a difficult class given how backward the instructor planned to teach something as straightforward as chemical reactions.

"I don't know." She didn't take her gaze from his and he couldn't look away, not when she had so many interesting nonverbal things she was saying. "But it's not right this minute. We have plenty of time to worry about that later."

College classes had definitely shifted his advantage and he was nothing if not prepared to press it.

Awareness saturated the atmosphere. So maybe she was looking for a distraction. One that had a much more explosive reaction than those detailed on her screen.

"McKenna," he murmured, and her face tipped up to the perfect angle for him to take her mouth with his, which he planned to do as soon as he was clear on whether he'd been reading her signals correctly.

Once he kissed her, he didn't plan to stop. Therefore, it would be prudent to make sure that's what she wanted.

"Desmond," she murmured back.

The way she caressed his name with her raspy voice settled low in his gut, flaring out with sensual heat that would take little to stoke higher. The virtual chat had gotten him good and primed already, especially with all the talk of magic buttons.

He should have installed a chat tool weeks ago. Who knew that would be the mechanism to get his wife to flirt with him?

But virtual chatting only went so far. Being in her presence heightened the reactions her sexy talk had started and he craved the experience of connecting with her in the flesh. There was so much to discover between them, nuances of emotion and heights of pleasure to catalog. He couldn't wait to start exploring.

"I'm going to kiss you," he informed her. "If that's not what you want, you should tell me to leave. Immediately."

Her dark eyes speared him to the core, blazing with unmistakable heat. "My mouth is one of my buttons."

As invitations went, that couldn't be much clearer. But they'd been at this spot before and she'd backed off. Twice. He wasn't going to make that mistake again. "And I definitely plan to push it. Along with several others. If that's not okay, I need to know that now."

"I want you to kiss me, Desmond."

Her exasperation came through loud and clear but he'd been exasperated for nearly a week. She could deal with it until he had the answers he needed.

"What about the complications?" he asked.

She stood so fast that the chair shot backward and tipped over, but he could hardly focus on anything other than the beautiful woman who'd stepped into the gap of his thighs. He widened his legs to give her plenty of room, aching to slip his hands around her waist and yank her closer to his center. Her heat was exactly what his throbbing erection needed.

"The only complication I'm dealing with right now is the one between your ears," she said with a half laugh as her hands slid over his shoulders. "I'm starting to see how you could be described as difficult."

Apparently impatient with waiting, she wound her fist in his shirt and pulled. He let her because… *Hell, yes*, this was the chemistry he'd come for. If she wanted to move things forward at her own pace, he wasn't going to argue.

And then their mouths aligned, both rough and tender at the same time. It was such a rush of sensation that his entire body jolted. The kiss deepened without any effort on his part as she inhaled him, drawing him into her spirit and essence with nothing more than the conduit of her mouth.

She was molten and fluid, eager. Best of all, she'd granted him permission to drop down the rabbit hole with her.

Now he could touch. With the threat of losing this moment eliminated, he smoothed his palms down her back, reveling in the firmness of her body against his fingertips. *His wife.* The mother of his child. She felt unbelievable and that was saying something considering how often he'd fantasized about having her this close, this available for his investigation.

And the kiss deepened even further, destroying him from the inside out as she nestled against the planes of his torso, thigh to thigh.

Her hot tongue slid forward, seeking and... Oh, yes, he craved more of that, already anticipating the way she filled him with her taste. He took each thrust, felt it in his bones, his blood, his groin. She crawled inside him easily and he didn't try to stop the flood of McKenna. She was right where he wanted her.

He let her have her fun for four seconds. *My turn.*

Nearly drunk on her, he wrested control of the kiss away from her in one fell swoop, spinning to capture her against the desk. His thigh spread hers and she gasped, but opened to him beautifully, accepting his hard length at her center with surprising willingness. Stars exploded across his vision as he absorbed her heat through his clothes.

She was so ready for him. Probably slick with it and swollen. He could feel her desire under his skin, where the empathy was always strongest, and it built his own need to a fevered pitch.

More. Now. He gripped her jaw and slanted it, plunging into her mouth with a ferocity he had no idea he possessed. But she met him halfway, seemingly as impatient for it as he was. Desperate little moans vibrated from her throat and it thrilled him to incite such sounds of abandon from her.

She wanted him. Wanted the connection he'd felt from the first. The sense of isolation and loneliness he'd carried for most of his life vanished in a snap as he opened his soul to what she was offering him.

Warm hands branded his back as she explored under his shirt. He returned the favor, yanking the fabric of her T-shirt from her pants and letting his fingers do the talking. Beautiful. Velvety. He couldn't get enough of her skin. Too many clothes in the way.

"Desmond," she breathed against his mouth.

He scarcely had enough of his senses left to recognize his own name. "Hmm." Her throat had the tenderest little area that his lips fit into perfectly and he got busy acquainting himself with it as he slipped the T-shirt off her shoulder to give him better access.

"I hate to mention it, but I'm, um…not on any kind of birth control. I wasn't expecting this."

That heavy dose of reality put a pall over the wonders of her skin against his tongue. He lifted his head, his mind clicking through all the possible scenarios as the critical pieces of information fell into their buckets. She didn't want to get pregnant again. Of course she didn't. And, idiot that he was, he hadn't been expecting her to remove all the obstacles between them so quickly either. Why hadn't he had an entire truckload of condoms delivered? Some genius he was.

But surely he was smart enough to salvage the situation.

"No problem," he murmured and slid a hand under her shirt to toy with her bra strap. "We're just getting started. There's a lot of you I haven't seen yet and a lot of ways I can make love to you that don't require birth control."

Her eyes darkened. "I'm thoroughly intrigued by that statement."

"Let me demonstrate."

He lifted the hem of her shirt and whipped it off. The catch on her bra came apart in his fingers with a small snick and her lush, full breasts spilled out before he could fully peel the fabric from them.

Groaning as he tossed her clothes to the floor, he packed both palms with her engorged flesh. Erect nipples chafed his hands and the heat of her zinged through his erection. There was no way he could have been more turned on in that moment.

"I need to see the rest of you," he said hoarsely, and she nodded, pulling off her pants and underwear in one motion.

Naked, she perched on the desk without an ounce of embarrassment. Slowly he settled into her desk chair and caressed her thighs, trailing down to her knees. Then pushed, opening her until she was spread wide. She didn't protest, just shoved the computer aside so she could lean back on her elbows, letting him look his fill. It was the most humbling experience of his life, except for the first moment he'd held his son. This woman had given him both.

"McKenna," he murmured and it fell from his lips like a prayer. "I can't believe how gorgeous you are."

Laying his lips on her thigh, he worked his way toward

her center. She squirmed restlessly, gasping as he abraded her tender flesh with his beard, which he'd thankfully trimmed not too long ago. It was about to come in very handy as he pleasured his wife.

The first lick in her slick center pulled a cry from her that thickened his erection past the point of all reason. *How* was she so sexy, so disturbing, in all the best ways? He'd barely started and her taste exploded against his lips as she rolled her hips, shimmying closer to his mouth.

Obviously she wanted him to go deeper. That worked for him. He gave it to her, grasping her hips to hold her still as she couldn't seem to manage that on her own. Excellent. He loved that she got so into it, crying and panting with little feminine noises as he licked her harder.

He twisted two fingers into her slick channel, gently because he was nothing if not overly sensitive to the fact that she'd recently given birth to the miracle that lay sleeping down the hall.

She bucked, her muscles clamping down beautifully on his fingers in a release that tensed her whole body. Throbbing with his own desire, he nibbled at her core until she came again, crying his name and rocking against his tongue.

The most amazing feeling washed over him and it was so engulfing, so beautiful. He couldn't sort whether he'd sensed it from her or it had bloomed from his depths. Didn't matter. They were so entwined, so connected, they'd probably generated it together. Simultaneously. It was nearly spiritual. He needed more.

"Again," he murmured and started all over.

She shook her head and tried to move out of reach, but he clamped down on her hips.

"I want to return the favor," she insisted weakly, levering higher on her elbows to capture his gaze and, without looking away or letting her do so either, he took a long, slow lick at that precise moment.

She shuddered, banked embers in her depths flaring to life in a raging fire that stoked his own.

"That can wait," he informed her. "This can't. I've dreamed about having you at my mercy, exactly in this position. You took biology. You know the tongue is the strongest muscle in the body. I can do this all night."

Her eyelids fluttered closed as he spread her again with his thumbs and proved his point by giving her the flat of his tongue. Her swollen folds welled again as she orgasmed a third time in mere seconds.

"Stop, it's too much," she gasped and then cursed as he ignored her, wholly unsatisfied with how little he'd done for her. How could a few orgasms possibly compare with what he owed her? She'd sacrificed a year of her life in pursuit of his plan for a family and delayed medical school to nourish his son.

"It's not enough," he corrected, his lips still buried inside her. "I'm only just beginning to learn which buttons to push. I need a lot more research between your thighs before I can possibly stop. For example, what does this button do?"

He rubbed his beard right in the center of the bundle of sensitized nerves. She cried out as she came again, her back lifting off the desk in an arch that thrust her breasts skyward. It was such an erotic pose that he nearly lost the iron grip he had on his own release. The need to fill her, to finally empty himself inside her, overwhelmed him and he almost couldn't stand it.

"Please, Desmond," she nearly sobbed. "I want...need. Something. More. You."

Maybe they'd both had enough. It was all he could do

to keep from stripping down and giving her what she'd asked for. No condom, just flesh on flesh for an eternity.

Reluctantly he pulled back and kissed her inner thigh. This interlude had merely been the precursor and he wasn't opposed to giving her time to recover. "We'll have it your way. More of that later tonight."

"I don't think I'll be recovered by then," she muttered and then shot him a sly smile. "And don't think I've forgotten how merciless you are. I will definitely be returning that part of the favor, as well."

We'll see about that. He had several hours to get condoms into this house and maybe a few other surprises that would guarantee she wouldn't back off again.

That was the most important thing. The less time he gave her to second-guess what was happening here, the better. He wasn't nearly finished exploring how deep this unbelievable coupling between them went.

Funny how he'd once been so determined to deconstruct their attraction solely with the intent of making it stop. Now that he'd started, he never wanted it to end.

Desmond finally left her alone after promising he had something special in mind for later that night. McKenna ate dinner in the kitchen with Mrs. Elliot and a couple of the groundskeepers, which was fairly typical, but she couldn't seem to swallow.

Anticipation kept her whole body keyed up. Throwing caution to the wind had allowed for an amazing experience at the hands—and mouth—of her husband. Frankly she couldn't imagine what else he might come up with that could top earlier. But she was totally game to find out.

After dinner, McKenna fed the baby and put him down for the night. If true to form, Conner would sleep until midnight. Four hours away.

As she hurried to her room to get dressed for her date with Desmond, she didn't pretend to have anything on her mind other than what might be considered "special." The things he'd done to her body... She hadn't realized she could come that hard or that many times in a row. Or that she'd married a man who wasn't done after giving her one orgasm. He should teach a class—in her experience, that wasn't the typical philosophy of the male gender as a whole. So far, she was a huge fan of Desmond's brand of lovemaking.

And if all the stars aligned, she'd get to learn a lot more about his philosophies. She shuddered as her body got in on the anticipation in its own way, soaking the tiny scrap of silk underwear she'd slipped on. So much for wearing sexy lingerie for her husband. Maybe he'd like it if she went commando.

Why was she so *nervous*? It wasn't like she'd never had sex before. And, for all intents and purposes, she'd *already* had sex with Desmond. The big difference, of course, being that this time he'd be participating.

The knock on her door nearly separated her skin from her bones. She smoothed the skirt of the dress she'd painstakingly picked, though it probably didn't matter. It would likely be on the floor shortly.

She opened the door and her breath caught as Desmond's gaze devoured her whole.

"Come with me," he said simply and held out his hand.

Her palm in his, she let him lead her down the hall to his bedroom. All righty then. No preamble apparently. This wasn't a date in the traditional sense, with wine and flowers. They were just going to hop into bed? Of course, given her abandon earlier, she couldn't exactly claim a sense of modesty or that she needed romance to get her motor going. Desmond pretty much just had to look at her and her panties melted.

But then he ushered her through the double doors, clicking them closed behind him as the darkness of the room surrounded her. Her pulse leaped, hammering in her throat as her pupils fought to adjust to the black.

"I hope you meant what you said about liking thunderstorms." His voice slid across her skin like silk a moment before a rumble sounded from the far wall.

A bolt of lightning forked across the ceiling in a brief flash of light. Awestruck, she watched as another one streaked across the wall. "You made me a thunderstorm?"

"I did." Another rumble of thunder interrupted him, louder this time, as if the storm was growing closer. "Surprise."

"It's brilliant." Lightning lit up the room for another brief second, revealing the four-poster. Somehow, the faux storm swirled around it, beckoning her straight into the center.

But Desmond didn't give her a chance to take one step. Sweeping her up into his arms, he carried her to the bed, laying her out on the comforter. "It took some doing. I think it turned out well."

The patter of rain echoed behind her head, coming faster now as more thunder crashed through the bedframe, shaking it with shocking realism. "I don't think you could have made it more real."

"Let's just see about that, shall we?" Lightning illuminated half his face, revealing a wicked smile that put a tingle in her breasts.

Faint music danced between the crashes of thunder, something electronic and fast with no lyrics that kept time with the storm perfectly, as if one fed the other. The divine maestro himself rolled onto the mattress, sweeping her into his arms and into the maelstrom with a hot, hungry kiss.

Instantly her body electrified. With her eyes closed, she could scarcely credit how real the storm seemed. Desmond's tongue circled hers, demanding and insistent. White-hot desire split her core, flooding her with the thick, achy need that only he could satisfy.

In the space of one peal of thunder, he pulled off her dress and crouched over her. The next time the room lit up, his gaze traveled over her, hot and heavy.

"I, um, thought it was going to be my turn to be merciless," she squeaked as he bent to mouth her throat. Her head tipped back involuntarily to give him better access. When his fingers slipped under the cups of the bra to lightly play with her nipples, her back bowed off the bed, grinding her pelvis into his.

Every erogenous zone on her body was far more sensitive than she was used to but her breasts were the worst. Best. His touch penetrated her to the marrow, swept a volcanic wave through her blood until she was writhing under the press of his hips, silently begging him for what she'd only gotten a taste of earlier.

"Please," she rasped. "I want your mouth on me again."

His lips were nearly poetic, strong, full, talented. And she wanted his French kiss between her legs immediately. She'd get busy pleasuring him very, very soon, but she couldn't help how much the earlier session on the desk had prepped her for a repeat.

"Absolutely in the plan," he murmured. "We have hours and I intend to use every last second to worship your body."

His fingers tangled in her bra straps, pulling them down off her shoulders until both breasts burst free of their confines. The first scratch of his beard against a nipple raced down her spine, unleashing a shiver. But he didn't draw the aching tip into his mouth like she'd expected, somehow cluing in that she'd had enough stimulation in that area lately.

Instead he laved at the underside, finding new places to nibble that she'd have never called sensitive, but he lit her up with nothing more than carefully placed teeth.

Gasping, she twisted against the onslaught, nearly weeping to get more of him against her flesh. He complied, inching his way down her stomach with his fiery mouth, leaving trails of sensation as he went until he hit the juncture of her thighs, where she ached for him most.

"You're not wearing any panties," he announced, a thread of pure lust lacing his voice. "It's almost as if you're asking for me to spend a lot of time down here."

Breathless, she choked out a laugh. "You read my mind."

By way of answer, his slightly rough and wholly talented hands slid up her thighs and pressed, opening her wide until her knees hit the comforter on either side. His hands—she couldn't get enough of them on her. They spoke a language all their own as his thumbs explored her center, rubbing, dipping, whirling her into an oblivion of sensation heightened by simultaneous booms of thunder and the drumming of rain.

The heat and pressure of his mouth at her core as he finally added his lips and tongue tensed her whole body, and the gush of wetness was almost embarrassing, except he groaned, lapping it up.

"So gorgeous. So responsive. I love how I can do this to you," he said and swirled his tongue with exactly the right motion to send a shower of heat through her as she slid to the edge and over, rippling through the first of what would likely be many spectacular climaxes.

"Again," she commanded, instantly addicted to his talents, delirious with the pleasure of his hands. "But this time with you."

She'd waited long enough. She wanted to see him, to touch. To bring him to climax and hear him cry out because the release was too big to keep inside. Rolling away from him before he could clamp down on her thighs again, because she knew his tricks now, she knelt on the bed and pushed at his shoulders, insisting he sit up from his position on all fours.

It clearly amused him to do as she directed since he did it. Otherwise she'd probably never have moved him. Honestly, it was a crapshoot on whether she'd have rolled back under his mouth if he hadn't. Her core still quivered from the climax and she well knew the second one would be even better. Her body craved it, demanded it, sought it with little circles of her hips even as she fingered her way down his shirt in the dark, unbuttoning as she went.

He was lucky she didn't tear the thing from his body, shedding buttons like flower petals ripped from their stems. Finally she drew off the shirt and couldn't resist her first taste of Desmond's body.

Without hesitation, she bent her head and kissed his shoulder, then dragged her tongue across his clavicle. His hands gripped her waist, holding her in place as he sucked in a breath. Bolder now, she nipped at his throat, nibbled her way up the column to his ear and laved at his lobe, eliciting a groan deep in his chest that thrilled her.

This was her turn and she suddenly wanted to lavish him with as much care as he'd showed her. She pushed him back onto the mattress and rid him of his pants and underwear. She wished she could have done a slow reveal but she wanted to touch.

Warm flesh pulsed under her palms as she covered

him and, in that moment, the thunder and lightning crashed simultaneously, lighting up the bed well enough for her to see the gorgeous length. Tongue to the tip, she licked, her eyes on him, his eyes on her.

Darkness fell again but the half-lidded expression of pure pleasure on his face had burned into her mind. She sucked the whole of him into her mouth, rolling her tongue around his shaft until he groaned out her name, hips pistoning under her palms.

"Enough," he growled and she almost ignored him as he'd done to her earlier, but he easily lifted her off him and set her back against the pillow, thumb sliding across her face in an apologetic caress. "You can have many orgasms but my physiology isn't as evolved and your mouth is amazing."

Fair enough. A rustle indicated he'd likely donned a condom and delicious anticipation filled her. This was it. The consummation of all of this foreplay.

Thunder cracked again and again, heightening the low throb in her core. He didn't make her wait. Before she could blink, he'd gathered her up and laid her down, covering her with his hot, firm body. But instead of gearing up to plunge in, he captured her lips in a long, tender kiss.

Slowly his tongue explored hers. The rush swept outward, languorously stealing over her skin as he made love to her mouth. This kiss wasn't about the mechanics of sex, which he'd proved again and again he had down pat. It was the basest form of communication and she absorbed all of what he was saying, grasping it eagerly with every fiber of her body.

"I want you," he said over and over, and it was a delicious kick to be the object of his desire. His hand drifted down her arm, caressing, lingering, then eventually working south to her waist, her thigh. The gorgeous,

heavy press of his body on hers grew more insistent. He shifted, hips rolling suggestively against hers. The kiss deepened, grew urgent, and she answered with her own suggestive shimmy and slid her thigh along his, opening herself up into a wide cradle.

"McKenna."

He murmured her name so reverently it curled through her senses. Her head tipped back against the pillow as she felt him slide into place at her core. Then he pushed and his thick length filled her, and it was so right, she gasped. Urgency overtook them both and they came together in perfect tempo with the music and the rain and the fevered ecstasy he was building in every pore of her body.

Soaring, she gave up all thought, reason, let him fill her to the brim with the pretty phrases he drizzled down on her as they wound each other higher and higher. At the crescendo of the next round of thunder, his gifted fingers danced across the button at her center, firm, hot, and it shattered her. Boneless, she came, rippling around his length in a powerful release that eclipsed anything she'd ever known. Wave after wave of something divine swamped her, spiraling her into a near out-of-body experience.

But she didn't want to be out of her body, not when Desmond was still powering through the finale of his own release. Hands on his back, she urged him on, whispering encouragement until he tensed against her thighs with a hoarse cry.

It was so beautiful, tears slid down her face.

Collapsing to the mattress, he rolled her into his arms, holding her tight against his body, wordless. No matter. The nonverbal spoke loudly enough in the darkness. *Wow.*

After a long, delicious eternity of nothing but naked

skin against hers, he nuzzled her ear. "Tell me that was fantastic for you."

She nodded far less enthusiastically than she'd have liked but her muscles were still recovering. "Fantastic is an understatement."

"I...felt it," he murmured, sounding hesitant for the first time since he'd swept her into the room. "Your pleasure, I mean. It was like a second presence and it was unbelievably amazing. It's hard to explain and now I'm sure you think I'm as weird as everyone else does."

He trailed off with a half laugh but she sat up, scowling, even though he couldn't see her until lightning forked across the ceiling on the next wave.

"Stop it. I do not think you're weird." *Different*, sure. But in a good way. "You're brilliant and kind and you made me a thunderstorm. If that's weird, then weird should be considered the new sexy."

"You think I'm sexy?"

Her eye roll was so loud, it was a wonder he hadn't heard it. "Duh. I can't even count all of my orgasms today."

"Six. So far."

Dear God. "No. Not *so far*. Absolutely no more. For me anyway. It's your turn."

He'd stopped her before she could finish the job she'd started earlier and if any more orgasms happened tonight, they'd be all his.

"I'm afraid that's not going to work for me." His hand found hers, clasped it. Twined their fingers together. "I like it when you come and I like having my mouth on you when it happens. It's so much better than anything I've ever imagined."

He yanked on their clasped hands, pulling her off balance. She fell to the mattress and he covered her immediately. She squirmed and only succeeded in grinding against his semi-erection.

"That was dirty," she snapped as he trapped her against the pillow, arms above her head.

"Not sorry. By the way, if you think you've experienced the full extent of my imagination, you'd be wrong."

She shuddered as he slid down the length of her body to nip at the juncture between her legs. There was a half second when she considered clamping her thighs together to prove a point. But then her knees fell open almost without any help on her part as he pushed on them. Who the hell was she kidding? As if she had the power to deny him access to whatever he wanted to lick, touch or bite on her body.

Delirious instantly, she thrashed under his hot mouth, so many emotions bleeding through her chest. His teeth scraped across her nub and she nearly screamed as white-hot pleasure crashed against the realization that her feelings for him went far deeper than she'd guessed.

The flood of everything crested up and over as he increased the pressure exactly as he'd learned—so quickly—would splinter her into a million pieces. The wave of her release spread like molten lava, eating up all her cold, empty places and filling them with Desmond.

This was not supposed to be happening.

Furious with herself for letting things get so out of hand, she clenched against her release, cutting it short through sheer will.

"McKenna," he murmured. "Let go. Don't deny yourself because I wished to pleasure you instead of letting you have your way."

She nearly laughed and then choked on it as he did something new against her core. The sensation gripped her in steely claws, coaxing her back to the edge. And then he pushed her over with a shattering climax that put the other six to shame.

Her husband commanded her body as easily as he'd commanded her to wait for the divorce. She'd given him that power by choosing intimacy and it scared her all at once. She didn't know if she *could* deny this draw between them.

"That was so beautiful," he said and curled her against his side. "You're my wife and you deserve to be treated like a queen. Think of me as your vassal. Sleep here. I'll bring Conner to you and put him back to bed. You do nothing more strenuous than lay here until morning. Sleep if you want. Or tell me to pleasure you again."

She blinked and settled her palm on his chest, content to lay half on top of him because he felt delicious against her overused muscles. That was the problem with Desmond. He made it sound like she'd gotten it all wrong, that he was the most selfless human on the planet. She didn't have to do anything but lounge around and wait for the next time she felt like ordering her husband to make her body sing?

If there was a downside to that, she couldn't find it.

Eight

Carefully, Desmond eased back into the bed after checking on the baby for the second time. Conner had started waking up at 6:00 a.m. two nights ago, but both times Des had been able to get him to go back to sleep without nursing.

The material he'd read suggested that if he let the baby eat, he would eat. If his father talked him back into bed without giving him what he wanted, Conner learned that he didn't have to eat just because his eyes were open. So far, so good.

McKenna lay in Desmond's bed, eyes closed and face tranquil. He'd kept her awake far past when he should have but once he'd started exploring the wonders of her, he couldn't stop. She hadn't complained. And he intended to ensure that continued to be the case.

Des had turned off the storm machine before the baby's midnight feeding, which was a necessary shame. That had been inspired and McKenna had loved it. Conner wouldn't have. Last night was the first time his wife had breast-fed his son in Desmond's bed. That unprecedented event deserved respect, as did the fact that she was still in his bed.

The first of many nights if he had anything to say about it.

He had no practice at sliding between the covers without waking another person. Somehow he levered himself onto the mattress without rocking it, then got most of his body into position, a feat considering McKenna slept with abandon, flinging an arm across his pillow and curling her legs up onto his side. He didn't mind. She had gorgeous legs.

But when he pulled the covers up, they caught on something. He yanked before realizing she'd balled up a good bit in her fist.

Her dark eyes blinked open and she smirked. "Don't tell me you're an early riser. That's grounds for divorce."

He smiled because he couldn't help himself. When he looked at her, it was like seeing the sun peek through the clouds after three days of gray. "I was checking on Conner. I didn't mean to wake you up. If you weren't hogging the covers, you never would have known I'd moved."

Long, dark hair spilled over his pillow and he resisted the urge to gather it in his hands. Barely.

"Oh, I see. This is all my fault. The fact that you handcuffed me to the bed and wouldn't let me leave doesn't have anything to do with it."

His brows shot up involuntarily as he eyed her. "Even without an eidetic memory, I would have remembered if handcuffs had been involved at any point."

Had she felt like he'd forced her to sleep here last night? That was so far from his intent.

He ran through the events again, calculating, reevaluating. She'd been so into everything, eager, enthusiastic. Nearly crippling him with her desire at times as his empathy soared along with her.

There was no way he'd misread her pleasure. Or that she'd been more than willing to sleep in his bed. When he was this in tune with her, he'd know if she'd been unhappy.

"Seven orgasms," she said, holding up the requisite number of fingers in case he wasn't clear on the count. "What woman in her right mind would sleep alone after that?"

"I see. You're a slave to my attention, is that it? I've shackled you with my orgasms."

She sighed lustily. "Yeah, I guess that's true."

Something eased in his chest and he didn't hesitate to gather her up against his body so he could say good morning in a much more hands-on fashion. "In that case, we have a couple of hours until breakfast."

She groaned. "Seriously? I'm not used to this much, uh…stimulation. I haven't used some of those muscles in years."

That pleased him to no end. They'd had little to no communication about their respective love lives, but he'd envisioned that she'd been in school long enough to have avoided personal attachments. Of course, last night had been confirmation that she didn't have a boyfriend waiting in the wings.

He frowned. That was a huge assumption on his part. Women had multiple sexual partners all the time.

A growl nearly erupted from his throat but he bit it back. McKenna was his wife and after last night, he wanted to keep it that way. "Seriously. Was I not clear enough that you don't have to move? I do all the work. You have no other job than to issue instructions as you see fit. 'Harder, Des' works. 'Put your mouth on me.' These are not strenuous sentences to utter."

She laughed and flipped over to curl up in his arms spoon style. "You were clear. But the only thing I want right now is a massage."

Her shoulder nudged his chin and he didn't hesitate to put his hands on her. Cradling her firm rear with his hips, he nestled her closer and rubbed her arms with long, slow strokes. Her lengthy sigh had all the hallmarks of a woman relaxing and it settled the beastly possession that had welled up a moment ago. Mostly. He needed to get a lot more of her under his fingertips before he'd fully unwind.

McKenna. He got serious about her request and moved into a better position to take care of the one need his wife had at this moment. They'd both shed their nightclothes after the midnight feeding, which meant there was nothing in his way. He touched her at will, reveling in the soft silkiness of her skin, kneading her shoulders, curling his thumbs around the base of her skull to press along the meridians his one foray into Shiatsu had taught him would relieve her soreness.

The strongest sense of peace radiated from her flesh as he touched her and he absorbed it like a sponge. She moaned as he shifted his fingers to the top of her head, but he didn't need the additional verification that he'd also soothed her as he soothed himself.

As his fingers drifted down to caress her neck and shoulders, she arched her back, intensifying the rub of her very fine backside against the beginning of an arousal that was about to get out of hand if she didn't quit with the sensual contact. She'd asked for a massage. That's what he was giving her, as ordered.

The second time she circled her bottom to brush his

erection, fire shot through his groin. A groan rumbled from his chest. If that was an accident, he'd apologize profusely for the mistake. Later. He slid a hand down her stomach to hold her still as he ground his hips against her gorgeous, firm rear, sliding straight along the crevice. Hot. Tight.

She gasped, desire drenching her aura. And her center, as he discovered the moment he dipped his fingers into the valley between her legs. Nudging his knee between hers, he created a gap that gave him just enough access to explore.

"Desmond," she muttered breathlessly. "What happened to my massage?"

"Still going on." To prove it, he rubbed her nub with two fingers and kneaded her buttocks with the other hand, separating the twin globes enough to slide between them much more deeply than the first time.

His eyelids shuttered closed as the pressure built. He needed to be inside her, to let her take him under, to experience all of her glorious emotion in tandem with his as he built her toward release.

"That feels…i-incredible," she stuttered. "I didn't know that was one of my buttons."

"Now we both know." The heat engulfed him as he teased her backside and he couldn't hold on. Yesterday his restraint had been…well, not easy, but *easier*, solely because he hadn't yet coupled with her. Now that he had, his body had a mind of its own, desperate for her, for the sensation of being one with this woman.

Just as he was about to notch himself in the center of her slick heat for the long, slow slide to perfection, she half rolled away.

"Where are the condoms?" she asked. "You're going to need one after all."

Uh, that was a minor detail he'd conveniently forgotten. Blindly he felt around for the dresser behind him until his fingers closed over the knob and then the packets inside. Thankfully he managed to hang on to the one he grabbed and get it on before he lost his mind.

In moments, his wife's core enveloped him fully and he paused to let the scorching, flawless, rightness of her wash over him. She squirmed restlessly, not on board with slow, apparently. The decision was taken from him as his body began to crave the sweet burn of movement. As she urged him on with small hip rolls that drove him deeper inside, he rode the wave, spiraling higher and higher toward bliss.

But the real bliss lay in her reactions, every cry, all the nuance of her pleasure that heightened his own. It was everything he wanted and nothing he'd ever experienced.

Before his brain could engage, she guided his hand back to her center and he willingly started all over with the massage, but with laser focus on her erogenous zones until she rippled and squeezed through a release that shot fireworks through his gut.

Imagine if she hadn't insisted on condoms. This dazzling experience could include so much more than just an orgasm. He could impregnate her. Today. If she conceived, he could watch her grow round with his child. He'd missed that the first time and it was an injustice he ached to rectify.

His own release exploded from his depths without any warning. As he cried out through the tense burst that left him emptied, he held her close in case she had a mind to roll away. He didn't want to miss a moment of being inside her. Not one moment of making love to his wife.

She was far more than the mother of his child. She was a crucial part of the fabric of the family he'd been trying to create. How had he missed that a family of two was nice but three was so much better, especially when they were so tightly knit together already?

McKenna resettled his arm across her stomach more closely, burrowing against his chest to let him hold her as snugly as he wanted. The problem was that she'd eventually leave the bed. And his life. For all the talk about handcuffs, he had few mechanisms at his disposal to convince a woman that she should wish to stay exactly where she was.

"I need a bath," she murmured. "And maybe a nap. By *myself*."

The stress on that part came with a playful smack to his hand, which had apparently gotten too friendly with the curve of her breast. "That's the exact opposite of what I need."

"Well, I can't lie. This has been amazing. But maybe it's best if it's a one-time thing."

Something cold and sad crowded into his chest. Of course that was her thought. She'd been backing away from him since the beginning. Except now he had a stake in convincing her she didn't want to do that.

"Best for what?" he growled. "Did I dissatisfy you in some way?"

"What? No." She laughed and half rolled toward him, which pulled her from his arms. "This was just a… I don't know, a fling. An affair. I have no idea what kids call it these days. But it's not the kind of thing you keep doing, no matter how great it is."

That literally made zero sense. "Why not?"

"Because. We're getting a divorce." Exasperation laced her tone, inciting his own frustration. "This is a temporary situation until we can sort something out to get the baby weaned."

"Which we've already established may not happen for several months. Why put an arbitrary end date on something we're both happy with?" he countered far less smoothly than he'd have liked. But she was growing upset and empathy bled through him in a wholly unpleasant internal storm.

The blackness crowding his chest wasn't just his own reaction to the subject, though he had plenty of gloom vying for space. His was because he didn't know how to let her go. Hers was because she wanted him to.

"I'm just not the type to sleep with a man solely because he's generous in bed." She'd moved back to her pillow, clutching the sheet around her breasts in an ineffective cover that did nothing but heighten her sexiness. "This was maybe a blip in judgment at best. You're very difficult to say no to."

By design. He left nothing to chance, not when it was something he wanted. That meant he still had work to do if he wished to create the family he saw in his head. Everyone else in his life spent a great deal of energy trying to get away from him. McKenna was no different.

She was just the first one he wanted to stop from leaving.

The connection he craved, the one that had driven him to create a son with this woman, had flourished with McKenna in ways he'd never have imagined—and he had a great imagination. He couldn't cut it off, didn't have any desire to.

He nodded as if he agreed, his mind sifting through a hundred different scenarios that might work to change the tide of his future. If his wife wasn't the type to sleep with a man solely because he was generous in bed, then maybe she was the type to do so if he was generous out of bed.

Divorcing McKenna was not what he wanted any longer. He liked being married. To her. If she hadn't come to the realization that her future lay with him, then he would have to help her along. Provide incentives.

Orgasms were only one of many things he could offer that might convince her she'd found a permanent home in his bed and his life.

McKenna took her newfound sense of propriety and left Desmond's bed, determined not to repeat the mistake of yesterday. And last night. And again this morning. Twice.

While she'd been fumbling around for the proper terminology to describe the act of sleeping with one's husband—besides the obvious one called *marriage*—he'd been quietly campaigning to prove her completely incapable of resisting him.

As if the first time hadn't been enough of a clue. *Massage.* Leave it to Desmond to redefine that word into "explosive sexual encounter." And then follow it up with a second round that had somehow ended up with her on top, riding him with fluid, delicious motion that put the most sensually hot expression on his face. She could have watched him get lost in pleasure for an hour.

It was high time for a break from the maestro of the storm who'd lured her into sleeping with him all night long and confused her with his insistence that he was at her command instead of the other way around. She'd already been confused enough, what with her chest hurting at the thought of leaving the baby behind when the divorce was finalized.

Schoolwork beckoned. It was no easier to concentrate at her brand-new desk than it had been yesterday. Harder actually. The little blue icon in her system tray beckoned her to open it and connect with the man on the other side.

The chat tool had kindly alerted her that Desmond was online about halfway through her attempt at the second conversion exercise in her biochemistry class.

She ignored it and focused. The concepts were supposed to be a review of what she'd already mastered. So far, all she'd proved was that she could only get through this with the help of someone much smarter.

No. She wasn't too dim-witted to figure this out. She was just…preoccupied. Slowly she fought through the web of Desmond and Conner spinning through her mind and found a rhythm to the chaos. This was medical science. Her wheelhouse. A man and a baby would not—could not—distract her from getting her degree. Being a wife and mother was nothing more than a temporary glitch in her life. Nothing she'd ever wanted or seen for herself.

Her concentration improved drastically when she finally accessed Desmond's magic portal. It wasn't just a flippant label; the thing really was magic, producing results easily from her search terms. Why had she resisted this so long? He'd offered it to her and she'd pretended it didn't exist, just like she was pretending the man didn't exist. Both to her detriment.

She found some great papers online at Johns Hopkins University that walked her through the concepts in a whole different way that suddenly clicked everything together in her brain. The rest of the exercises were easy once she had the foundation straight.

Or they would have been if she'd had a chance to finish. A knock on her open door interrupted her near the end. *Desmond.* Here for the next round of nursing. Total and complete awareness of his presence invaded her very pores, skimming along her skin, raising the hair on her arms.

"Sorry to bother you," he said.

He definitely needed to find a different greeting. "I'm pretty sure I've told you it's no bother."

Conner's little baby noises finished killing her concentration where Desmond had left off. She stood from the desk to get comfortable in the rocker, already familiar and content with the routine Desmond had instituted where he took care of everything and fetched whatever she needed.

At her command. What a kick that was to have such a sensual, intelligent man wallowing at her feet.

Something far deeper than mere awareness of said man with the baby in his arms walloped her out of nowhere. He'd always drawn her eye with his energy, his classic cheekbones and dark swept-back hair. But now she knew every contour under that powder blue buttondown, both visually and by touch.

Her tongue dried up as he gathered her hair gently to waft it down her back, instinctively moving it out of the way without her having to tell him, then settled the baby against her bosom. It was so…domestic and tranquil and a host of other things she shouldn't be wishing could continue.

This fairy-tale land Desmond had dropped her into was temporary. It couldn't be anything else, especially when he wasn't offering her more than his home and his bed. Especially when she was already having such a difficult time focusing on biology, the first love of her life. At best, she might have another few weeks of having her body worshipped in Desmond's bed, but he'd never unbend enough to want a permanent third person in his son's life.

That wasn't what she wanted either, never mind that she could easily get carried away with a fantasy about what that looked like. Fantasy—hell, it looked a lot like this, with Conner in her arms and Desmond doting on her because he'd fallen madly in love.

Lunacy. She'd never dreamed of a man falling in love with her and handing her the moon. Not once.

Until now.

After father and baby left, McKenna lost the ability to do anything other than stare off into space and replay the memory of this morning in bed, when she'd finally had the opportunity to burn images of Desmond's body into her mind. She couldn't decide if the dark was better because she had to feel her way around him or if light was better because she could watch him in the throes of passion.

If Desmond could be believed, he would give her the opportunity to do both. Every night. For how long? Until he kicked her out of his life and the baby's?

The idea of sleeping with him until then was ridiculous, a ripe situation for her to mess up and start caring for him far more deeply than she already did. The little hooks in her heart were going to hurt like hell when he finally ripped them out. She'd already been ten kinds of a fool for letting things go as far as they had.

Best thing would be to get some healthy distance. She was way overdue to visit her parents, who'd come by the hospital briefly to check on her after the birth but otherwise had stayed out of her decision to breast-feed the baby she'd given up. Who better to provide solace than the people who cared about her most?

Before she could change her mind, she slipped her phone from her bedside table and texted Desmond that she was going out, shoving back the guilt that welled higher with each letter under her thumbs. Yeah, she was intruding and forcing him to respond to an electronic communiqué he would likely hate. But seeing him in person would just give him an opportunity to ensnare her more firmly in his web of pleasure.

Desmond immediately texted her back.

I'll have the limo driver waiting for you in the roundabout at the front steps in five minutes.

She nearly groaned. So not necessary. And so ostentatious to arrive like the lady of the manor, wheeling through the middle of the place she'd grown up, especially given that a lot of the residents in the community shunned cars. But she didn't want to seem petty so she sent him back a thank-you and changed clothes, scurrying out of the house before Desmond said he could easily pack up the baby and accompany her.

She was afraid she'd agree. And allowing tagalongs wouldn't give her the distance she sorely needed.

Her pretend family dominated her thoughts as the limo cut through the swath of trees surrounding Desmond's property. This marked the first occasion she'd left the house since moving in with Desmond, which could well be the whole problem. Regular outings into the real world *should* have been a daily part of her regime. At the very least, it would have created more of a delineation between her and the Pierce males.

Desmond and Conner were the real family, no moms need apply. She'd married the man solely for convenience. It was an easy way to avoid the legal tangle of receiving a fully paid medical degree via a divorce settlement, yet, so far, nothing about their relationship felt convenient or easy. It felt like a slippery precipice with nothing to grab on to once she inevitably lost her footing.

Oddly enough, it had only just occurred to her that

she could legally adopt Desmond's last name, too, if she so chose. There was literally nothing stopping her other than the paperwork hassle times two, because she'd surely end up back at whatever office did that sort of thing to change it again when Desmond whipped out his pen to make the divorce final.

Though no one could force her to give it up, if she did do something as crazy as change it in the first place. Desmond didn't have all the power, whether he liked that reality or not.

The limo was plush, with leather seats that smelled divine and a small bar built into the sidewall that held glasses and a tub of ice with bottles of water stuck deep down in the cubes. Nice touch. She still couldn't drink alcohol while breast-feeding, a sacrifice she didn't mind since she wasn't much of a drinker anyway. Desmond's attention to detail warmed her far more than it should have.

Once the driver left Astoria, he veered inland and the forest swallowed the car. Long, dark shadows kept the limo in partial sunlight for the rest of the drive to Harmony Gardens on the other side of the Clatsop Forest where her parents lived.

Yes, she definitely should have done this much earlier. The quiet hush of the trees bled through her soul, calming her, filling her with peace. The forest had been here long before she was born. It persevered, growing and thriving despite all the forces working against it.

She would, too.

Her mother waited for her in the small yard of the clapboard house near the center of Harmony Gardens. It had been McKenna's grandfather's house before he passed and her parents had moved in to care for him a month before her twelfth birthday. Grandfather's long battle with cancer had kept him in and out of different healing centers until he'd taken his final breath in the back bedroom. While a terrible ordeal for everyone, it had sparked the kernel of McKenna's dream to be a doctor.

The care Grandfather had received had been loving, patient. But ultimately ineffective. She'd begged him to see a medical doctor, to try radiation. *Not for me*, he'd insisted as McKenna's mother took him to yet another shaman or crystologist. Would the cancer have killed him even with western medicine? No way to know.

But McKenna could surely replicate the kindness the alternative medicine practitioners had demonstrated as she sought to heal people with the methods *she* trusted. No one else had her unique mix of drive, determination and a husband with deep pockets.

The plan would have been flawless if Conner hadn't developed formula allergies. If she hadn't started to feel things for Desmond that she shouldn't.

The driver parked near the house and swept open the back door of the limo, holding out his hand to help McKenna from the seat. She smiled her thanks, stepping back in time as she turned to follow the trail of worn brick pavers leading to her mother.

"My sweet darling," her mother crooned as she embraced McKenna.

Love enveloped her instantly, soothing her raw nerves and drawing her into a place where everything in her world made sense.

"You didn't have to hang around outside," she chided her mother gently. "I know how to knock."

"I couldn't sit still. I haven't seen you in months, except for thirty minutes in that dreadful hospital." Her mother's long, dark braid danced as she shook her head.

It was a rare occasion that the braid, now shot with a few silver strands, wasn't hanging down her back.

A tinge of grief gripped McKenna's stomach as she realized her mother was aging. Of course she was. Though in her early fifties, Rebecca Moore still looked forty, with beautiful skin that had started to sport small crinkles at the eyes and thin lines around her mouth. She looked exactly the same as she had the last time McKenna had seen her barely two months ago, after Conner had been born.

This was just the first time McKenna had a benchmark. Giving birth had done that somehow, where six years of school had not. One year had blended into the next and, finally, she'd graduated. A baby, on the other hand, grew and aged alongside you—or at least that was how it was supposed to work. McKenna's baby wouldn't come visit her when she was in her early fifties and carry along with him all of the memories of watching him grow up, of raising him, loving him. Seeing his first steps, first lost tooth, first date.

A tear slipped down McKenna's cheek before she could catch it.

"Oh, honey." Her mother clucked. "Come inside and let me get you a drink so you can tell me what's bothering you so badly that you came all the way down here to see me."

So much for trying to keep her inner turmoil in check. But gaining some clarity was the whole reason she was there. Why not tell her mom everything?

McKenna followed her mother into the small, ancient house. Her parents had done their best to preserve the interior in a snapshot of the way Grandfather had kept it. His old chair still sat by the fireplace where he'd spent many hours warding off the chill that had constantly haunted him in his last days. Photographs of her mom and dad as kids playing together lined the walls. They'd known each other their whole lives, just like many of the couples who comprised the community. Growing up, McKenna had always understood that the beliefs of many of those who resided in Harmony Gardens didn't reflect societal norms, thus they tended to stay insulated.

She'd rocked the boat by leaving. Embracing her dream of being a doctor. Moving to Portland. Having a baby and giving him up.

"I know you don't approve of my choices..." she began, but already her mother shook her head, braid bouncing against her shoulders.

"That's not what's bothering you." Her mother handed her a glass of water and pulled McKenna onto the couch that had seen many years of wear, most of it happy, and some tears. Like now. How did her mother see through her so easily?

"But I need you to hear this," McKenna said as the next tear slipped down her cheek. "You don't seem to understand how important being a doctor is to me."

Her mother slipped an arm around McKenna's shoulders, holding on tight like she used to when warding off the boogeymen when McKenna had a nightmare about creatures creeping out from the surrounding forest and standing outside her window.

"I've never questioned your commitment to following your dreams," she said. "What I've tried to do is help you see that there are other factors to consider."

"Like having lots of babies is a factor I should consider?" Frustrated all at once, McKenna shoved off the couch and out of her mother's reach.

"No," her mother countered calmly. "Like the fact that sometimes one is all you get. You know your father and

I weren't able to have more children. We wanted more, desperately. Not because you weren't enough. You're amazing and special. We wanted to give you brothers and sisters."

"And do your part to populate the community." It wasn't a secret that her parents had long held that belief. Children were not only a happy gift from God, according to them, but Harmony Gardens sustained itself by every member pitching in. The more members, the better.

But McKenna felt crappy bringing it up when the sole reason was to detract from the aching hole that had just opened up in her chest.

Sometimes one is all you get.

Was that her fate, too? Conner could be her only child. The endometriosis that had rendered her mother infertile could very well be in McKenna's DNA, too, waiting to strike after she'd birthed her first baby. That would be now.

She shook her head, shoving back the wave of emotion. "It doesn't matter. I don't want children."

The sentiment rang so much hollower than it had in the past. While she didn't want the nebulous term that encompassed "children," she couldn't include Conner in that statement. He was a baby that already existed, one she never should have come to care for.

Her mother's eyes softened. "Sit with me. Let's talk about that for a minute."

Warily, McKenna complied. "You can't talk me into wanting children. I made a deal."

"Yes, let's not dwell on that, shall we? You've made your choice and I understand that you've signed agreements that you'll never have contact with the baby, which by default means we'll never know our grandchild. What's done is done." Folding her hand around McKenna's, her mother squeezed, gracing her with compassion she didn't feel she deserved all at once.

"I…" She'd never considered that she was punishing her parents as well as herself by giving up Conner.

"Not dwelling on it," her mother reminded her. "Instead let's talk about why you don't want to have children."

"Because women don't have the same choices as men," she burst out. "Especially not in a place like Harmony. They have their first baby at eighteen or nineteen and, before you know it, they have nothing more defining them than being a mother. They're sucked dry with no time or energy left over to make a difference."

Quietly her mother stroked her hand. "The point is that having children is making a difference in their minds, and that's *their* choice. You never saw that. Nor have you recognized that some people do have careers and children. With you, it's always been either-or."

"Having children while going to medical school is not an option," McKenna countered. She could barely take two classes and maintain her sanity with a baby and a sexy man in the house. Not to mention that online classes that counted toward a medical degree were few and far between. "Besides, it doesn't matter. That's not an option."

"And that's the problem." Her mother nodded sagely as two more tears slipped down McKenna's cheek. "I was worried this might happen. You're so matter-of-fact about your decisions and you don't honor your feelings enough."

"Emotions are not a good thing to base decisions on." So easy to say. Thus far, it had been easy to do. She'd always had a practical nature, which was part of the reason being a doctor appealed to her.

How could she have predicted that she'd ever have so many impossible dreams racing through her chest, ones that hurt when she contemplated them?

"You're right." McKenna shut her eyes for a moment, willing back the next flood of tears. They were right there, threatening to well up as she forced herself to reconcile what her mother was telling her. "The problem isn't that I feel a certain way about anything. It's that I don't have a choice."

"You don't like not having choices."

This was not a new conversation. They'd had this argument many times, especially when she'd first sprung the concept of being a surrogate on her parents and they'd accused her of picking this option deliberately to thumb her nose at the concepts they'd long held dear. "That's n—"

It was true.

She knew it was true. She liked having control over her own life. Why was she about to argue that fact? Because she'd just realized she had more in common with Desmond than she'd credited?

It was the whole reason she didn't appreciate his attempts at manipulation. Perceived attempts, she reminded herself. She didn't know his motivation for being so helpful when it came to breast-feeding or in being so greedy for her pleasure in bed either, for that matter.

But it smacked of control and that she would not tolerate. Especially when he'd already made it so clear that he insisted on absolute control when it came to Conner. Fine. That was set in stone and she couldn't change it now. But she did not have to let him control anything else.

She should demand that Desmond hire a nanny. Today. She'd avoided that subject because of all the waffling going on in her heart about leaving. No more. Not only did she need a nanny in the house as soon as possible, she wanted a date on the calendar for the divorce. That was how she could maintain control over her choices.

"I see your wheels turning," her mother said with a small smile. "Keep in mind that I love you as I say this. The world is not black-and-white. You tend to think of your choices that way, when in reality, things are not so easily put into your either-or buckets. Especially not when you start to have feelings for someone."

She scowled. "I don't have feelings for anyone. What are you talking about?"

"That you want to feel like you have control over your emotions and, sweetie, it just doesn't work that way. When you meet the one, you don't have a choice. You just…fall."

"In love?" she squawked. That wasn't what was happening to her. It couldn't be. "I'm not—I mean, okay, Desmond is kind and unexpectedly…"

Hot. Wickedly talented in bed. His mouth alone should have a warning label. None of that seemed to be the kind of thing you said to your mother. Neither could she actually admit that her mother was right.

The knowing look on her mother's face said she'd already figured it out. "Go home to your husband, McKenna, and give the unexpected a chance. You might find that you have more choices than you originally thought."

But the one choice she desperately needed wasn't open to her. She could not choose to stop falling in love with Desmond. That was a done deal.

Nine

Despite promising himself he wouldn't listen for the crunch of gravel under the limo tires, Desmond did it anyway. So he knew the instant McKenna had returned from wherever she'd gone. Finally.

He'd missed her. The house had felt empty without her in it, as if it had been drained of something vital. She'd been gone for four hours and it had felt like a lifetime. He was in serious trouble here, with little to no idea how to put the final threads in the fabric of the family he wanted. But nothing would stop him from trying.

She came inside and stopped short when she saw him hanging around like an idiot in the foyer, pretending to play with Conner, as if the kid didn't have a nursery, a recreation room and maybe five other places more hospitable to a baby than a drafty open area near the front door.

Her smile lit on the son they shared and Desmond soaked it in, enchanted by the way she filled his space with her presence and still mystified why the invasion didn't bother him. It should. Not one but two people were in his sanctuary. He liked them here. And she'd been responsible for both.

"Hi," he said and it sounded as lame out loud as it had in his head. The other stuff he'd practiced dried up as her gaze skittered away from him.

Something wasn't right. His senses picked up on it instantly.

"Hey," she said.

A dark shadow moved through his consciousness as he internalized her response. He tried to ignore it. "Did you have a good time?"

"Sure."

That was supposed to be an opening for her to tell him about her day, mention where she'd gone.

"I—"

"I'm tired, Desmond." She wouldn't look at him. "I'm going to take a nap before dinner."

He let her go and tried not to stress about her mood. After all the amazing things they'd shared, it was frustrating that she didn't want to open up to him. He did *alone* better than anyone, but he'd found a reason not to be and would stake his life on the fact that she'd felt something binding them together just as strongly as he had.

For some reason, she wasn't engaging.

Without any more answers, he retreated to his workshop after dinner—which McKenna did not eat with him—and played with Conner. He put the boy to bed and fiddled around with one of the analog switches in his robotic humanoid, but his mind refused to participate in what was largely a distraction anyway.

The computer dinged to alert him that McKenna had

come online. It didn't take but a quarter of a second for him to envision her sitting at her desk studying, brow furrowed in concentration as she swept that gorgeous fall of hair behind her back. He'd like to visit her again, offer to help with her homework, but given her earlier reticence he had a feeling it would be a short conversation.

Of course there was only one way to find out.

His footfalls outside her open door must have alerted her to his presence because she'd already turned the chair a half twist as he drew even with the threshold. Maybe she'd been anticipating his arrival, remembering the last time he'd come to her room to help with her chemistry problems.

They'd resolved all of them, one way or another. But his favorite was still that first orgasm, when she'd come so fast he couldn't wait to do it again.

"I'm glad you're here," she said with a tentative smile and motioned him inside. "I think we should talk."

That was probably the last thing on his mind. And should be the last thing on hers. Lots of work to do here if talking was the first thing she wanted to do. Casually, he leaned on the edge of the desk to disguise how tense his body had grown with the effort to not sweep her into his arms. "About your homework?"

Seeing her in the flesh still kicked him in the gut, but the feeling had so many more teeth now, slicing open nerve endings and fanning through his blood with sensual heat that only she could tame.

Her gaze locked with his and she swallowed. But didn't look away, like she had earlier. "No, um... Let's start with Conner. That nanny-finding service is really falling down on the job. Maybe you should hire another one?"

"I can take care of my son," he said gruffly, still reeling from her nearness.

He'd made love to her twice just that morning. How many times would be enough to still this raging need inside?

"I know." She bit her lip, eyeing him as he moved a few centimeters closer. He couldn't help it. She smelled so good. "But the nanny will do more than just care for Conner. I feel like we've had this conversation a hundred times. I need to start figuring out how to wean so I can move back to Portland."

Well, that put things in perspective. If he'd wondered whether she'd ever thought about sticking around, he didn't have to wonder any longer. Even after last night, she still couldn't wait to be rid of him.

He needed to put some more icing on the cake.

"It's barely been two months," he countered and somehow kept the hitch out of his voice. "We agreed the baby would likely need you for a few more months yet. Are you feeling restless? I'll have a car delivered tomorrow so you can come and go at will."

She blew out a breath. "That's very generous but—"

"I seem to recall a few other ways you've enjoyed my generosity recently." He picked up her hand and held it to his lips, inhaling her scent. "I'm thinking of expanding on that. Right now."

"Oh, um…" Her eyes widened as he sucked one of her fingers into his mouth. "That wasn't what I wanted to talk about."

"So talk," he said around her finger and laved at the tip. "Don't mind me."

Her eyelids fluttered closed as he mouthed his way across her palm and nibbled at her wrist. "It's hard to think when you're doing that."

"Hint. That means you like it," he whispered and concentrated on her elbow where his tongue got a groan out of her that hardened him instantly.

"That's the problem. I don't want to like it. I want to talk about how we're going to get the baby to a point where I can leave—"

"McKenna." It was a wonder he got that out around the vise that had clamped around his throat. "Stop talking about leaving. Let the future take care of itself. In the meantime, if you're unhappy, say so. That's the only way I can fix it."

Her hesitation bled through him, ruffling the pit of fire near his groin. "I'm not unhappy. Don't be ridiculous. I'm just…concerned. I don't see any kind of exit plan and—"

"No exit plan. We can come up with one later." *Or never.* "Right now, I want to enjoy you. And help you enjoy yourself. Let me."

"I don't know what you're asking me to do." She shook her head, gripping his hand tighter instead of slipping free like he'd have expected.

Crap, he was botching this. He needed more time to figure out how to persuade her. Except she'd been so quiet all afternoon. There was no telling how long he had before she'd shut down again and, besides, he wasn't much of a verbal dancer.

"McKenna." He pulled her into his arms with a growl, determined to get her over whatever was going through her head that was keeping them apart. "I want you in my bed. I want to watch you care for my son. The shape of what I want is already there. What it's called is a question for another day."

He already knew what to call it—his family. The vision in his head would shatter without the integral third she represented. Somehow he had to communicate what was in his mind and his heart whether he had all the right words or not. There was only one surefire way to do that in his experience.

Before McKenna could blink, Des swept her up in his arms and carried her out of her room. Her gorgeous hair draped over his shoulder and he couldn't wait to get his hands on it.

Breathlessly, she sputtered, "Wh-what are you doing?"

"Taking you to my room," he growled. "Where you belong. You sleep there from now on, where I can properly take care of you."

"Or what?" she challenged as her pulse picked up, beating hard against his fingertips. It was a clear indication he'd gotten her attention.

But because he wasn't a complete beast, he laid her out gently on the bed and stepped back, giving her plenty of room to breathe, bolt or bare herself to him, pending how well he'd gauged the swing in her mood. "There's no 'or what.' Give me two minutes to convince you this is what you want."

Arms crossed, she contemplated him, her eyelids at half-mast. But that wasn't enough to conceal the intrigue and excitement his challenge had stimulated. "While I'm dressed?"

"Hell, no, you won't be dressed," he shot back. "The point is that I want you in my bed *naked*. I want you to be here when I go to sleep, when I wake up. When it's time to nurse the baby and all the times in between. I—"

As he choked on his own emotion, her gaze softened and she held out her hand. "Come here. Instead of slinging ultimatums and deals around, lie down. *Dressed*. Talk to me."

That, he could do. He stretched out next to her and laid his head on his bent arm as she caressed his temple, threading his hair through her fingers soothingly. It wasn't sexual. It was…nice.

"I don't know how to do this," he confessed. This was barely *his* room, let alone hers. But he knew he wanted to be in it. With her. She brought his entire house to life just by being there.

"I know. This isn't what I expected either." Tenderness bled through him as she let her hand trail down his jaw to rest against his neck. "Just cool your jets for a minute and stop trying to manipulate me with sex."

"That's not what…" Yeah. It was exactly what he'd been trying to do. Give-a-woman-enough-orgasms-and-she-stopped-looking-for-the-door kind of philosophy. That clearly wasn't working. "What can I do to convince you that I genuinely want to spend time with you?"

"Tell me." Her expression warmed. "I like to hear the truth. I also like to have choices."

As insights went, that was a big one. "I'm sensing you don't mean a choice between making you come with my fingers or my mouth."

She arched a brow. "Well, I can't lie. That's not really a choice because my answer is always both. No, I mean the fact that you don't like to give me any control when it comes to things like hiring a nanny. I worry that sex will cloud the issues."

Nodding, he filtered through what she was saying, her nonverbal cues and how to reconcile all of that with the aching need to keep her by his side. She clearly wasn't balking at his desire to sleep with her, just the fact that he'd been grasping the strings of his life too tightly.

Control was his default. It shielded his vulnerabilities. But she was saying he had to give or she'd walk.

"So hiring a nanny will help you feel like you've got choices?"

"Well, sure. Because it means you're not so stuck in your control-freak land." She smiled to soften the sting of her terminology but, honestly, she wasn't off base. The thought of losing her hurt far worse than being told the truth about himself.

"I don't want to hire a nanny." He held up a finger as her expression darkened. "But not because I'm trying to control you. Because I should be the one taking care of my son. I have a problem connecting with people. I don't want that to affect our relationship. If I'm all he knows, he'll come to me for a Band-Aid."

Her warm hands came up to cup his jaw as she re-settled on her pillow much closer to him than she had been. "Oh, honey. I didn't mean for that to be such a defining moment in your decisions as a father when I pointed that out."

"But it was. And it should have been." Because it felt natural and right, he tucked an arm around her waist, drawing her body up against his. They were still fully clothed but their position was by far the most intimate thing he'd ever done with anyone. "I needed to hear that. I've been reading up on how to wean a baby with formula allergies. I'm going to help you."

He should have started long before now but, as always, she saw him more clearly than he saw himself.

Something raw and tender exploded in the depths of her eyes. "Really? You'd do that for me?"

"Well, yes. Of course."

The gruff note in his voice wasn't due to uncertainty like usual. It was pure emotion. She was softening; he could feel it. Feel them binding together in this quiet moment that had nothing to do with sex. All because he'd loosened his grip. That was as much of a defining moment as anything else.

He needed McKenna to push him like this, to help him see that giving a woman choices didn't mean she'd immediately stomp on his emotions.

The sweet kiss she laid on his lips was just as raw and tender, sweeping through him with the force of a tidal wave, clear-cutting a path through his body straight to his heart.

"McKenna," he murmured against her lips, and she burrowed closer with a soft sigh, wedging a thigh between his as she deepened the kiss.

Everything shifted in the space of a moment. Urgency built, a yearning to touch, to revel, to feel.

To experience. Not to claim.

Reverently he took great handfuls of her hair. She moaned as he levered her head back to allow him access to taste her throat, the hollow behind her ear, her lobe, anything he could put his mouth on. Then he ran out of skin.

Stripping her became an act of adoration. Each button slipped free of its housing, revealing another slice of her, and he christened what he'd uncovered with a kiss. She shifted restlessly, her desire mounting so fast his head spun.

When he spread the fabric of her shirt wide, she arched her back, pushing closer to his mouth, so he indulged them both, laving at her exposed flesh and dipping under the fabric of her bra as he worked at getting her pants off. It was a much bigger trick when she was lying on the bed and he was facedown in her breasts, a problem he didn't mind solving the old-fashioned way—brute strength. He picked her up by the hips and tore off the offending garments until she was fully bared.

He took a moment to let his gaze sweep over her, lingering at her breasts, hard nipples taut and gorgeous.

Her lungs audibly hitched as he reached out to stroke. Looked like she wasn't of a mind to bolt or breathe. That worked for him.

Ripping out of his clothes in record time, he resettled next to her on the bed, stroking whatever he could reach and murmuring nonsense about how beautiful she was. His brain was a tangle of wants, needs and absolutes, all of which began and ended with McKenna. The more he stroked, the higher the urgency climbed until he was nearly writhing as much as she was.

Because he couldn't hold out much longer, he knelt to take her over the crest the first time, gratified that he could sense exactly where to put his tongue to wring the tightest, strongest orgasm from her. What a total high to discover he could use his empathy in such a pleasurable way.

She gasped and moaned her way down from the peak, eagerly collapsing against his body as he pulled her into his arms.

"More," she croaked, and he couldn't hear that enough.

But this time he needed to be with her, soaring alongside. In a flash, he had himself sheathed and pushing inside to bathe in the bliss of her body as she accepted him to the hilt, so hot and ready for him that it took his breath.

"Yes," she cried and wound her hips in a slow circle, drawing him deeper still until he was lost in the sensation. "You feel amazing."

That didn't begin to describe the way they mated spiritually as well as physically. But he wanted more and wasn't going to stop until he got it.

"Imagine how much better this would feel if we didn't have to use condoms," he risked saying aloud.

He wanted to spill his seed in her, to see if he could sense the moment when she conceived. They'd hold hands as they took a pregnancy test together, waiting with breathless anticipation to confirm what he already knew in his soul would be a plus sign.

The ghosts that had haunted him since Lacey would finally vanish.

McKenna half laughed and let her head tip back as he nuzzled her neck. "Yeah, if this is how the next few months are going to be, I should definitely see about a more permanent form of birth control."

Cold invaded his chest and he willed it back. He had months to convince her of what was happening here but, for the first time, everything seemed to be falling into place. No longer would he live in fear of his family being ripped apart by forces beyond his control.

He changed the subject by hefting her thigh higher on his hip and driving her into the heavens a second time before following her into the white light of release.

McKenna was his and he was not letting her go.

Days bled into a week and Desmond waited for McKenna to come up with another argument against living as husband and wife. But she didn't mention leaving again. At night she slept in his bed and during Conner's naps she sat in the corner of his workshop with her laptop, blazing through her online classes brilliantly.

It helped that he was right there to help, cheerfully stopping whatever he was doing—usually watching her out of the corner of his eye—to answer a question or to call up a resource from his knowledge bank.

By the middle of the second week Des didn't know what to call this euphoria. The only term he could think of was *happiness*. That had never been a goal of his and he'd never have thought it would be the result of getting what he'd asked for. But what else could this be?

True to his word, Desmond bought McKenna a breast pump and they worked together to get Conner used to taking his meals from a bottle. The baby's pediatrician proved a great help, suggesting they alternate a hypoallergenic formula with breast milk and gauge how he responded.

They kept careful watch, took notes, switched formulas as Conner reacted to the elements found in one or the other. McKenna hated the process, sometimes crying at night in Desmond's arms as the formula caused hives to break out on the baby's skin or he constantly spit up.

"I'm the most selfish person on the planet," she wailed, her distress eating through Des as he held her, stroking her hair, forehead, whatever he could get his hands on, though nothing stemmed the tide of her bleakness.

"No. This is an important step for him," he told her, quoting the doctor. "This is not just something we're doing so you can stop breast-feeding. We have to know what he's allergic to as he may have sensitivity to milk and soy his whole life."

Her tears soaked his shoulder, running down into the mattress below. "But I'm making him deal with this while he's still so tiny. I could breast-feed for a year. Two. People do it all the time."

"Sure you could. But at what cost?"

What kind of hell was this where he was forced into the role of convincing her that weaning was the right thing for everyone? Once she didn't have to feed the baby any longer, she could leave whenever she wanted. But he was slowly conceding that she needed options. He had to believe that when push came to shove, she'd choose Desmond and Conner. The concessions he'd made internally to get himself to this point were enormous. And so worth it.

"Sweetheart, listen to me." He levered up her chin with one finger until she met his gaze. "We're going to get through this. Together. I promised you."

She nodded and sighed, wiping at her leaking eyes. "Take my mind off it. Right now."

Her busy hands made short work of removing the drawstring pants he wore at night, leaving no room for him to misinterpret what she intended for him to do to grant her oblivion.

That was one thing he never minded letting her control. "Gladly."

In the morning they started all over again with the baby. Finally they settled on a rice-based formula that proved the least problematic.

After the third time feeding him without a reaction, McKenna glanced up at Desmond, her eyes bright as she held Conner to her shoulder, his little head listing against hers as she burped him. "I think this is it."

He nodded, afraid to upset the status quo with something as irreverent as speech. What would he say that could mark such a momentous, emotionally difficult occasion?

"It's kind of hard to believe I'm done," she said with a catch in her voice.

Conner made one of his baby noises and Des retrieved him from his mother in the same manner as he had almost since the moment of his son's birth. Only this time he did it to cover his own melancholy reaction to the passage of a ritual he'd grown to love.

Watching her breast-feed had been holy and beautiful. He'd never imagined he'd mourn the loss of it and regret that the last time he'd get to experience it had already happened. He'd have commemorated the occasion, or savored it longer, if he'd realized.

It was too late now. They'd reached the goal they'd set for themselves. Now McKenna could make a choice to stay with a clear head and no sense of obligation. He couldn't contemplate another scenario.

He cleared his throat. "You were fantastic. The whole time. So amazing. You sacrificed so much for our son. I—"

"Your son," she corrected. "Now that he's weaned, he can be totally your son again. I wasn't going to bring it up so soon, but while we're on the subject...let's talk about the divorce."

A roaring sound in Desmond's ears cut off the rest of her speech. "What are you talking about?"

She recoiled, her mouth still open. "Our agreement. The baby is weaned. The new semester starts in a couple of weeks. The timing is perfect for me to register. But I can't until I get the settlement money."

The baby squeaked as Desmond hefted him higher on his shoulder. Before he could have this conversation, Conner came first. He settled the baby into the bouncy seat that served as his primary residence when he wasn't asleep or being held. The stuffed giraffe hanging from the center bar caught the baby's attention and he kicked at it, his eyes tracking the trajectory of his foot.

When Des thought he could be a touch more civil, he turned back to McKenna who was still sitting in the rocker that she'd moved from her former bedroom to the one she now shared with him. He'd practiced how to approach the subject of her tuition but, honestly, he'd talked himself out of believing she'd bring it up.

The shock of her decision still hadn't faded. He swallowed as he absorbed her taciturn expression. Had the last few months meant nothing to her? He'd been falling into her, falling into the possibilities and he'd have sworn she was too. He couldn't be so out of touch that he'd mistaken that. No way was he alone in feeling these big, bright emotions.

"We have an agreement, Desmond." Her quiet voice cut through him.

"I'm aware," he said more curtly than he'd have liked, but his entire body had frozen. "I had hoped you'd reconsider."

"Reconsider what?" Her mouth dropped open as understanding dawned. "You thought I'd reconsider becoming a doctor?"

"No, of course not. I meant reconsider the divorce."

"You're not making any sense. Our agreement was that you'd file for the divorce once I gave birth. Then the formula allergy happened, but I always expected you to come through with your part of the promise." The tight cross of her arms over her still ample bosom drew his attention and that's when he noticed her hands were shaking. "Conner doesn't need me anymore. I have to go."

"I need you!" he burst out before thinking better of how such a statement gave her power to cut him open. "What do you think we've been doing here but building something permanent?"

Her eyelids fluttered closed. "No," she whispered. "We can't. That's not the deal."

"Screw the deal. I want you to stay." *I want you to feel the things I feel.*

"Forever? That's impossible!" She leaped to her feet as Conner started crying. "Now the baby is upset. I can't stand it when he's upset."

She couldn't stand it? The twin streams of black distress—Conner's and McKenna's—sank barbed hooks into Desmond's consciousness, wringing him out like a wet rag. Conflict was not his forte, especially when he hadn't been expecting it, and he did not handle it well.

McKenna hurried to the bouncy seat and scooped up the baby, cradling him as if she never meant to let him go. Didn't she see that she belonged here, holding Conner, caring for him? Didn't she see how much control Desmond had conceded to her, laying himself bare?

"I'm going to take Conner to Mrs. Elliot," she said firmly. "And then we're going to finish this conversation once and for all."

She wasn't gone long enough for his empathy to settle or his temper. The words in his head refused to gel into coherent sentences. He was losing her and he couldn't grab on any tighter.

"You can't leave," he told her grimly as she stopped a half foot over the threshold of his bedroom.

"Or what? You'll tie me to the bed?"

She let her head drop into her hands and her shoulders quaked for a beat. But then she lifted her face to reveal the deepest agony he'd ever seen. It bled through him, nearly crippling him with her grief.

"You can't keep me here. Don't you see how it's killing me to leave Conner? Sometimes I think everyone would be happier if I gave up my dreams. Everyone except me. I can't be a mother and a doctor. It's not in my makeup. I have to choose. And you have to give me that choice."

"I've given you choices," he growled even as he sensed that what she was saying was the rawest form of truth. These were things she felt deeply. Just as clearly, he got the sense she did care about him. Not enough to stay, though, and it was killing him. "Lots of them. This is not the same situation as before, when you needed to feel like you had some measure of control—"

"Yes it is!" Clearly bewildered, she shook her head. "Yes, you gave me choices with Conner and I appreciate them. But you were the one who held me when I cried and said it was important that I wean. That if I kept breast-feeding, it would have too high a cost. The cost would have been my medical degree. I thought you knew that. Agreed."

"The cost was to Conner," he stormed as the barb she'd sank into his heart cleaved through it with so much pain that it was too hard to sort out whether it was hers or his. "There was never a point where I thought we were weaning so you could leave us. I thought—" *You were happy here.*

That she was falling for him as he was falling for her. Hell, there was no falling left to do. He'd opened himself emotionally, sometimes against his will. Though, to be honest, the dominoes had started lining up the moment he'd spied her for the first time in that hospital bed.

"I gave birth to Conner for *you*. I wanted to give you a family. But that's all I can give." Wide-eyed, she surveyed him, her expression so stricken he nearly yanked her into his arms so he could soothe her. "I didn't expect you to be kind and amazing. It's hard for me to leave you, too. But this is what I have to do, Des."

She'd never called him that before. It was almost an endearment. In the final hour she'd conceded that she did have feelings for him. But her feelings didn't seem to matter.

"What do you want?" he whispered and bit back the flood of words he wished he could say. *I love you* being first and foremost. But he couldn't stand the thought of stripping himself even more emotionally bare.

"The choice," she answered simply. "File for divorce."

No. His soul cried out the word but he couldn't force it out of his throat.

"Don't you get it?" she continued when he didn't im-mediately agree. "You've supported me for over a year with a golden handcuff. I have nothing on my own. If you don't grant me the divorce, you've simply transferred your need to control things from one area to another. It's so hard for me to make this choice. I don't need the ad-ditional complexity of not being given one."

He nodded once. How ironic that his greatest life les-son would come at his own hands. He'd structured the agreement expressly so she had no control and, thus, no ability to hurt him. Instead she was following the agreement to the letter—and tearing him apart at the same time.

"You will still choose to become a doctor."

It was inevitable. Final. Incentives, orgasms, choices—his heart—none of this had been enough. If only he could lie to himself, he might be able to salvage the situation. But in the end, he knew the truth: he had to give her what she'd requested.

She nodded. "I have an obligation to myself. I've been working on saying goodbye this whole time. You have to let me do that."

Once again McKenna was pushing him out of his com-fort zone, forcing him to look in the mirror. The family, the connections he'd been building, weren't a beautiful creation but a mirage. And if he didn't let her go, he'd be the monster instead of Dr. Frankenstein.

Ten

The university had walking paths, one of which ran right behind the little house Desmond had bought for McKenna. She'd expected to live in the dorm but he'd insisted she'd want the peace and quiet, so she'd accepted the key from the Realtor and kept her mouth shut when furniture arrived via a large van with the name of an exclusive store stenciled on the side.

This was what she'd asked for. Maybe not the part where the contents of the small house were worth more than her parents made in a year. But she did like the French country style that took shape around her, especially the functional desk she'd directed the movers to put in the dining room that would act as her office, where she'd study.

She had zero plans to entertain. Medical school was as demanding and difficult as she'd envisioned. Desmond had prepaid for her entire degree, citing the divorce might take too long to be finalized, thus he might as well pay for everything now.

One nice benefit to the house being off campus: she didn't feel compelled to take part in any of the campus activities and instead could focus on her class work, which she did, every night.

After three or four days she forced herself to drive to the grocery store in the practical Honda that Desmond had given her with express instructions to take it somewhere to have maintenance done every five thousand miles. Since she drove it less than ten miles a week, it would take about ninety years to reach that first milestone.

Of course, every time she got behind the wheel, she thought about driving it to Astoria and straight up the drive to the remote mansion along the Columbia River. What she'd do when she got there, she had no idea. This was her life now. The one she'd planned, envisioned, fought for.

The life she'd left behind at Desmond's was not hers, not real, not possible. How dare he act like that was a choice, like she could just stay there in the lap of luxury and let him take care of her while she gave up her dreams? While she ached to understand how he really felt about her without all the fantastic sex to muddle things?

The complications that had always been there had gotten worse. Mostly because Desmond had climbed into her heart and taken up residence when she wasn't looking. She had no idea what to do with that big, frightening reality.

What if she stuck around and the way she felt about him got bigger, scarier, more painful? Then she'd have no choices and a broken heart when he got bored with her and *then* filed the divorce papers. They were already signed, had been since before she'd conceived. The only thing he had to do was to take them to the court and it would be done. All part and parcel of their agreement. He had always had all of the power and no apparent qualms about throwing it around.

She'd demanded the choice and when he'd given it to her, she'd taken the opportunity to leave. It was the only way she could stay sane. After all, she ached to be with both Desmond and Conner past the point of reason, and it was killing her to be apart from them both, regardless of how necessary it was.

McKenna walked to her 9:00 a.m. pain management course on Monday, marking the first time in several days rain wasn't falling in a continual downpour. She'd tucked an umbrella into her bag because it was still Portland. Rain was predictable.

When she got to the building, one of the many guys in her class stood by the door. She started to brush past him but he stopped her with a nice smile.

"McKenna, right?"

Uh-oh. Was she being hit on? With Desmond, it was always completely obvious what had been on his mind, probably because it had been on hers, too. She missed that, missed his straightforwardness and wicked way with his hands. The ever-present ache in her chest got a whole lot worse as she drowned in memories.

And the guy was still smiling at her.

"Yes. I'm McKenna." She scouted her memory for his name but came up blank. There was a sea of faces on campus and none of them stuck out.

"It's Mark," he supplied easily with another nice smile, and she really wished she could smile back but she didn't want to encourage him.

"So, listen…" he continued. "I was wondering if you had some time this afternoon to go over the notes from last week. I missed a lecture because my daughter had an appointment."

"Oh. Um. Sure." Then what he'd said registered. "You have a daughter?"

"Yeah, she's great. My wife is a champ, taking care of her and working at the same time while I go to school. Do you have kids?"

She shook her head automatically. Conner wasn't hers and for all of Desmond's talk about keeping her around, there'd never really been any give on his part regarding that. He wasn't asking her to be his wife and his son's mother. Just the woman in his bed.

"So, about the notes?" Mark asked again, obviously interested in school not flirting. "I know it's an imposition, but I couldn't miss my daughter's appointment. It's a balance, but worth it, you know?"

No, she had no clue how someone could balance medical school and being a parent, let alone being married. "Sure, no problem."

They exchanged phone numbers and she sat through the class, half listening to the professor's long-winded lecture about chronic pain. Actually she had a pretty good idea how someone balanced medical school and life. She'd done it with Conner and her online class, with Desmond's help. And once she started thinking about how often the man she'd married had stepped up to assist her in all aspects of motherhood, classes—orgasms—she couldn't stop.

Somehow she got through the day, met up with Mark in the library to let him copy her notes, and wandered back home at the end of her last class. It had started to rain, no shock. But she didn't put up her umbrella, letting the light drizzle soak through her hair and clothes before she'd even noticed.

The phantoms she sometimes heard late at night were growing more active during the day. When she walked into the small house she could have sworn she heard Conner's baby noises wafting from the ceiling. Impossible. She shut the door and tried to care that she was dripping water all over the new throw rug covering the hardwood floor.

Her chest was on fire, aching to hold her baby, aching to be with her baby's father. But how could she stay under Desmond's thumb and never go to medical school? People who got sick like her grandfather needed an advocate in their corner. Someone to convince them that medical care in a hospital wasn't the evil they thought it was.

What choice did she really have?

Instead of sitting at her beautiful desk and working on her exhaustive list of assignments, she stripped out of her wet clothes and fell into bed, pulling the covers up to warm her chilled body. It didn't help. The cold penetrated straight to her core.

Choices. They haunted her. The ones she'd demanded. The ones she'd made.

It was the ultimate act of selfishness, wishing she could somehow have everything—the man she'd fallen in love with, the baby she'd never dreamed she'd want to keep *and* earn the medical degree she'd long believed was her path.

She slept fitfully only to wake at midnight, hot and uncomfortable under the pile of blankets. Throwing them off, she lay there naked, welcoming the cool air. No way would she go back to sleep now. And she had an assignment due in ten hours that she hadn't touched. Homework was the last thing she wanted to do. But this was the lot she'd chosen and she had to persevere.

When she booted up her laptop, the little blue icon popped up to let her know Desmond was online. Shocked, she stared at the message until it faded. He hadn't uninstalled the chat program? Had he found someone else to chat with? Also, geez. It was midnight. Was he up because he couldn't sleep? Maybe he'd been lying awake aching to hear someone else's heartbeat next to him in the bed. Doubtful. That was probably just her.

More likely Conner had woken up looking for a bottle. Oh, God. What if he was crying because he wanted his mother and was confused and frightened because she wasn't there? She had to check.

She'd clicked open the chat window and typed *hi* before fully thinking it through. If Desmond was in his workshop online, the odds were good that he wasn't taking care of Conner.

Too late now. He'd know instantly that she was messed up.

The message sat there blinking with no response and she nearly shut the program down. But then came the very cryptic return comment.

Desmond: *hi.*

Not capitalized, no punctuation. What the hell? Aliens had surely possessed the body of the man she'd married. And what was she supposed to say back? *Don't mind me, I'm just sitting here regretting everything I've ever done up to and including typing hi.*

McKenna: *Sorry to bother you.*

She nearly groaned. That had always been his line. For the first time she had the opposing perspective as the one doing the bothering. Except she'd never felt like it was a bother when he'd sought her out and, secretly, she'd always reveled in Desmond's attention.

Desmond: *Is everything okay?*

McKenna: *Peachy. Why do you ask?*

Desmond: *It's midnight.*

McKenna: *Yes, I noticed that. I was worried about you.*

She swore and tried to click on the message to recall it so she could correct that to *Conner* but he was already typing.

Desmond: *Don't do this. The adjustment is hard enough.*

She blinked. Don't do what? Be concerned? Talk to him via the chat tool he'd installed? The list of things he might be asking her to refrain from doing was long, but the better question was why he'd even say something like that.

McKenna: *What adjusting do you have to do? I'm the one in a new place.*

Desmond: *That was your choice. I have plenty to adjust to. I haven't ever been a father by myself. I miss you.*

Oh, God. She missed him, too. More than she could stand sometimes. Before she could react to that—unfreeze her fingers, breathe, *something*—he sent another message.

Desmond: *I can't do this with you.*

And then his status immediately flipped to offline. Stunned, she stared at the screen, her mind racing through that pseudo conversation, trying to pinpoint how she'd upset him. And it was very clear that she was indeed the problem. *I can't do this with you* sat there as a silent accusation, as cryptic as his initial unpunctuated and uncapitalized "hi."

Desmond missed her. It was right there in black surrounded by a blue bubble. She couldn't stop staring at it as she internalized that he might have a much bigger emotional stake in their relationship than she'd supposed. And if that was true, their conversation was far from over.

Oh, God. He missed her. He wasn't sleeping.

Everything but Desmond drained away.

She'd made a huge mistake.

Medical school could wait. Her family couldn't.

She yanked out her phone and texted him. Can't do what?

Let's see how you deal with that, Desmond H. Pierce. She'd entered him into an unbreakable social contract that required him to communicate back.

Except he didn't.

McKenna texted him again. Talk to me.

Thirty minutes later he hadn't complied. Furious with herself for caring whether or not she'd made a choice without all the facts, she stalked to the car and did the one thing she'd sworn never to do. She drove to Desmond's house. Ridiculous, stupid plan. But the panicky feeling in her stomach wouldn't stop and her brain kept turning over the fact that she hadn't really asked Desmond what her choices were when it came to what he was proposing.

The gate admitted her car without any trouble, a telling sign since it was automated to scan the license plate. Desmond had added her Honda to the list. Why?

At the front door she sent another text message: I'm outside. Come tell me to go away. She was going to get him to talk to her one way or another.

The front door cracked open less than thirty seconds later. Light spilled from the foyer, casting the man who'd opened it in shadow.

"It's late," Desmond rumbled into the darkness. "What are you doing here?"

His voice washed over her and her knees went a little weak. What *was* she doing here? She'd left this house because she hadn't seen any way to stay that wouldn't make her insane. Apparently sanity wasn't the goal because here she was again, begging for this man to talk to her, to change the tide, to force her to choose happiness instead of duty.

"Do you know what my favorite quality of yours is?" she asked instead of answering his question. Mostly because she didn't know how to answer it. Her mind was a riot of illogical, fragmented thoughts.

He sighed. "I must not have been clear. I don't want to talk to you. You made your choice to walk away. But I can make a choice to not let you back into my life."

Yes. She'd walked away. Toward a medical degree, which had long been her goal, but she'd also left something precious behind.

"That's my favorite quality of yours." She poked him in the chest because she couldn't stand not touching him a second longer. "You tell me exactly what's on your mind. Except when you don't. And that's what got me into the car, Desmond. Our conversation wasn't finished."

"Yes, it was, McKenna. There's nothing left to say."

The pain lacing his voice nearly stole her breath. She'd *hurt* him. *That* was why he kept shutting her down. While she'd been determined to get his attention strictly for her own peace of mind, he was trying to push her off because she'd hurt him.

She'd had no idea he cared that much.

What else didn't she know?

"I beg to differ," she countered softly and curled her hand around the open neckline of his button-down, holding tight and totally unsure if it was to keep him from fleeing or to keep her from dissolving into a little puddle at his feet. He wasn't dressed for bed, which might be the most telling of all. "I think there's a lot left to say. Like why you let me leave."

"Why I *let* you leave?" His short laugh raked through her. "I don't recall being given the choice. You demanded all the choices and then made your decision. What else could you possibly expect me to say other than I simply stepped out of your way."

It wasn't a question. It was a statement. A conviction. He'd done exactly as she'd told him to. Instead of having a conversation, she'd slung her own need for control around, forcing him to step back. What else might he have said if she'd shut her mouth?

She stared at him as he let her glimpse the anguish her choices had caused. Or maybe the things he felt were too strong to keep inside. "I expect you to tell me I'm selfish and I messed up. That I walked away from my family because of stupid pride and a need to do things my own way. As a result, I lost the two most important things that ever happened to me."

"That's not true." His gaze turned indignant as he argued with her. "Medical school was always important. You're incredibly intelligent, personable. Driven. You'll make an excellent doctor."

That curled up in her chest in tight, warm ball. "That's the nicest thing anyone's ever said to me."

He shrugged. "That's why I stepped out of the way and smoothed your path. I owed it to you, as you pointed out time and time again. I let you leave because it was never my right to force you to stay."

Her heart cracked open, spilling out love and pain and adoration and regret. He really did get it, displaying a wealth of understanding and willingness to change, which she'd failed to value. She did now.

"You couldn't have forced me to stay. Instead you set me free. That one act allowed me the time and distance to see where I wanted to land. It's here. With you. And

Conner. I made a mistake." Desperate to make him understand, she gripped his shirt tighter. "Please tell me it's not too late to pick up the pieces of our marriage."

He shook his head. "It's too late, McKenna. I can't let you go again."

"But that's not what I'm asking you to do," she whispered. "I'm not going anywhere. I choose to stay this time."

The short, simple phrase bled through Desmond's chest, slicing open new wounds as it burrowed toward his heart seeking asylum. "You can't say things like that."

Not now. Not after he'd already reconciled that his family had been torn apart. He'd cataloged all the emotion, analyzed everything that had gone wrong and arrived at the conclusion that he wasn't cut out for this madness.

Some people were natural artists, others were gifted musicians. Desmond's talent was trusting a woman with life-altering power. And when the woman exercised that power, she dug big, gaping holes in his soul that would never be filled. Loneliness and isolation plagued him and he lacked the ability to resolve either.

"Why?" she asked. "Is the invitation to stay rescinded? I didn't hear a time limit attached."

"Please don't do this." It was too much for him to breathe her in and let his senses get that one long taste of her. "You're enrolled in medical school. The die is cast."

"Then why haven't you filed for the divorce yet?" she countered quietly.

That nearly broke him. She wanted truth?

"Because you're still my wife, no matter what," he admitted.

Her expression veered wildly between extremes and finally settled on tenderness. "Yes. I am. And I want a chance to see what that looks like when we both give up our need for control."

"I've already done that once, McKenna. Never again." Harsh. Although still just the plain truth. If nothing else, he'd learned that life did not go as planned simply because he willed it to be so, but he could certainly curtail the damage by never opening himself up again. He'd spent years hiding, which suited him fine. Nothing had changed.

"I hurt you." At his curt nod, both of her hands slid up his arms to squeeze his shoulders and her touch almost knocked his composure away like a cat amused by a ball of yarn. "I'm sorry. I didn't honor how difficult that was for you, to give me the choice to leave. I made the wrong decision because I couldn't see myself as anything other than a doctor. I'm not good at failing and I didn't handle the dynamic between us well."

"What dynamic?" he couldn't help but ask and then wished to bite off his tongue. He might as well come out and ask if she'd developed feelings for him that she'd yet to share. Pathetic. Hadn't he learned his lesson? Women were treacherous.

"The one where I wanted to stay but couldn't see how that would work."

Her warm hands hadn't moved from his shoulders and he leaned into her touch, craving it and cursing himself for the craving at the same time. But he'd long ceased looking for a way to resist her because that was the very definition of insanity—doing the same thing over and over again without better results. Resisting her was impossible.

"The one where I fell into your world and couldn't

break free," she whispered. "You opened your door and eventually your body, your mind, your heart, and I... loved all of it. Especially your mind."

"Again, very short list of people in that category," he countered, not at all shocked that the gruff note in his voice perfectly matched the insurrection of emotion exploding through his chest. "If you wanted to stay, why didn't you?"

"I'm selfish and stubborn, or didn't you get the memo?" she asked wryly, and he refused to smile, though it was clear she'd meant for him to.

"You're the least selfish person I know. Everything you've done since I've met you has been for someone else. You'll be a great doctor," he repeated because the point couldn't be made clearly enough. He couldn't stand the thought of her resenting him for standing in her way. "You're also an amazing mother and the only wife I could imagine letting into my world."

Her eyelids fluttered closed as she processed that and, when she opened them, the clearest sense of hope radiated from her eyes. "You've always seen me as more than I do. I didn't believe in myself nearly as much as you did. I never thought I could be more than a doctor. It was too hard to concentrate when I had Conner and you right down the hall."

That was definitely something they had in common. He'd been unable to focus on anything other than her since that first moment she'd invaded his workshop without invitation, barging into his consciousness without fear, and he'd never been able to let her go in all the days since.

Even this one. Case in point. They were having a conversation at one in the morning instead of sleeping. Nothing worked to exorcise her from his mind, her scent from his head and the ghost of her in his bed.

"Then I have to ask. Did it get easier when you left?" If it had, he'd move in an instant to somewhere he could concentrate without her invading his everything.

"No." She smiled and it grabbed hold of his lungs, heart—hell, all of his internal organs at once. "I'm afraid it only got worse. So the problem is that I can't be a doctor without you. I can't be a mother without Conner. So here I am. Now what?"

Oh, no. She wasn't throwing that ball back in his court. "That's not my choice. It can't be."

"Then that makes it mine by default. So you're stuck with me," she informed him loftily. "The only thing is that you have to forgive me for wasting your tuition money. It's too late in the semester to get a refund."

"You're quitting school?" Incredulous, he stared at her. "You can't do that. *Why* would you do that? That's the worst possible choice you could make."

"Please, Desmond. Don't lock yourself away from me. I'm begging you for another chance." She shook him fiercely as if trying to knock that chance loose by sheer force. "Are you listening to what I'm saying? I'm not leaving again. I can't. I love you too much."

So many wondrous emotions radiated from her skin and burrowed under his, winnowing toward his soul too fast for him to catch it all or block it somehow. Too late. She swept away the shadows that had crawled inside him since she'd left.

"You shouldn't," he countered as his heart knit back together so fast he went light-headed. "I'm difficult to love—"

"Shut up. Stop saying stuff like that. What's difficult is when I try to stop loving you." She laughed and one tear slipped down her face as she shared what was inside her. "I don't know how to be in love. It's scary. It has no way for me to control it. Instead of telling you this, I left."

"To be a doctor. You had a dream that I wasn't a part of. I respected that even as it tore me apart."

"I know." Her head bowed for a brief moment. "That's what finally broke me, I think. That you were willing to sacrifice for me in spite of everything."

"I still am," he admitted gruffly. "It's the least I can do for what you sacrificed to give me Conner. Please don't give up medical school."

"It's okay, I have something better. A family."

That was the part that broke *him*. He swept her into his embrace and clung, scarcely able to believe he was holding her again.

"I love you," he murmured, unable to stop the flow of words. "So much. Too much to let you make such an irrevocable choice. There's absolutely no reason you can't keep going to school. I'll move to the house near campus. Tomorrow. Conner and I will take care of you while you become a doctor."

"You'd do that?" His shoulder muffled her broken whisper but he heard the question inside the question regardless.

"Of course I would. I'm already the nanny. Why not the househusband? I would live in a shack on the side of the road if that's what you wanted. As long as you were in it." He tipped up her chin to lay his lips on hers in what was only the first of many kisses to come. "This is just a house where I build things. If I have a family, I've already built the most important creation of my life. Anything else is just icing on the cake."

She smiled through her tears. "That sounds like an easy choice then."

"None of this is supposed to be hard. I told you, all you have to do is lie there and command me to do your will."

"I don't understand why you would do all of this for me."

Because to her he wasn't a beast. He wasn't the weird, awkward kid no one wanted to sit by. She'd chosen *him*. That was awe inspiring. And probably the only thing that could have enticed him out of his reclusive fortress designed to keep out the world.

But it turned out he didn't have to. McKenna had brought the world to him.

"Also not hard. I love you and you gave me Conner. The real question is what I could possibly do to repay you for the miracle of our son. I still don't know. But I'm going to spend a very long time trying to answer that. If you'll allow me to rip up the divorce papers."

She nodded furiously. "I'd like to burn them. In the fireplace. So I know for sure they're gone forever."

"Done. Except you'll have to wait until morning because I plan to be very busy between now and then." He couldn't stand to let her go as he led her toward the stairs and the bedroom upstairs that had been cold and empty without her.

"Oh, what did you have in mind?" she asked saucily with an intrigued expression that wasn't difficult to interpret. She was game for whatever he could envision, which excited him to no end. He had a great imagination.

"Sleep," he said with a laugh. "I haven't done that since you left and I'm looking forward to many nights of recovery."

She scowled without any real heat. "Sleep? I drove all the way from Portland to tell you my life is meaningless without you and you want to go to bed to *sleep*?"

"Maybe in a little while. I have some lost time to make up for first." And then he claimed his wife's lips in a kiss that was the second miracle he'd experienced in his life. He couldn't wait to find out what the next one would be.

Epilogue

McKenna swept Conner up for a hug, kissing him soundly on the cheek, but the precocious, dark-haired three-year-old was having none of that. He squirmed out of his mother's grip and ran off to play with Mark Hudson's daughter, the only other little person at the university's graduation ceremony.

Desmond smiled at his wife as she paused to exchange hugs with Mark's wife, Roberta. They'd socialized with the couple occasionally as Mark and McKenna worked through residency, but more often than not, Roberta and Desmond traded babysitting duty to give the other household a break during the grueling three years of medical school their respective spouses had endured.

It was over now. They'd both graduated with honors and earned their medical degrees.

"Dr. Pierce," Des murmured in his wife's ear as she paused at the reception table for a bottle of water. Happiness radiated from her, nearly dripping from her skin. "I've been waiting a long time to call you that."

She grinned and leaned into his embrace, which worked for him because that was where he wanted her. Always.

"Only because you're tired of being the only Dr. Pierce in our house."

Home. Not a house. They lived in a home, barely twelve hundred square feet worth, but he loved it. Had watched Conner take his first steps in the living room. Kissed McKenna at the dining room table as she'd applied for her second year of medical school, her residency, her name change.

"Perhaps," he conceded with a nod.

But more to the point, they'd agreed that once she'd earned her diploma, they'd throw caution to the wind and see what happened when McKenna stopped taking her birth control pills. For three years he'd been patient, letting her focus on medical school as promised.

She'd graduated. Tonight was his turn.

"Come with me, Dr. Pierce," he growled as the festivities wound down. "The Hudsons are taking Conner home with them for the night. You're all mine."

"Why, Dr. Pierce, whatever do you have in mind?" McKenna shifted her long dark hair off one shoulder as she contemplated him with a saucy smile. "A little graduation party for two?"

"Yes."

She laughed and the clear sound trilled through him. "Glad I'm not a big fan of suspense. You're as transparent as glass."

Still her favorite quality of his, as she told him often. Good thing. Saved him a lot of trouble explaining things.

"Then it should be no surprise what I've got planned. Kiss your son and let's go."

He waited impatiently as she gave Roberta a few instructions, including the one about making sure Conner had his elephant, Peter, to sleep with. And then, finally, he got her snuggled into his embrace for the five-minute walk to their little clapboard house that had not one robotic humanoid inside its walls.

The remote mansion on the river sat untouched, a monument to the man he'd once been and never would be again. But he couldn't bear to sell it because it was still the place where he'd fallen in love with his wife, where he'd first made love to her. One day, Conner might want to live there and have access to all the luxuries. But for now, all they needed was each other.

Once she cleared the door, McKenna turned in his arms, trapping him against the wood. There was no place on earth he'd rather be. His arms were full of light, desire, happiness. So many emotions raced through her, he could hardly sense one before another took over.

"Tonight's the night," he told her. "If this isn't what you want, you should tell me now."

He really didn't have to clarify. But it was always nice to hear her voice.

"Which part?" she murmured against his throat as she nibbled his skin. "Where I command you to strip me naked and have your wicked way with me?"

"The part where I get you pregnant," he corrected, his voice so rough with need it was a wonder she understood him. "Finally."

But then, she'd never had a problem understanding him.

"I've been waiting three long years for this, Des." She smiled, her hands busy unbuckling his belt. "I want to conceive your baby and, alongside you, watch it grow in my tummy. I want a brother or sister for Conner. A legacy that has everything to do with love."

That sounded perfect to Desmond. "Then come here and let me love you."

He swept his wife into his arms and took her to bed where the only thing that stood between them was skin. He did his best to savor each moment, to pay attention to the subtle cues so he could pinpoint the exact moment of conception. But in the end there was too much going on and he let the sheer pleasure of her reign supreme because what else mattered?

"You know it might take more than one try to conceive," she murmured later as they lay content in each other's arms.

"I'm nothing if not ready, willing and able to try as many times as I need to."

Smiling so wide it hurt his face, he stroked her arm. A baby would be amazing. A fantastic addition to the family he'd built, that they continued to build every day. McKenna had drawn him out from behind his curtain into the real world. And they had lots of opportunities to perfect the art of baby making. They should probably start over right now.

* * * * *

*If you liked this story of a wealthy tycoon
tamed by the love of the right woman—and baby—
pick up these other novels from
USA TODAY bestselling author Kat Cantrell.*

*THE CEO'S LITTLE SURPRISE
A PREGNANCY SCANDAL
THE PREGNANCY PROJECT
FROM ENEMIES TO EXPECTING*

Available now from Mills & Boon Desire!

***

*And don't miss the next
BILLIONAIRES AND BABIES story
HIS ACCIDENTAL HEIR by Joanne Rock.
Available June 2017!*

***

*If you're on Twitter, tell us what you think of
Mills & Boon Desire! #MillsandBoonDesire*

"Now, how can you possibly know about my love life?"

"Word gets around about you," Meg replied, teasing.

"Well, what do you know," Gabe said with a smile. "You've been discussing me with others."

"Don't flatter yourself—I may not be the one bringing up your name, you know."

He laughed. "I better back off right now. I know you well enough to know when my teasing is getting to you."

"You don't know as much about me as you think you do. The last time you teased me I was fourteen years old."

He tilted her chin up. "We're in a spotlight from the security light. Just in case anyone is observing us, let's make this look like the real thing."

"No one in this neighborhood is paying attention to us." Gabe slipped his arm around her waist. "You know, Meg, we've never kissed."

He leaned closer and her heart beat faster.

When his mouth brushed hers, heat swept through her. His arms tightened around her, drawing her against his hard length as his mouth covered hers.

Oh. She was in trouble.

* * *

The Rancher's Cinderella Bride
is part of the Callahan's Clan series—
A wealthy Texas family finds love
under the Western skies!

THE RANCHER'S CINDERELLA BRIDE

BY
SARA ORWIG

MILLS
BOON

First Published in Great Britain 2017
By Mills & Boon, an imprint of HarperCollins*Publishers*
1 London Bridge Street, London, SE1 9GF

© 2017 Sara Orwig

ISBN: 978-0-263-92818-1

51-0517

Our policy is to use papers that are natural, renewable and recyclable products and made from wood grown in sustainable forests. The logging and manufacturing processes conform to the legal environmental regulations of the country of origin.

Printed and bound in Spain
by CPI, Barcelona

Sara Orwig, from Oklahoma, loves family, friends, dogs, books, long walks, sunny beaches and palm trees. She is married to and in love with the guy she met in college. They have three children and six grandchildren. Sara's one hundredth published novel was a July 2016 release. With a master's degree in English, Sara has written historical romance, mainstream fiction and contemporary romance. Sara welcomes readers on Facebook or at www.saraorwig.com.

One

Gabe Callahan sat on the porch of his ranch house with his booted feet propped on a rail as he watched a red pickup race up the road and onto the circular drive in front of the house. Aldridge Landscape Design was in red letters on the side, against a white circle background. Having known the driver as far back in his life as he could remember, he couldn't imagine what could have made her so desperate to call him, let alone to drive the two hours southwest from Dallas to his ranch. Unless she had been in Downly, the nearest town and only thirty minutes away from him. For Meg the drive would be longer.

As the truck screeched to a stop, he winced and stood, walking to the top of the steps. He waited there till Megan Louise Aldridge popped out of the pickup and charged toward the porch.

"Good morning, Meg," he said, addressing her the way he had since she had been in preschool and he had been in the first grade. He nodded toward the pickup. "When are you going to learn to drive?"

She didn't laugh or even smile at his usual teasing, so whatever the problem was, it was big.

"Let's go inside," he said quietly, realizing something was really wrong. That alone was startling because Meg was usually cheerful. At least the Meg he remembered. He hadn't seen much of her the past few years.

"Let's sit in the library," he directed as he motioned her into the house.

As she walked beside him, he caught a whiff of the familiar lilac perfume she had worn since middle school. He gave her a sidelong glance. She hadn't changed much. Though she was taller now, her long pale brown hair was still held back from her forehead by a blue headband—the same style hairdo she'd worn since preschool. Her hair had always been either caught by a headband or braided in pigtails. And once again, she wore no makeup. Frank, honest, sweet—that was exactly how he'd describe the Meg he remembered. And exactly how she looked right now.

Though these days they kept in touch mainly through social media and through the grapevine, back in the day Meg had been a great friend—and in the earliest years, his best friend. As kids, she had been there for him during the bad times and he had been there for her. All that despite a family feud that had put a wedge between the Callahans and the Aldridges.

Sometime after his high school graduation, they'd begun to drift apart, seeing each other less, and to his relief, as far as he knew, neither one of them had had as many problems as they'd had growing up. At least not until now. Something was definitely wrong in her life to send her to his ranch looking as worried as she did.

He closed the double library doors, glancing around a room that had three walls covered with shelves of books that he loved. From the day he moved in, this room had been his sanctuary. Crossing the room, he placed his hands on her slender shoulders. "It's been a long time since we've really talked, Meg. It's good to see you again."

"It's good to see you, too," she said, giving him a tight smile.

"I appreciated you coming to the memorial service for my brother and sister-in-law."

"I was sorry about Nathan and Lydia."

"Thanks. We've both lost brothers," he stated. "That isn't why you're here. I get the feeling something's wrong." He searched her eyes. "What is it? Do you need something from me?"

She looked directly into his eyes, and her expression was firm yet unreadable. Then she nodded. "Yes, Gabe, I need something. I need us to get engaged."

The laugh burst out of him like a popped balloon. "Nice one." He wasn't used to Meg being the jokester in the relationship, but he enjoyed a good laugh as much as anyone.

But Meg didn't laugh, or even smile. She merely stared at him and then said bluntly, "I want to get engaged to you for about a month. I want you to propose marriage."

So she wasn't kidding?

Not knowing what to think, he wiped away his grin and looked down at the floor while he pulled himself together. Then, frowning, he met her gaze once again. He could only manage one word. "Why?"

"To get my family off my back."

The explanation may have made perfect sense to her, but he felt as if he'd come in on the second act. He had no idea what she was talking about.

Before he could ask her to explain, she went on.

"Of course, it wouldn't be for real or for long. Just long enough to get my family to back off, settle down and let me live my life." Now her eyes went wide and he saw the emotion in them once again. She was deeply troubled. "They want me to marry and I don't want to get married. But they don't seem to care. Mom and Dad are pushing me even when they know I don't want this."

"But everyone in these parts knows we've never been in love or even dated. Why me?"

"Because you're my friend. I know we're not as close as we were, but in a lot of ways, Gabe, you're still my best friend. Who else would I turn to?"

"Meg, you're my best female friend—" He paused and studied her. "In fact, you may be my best friend except for my brothers, and I've told you secrets I haven't told them." What was he saying? Instead of strolling down memory lane with her, he needed to talk some sense into her. He took her by the hands and led her over to two chairs. "Let's sit and talk."

Clamping her lips together, she sat. Leaning back in his chair with one foot on his knee, he gazed at her. She looked about the same as she had the last time he had seen her, over a year ago. She had on a baggy gray sweatshirt, worn, faded jeans and scuffed, dusty boots. From what he'd heard through the grapevine, her landscape design business in Dallas was growing and successful.

It felt good to see her again, to talk to her again.

They'd always discussed their problems, but he had to admit, this one was a doozy. "Talk to me, Meg. What's the deal? You have a nice family."

"Not about this," she said, frowning, worry filling her big, thickly lashed dark brown eyes. Really pretty eyes. That thought surprised him because he had never been physically attracted to Meg. She wasn't his type of woman.

"I need your help," she said, leaning forward and taking his hands in her dainty ones that were as cold as ice.

"You're freezing," he said, covering her hands with his. "Calm down. I'll help you. Any way I can."

"I hope you mean that," she said in a low, intense voice. "Because I really need you to ask me to marry you."

He pulled his hands back, but she grasped them tighter. "It's temporary, very temporary," she said quickly. "I think one month should do it. And it wouldn't be a real engagement, of course." She leaned closer and her voice took on a more earnest tone. "I need your help, Gabe. Please," she begged, as if he had threatened to toss her out of his house.

He did what he did best. He tried to lighten the mood. "Hey, remember, you're talking to me—best friends since forever."

"I'm serious, Gabe, and I'm desperate."

"I believe you," he said, getting more worried.

She took a deep breath and looked as if she faced a firing squad.

"All of them—my parents and both sets of grandparents—want an heir. And they all want a grandchild."

He shrugged. "Tell them that will happen in due time."

"Time is part of the problem. They're all getting

older. You know Todd, my oldest brother, is career military and he's in Afghanistan now and isn't getting married anytime soon. Caleb, my married brother, has a good part in a Broadway play alongside his wife, Nora. They don't want children to interfere with their careers," she said, rattling off her reasons and sounding more panicky with each one. "And Hank is gone," she said, a wistful note of sadness in her voice that made him want to offer sympathy again over her brother who was killed in a crash when he was flying his small plane. "My family is desperate for a baby and I'm the prime candidate."

He managed to extricate his hands and sat back. "I get that, but—"

"There's more. Someone wants to marry me and my family knows it," she said, looking distraught and sounding as if she were caught in a huge calamity.

"Who wants to marry you?"

"Justin Whelton—fourth generation of successful Dallas lawyers."

"I know Justin," Gabe said, frowning and thinking he could see why she had no interest in marrying him. Gabe had known Justin as long as Meg had known him. Their parents moved in the same social circles and now that he and Justin and Meg were grown, they crossed paths at social events. Gabe didn't like Justin and suspected he had done some underhanded things to win cases.

"Justin and I dated in high school. It meant nothing to each of us except convenience. It's the same now, but the minute we went out a few times this past year both sets of parents came up with the idea that we should marry. Justin's folks want him to marry because he has big political ambitions and they think being married would give him stability and better voter approval. And I'm the perfect candidate to be his wife as far as his parents and mine are concerned. I've told mine I don't love him but they think we would fall in love because we're apparently so compatible and we've known each other all our lives. My mistake was ever going out with him, just because he was a friend. There never has been any romance between the two of us, no more than there was any between you and me. We're friends. Period. I don't like to kiss him and we rarely have. How do you marry someone you don't like to kiss?"

He couldn't help it. Despite her seriousness, he chuckled.

"Gabe, don't you dare laugh at me. It isn't funny."

"I'm not laughing," he said, trying not to, "but I'm surprised Justin wants this if you won't kiss him. If you and I get pretend engaged, will you kiss me?"

"I'm serious here," she said, anger flaring in her big eyes.

He had to bite back another laugh and realized he shouldn't tease her now. She was too upset to see humor in it.

"Yes, I'll kiss you," she said through gritted teeth and her cheeks turned red.

He couldn't hold the grin that came that time.

"Gabe, so help me—"

Impulsively, he hugged her. "I'm teasing, Meg, and you know it. You just get so riled up that I can't resist." He released her, but not before he noticed she was soft to hug and far different from when she was a skinny middle school kid.

"His dad and grandfathers have offered him so many financial incentives—you can't imagine."

"That's no incentive if the lady doesn't like you. I'd

think your family would listen if you firmly tell them you don't want to marry him."

"They're *not* listening, Gabe. That's the problem. They're all pushing, including Justin, who thinks this would help his career. He's laying the groundwork to run for the Texas legislature, but he wants to be in Washington and he thinks I would make—to quote him—'the right kind of wife.' What a reason to marry!" She grabbed Gabe's hands again. "You can't imagine the pressure my family is putting on me. Please, just think about a pretend engagement," she begged.

He kept telling himself this was ridiculous, she was exaggerating and he wanted no part of it. But as she held his hands in hers, he looked down into imploring brown eyes and felt himself sinking into quicksand.

"I'm friends with Justin's secretary, Gretchen," she went on. "She told me Justin is planning to propose at the big anniversary dance this month at the country club. If I turn him down in front of all those people and our families, it'll be dreadful."

Gabe pulled back and stood up. "Dammit, Meg. Justin isn't planning that because he loves you and wants a fun memory for you. He's doing it to get attention for himself."

"I know that." Her eyes went watery and he was afraid she'd start to cry. "You're not going to have to go through with marrying me. Just a pretend engagement for a month and then you can tell all your lady friends that it was a sham. I'll tell them if you want."

Shaking his head, he gave her a brief crooked smile. "Geez, Meg, I don't have a harem. You don't have to reassure anyone that I'm available." He ran a hand through his hair. "You've never been dishonest or hidden things from your folks in all your life. How are you going to look them in the eye and tell them we're engaged?"

She took a deep breath. "That's worried me the most, but they are really pushing me to marry a man I don't love, so I can do it and later I'll apologize and remind them that they forced me into this and I was really desperate."

"Ah, Meg, this isn't like you and it isn't like me. No one would believe us. Remember, we've never even had one date."

"They'd believe me. You know they would."

He stared down at her, the sinking feeling growing in the pit of his stomach. Much as he hated to admit it, she had a point. Meg was the most honest, frank person he had ever known, so a pretend engagement was so foreign to her way of living that people might never suspect it. But... "There is not another person on this earth that I know who could carry a pretend engagement off and get people to believe it, but I'm not sure you can, either."

"Gabe, it would only be a short time and—"

"I still say people won't believe us."

She stood up, dug in a hip pocket and pulled out a small velvet box. Opening it, she held it out to him. "They'll believe it when I announce it with this on my finger," she said.

He took the small box in his hand and looked down at a dazzling diamond ring. Then he looked at her. "Is this real?"

Her cheeks turned pink. "Of course not. I can't afford a diamond like that, but if it were real, you could afford it."

"Megan, your family doesn't like me or my family. Except for you and your brothers, the Aldridges haven't spoken to me for years." The silly feud had seen to that. Decades ago, both their fathers had been business partners, until his dad had bought out her dad and caused a rift that had never healed.

"Don't you see, Gabe? That's exactly why my plan is perfect. If they think I've gotten engaged to you, they'll back off pushing for marriage so fast," she said with a grim determination in her voice. "Just one month, Gabe."

He gazed into her big brown eyes and his spirits dropped another notch. "Ah, Meg, I just don't think it'll work. If it does, everyone will think I've gotten you pregnant."

"I don't care because in time, they'll know that you haven't. That's no problem."

"We've never had one date," he insisted.

"So we start dating. Gabe, I'm desperate," she cried.

Gabe patted her soft hand while he thought about what she had just told him. He had always promised her he would help her if she ever needed him, and he was letting her down now, when she needed him most.

Meg was relentless. Her barrage of persuasion persisted. "If we get engaged, everyone will talk about it and Justin and I will vanish from the center of conversations in our families.

"You ought to be at my house for dinner any night and hear them badgering me. My dad has offered to give us enough money to buy a house. My grandparents have offered the deed to one of the ranches they own. They're so earnest. One set of grandparents will fly me and my mom to New York for me to have a makeover and buy an entire new wardrobe. It's ridiculous."

She tightened her cold fingers around his hand, leaning closer, looking as if she would burst into tears.

"Please. It's just pretend, so it doesn't matter how we feel about each other."

No matter how many reasons she gave him, he still thought the ploy wouldn't work. It would be disastrous and only make her family dislike him even more. And he wasn't sure it would help her at all. In fact, the only one he saw coming out of this well was old Justin, who'd save face by not getting rejected during a dumb public proposal.

No, he thought, *this was not a good plan at all.*

Reluctance filled him. He squeezed her shoulder gently, her soft hair falling on his hand. He looked deep into her eyes and prepared to decline, no matter how much it hurt him to not be there for her.

But he couldn't believe the words that came out of his mouth.

"I'll be your pretend fiancé if that's what you want."

The words had just spilled out. Who was he kidding? He could never resist helping her.

"Oh, Gabe, thank you," she cried, hugging him.

He wrapped his arms around her, still feeling as if she were the sister he never had. Except when he hugged her, it was a curvy woman's body pressed against him and he had a fleeting curiosity about what she'd look like out of that shapeless sweatshirt she wore. She was soft and smelled sweet, the same lilac scent he'd always remembered. As a little kid, she'd told him her grandmother got her lilac soap. He released her and gazed into brown eyes and a big smile.

"You're pretty, Meg. There ought to be all sorts of guys wanting to take you out."

She shook her head. "Not anyone I want to go out with and not anyone I'd trust with a pretend engagement. I'm probably too bossy because I'm used to running my own business and giving orders."

"I don't recall thinking you're too bossy."

A brief smile flickered on her lips. "That's because you're bossier."

"You never told me that. Well, maybe a time or two."

"You can be as bossy as you want. Thank you, Gabe."

"If we're going to do this, and you want to stave off a public proposal at the dance, let's get with it. Today is Thursday. I think we should have a first date this weekend if you can make it," he said.

"I sure can," she said, wiggling with eagerness that made him remember times in the past when she would get her way and be very happy. "Say when."

"Saturday night," he answered, wondering what she was pulling him into with this pretense and how much explaining he would have to do with some of his close female friends.

"Saturday it is."

"How are you going to tell Justin about going out with me Saturday night?"

"I won't have to yet because he's going out of town this weekend on business. He'll be back Wednesday and by that time, he'll know we went out. Even one date with you will make him call off a public proposal."

She turned to leave, but spun back around. "I almost forgot. Saturday night, do you want me to be at my house in Downly or my house in Dallas?"

"You have two houses?" he asked.

"It works out better with my landscape business. You probably don't even know I'm not living at home with my folks anymore, do you? My maternal grandparents do that."

"Which place is more convenient for you on Saturday?"

"Downly."

"Then I'll pick you up at your house in Downly. I need an address."

"I'll text you," she said. Then her eyes narrowed as she looked at him with an expression he couldn't read. "Do you think it's going to be weird to 'date'?"

"No. We've always had fun together and Saturday night won't be any different." He leaned into her, bumping her shoulder with his.

"I suppose you're right." She grinned at him, then came back with another suggestion. "Later, after a few dates, maybe I can stay at your ranch so it will look as if we're serious, and sometimes at your house in Dallas, so I can go to work from there. It won't be for long and I'll stay out of your way."

That might not be the best idea, but he couldn't say no at this point. And actually part of him looked forward to seeing her more because she was always good company. "That's fine if you want to," he finally said. "I have big houses with plenty of room."

Her grin turned into a full-fledged smile. "In case I forget to tell you this a thousand times over the rest of my life, thank you, Gabe. You always promised I could come to you for help and now you're going to help me," Meg gushed, her eyes getting a sparkle that made him feel a degree better.

"I don't want a loveless marriage and I don't want to marry Justin. None of them can understand it. When I marry, I want the love and closeness my grandparents and my parents have had."

He knew she did. That was the kind of woman Meg was.

"Then I hope this ploy works, Meg. For your sake."

"Oh, it will. You'll see. We'll convince my family and Justin's, and they're the ones who count. And then you can go on your way knowing you have been the knight to the rescue." She patted his hand. "My wonderful, handsome knight."

It might not be a role he was accustomed to, but he had to admit he was going to like it. But before he got knighted, they had a lot of work to do. He only hoped they'd pull off the charade as easily as Meg seemed to think they would.

While Meg had always been a good friend, there had never been anything romantic between them. Nor would there ever be. As great as she was, she wasn't his type and he wasn't hers. They were just too opposite. She was too staid and fearful of the daring things he liked to do. And then there was the feud between the older generations of their families. No, Meg wasn't the woman for him and he wasn't the man for her. But now they had to convince the world they were. He hoped this charade did not have to last long. He liked his other women friends and partying too much to be tied up in Meg's pretense.

She still held his gaze as she said, "You are an absolute angel coming to my rescue."

He laughed. "I've been called a lot of things, but 'angel' has never been one of them."

She smiled sweetly at him and patted his cheek. "You're definitely my angel." She ran her hand lightly over the stubble on his jaw. "You've stopped shaving close. It gives you a rugged, devil-may-care look even more than before," she said, tilting her head to study him. "I like it. You know, I wish Hank could know what a huge favor you're doing for me."

"If your brother knew, he would roll on the floor with laughter. But your family... They're going to hate me when they learn the truth."

"They don't like you now because you're a Callahan. This will get them to stop talking to me about Justin and start talking to me about breaking up with you. And Hank wouldn't roll on the floor and laugh at us. He'd thank you and tell me to go for it because he wouldn't approve of them trying to push me into a loveless marriage."

She turned to leave again.

"I better run, Gabe," she said. "Oh, I almost forgot. You keep this ring, and soon you can give it back to me to wear." She thrust the small box into his hand.

"Sure, Meg," he said, thinking he had to after all their years of friendship. She'd always been there for him when he was young and hurt by his dad. When his dad wasn't around for graduation or games or awards or holidays, she had supported him and cheered him up. "I owe you this because you stood by me when I was ignored by my dad. He never gave me or any of my brothers his love, his time or his attention. It was worse for our stepbrother, Blake, because our father didn't even acknowledge Blake as his son. At least I had your friendship when I was so hurt."

She smiled at him as she walked out to her pickup. "That's what friends are for, and you're the best I've ever had."

"I think you used that same line with me when you were nine years old," he remarked drily and she laughed. She had a contagious smile, and under ordinary circumstances it would have been good to see her again, he admitted.

"I probably talked you out of some of those fancy

marbles you used to have. I thought they were the most beautiful marbles ever. I still have them."

"You always were easy to please so I guess I don't have to rack my brain over where to take you to eat on Saturday."

"This first time let's go somewhere we'll be seen and where people will talk about us."

He grinned. "Whatever you want to get this show on the road. I'll see you at seven Saturday night," he said, opening the door to her pickup.

With a quick pat on his hand, she climbed in and he closed the door. "You know, there is a way you can cut the dating time in half and end your folks pushing you to marry."

"What's that?"

He placed his arm on the door and leaned in closer. "Move in with me."

"That's actually a wonderful idea, Gabe."

He laughed. "I think we have different views of living together."

She wrinkled her nose at him. "I'm just thinking of staying under one roof."

He leaned down. "Shucks, Meg, I'm thinking about staying in the same bed. We didn't discuss that. We should have some fun with this deal."

"Will you cool it? We're not going to bed together," she said while her cheeks turned pink and he laughed.

"I've sure had worse ideas." He grinned and she shook her head, but she smiled at him.

"Stop teasing me. You haven't changed any. See you later."

Laughing, he watched her drive away and wondered how much Meg was going to complicate his life. She said this would only be a month and then it would be over. But the month was going to be interesting—Meg living in the same house with him. He was sure she was old-fashioned. And he would try to curb some of his teasing, but it was hard to resist getting a rise out of her. All in all, he looked forward to spending the time with her. How much had she changed since she had grown up?

He turned the velvet box over in his hand, thinking about the dazzling ring that was as fake as their engagement would be. Would a month's pretend engagement really have any impact on his life?

Two

Meg closed the door of her small house in Downly, and glanced around at familiar surroundings without seeing any of them. She threw her arms up and spun on her toes, joy and relief overwhelming her. Gabe would help her. He was going along with the pretend engagement and she couldn't wait for their first date.

A date with Gabe. The thought stirred tingles of excitement that surprised her. She didn't want to feel any attraction to him. He was a wild man with wild ways. He loved the ladies. And he was not her type. Whatever excitement she felt over being with him would vanish, she was sure.

She poured a glass of water and stepped onto her patio while she thought about Saturday night. Saturday was a big day in the landscape business, but she could get off early. She wasn't going to say no to any date Gabe suggested as long as it was soon. She knew she should head to work now, but she wouldn't be able to focus on anything except jubilation that Gabe would bail her out of her problem.

She remembered how she had tried to cheer him up and comfort him as a kid when his dad wouldn't come home or ignored Gabe when he was home. Through the years, Gabe had repeatedly promised that he would help if she ever had any problems and he'd insisted she promise she would come to him with them. That was all childhood history, but he had come through on his long-ago promises to her today.

She went to the room she had turned into an office. Shelves lined the walls with books, pictures, trophies, awards and stacks of papers. She crossed the room to pick up a small picture and looked closely at it. It was a snapshot of her and Gabe in her backyard. He held her pigtail in front of his face like a mustache while he grinned at the camera. She smiled as she looked at it. "Thanks for being my friend always," she said to his picture.

She was going out with him Saturday night—their first date. But one where she needn't worry about what to wear. Gabe wouldn't care. Going out with him would be like an evening with one of her brothers. The thought reminded her of Hank again. Hank and Gabe had been close friends, and they were a lot alike. Hank had taken risks like Gabe did and had loved life on the wild side—flying, competing in rodeos, taking out party girls and never getting serious. Gabe was slightly older and her family felt he had been a bad influence on Hank. In the early years when her dad had worked with Gabe's dad in their own business, both families had been close and Hank thought Gabe was great. Later, her family was so bitter over the way Dirkson Callahan had cut her dad out of the business that they stopped speaking to any of the Callahans and didn't want any of their children to speak to them, either. While the grandparents felt the same as her parents, the feud had never carried over to her generation, and as much as possible, her generation had stayed friends with one another.

Her family wasn't going to want her to marry Gabe, and with a ring on her finger from him, she expected them to stop pushing her to marry.

She hugged the picture. "Thank you, thank you," she whispered, remembering when he had hugged her today. His broad shoulders and strong arms were a physical reassurance that made her feel safe, as if her problems were solved. She looked more intently at the picture. When had that skinny kid grown into a tall, strong man whose hug could make her feel that she was safe and all would be right with her world? He had grown up to be a good-looking guy, which she had never thought about before in her life.

"You're definitely my best friend," she whispered to his picture.

Still smiling, she placed the picture back on the shelf and went to her desk to check emails on her laptop.

Like her brother Hank who had been in commercial real estate, Gabe had gone into business with his older brother Cade in commercial real estate with a large office building in Dallas. She knew through the years they had oil and gas investments and business ties with Gabe's stepbrother, Blake, who was a hotel mogul. She didn't know whether Gabe spent more time in Dallas now or more time on his ranch. He could afford to do whatever he wanted.

Briefly, she concentrated on her emails, answering quickly and then gathering things to take to Dallas to her office, which was almost a two-hour drive away, depending on traffic. Before she left the room she blew a kiss toward Gabe's picture. "My handsome knight to my rescue," she whispered.

Relieved, happier than she had been in a couple of months, Meg gathered her things and left for her office, able to concentrate fully on business and work that she had planned for the day.

Saturday came swiftly and at the end of the day, she rushed home to get ready to go out with Gabe. She showered and dressed, selecting clothes that might get her noticed—not by Gabe but by other diners. She chose a pair of her fancy skintight jeans, her best black boots and a bright red sleeveless vee-neck shirt, and a matching red headband.

Gabe suggested they go to the best barbecue place near Downly, where they could have ribs along with some boot-scootin' fun. Because many people from Dallas were there on the weekend, word would spread back to Big D real easily. Not only would that put the kibosh on Justin's proposal, but she would have fun with Gabe in the meantime.

Promptly at seven she heard a car door slam and seconds later her doorbell rang. She hurried to open the door to Gabe, who wore a black hat, black shirt, jeans and black boots. He had never looked as appealing as he did at that moment because he was going to deliver her from a worrisome dilemma.

"Are you ready for a new adventure?" he asked, grinning at her.

"You can't imagine how ready, you handsome cowboy. I want you to sweep me off my feet."

"That sounds like my kind of task," he replied as his gaze swept over her from head to toe. He whistled.

"Wow, you grew up in the most delightful way. You look pretty."

"Thank you. I hope I'm pretty enough for people to post our picture on all sorts of social media." She reached for her keys. "I'll show you my house some-time, but right now, I can't wait to get out there and let every Texan possible see us together."

"Slow down, Meg," he said, laughing. "I promise, you'll be noticed."

Grabbing her broad-brimmed black hat, she locked up and left, walking beside him toward his shiny black pickup. "You know, I never noticed what a good-look-ing guy you are."

His smile widened. "You've gotten what you want, Meg, so you can cut the flattery. Or are you buttering me up for more? I'll tell you now—I agreed to a pre-tend engagement but I draw the line at a pretend mar-riage. I'm not the marrying kind, real or even pretend."

"I wouldn't think of asking you to do one more thing," she answered with exaggerated politeness.

"I seem to remember a few instances when you turned on the sweetness and charm with a definite goal in mind."

"You exaggerate, but that's okay. With time your memory has embellished circumstances. I can't tell you how happy I've been the last couple of days, and how relieved. I feel as if I've escaped prison."

"Yeah, I've had a few relationships that I ended and then felt the same way," he said with a smile.

She wrinkled her nose at him and shook her head. "Well, this is a once-in-a-lifetime dilemma for me. I will never again get myself in this kind of situation with a guy."

"Watch what you predict. Life has a way of sending

us all kinds of surprises. Did you ever think we'd be going out on a date?"

Shaking her head, she laughed. "I'm sure on this one," she said as he opened the pickup door and she slid into the seat to watch him circle the pickup. He was good-looking, something she hadn't given much thought to in past years. A Dallas magazine had listed Gabe as one of the top twenty most eligible bachelors in the area. But Gabe's looks and sex appeal wouldn't interfere with her plans.

Tonight she just wanted to have fun, to celebrate her freedom that was coming, freedom to live her life her way without a constant war with her parents and grandparents.

Gabe drove to a log building with a long front porch. Rocking chairs and pots of blooming flowers created a relaxed, inviting ambience. Inside, lights were low, and ceiling fans turned slowly above dancers circling the floor as a fiddler and a drummer played. Gabe got a table at the edge of the dance floor where couples were already into a lively two-step.

"This is perfect. Everyone will see us at this table."

"Unless someone is blind drunk, you're probably right," Gabe remarked drily. "Now order up. And relax, Meg. You'll get what you want. You look ready to jump out of your skin."

She laughed. "I'm so excited and happy. Let's dance and then more people will see us."

Laughing, he shook his head as he stood and took her hand. In seconds, he held her hands while she danced at his side in another fast two-step. He turned her around and when he caught her to stop her from turning again, he pulled her slightly closer. Flashing another smile, she looked up at him. "You adorable man. You're the best friend possible," she said, hoping she looked like a woman falling in love.

"Don't overdo it," he said, laughing at her.

"There's no way to overdo what I feel, and since I want people to think I'm falling in love with you, I have to look as if I'm having the time of my life. Which I kind of am."

"You're shameless, Meg. I keep telling myself not to be flattered that you asked me to be your pretend fiancé, because any guy would have fit the bill. Except you knew that because of our friendship, I'd do this without any demands on you."

"Not so. I wouldn't trust any other guy. Besides, with another guy no one would believe me. But you fit all the qualifications. I've known you forever. You're handsome, sexy, fun, popular, wealthy—"

"Stop with all the flattery. You've already got what you want. If I were all that you said, the ladies would be lined up at our table waiting to dance with me."

"I'm surprised they aren't, but they're watching you, which means they're watching us, which is good. Hey, you're a good dancer, too."

"Don't sound so surprised. What do you think I've been doing on Saturday nights?"

"Well, you just seem so into planes, motorcycles and bull riding that I didn't expect you to be so light on your feet."

"Maybe you're in for all kinds of surprises from me," he said with an exaggerated leer that made her laugh.

"Bring 'em on, cowboy. I'm ready for some excitement in my life."

"I told you before—and you know the old saying— watch what you wish for. That's a challenge you just gave me, Meg," he teased.

"I'm ready for you." She twirled and came back beside him. "It's fun to be with you again." When he was about to protest, she said, "I mean it. You have to admit, it's different from when we were little kids."

"Is it ever, darlin'. And vastly better," he said, his gaze drifting over her again, making her laugh and feel a surprising tingle.

The dance ended and he held her hand as they returned to their table. She stopped to say hello to some people on the way. As soon as they had ordered, she stood. "I'll be back in a minute. I'm going to the ladies' room."

"Yeah, I know. You're going so more people will see you."

She smiled and left, knowing that Gabe would be good-natured about this fake engagement. Excitement bubbled in her and she wondered how much of it was knowing her problem would soon be a thing of the past—and how much was just pure excitement from being with Gabe.

When she returned to their table, they ordered and shortly had platters with piles of ribs covered in red barbecue sauce, a mound of curly fries and thick, buttered Texas toast. While they ate, she tried to catch up on his current life.

As they laughed over a recent incident, Gabe took a sip of his beer and when he set it down, he smiled. "You're right—it's good to be together again," Gabe said.

"I'm surprised there's no woman in your life right now, but I'm glad there's not, otherwise you couldn't have gone out with me. Why don't you hold my hand," she suggested. "That would look good."

His grin widened. "This is the first time my date has told me how to come on to her."

"Well, I just want you to look as if you're falling in love and really want me. So far, with all the fun we're having, we look just like what we are—two old buds out together."

"Oh, darlin'," he drawled. "I think I can get beyond just buddies without you having to coach me," he said in a husky, breathy statement that was barely above a whisper. He stood, drawing her to her feet while he watched her intently. He slipped his arm around her waist, pulled her tightly against his side as they walked to the dance floor.

"Oh, my," she said, gazing up at him. "That's definitely on target."

"Just wait, darlin'." He leaned down to whisper into her ear, his warm breath stirring tingles that surprised her.

On the dance floor she turned to face him, winding her arms around his neck and gazing into his eyes as they moved in unison. Her satisfaction climbed over how well they fit together.

"Gabe, this is positively a dream come true," she said, dancing closer so he could hear her over the music. "Tanya is here, Justin's ex-girlfriend, and she's seen me. She can't stop glancing at me. When this dance ends, try to be near her and we'll go talk to her. I'll introduce you."

"Dare I hope she's the one in the skintight jeans and low-cut blue blouse that reveals a lot of her ink? No wonder his parents have focused on you. They're not the type for tats and blouses with vee necklines to the waist. As adorable as you are, I'm surprised Justin gave in so easily."

"I think I should feel insulted, but I don't. Justin's dad gave him incentives to give in. If he marries me, he gets a partnership in the firm after the first year of our marriage. If I'm pregnant, he gets an even bigger deal," she said, shivering.

"No wonder you want out of that. Damn. My dad gets an F in fatherhood, but he hasn't pulled anything like picking a wife for any of us."

"Until this, my parents have been wonderful. So have my grandparents, and I love them all dearly."

"We'll head Tanya's way. I won't protest meeting her," he said, dancing Meg her way.

The music stopped and she turned, smiling at Tanya and pulling lightly on Gabe's hand. Tanya's straight, waist-length blond hair fell loosely around her face. She wore a tight blue silk top with bling along the neckline that dipped in a deep vee, revealing half of a butterfly tattoo on the curve of her full breast. Curiosity filled her eyes as she watched Meg and Gabe approach. She glanced back and forth at each of them until Meg greeted her.

"Tanya, meet Gabe Callahan. Gabe, meet Tanya Waters."

Smiling, Tanya touched the arm of the man beside her. "Hi. This is Bobby Jack Lawrence."

As the men greeted each other, Gabe held Meg's hand lightly. They talked a moment until the music commenced again and then Gabe pulled her to his side for a two-step.

"That was absolutely perfect," Meg said. "I'm so glad we came here. I see Cassie Perkins from Justin's office. I think she's interested in Justin, so I'm sure she'll get the word out around his office."

Gabe looked down at her. "I didn't know you could be so plotting and devious."

"Only because I'm desperate," Meg said. Then she became quiet, enjoying dancing with him and thinking the evening had been a huge success.

"How in the world did you get involved with Justin in the first place?"

"Friendship. The way I am with you. We go to the same places and see each other. We like the same things—symphony, opera, contemporary art. His folks were giving him a terrible time about seeing Tanya and we talked about that. I just didn't realize what it would lead to and suddenly he was talking a marriage of convenience."

"Lesson learned there, I suppose."

"There's no danger of our families trying to push you and me into a marriage of convenience. Actually, this ought to set family tongues wagging about us going out together and get Justin out of the conversation."

"This fake engagement sure as hell isn't going to endear me to any of your family."

"I'm sorry about that, but they don't like any Callahans anyway, so it isn't like you're losing their friendship."

"Somehow, your logic doesn't cheer me," he said and she smiled.

It was after midnight when a number ended and Gabe spun her around, catching her and pulling her up against him. She looked up into his eyes and her laughter faded, her grin giving way to a sultry smile.

He gazed back and took her hand. "That look should convince the most doubting spectator. If I didn't know better, I'd be on fire now," he remarked.

"Well, I'm thankful you didn't laugh because that definitely kills the effect."

"What I felt wasn't laughter," he said. The smoldering look he gave her made her tingle, which surprised her. How shocking that she found him so appealing.

"I think we can leave now," he said, wrapping his arm around her waist and pulling her close against his side.

She slipped her arm around his waist, looking up at him and smiling, as if they were about to go home and make love. She hoped that's what others thought.

"That was fun, Gabe. You're perfect for this. You would convince anybody that we're a couple."

"Anybody who doesn't really know you," he remarked drily. "Otherwise, I think there will be suspicion."

"No, there won't," she assured him, supremely happy with the way the evening had gone and looking up at him as if she thought he was the most adorable man on earth. At the moment that wasn't even pretend.

Gabe drove to her small home in Downly in an older part of town with tall shade trees. Her bright front light illuminated the porch, the surrounding flower beds, the steps, the walk and half of her front yard.

"That's some porch light you have. Your house hasn't been broken into, has it?"

"Heavens, no. I just like a light when I come home. It's cheerful."

He shook his head. "It's like the one at the Hansons' lumber yard at night. Well, I'd say tonight was a success."

"Definitely. Next I think we should hit the country clubs in Downly and in Dallas. I'll get dressed up so I look more like the ladies you normally take out."

He laughed. "I don't think old Justin stands a chance."

After parking his pickup, Gabe stepped out to open her door.

She waited, hoping someone she knew would drive by and see them. Getting out of the pickup, she looked around. "I don't see anyone. My neighbors aren't the curious type and no one's ever on this street. Nonetheless, just in case someone is watching, I'll hang on to you, and you can put your arm around me," she said as he slipped his arm around her waist.

"This is a unique experience," he said with laughter in his voice. "Even my first date didn't tell me what to do and that was fifth grade."

Meg shook his arm playfully. "I'm not telling you what to do—at least not the entire evening," she added as they climbed the porch steps and turned to face each other. "Thank you, thank you. I am indebted to you and tonight was a roaring success," she said, smiling up at him as his hands rested on her waist.

"Meg, this night is not over yet," he drawled in a deep voice. He glanced around. "I feel like I'm onstage right now, under a spotlight." He looked up at her porch light. "I take it Justin doesn't mind the light."

"There is absolutely no reason for him to. Besides, we haven't gone out together in Downly."

"Are you going to let me kiss you?" Gabe asked, his blue eyes twinkling. "I don't think I've asked that question since my first date, either."

Knowing he was enjoying himself by teasing her, she smiled. "Yes, I will, but I'm not going to bed with you."

"Now you've flung another challenge at me that I'm going to have to deal with," he said, flirting with her.

Still smiling at him, she shook her head. "That was no challenge. It's an established, guaranteed fact."

"Oh, Meg, sweetie," he drawled, taking her hand and stroking it lightly while his eyes still sparkled, "you've done it now. I can't wait for our next date. My reputation with the ladies may be on the line here."

"Don't be ridiculous. If you slept with me, no one would ever know it except the two of us. I know you don't talk about your affairs of the heart," she said, trying to keep from laughing and also aware that his light caresses were stirring surprising sizzles. How could Gabe cause any sizzles? He had always been like a brother. She gazed more intently at him, thinking that brother image was being melted away by every stroke on her hand.

"Now, how can you possibly know about my love life?" he asked.

"Word gets around about you."

"Well, what do you know—you've been discussing me with others."

"Don't flatter yourself. I may not be the one bringing up your name, you know."

He laughed. "I better back off right now. I know you well enough to know when my teasing is getting to you."

"You don't know zip about the grown-up me. We haven't spent much time together since I was a teenager."

He didn't respond to that remark. Instead, he was focused on something else. "Let's go back to my question."

She knew the one he meant. *Are you going to let me kiss you.*

He tilted her chin up. "We're in a spotlight. Just in case anyone observes, let's make this look like the real thing."

"No one in this neighborhood will observe us," she said, amused, curious about kissing him.

Gabe slipped his arm around her waist. "You know, Meg, we've never kissed," he said, looking into her eyes.

She gazed back into vivid blue eyes that seemed to turn her insides to jelly. Gabe really was a good-looking man. When his gaze shifted to her mouth, to her amazement flutters tickled her insides.

He leaned closer, slowly, and her heart beat faster. When his mouth brushed hers, heat engulfed her. She closed her eyes, winding her arm around his neck. His arms tightened around her, drawing her against his hard length as his mouth covered hers and his tongue stroked hers.

She felt in free fall, her insides clenching while her heart pounded. She forgot everything except his kiss, his arms holding her tightly and their bodies pressed together. Tingles raced through her and she moaned softly with pleasure, sinking into a kiss that set her ablaze. Sliding her hand across his shoulders, she trailed her fingers over his nape and into his thick hair.

She had no idea how long they kissed. She only knew she didn't want to stop. When he finally raised his head, he gazed silently into her eyes and she felt as if she were seeing him for the first time in her life.

"Wow," she whispered. "Now I know why the ladies like you," she said, trying to keep the moment light though she was stunned how his kiss had ignited such desire in her. She stepped back and from the look of him, he was as surprised as she felt.

"Thank you, Gabe, for tonight," she said, or hoped she said. Her thoughts were still on his kiss and she fought an urge to walk back into his arms and kiss him again. "I had a wonderful time and we were seen by so many people." She felt as if she was babbling, but she couldn't think straight. Gabe's kiss had scrambled her thoughts and she was trying to return to the world as it had been before he held her tightly and kissed her.

"I think this fake engagement is going to be easier to do than I first thought it would," he remarked drily, still looking intently at her. "You and I wasted our time playing with marbles."

"Not really. Our friendship was important. Tonight was perfect and a million thank-yous for agreeing to the engagement."

"I'm beginning to look forward to it. I'll call you. I'll try to plan something where you'll be seen by another segment of people you might know."

"That would be excellent. I'll get a fancy dress for the occasion. I'll even wear makeup."

He grinned and touched the tip of her nose. "I like you the way you are. You know, now I'm glad you called me for help, and believe me, I'm willing to help you."

"Thanks. Calm down a little, Gabe."

"After our kiss? I don't think so, darlin'. Want to try again and see if we get the same result?"

She leaned closer and squinted her eyes to look at him as she poked his chest with her forefinger. "We're not going to fall in love."

The twinkle was back in his blue eyes. "You don't think?"

"I know. You can't get serious and I definitely will not get serious with you."

"That doesn't mean we have to avoid kissing, does it?"

"I know you're laughing at me again. No, it doesn't mean we won't kiss. Maybe all the ladies you kiss fall in love with you, but I won't, so yes, we can kiss."

"I'm so glad to get your permission," he said, his voice filled with so much laughter she had to smile. "You've given me another challenge, Meg."

"Oh, no. Once again, that's a fact. I'm not going to fall in love with you and you won't with me. We're definite opposites. Good night, Gabe. Thank you, and it was fun."

"Oh, darlin', was it ever fun," he said, suddenly sounding sincere.

She turned to unlock her door. "I don't think I'll invite you in tonight. We'll save that for next time, when I'll show you my house."

"Sure, Meg. I'll call you," he repeated as he headed toward the steps.

As he drove away, she closed and locked the door and leaned against it, lost in memories of his kiss. How could his kiss have been so sexy? Her lips still tingled and she wished she could have gone on kissing him. Had she gotten herself into a predicament with this fake engagement?

It had never occurred to her she would have the slightest sexual response to Gabe. She had never even thought about kissing him. She had known him all her life without that happening and she hadn't given it a thought.

Till now.

Tonight he had turned her world upside down. And she no longer saw him the way she had before. Would she ever in her life see him again without that hot, tingling response she felt?

Gabe would be aiming for seduction. As he said, he liked a challenge. He also liked the ladies and parties…and a daredevil lifestyle that took her breath away, because it was the same as her brother Hank's lifestyle had been, and that wild living had gotten him killed.

Surely she wouldn't succumb to Gabe; she wouldn't go to bed with him. She had known him all her life and would never run the risk. One hot kiss wouldn't make a difference.

Except his kiss was different from all other kisses she had ever experienced. Not that there had been lots of different guys, but she suspected if there had been, Gabe's kiss still would have melted her. "Mercy me," she groaned. The man was sinfully sexy, and she suspected she'd never view him the way she once had again.

What was she saying? She could not be attracted to Gabe. Absolutely not! Kisses were one thing. Falling into bed with him was another.

She moved through her house, switching off lights and going to her room. She just needed some sleep. But when she crawled into bed, sleep was the last thing on her mind. She lay there, gazing into the darkness, her lips still tingling and memories burning their way into her thoughts. She may not want to admit it, but she still wanted to kiss him again.

She sat up in bed. "I'm not going to fall into bed with you," she whispered in the darkness. That wild, woman-chasing cowboy would be nothing but heartbreak. It was just one month. One month wasn't a long time. Surely she could resist him for that long. It could be a lot of kisses though, because it wasn't going to be just weekend dates. She planned to stay at his house with him. She'd simply have to guard her heart and keep kisses to a minimum.

Did she have the willpower for that? She suspected it was going to be difficult to resist him. He wouldn't have trouble resisting her, so maybe there was nothing to worry about. She just had to take care, remember who he was and how he felt about a serious relationship, and that wild lifestyle he had. He raised rodeo bulls for a living—big, mean, thousand-pound animals. He liked to compete in bull riding. He flew his own plane. He had a motorcycle and a sports car. And he loved the ladies and parties. There wasn't a serious bone in his body.

She had to make each date move things along to convince her family and Justin that she and Gabe were serious. The minute Justin was out of her life, she would thank Gabe and send the sexy hunk on his way.

When had Gabe changed to a "sexy hunk" from the friendly kid she grew up knowing? She hadn't been around him in the past few years because they moved in different circles after school. She knew a lot of local ladies loved going out with him. She paid little attention when one of her friends talked about wanting to date him. Such conversations left her slightly amused at most. But his kiss wasn't amusing. It was sexy enough to wrap around her heart and carry it away.

She punched her pillow behind her, feeling suddenly uncomfortable. "You may be my knight to the rescue, Gabe Callahan, but you're going to be trouble," she said in the dark, empty room. Moonlight spilled in the window. All she could see was Gabe's blue eyes and his cocky smile. "About six feet, three inches of sexy male and you've already rocked my life. We'll kiss, but I will not go to bed with you. I mean that," she whispered, and sighed. She knew she'd better stick to that conviction if she wanted to get through this pretend engagement with her heart intact.

She sighed again, getting up and opening a bottom

drawer to rummage through sweaters. She pulled out a raggedy brown bear and shook it. Gabe had given it to her on her ninth birthday. "Why didn't he stay the way he was when he gave you to me?" she asked the bear. "A nice kid I had fun with instead of this sexy man who makes me want to keep kissing him all night."

She hugged the bear that she had loved ever since receiving it, even taking it to college with her.

She went back to bed and sat cross-legged, putting the bear in front of her. "I will get through this engagement and Gabe and I will have fun like we always have. I will not go to bed with him and when the month is over—or hopefully, sooner—I will thank him, give him a big present and we'll go our separate ways. I am not going to fall in love with him like one of his women he's had an affair with." She poked the brown bear with her finger. "I promise and you're my witness."

She'd bet anything that Gabe hadn't even thought about their date or their kiss or anything else about her. He was probably wishing this month would zip on past. Either that or peacefully sleeping.

She'd asked him to take her somewhere fancy next time and told him she would look more like the women he usually dated. Right now, she was a million miles from that look, but wonders could be achieved with the right makeup, a new hairstyle and some knockout clothes.

She told herself that if she changed her look, more people would notice her, would see her with Gabe and believe their engagement.

Who was she kidding? She knew the real reason for wanting to change.

She was already annoyed with him for treating her as if she were a kid while she was having to fight an attraction to him. She'd make him see her as the grown woman she'd become.

After all, wouldn't it serve him right if he had a little fight of his own to deal with?

Three

Late Saturday night after he was home, Gabe sent a brief text asking Meg to go to a dinner dance at the Downly Country Club in honor of its renovation. She sent a return text immediately, accepting his invitation.

He thought about their deal—a month-long fake engagement. Her request had surprised him. But it was her kiss that had stunned him, and from the wide-eyed look he had received, she had been as shocked as he had. He had never expected kissing Meg to be anything except sweet and he had been amused when he'd teased her about it beforehand. He'd expected his request to throw her into a quandary, that they'd have a sweet kiss and that would be all there was to it. He had never envisioned what had actually happened. Maybe he should have guessed because he'd had a sexual reaction to her at the ranch, but he'd never dreamed kissing her would be akin to a nuclear meltdown.

Her searing kiss had shifted their relationship forever. He would never again view her the same way he had before. With that kiss he wanted her in his bed.

His common sense rejected that possibility completely. She was still Meg, still his best friend, still Hank's big sister. She was earnest, sweet, trustworthy, intelligent, and if she had a real relationship he was sure she would be into commitment and marriage. He suspected that had never really happened. They had lost touch through her college years and he didn't know if she'd had boyfriends, but he would bet the ranch there was no guy in her bed on a regular basis at any point in time.

Meg was the type to equate love, kisses and bed with vows, marriage and home.

Regardless, the woman had caused him a sleepless night. She had him all wound up and wanting to hold and kiss her. That reaction still stunned him. He'd never thought about kissing her and never for one second expected any kind of positive reaction on his part. Now Meg's steamy kiss was something he had to deal with in the coming month.

Just remembering her kiss could put him in a sweat. He wanted to pick up the phone and ask her out tomorrow night and seduce her. But that would make him a sneaking, dirty rat who could no longer be called her best friend, and he would feel like the jerk of the year if he didn't propose to her. Neither outcome looked good.

He hadn't imagined what he'd felt and it wasn't because he hadn't been out with a woman in a long time. And it wasn't faulty memory. As impossible as it seemed, Meg was hot and sexy.

He had thought, as sweet as Meg was, this fake engagement might get tedious before a month was over.

Now his worries had swung the other way. Now this fake engagement might be too tempting to resist seduction.

He didn't like Justin and was happy to see that she wanted to break off seeing him. But now he could understand why Justin was all for this marriage of convenience.

Gabe groaned. "Damn, how will I get through a month with her?"

He thought he would plan to be out of town on business a lot of the time. A month wasn't long. At least it wasn't long until he thought it would mean thirty nights when he might be with her, kissing her, having to resist temptation. He put his head in his hands.

When he told her he would go along with the fake engagement, he hadn't given a thought to kissing her. Now he couldn't stop thinking about it.

Saturday night he needed to keep a clear head and not do anything he would regret later. He had to keep one thought paramount in his mind: Meg was the marrying kind, and if he ever took her into his bed, he'd have to marry her for real.

And that was the one thing that could never happen.

After a restless night, the last thing Meg needed was a day with her family. But the next day, after joining her family at church, she took a homemade peach cobbler to her parents' house for Sunday dinner.

As they sat around the dining room table, eating slices of tender roast beef and mashed potatoes with brown gravy, the topic she was loath to hear came up.

"I saw Justin's mother last night and she said he was out of town. If we'd known, you could have gone to dinner with us last night," her mother said.

"Thanks. I ran into an old friend and we went out last night," she said, glancing around the table. Her dad didn't react; he was concentrating on his meal, the gray in his light brown hair shining in the dining room chandelier. He still wore his best brown suit and tie from church. Carlotta Aldridge, her paternal grandmother, sat on his right. Carlotta's short, straight brown-and-gray hair hung just below her ears. She was the grandmother who had spent hours reading to Meg when she had been small. Carlotta wore her favorite color, a frilly pink dress. Next to her was Meg's paternal grandfather, Mason Aldridge, whose thick gray hair was slightly curly above his long, thin face. He had been a rancher all his life and it showed in his weathered brown skin and rough, callused hands. He had taught Meg to ride a horse and take care of her pets.

Seated beside Meg was her maternal grandmother, Lurline Wills, whose round, jolly face had bright blue eyes and a perpetual smile. Meg and her brothers called her Lolo. Meg's maternal grandfather was Harry Wills, another oil and gas man who had worked with her dad most of her life and was as angry and bitter as her dad toward Dirkson Callahan. They were all talking, set to enjoy another delicious Sunday feast, and she was going to end their peaceful Sunday gathering.

"Who's the old friend?" her mother asked, passing hot rolls around the table. "Here's honey. Also raspberry jam," she said, passing small dishes.

"Gabe Callahan and I went out. It was fun to see him again," Meg said, taking a roll and aware all conversation had stopped and the room had gone silent.

"Oh, dear. Megan, we don't speak to the Callahans," Grandma Lurline said, frowning and pushing her glasses up on her nose to stare at Meg. "We haven't spoken to any of those dreadful Callahans for years."

Meg glanced around the table and smiled while everyone else frowned. Both sets of grandparents sat scowling at her. "Gabe and I have always been friends. We had a very good time," Meg said cheerfully. "And we do speak to each other. As a matter of fact, we're going out again next weekend."

Her mother dropped her fork. "Oh, no. Megan, you can't do that."

"Of course I can," Meg replied. "I've got a date with him."

"What about Justin?" her dad asked, his face getting red.

She took a deep breath. "I'm not dating Justin. I'm sorry if spending a little time with Gabe upsets all of you, but I have my friends and Gabe isn't responsible for what his father did or does. Dirkson Callahan hurt his sons, so don't blame Gabe for his dad's actions. And as for Justin—I've said all along, I am not interested in Justin and he isn't interested in me. We're not getting engaged or married. We're finished."

"Justin and his family think you're serious," her mother said. "Justin has said you are both talking about marriage and making plans. That's what Francis told me."

"That isn't my view because we're not making plans." She picked up her fork and speared a slice of meat. "Mom, you, Grana and Lolo have worked hard fixing a wonderful Sunday dinner. Let's enjoy this delicious roast."

For an instant, all of them stared at her in silence and then her mother smiled. "You're right. We can talk about it later. We did work too hard on this to let it get cold and go uneaten," she said, smiling at the others. The grandmothers nodded as her mother picked up two bowls to pass around the table. "Here are fresh squash and sliced tomatoes from Dad's garden."

Conversation picked up again and Meg relaxed, talking about the dinner and the garden, and avoiding any mention of Gabe or Justin.

It was late afternoon when she got in her car to go home and her mother came rushing out the back door.

"I wanted to talk to you before you go," she said after Meg rolled down her window. "I hope you rethink seeing Gabe Callahan. You know our families don't get along."

"Gabe and I had a good time. We've been friends forever," she said. "I'm going out with him next weekend." Difficult as it was, she faced her mother, realizing the woman had more gray hairs streaked in among the brown hair around her face. Meg felt a pang because she was going to worry her family, but she had to worry them or end up married to a man she didn't love.

"You know what kind of man Gabe Callahan is," her mother said. "Besides being Dirkson Callahan's son, he's got a reputation for being wild and taking risks. He was a terrible influence on Hank. Your father is so unhappy to hear you're going out with him."

Meg smiled at her mother. "I love you and I love my family with all my heart, but I have to live my life. I had a good time with Gabe and I want to see him again. Sorry, Mom, if no one in my family is happy with me, but I can't date someone to please my family."

She patted her mother on her arm. "I'm not marrying Gabe next weekend. I'm just going out with him. And he moves in the same social circle Justin does. Now stop worrying. It's just an evening with a friend."

She gave her mother a smile. "I better head home because I have a busy week ahead. Thanks again. Dinner was wonderful."

Her mother stood waving as she drove away. Meg sighed with relief because she felt another hurdle was over. Her family knew she was going out with Gabe.

Monday afternoon she received a text from Justin saying he wouldn't be in until late Thursday night and asking her to dinner Friday. She declined, telling him she had a benefit to attend with one of her friends. Instead, she made plans to meet him at the café for a quick bite Thursday night. Suspecting he had heard about Gabe, she wanted to make their breakup official then. She was anxious to break the news to him about Gabe and she didn't want to spend an entire evening with Justin to do so.

She hadn't heard a word from Gabe, but she hadn't expected to. This was a favor he was doing for her and there wouldn't be any reason for him to call to talk. She smiled at the thought. He probably wouldn't give a thought to her or his agreement until the end of the week.

Tuesday night Meg sat in her Dallas house and planned Saturday night at the formal country club where she and Gabe would be seen by Justin, his family and her family. She hoped Justin would be there with someone else. He hadn't gotten around to asking her and she was certain he expected her to attend with him. That was, he would until she broke the news to him Thursday night. Meanwhile, she still needed to get a dress for Saturday night, and her makeover.

She smiled in anticipation. Soon she would be free of her family's meddling, thanks to Gabe. Now, if she could just resist his kisses, all would be well. No wonder half the eligible women in the county liked to go out with him.

Thursday afternoon after work when she drove home, she was surprised to see Gabe's black pickup in her driveway. Curious, she parked in her garage, took a glance at herself in the rearview mirror before she got out and smoothed her plaid cotton blouse and faded jeans. She wore scuffed brown boots and she had a navy band holding her hair back from her face—everything about her as plain as ever, she thought. She walked out to find him waiting near the gate that led to the back door. As she looked at him, her pulse jumped. In his black Stetson, jeans, black boots and a Western-style blue cotton shirt, he looked every inch the rancher he was. He also was handsome enough to be a celebrity. Slight dark stubble shaded his jaw, giving him a rugged touch that added to his appeal. How could she have gone all those years without noticing how handsome he was? He took her breath away now just standing still and doing nothing. And the closer she got, the better she could see the fantastic, thickly lashed blue eyes that made her heart beat faster.

Another phenomenon that shocked her. Those blue eyes she had looked into all her life could make her heart race now. Go figure that one. She shook her head without realizing what she was doing.

"Why are you shaking your head at me? Would you rather I get in my truck and go? What am I doing wrong?" he asked as she stopped in front of him.

"You're doing nothing wrong. It's just that you're the same as ever and at the same time, you're not," she said, unable to stop herself from revealing her thoughts. "Maybe I just never really noticed you. You have sinfully wicked blue eyes." She was still shocked over his kiss and her reaction, and she couldn't keep from telling him what she noticed now about him because she liked him and was struggling with the attraction.

He grinned and placed his hands on his hips. "You're putting me on to try to get me to be convincing in this little scheme of yours. You don't have to do that. I'll take you out where we'll be seen and let you stay at my ranch. I've already agreed, so stop trying to pour it on and schmooze me into this fake love."

"You fantastic man," she gushed, amused how he had taken her remark. "I'm going to make you miss me when I'm out of your life again."

He stepped closer to place his hands lightly on her shoulders, and she was instantly aware of his touch, his proximity and her heart beating faster. "You're not going out of my life. That will never happen as long as we're both alive and well. I'm sure you're doing all of this just in case anyone is watching. Let's go inside and you can be yourself."

"Sure. What brings you to my house?" she asked him as she dug in her purse for her keys.

"I was in Dallas, so I decided to stop by and see you and catch up on where you stand with Justin."

"I turned down an invitation to go out with him Friday night. I have a charity event to attend with a friend, so it's no lie. He gets back into town tonight and I told him I would meet him for a bite. I'm driving myself so I can leave. It isn't a date. This is goodbye."

"I take it your friend is female and not someone else who could have done this fake engagement."

"She is female, and no one else could have done this except you. You're perfect. I told you that. I don't think you pay attention to me sometimes," she said.

"Darlin', since we kissed, you get so much of my attention you wouldn't believe it if I told you."

Stopping abruptly, she tilted her head and smiled at him. "Do I really? That's exciting to hear."

"Maybe. I didn't much think you wanted any real attraction to spring up between us."

Her smile vanished. "You sure know how to kill happy moments." She pulled out her key. "Come in and we can have a drink and I'll give you the tour."

"Yeah, give me the tour. It might come in handy if I can describe your bedroom, or at least sound as if I have an inkling of what it looks like."

She laughed. "I'll give you the tour, but you're not going to have to tell anyone about my bedroom and I doubt if you do that with anyone else you're with." She was aware of him at her side, his height and long stride. Had one kiss created this instant, intense awareness of Gabe that she'd never had before in her life?

"Of course I don't, but Justin might just suspect you of doing exactly what you are doing—faking an engagement."

"Oh, no, he won't," she declared. "Not when he hears Tanya's and Cassie's reports on last weekend. We looked convincing, I'm sure. And then your reputation—at least as far as seduction is concerned—will convince him easily," she said, thinking about all the reasons she had gone over several times in her mind. "Now, the fact that you are engaged to me will be a little more difficult to sell, but that's where my lifetime of being frank and honest to a fault will carry us through this."

He shook his head. "You've got this all figured out and I have to admit, you're right."

"Just wait until that ring is on my finger and I've been to the wedding store in Downly. There won't be a doubting soul in town," she said, thinking more about Gabe brushing against her lightly as they entered the kitchen. As he hung his hat on a rack by the door next to two of her hats, her gaze ran across his broad shoulders and down to his narrow waist. It took an effort to pay attention to what he was saying.

"Don't get me roped into showers and having to return presents later. Also, I want to tell my brothers the truth. They'll laugh and forget it. I don't want them planning anything for us or getting some lavish wedding gifts. Ditto my mom, although if I didn't let her in on this, I don't think she'd believe it until she received an invitation to a rehearsal dinner, and we're not going that far."

"No, we're not. Your mom wouldn't believe it?"

"I doubt it, but I want to let her know the truth from the start."

"Sure. Let your family know. I'm sorry to be deceitful with my family. I never have been, but they've pushed me into this. I'm desperate. Mom is looking at wedding cakes and showing me pictures. Yuk." She put down her purse and the papers she'd carried in from a job she was designing.

"At least my family knows I'm going out with you and will continue to do so," she told him. "That's a death knell for a serious relationship with Justin. I expect to tell him farewell the first minute we talk."

"And you think he'll just drift away without trying to convince you otherwise? I don't think so, Meg."

"That's why I want to move into your Dallas house. That will do it. He has strong feelings about a woman being faithful."

Gabe laughed and draped his arm casually across her shoulders. His touch made her tingle and she was intensely aware of him so close beside her. "I would have sworn you didn't have a devious bone in your body until this deal. My, oh, my, how I misjudged you," he said, looking down at her. "I misjudged you in other ways, too," he said, suddenly turning serious, and his solemn gaze made her pulse jump.

"I don't think I want to pursue what other ways," she said breathlessly, aware how close he stood and thinking about his kiss. The moment stretched and she realized how they were staring at each other.

"Last Sunday, dinner at my parents' house was grim for a little while. Mom was on my case. Dad looked as if he could eat nails. My grandparents were all horrified because you know how they feel about your dad."

"I hate it when people think I'm just like my father," Gabe said and lowered his arm, propping his hands on his hips. "Just because he ran roughshod over people and his family, that doesn't mean I do."

She patted his hand, a spontaneous reaction that she had done lots of times in the past, except now, tingles radiated from the casual contact and she yanked her hand away as if burned.

Gabe didn't seem to notice and she guessed he was lost in thoughts about his father.

"Do you want something to drink? Iced tea, cold beer—"

"Yes, I want something," he said in a husky voice that took her breath away.

Her heart skipped again. How had a kiss changed their whole relationship?

"A drink, Gabe. Do you want iced tea, cold beer—"

"You said the magic words—cold beer."

"Coming right up," she said as she went into the kitchen.

When she turned from the fridge, she was surprised to see him right in front of her. Her gaze ran over him, reminding her of standing in his embrace while he kissed her. She cleared her throat before she could speak. "Why don't you get cookies out of the cookie jar on the counter or get some pretzels from the cabinet while I get my juice." Truthfully, she just wanted to put some distance between them.

He rummaged in a cabinet and got a sack of pretzels while she poured her grape juice over ice.

"Come on and have a quick tour and we'll sit on the patio and talk. It's shaded from the sun after three or four and it's bearable. We have a breeze today."

He took a sip of beer and set the bottle on the table to follow her into the adjoining living area and he glanced around. He seemed to fill the small room and her gaze ran over him again. "I'm surprised that you like contemporary furniture. I figured you for the fancy, old-fashioned furniture you grew up with."

"This room is what I prefer, but I have both because Mom gave me my bedroom furniture."

He smiled. "I know what that looks like then. The big four-poster mahogany bed," he said walking around the living room and looking through an open door. "I'm right. There it is," he said. "Hey…" He disappeared through the door into a narrow hallway and she followed, curious why he went to look at something.

The minute she stepped into her room, she regretted not checking things over before she offered a tour. Gabe crossed the room to the bed and picked up the little brown teddy bear he had given her so many years ago.

He turned to look at her. "Is my memory right? Why have you hung on to this all these years? Or is it out here for Justin's benefit?"

"No, it is not for Justin's benefit, because Justin doesn't get invited into this room. I just thought I might need it so I got it out of the closet."

Gabe laughed and tossed it back on the bed. He crossed the room to her to put his hands on her shoulders again and his blue eyes twinkled with devilment. "So Justin has never gotten into your bedroom, but he expects to marry you? I've forgotten how old-fashioned you can be. Justin is probably being and doing whatever you want to get a ring on your finger."

"I told you that we're both being pushed by our families."

Gabe laughed and shook his head. "I'm ready to sit and drink my beer. I've seen enough to indicate that I know my way around the place." He started out of the room and she walked with him, stepping through the door ahead of him.

"I forget that sometimes you can be annoying."

"But you still love me, don't you? You even still want to be engaged to me," he said, laughing as he teased her. "You need me, so you can't really get mad at me," he said, draping his arm casually across her shoulders. Only his touch wasn't casual to her. She had a prickly awareness of him and a sudden vivid recollection of his kiss.

As if he knew her thoughts, he turned her to face him. "We could have a lot more fun if we spend our time kissing."

"Will you stop?" she said. "We don't have an audience, therefore there is no point in kissing."

"*Au contraire*, my darlin'," he said. He laughed and threw up his hands, walking away. "I can see my teasing is getting to you. We'll go sit, make plans while I drink my beer and then I'll go home."

"That's better."

Holding his beer and the pretzels in one hand, he draped his arm around her shoulders. "This is great, to renew our friendship. I'd forgotten how much I liked having you for a friend. And now that we're kissin' friends, I *really* like having you for a friend." They stepped out on her shaded patio and he held a black metal chair for her. After she sat, he pulled a chair beside her, sat and propped his booted feet on a low iron table in front of him. "So you'll tell Justin goodbye tonight and Saturday night you'll go out with me. Right?"

"Correct. Tonight I expect to break it off with him for good."

"Should I gulp down my beer and go? Am I keeping you from getting ready?"

"Heavens, no. It's only four in the afternoon and I don't see him until eight."

"I figured you'd be getting yourself all—"

"If you say 'beautiful,' I'm going to take your beer away from you and send you home now."

He smiled at her. "I can't resist getting you all hot and bothered. You always rise to the bait." He chuckled and sipped his beer.

"Hot and bothered, huh?" she said, half amused and half annoyed with him because sometimes he still treated her the same way he did when they were kids. She set down her drink and turned to face him. "I'll show you hot and bothered," she said. She stood, swung her leg across his and sat in his lap, wrapping her arms around his neck and kissing him on the mouth.

She poured herself into her kiss, wanting to get back at him for all his teasing and give him something to think about before he teased her again.

For an instant she assumed he was startled, but then

his arms circled her tightly and he kissed her in return. A passionate kiss that made her forget teasing and realize she might have set herself up for something more worrisome. She had wanted to set him on fire with her kiss, to make him see her as a woman and not the kid next door he could tease and torment and still be friends with. Too late, she realized she might have stirred up a bushel of trouble for herself.

She felt his arousal press against her and her heart raced while she, too, burned with desire. She was shaking with wanting him, hot with the need for more.

Remembering what had started their kiss, she stopped as abruptly as she'd begun. They stared at each other and then she moved off his lap and walked away. "That got out of hand," she whispered, not sure whether he heard her and not really caring because she spoke the words more to herself than him. Despite what she'd said, she wanted to turn around, go back to him and continue where she'd left off. And that scared her.

"On that note, I better take my cue and get the hell out of here before I try to carry you off to that four-poster bed," he said. "I'll call you, Meg. I know my way out."

She merely nodded. "Bye, Gabe."

She heard the back door close and walked to the window to watch him get into his pickup and back out down her drive. In seconds he was gone.

She touched her lips. She wanted him so badly, she wasn't going to be able to resist him. Suddenly she realized something: he hadn't been flirting this afternoon. Gabe had been teasing her, the way her brothers would have teased her. He didn't really see her as a woman like the women he dated.

She placed her hands on her hips in an indignant

pose. She'd show him she was a woman. Saturday night. Silently she thanked her friend Barb, who'd told her about a fabulous makeover she'd had when she had been hired for a commercial. Barb had set up her appointment in a Dallas salon for Saturday.

Tomorrow, she would rearrange her schedule so she could shop for a dress. One way or another, she'd make Gabe see her for what she was: a grown-up, desirable woman.

At the same time, common sense told her to leave the situation as it was. As long as he saw her the way he always had, she would be less appealing to him and he would be less so to her. She never wanted to fall in love with him anyway, so why get a makeover and attract his attention? On the other hand, he might forever see her as a kid and she didn't want that, either.

Unfortunately, she had no such problem seeing him for what he was. Gabe had grown into a handsome, sexy man who would carry her off to his bed and steal her heart away if she wasn't careful. To her, he was no longer the kid from her past, the boy next door, a fun friend she could trust, just Gabe, friendly, nice. Never in the past had he made her heart beat like crazy or her insides turn to jelly or the room suddenly too hot to bear. Back then she hadn't seen him as the most handsome man she knew. She hadn't wanted his arms around her and his mouth on hers.

She did now. And it wasn't good.

Common sense told her to cancel the makeover, and she got out her phone. She should let well enough alone. Get loose from Justin, tell Gabe thank you and go on her way, forgetting Gabe as she had for the past ten or eleven years.

That was the sensible approach.

Then she thought about Saturday night. At the country club it would be a formal dinner. Gabe would be in a tux and look handsome and she would look just like she did for her first-grade Christmas party, wearing the same hairstyle and type of dress. And she knew she couldn't do it. She was a woman and she wanted him to see her as one.

As foolish as it was, it was a risk she was willing to take. She knew what she had to do.

She put her phone away.

At eight o'clock she sat in a booth in the small casual sandwich shop and watched Justin come up the walk. She had come early and wanted to be waiting when he arrived. Slightly taller than Gabe, he was handsome by any standard with thick brown hair and thickly lashed pale brown eyes. His prominent cheekbones and straight nose added to his good looks. She guessed he was probably at least an inch taller than Gabe. Both men were broad-shouldered, but Gabe was definitely more muscular. In a charcoal suit, white dress shirt and red tie, Justin looked handsome, successful and filled with energy. He had come directly from the airport. Justin had dated other women in his social circle who were beautiful and probably in love with him, and Meg would never understand why this marriage of convenience appealed to him except for family pressures. He had been engaged once to another woman whose family moved in his social circle and Justin had been the one who had broken it off. He had talked about the breakup with her, explaining that he hadn't known whether he could really trust his ex-fiancée to be faithful, and that he had to have that in a wife. Meg had listened to him talk, wondering what he was leaving out, because his reasoning had had some gaps, but she hadn't quizzed him about it. She knew Justin had women who would have his parents' approval who wanted to go out with him, so this crazy pressure for them to marry made no sense to her. Granted, Tanya wasn't one of those women, but from the little things Justin had said, she suspected he truly loved Tanya.

Justin kissed her forehead and they exchanged pleasantries before he got to the point.

"I might as well explain why I wanted to see you tonight. I heard you went out Saturday night with Gabe Callahan."

"Yes, I did. You and I have no commitment."

"We're on the verge of one," he said, frowning. "A huge commitment."

"I've told you I'm not interested in a commitment. I don't want a marriage of convenience. Gabe and I have been friends since I was three. We went out last weekend and had fun talking about old times. I have a date with him Saturday night to the country club dedication of the new ballroom."

Justin leaned across the table. "Break the date with Callahan. It will be unpleasant for everyone if you don't. Our parents and your grandparents will be there."

They paused when a waiter came to take their orders and as soon as he left, Justin leaned forward again. "I intended us to go together," he added.

"You didn't ask me," she said. Justin wore a scowl and his jaw was clamped shut. She knew he was angry, but her peace of mind and her freedom were at stake so she had to end this.

"I've accepted Gabe's invitation and I'm going with him. I'm not ready for a commitment to you. No one has listened to me. Not you, not my parents and not yours."

"Dammit, Megan. You're ruining everything. You're throwing away a future to go out with a wild, party-loving cowboy who will toss you aside in no time."

Their waiter came and Justin became silent while their drinks were placed on the table with their sandwiches.

"You're tossing aside all plans of us marrying, aren't you?" he asked.

"Yes, I am. We're not in love."

"Our parents want us to marry. We fit together. We're the same social circle, the same background. It would be perfect. You know I want a political career and you would be an asset."

"Thank you, Justin. But you'll be happier if you marry someone you love, a person you're thrilled to be with and you can't wait to come home to."

"I've been honest with you and I've told you what I want and what my family wants. I've told you what's in it for us and it's a lot of money and opportunities. My dad wants us to marry and he wants a grandchild. I'll get a partnership in the firm after you and I are married a year."

She studied Justin while he talked and her gratitude to Gabe for the fake engagement soared with every word.

"I'm so sorry to cut you out of a partnership, but you could go to work for someone besides your father. You're sharp and a good, successful attorney who will do well wherever you are. You don't have to work for your dad to be successful."

"I'll move up faster with my dad."

She could see she was getting nowhere with him. Hurtful as it might be, she had to be frank. "Justin, I'm going out with Gabe Callahan. You and I are finished even discussing this." She fumbled for her wallet. "I'll buy the dinners—"

"Dammit, Megan. I'll get our damn sandwiches. You're making a big mistake. You keep dating Gabe Callahan and we're through," he said.

"I understand that," she answered and his face flushed. She stood and he came to his feet, too. "Good-bye, Justin, and good luck."

"Gabe Callahan will not marry you, so don't count on that. He's not marrying anyone."

"I know that."

She turned and was out the door in seconds. She took a deep breath as she hurried to her car, eager to get away. She was finally free of Justin. She wanted to grab Gabe and hug him for being the catalyst that got her out of the sticky situation.

Once she got home, she went to her bedroom, grabbed the brown teddy bear and danced around her room with it. "I'm free."

Saturday night she would get engaged to Gabe, a silly fake engagement, but it would be exactly what she needed to make this breakup last. Up till now her life had been filled with doing what other people wanted her to do. From now on, she'd do what she wanted to do for herself. Starting with her makeover. And then she'd get engaged to Gabe and move into his house.

It was finally happening. Living her own life.

Amid her elation, she had one disturbing thought: Could she really do it? Live under the same roof with Gabe without ending up in bed with him?

Four

Gabe tried to keep his mind on business the next day, but it was difficult. He kept thinking about Meg, remembering when she had suddenly straddled him, sat on his lap and kissed him. The kiss had made him feel as if he would burst into flames, had set his heart pounding so hard he'd thought she could hear each beat.

He couldn't resist teasing her sometimes, because it was fun and because he knew it annoyed her. But she did the same thing back to him in her own way. She kissed him until he lost all rational thought.

How did she do that?

All he knew was that he wanted her in his bed, but each time he thought that, his conscience tore at him. She was his childhood best friend who trusted him completely and she had come to him for help, not for seduction. He could not seduce her.

"Damn," he said aloud. From the minute she told him what she wanted, he had known she was going to drag him into trouble with her plea for a fake engagement. And it was only going to get worse, because this weekend she was moving in with him.

He dreaded all of it. He wouldn't back out of his agreement to help, despite the fact that she complicated his life more with each passing minute. And if he wasn't careful, he might end up with a real engagement instead of a fake one, and he was not ready for that.

"Damn," Gabe said again, shaking his head.

He couldn't wait for tomorrow night at the country club. Justin's parents and Meg's parents would be there. He'd be relieved when that evening was over because it ought to finish Justin's dream of a marriage of convenience. Did he ever pick the wrong woman to try to push or bribe into a loveless marriage.

Gabe grabbed his hat and left to throw himself into working with his men on moving cattle from one pasture to another.

Meg took a few hours off work Friday to shop for a new dress and shoes for Saturday night's formal dinner dance. She found a sleeveless black crepe dress with a deep-vee neckline, a straight, ankle-length skirt and a high slit on one side. She paired it with stiletto-heeled black sandals.

On Saturday she had her makeover. It took all day, but that night while she waited for Gabe, she stared at herself in the mirror and couldn't believe what she saw.

She twirled in front of her full-length mirror and smiled. She barely recognized herself and she hoped Gabe wouldn't recognize her at all.

* * *

Gabe rang Meg's doorbell and as he waited, he gave himself a pep talk. That morning, somewhere between feeding the stock and mending a fence, he'd come to a realization. One he'd reiterated to himself again and again. Meg was just Meg—a childhood chum and now a friend he intended to help before going on his way. During the normal course of life these days, they rarely even saw each other. He'd simply missed her in his life—that's why she suddenly seemed so attractive. It wasn't the hot kisses, he told himself. Meg was filled with life and he was glad to be back with her. And this was just a temporary situation that would be over in three weeks.

Reinforced by his thoughts, he punched the doorbell again. What was she doing?

The door swung open and he was startled. For one brief moment he thought he had the wrong house. His gaze raked over a very tall stunning blonde, her silky hair falling to her shoulders in spiral curls. Her stylish black dress emphasized her creamy skin and luscious long hair while the vee neckline revealed full curves that made his temperature soar. She had a tiny waist and long legs with shoes that gave her additional height.

"I'm sor—" He stopped and peered at the woman while his pulse pounded and the world grew warmer.

"Meg?" he said, for once in his adult life feeling like an awkward teen with a new date—a feeling that he had rarely experienced even as a teen. "Meg?" he repeated, unable to believe he faced her. Shocked, he could only stare.

She smiled, a smile that lit up her perfectly made-up face.

"Why don't you come inside, Gabe." She stepped

back, took his arm and drew him inside. He merely followed, unable to take his eyes off her, unable to speak.

"You look very handsome in your black tux. Sophisticated and wealthy and elegant."

Again, he remained silent. He was absolutely flum-
moxed by the sight of her.

"We'll go inside until you're finished looking at me,"
she said, sounding amused. "From your expression, I
take it you like what you see?" When he didn't reply,
she walked into the living room.

He followed her, captivated by the slight sway of her
hips, the clinging ankle-length skirt, the glimpse of a
long leg through the slit in the side of it. He inhaled
her intoxicating perfume, a brand that was definitely
not lilac scented.

When he'd taken in every inch of her, he slowly came
out of his shocked stupor. He tried to collect his wits
and act like a normal guy ready to go out for the evening. But it wasn't easy when his brain could form only
one thought: *Wow!*

When she crossed in front of him, he caught her arm
lightly and turned her to face him, then placed his hands
on her hips, feeling as if he faced a stranger. He could
feel her warm body and her soft curves, the silky material of her dress beneath his hands.

"You're stunning. You look gorgeous," he said in a
raspy voice.

"Thank you. I'm glad you noticed and like the change."

"I'd have to be blind or dead not to notice or like
how you look. You take my breath away." Suddenly, he
could feel himself sinking even deeper into a quicksand
of complications in his life. He had never expected to
take out a stunning blonde who could kiss him into a
raging fire. This pretend engagement was going to re-

quire every ounce of his willpower to keep him from trying to seduce her. He didn't want to take her to the club tonight. Right now, he wanted to take her to bed.

He inhaled deeply. "Oh, darlin', the single guys are going to want to take you home tonight, and this is not the way to get rid of Justin. He won't want to give you up now, even if it becomes a life-or-death fight with me."

She laughed softly. Where did Meg get the soft, seductive laugh? She'd made a total transformation and for one single second he wondered if someone else was trying to pass herself off as Meg tonight. "Are you really Meg?"

"I'm really Meg," she replied, sounding more like herself. He felt tied in knots. He was still in shock from the neck up, his brain unable to process the change in her, but from the waist down he was hot, aroused and ready to pull her into his arms and kiss her until they made love.

"I guarantee you, after Justin sees you tonight this is going to be a battle."

Her smile faded and her brow furrowed as worry clouded her big brown eyes that were now thickly lashed, lined and lidded with a smoky hue. Her makeup was flawless, as if she had come straight from making a movie.

The worried expression didn't last. She drew herself up slightly and smiled, a smile that kept him aroused, aching to make love and still unable to believe his eyes.

"Gabe, if you're worried about Justin and his reaction, I can get someone else to take me. I do have some other guys who are friends."

"I'll bet you do. No, I'll take you, Meg. I just think you've made a move here that will keep Justin trying his damnedest to marry you. I don't think it will be simply a marriage of convenience he's after once he sees you looking like this."

She smiled. "You're sweet. I have two big bags and a carry-on packed—one bag to take to your ranch and the other bag to take to your Dallas house. I'm still going home with you tonight, right?" she asked with an air of great innocence.

"Damn right, you're going home with me. Oh, yeah," he said, wondering if he would be able to resist her once he got her there alone.

"Then we'll get my bags now," she prompted.

"Sure," he said. But he stood there, lost in thought about taking her home with him.

She laughed. "Gabe? My bags?"

"Oh, sure. I'll get them now and we'll get going," he said, coming out of his stupor. "Unless you'll let me kiss you a few times first."

She laughed and shook her head.

"Not on your life. You would mess up my makeup and probably my dress. We're going to the club now."

"It's going to be an effort to stop looking at you long enough to drive. You really are stunning."

"Thank you," she said, and he wondered if she was making fun of him. He didn't care. He could hardly stop looking at her. How had he known her all his life and not seen how gorgeous she really was?

He carried out her bags and then returned for her. "Let's go," he said, taking her arm.

As they stepped outside she frowned. "Oh, you've taken your sports car."

He grinned. "Half the world drools when they see this car. You look as if you want to run and get your pickup."

"I've gotten more nervous about speed and risks since Hank was killed. Do me a favor and keep it at the speed limit or lower."

"Sure," he said, smiling and shaking his head. "I might as well have brought my old car. Okay. We'll go slowly because I don't want a white-knuckled passenger. You didn't used to be this way."

"I used to have Hank."

"Sorry, Meg," Gabe said, hugging her lightly. "I miss him, too. But you know, he wasn't as wild as you think."

"Yes, he was. You don't know the difference because you're the same way."

"Are we having an argument at the beginning of the evening?"

She flashed a radiant smile that felt like a blast of sunshine. "Absolutely not. I think you're a wonderful driver and I can't wait to ride with you, my handsome prince to the rescue."

"This prince can't wait to kiss his princess goodnight at the end of the evening."

"I'll try not to disappoint you," she whispered.

"I'd be willing to bet every cent I own that you will not disappoint me at all."

She smiled. "We'll see."

He could only stare at her full, stunning red lips. Her eyes might be gorgeous but her mouth was pure temptation. Damn, he was getting hotter by the second.

His voice was husky when he finally spoke. "I'm about ready to go back inside now and get some of those kisses."

"Oh, no," she said, not a bit rattled. "I want Justin and my family to see us."

"Absolutely. And I'll be drooling over you all evening."

"Frankly, I hope not," she said and they both laughed.

Once they were on their way, he made an effort to keep the sports car well below the speed limit and his attention firmly on his driving, even though he'd have preferred to just sit and look at her. How could she have changed that much from just makeup and hair color? Part of it was also the dress, he admitted. He had never seen her in a sexy dress like the one she was wearing tonight.

"Your parents and Justin's are still coming tonight, right?"

"Oh, yes. And both sets of my grandparents. Justin has a table reserved with friends so he's going to have to explain why I'm not with him, which is good. You know he's listed as one of the twenty most desirable bachelors in the Dallas area. And so are you, for that matter."

He shrugged. "I don't know why the hell I'm in there. I'm a cowboy. I don't give a damn about these country clubs. I only belong to this club because of family and because it's convenient sometimes since it's in Dallas and near the area where I live. I shouldn't be on that list."

"Of course you should," she said, rubbing his knee lightly, her voice a sultry drawl. "You fantastic man— you are *sooo* sexy and handsome."

He knew she was teasing and he glanced her way to give her a smile. He had to drag his eyes back to the road. Three days ago he would have laughed, paid no attention to her and gone on to some other topic. Right now, he was breaking into a sweat, on fire and thinking of getting her into bed. She sounded like the same ol' Meg, but she didn't look the same and it made a boatload of difference.

"We'll sit with my family—not my parents, of

course," he said, trying to get his thoughts on their conversation and off erotic images of them scorching the sheets. "My dad lives out of the country and my mom is out of the country with friends now. We'll be with my half brother, Blake, and his wife, Sierra. And my brother Cade and his wife, Erin."

"I don't know Blake very well. He wasn't around those years you and I saw a lot of each other."

"My half brother and I have different mothers and those mothers didn't get along. Cade and Blake became friends in high school and Cade pulled him into the family—at least as far as the brothers are concerned."

"I've met Blake, but not his wife."

"Sierra is great. You'll see. And so is Cade's wife, Erin. When Nathan and his wife were killed in the car wreck, Cade became their little girl's guardian. Amelia is a doll." Cade had stepped up big-time at a dark hour when the family had been devastated by a drunk driver. Gabe had a lot of respect for his brother.

"Blake and Sierra have a little girl, too," he explained. "Emily, born in January. The kids won't be there tonight, but you'll get to meet them at some point." He glanced her way and saw a sadness overtake her face. No doubt, talking about his late brother reminded her of her own lost sibling. He quickly changed the subject. "I can't wait to see your parents go into shock when they see you."

"I went by their place before I went home to dress. They know I'm a blonde now. And they know I'm going with you."

He scoffed. "I can imagine the reception I'll get."

"Well, you've lived with that attitude since your dad bought mine out. My family hasn't spoken to you or any Callahan in years and tonight won't be an exception."

"No doubt you'll be hearing from Justin tonight. I wouldn't be surprised if he shows up on your doorstep."

"I'm not going home tonight, remember? I'm going home with you. My moving in with you should put an end to Justin."

Gabe grinned. "Justin is burned toast. I hope he realizes it."

Minutes later, as they approached the club where valets waited, Gabe slowed the car and glanced at her. "Here's your last chance. I can still drive out of here and take you home. I guarantee you when Justin sees you tonight, he isn't going to want to give you up. He'll want to marry you more than ever. A whole lot more than ever."

"Don't be silly. I'm still me. I don't look that different."

"Oh, yes, you do. For a while, I didn't recognize you. I promise you the 'new you' will change how Justin feels about you."

"That's exciting to hear. Maybe I should act sexier," she said in a sultry drawl. "That way I won't seem like such a kid to you. Has my new appearance changed how you feel about me?"

He pulled the car over to the side of the road, so other vehicles could pass them, and turned to her. As he wound his fingers in her hair that was now so soft and silky, he looked at her wide-eyed expression.

"Meg, I'm trying to be your friend, like a brother to you. Don't push the sexy come-on tonight unless you want to face the consequences. Kissing you is fantastic and I'm no saint. I can only resist so much. The way you look now makes me forget completely the relationship we've always had. Be careful what you get yourself into, unless that's really what you want."

This close, he felt her sweet breath on his face and all he wanted to do was lean in and kiss her. That and peel her out of that enticing black dress.

"Okay," she said. "Friends forever. I get it. Don't worry. In a little while I'll look like my old self again."

Reluctantly Gabe released her and turned to drive up to the valet.

"I can feel my freedom already. I'm so happy, Gabe. Thank you again."

"You can show me your appreciation when we get back to my place tonight," he said, smiling at her, and she laughed. Taking a deep breath, he tried to relax and get back to their familiar relationship, but he suspected that wasn't going to happen again in their lifetimes. There was no way to forget how she looked tonight. Or how she could kiss.

He couldn't wait for the evening to end. He had looked forward to seeing his brothers and their wives, but now he wanted to have Meg all to himself, which surprised him.

Everything about her surprised him now.

He got out of the car and walked around it while a valet held the door for her and she stepped out. She was poised, radiant and absolutely breathtaking. He couldn't stop looking at her. Her new appearance pushed him into more complications, yet now he looked forward to spending time with her this evening, not his family.

The event schedule was a cocktail hour, dinner, some speeches and then dancing, and he intended to enjoy every minute with her.

He took her arm and they entered the club, turning toward the refurbished ballroom where piano music could be heard. They didn't get far before they encountered Justin and his date.

Meg had turned to speak to someone nearby while Justin addressed Gabe. Justin started to look away when Meg turned and said hello to him, and Gabe saw the man's jaw drop. He recovered swiftly, his gaze sweeping over her once more, and Gabe couldn't resist slipping his arm around her waist—getting a look from Justin that expressed unmistakable hatred and anger.

"If looks could kill, I would be a dead man now," Gabe said when they walked on.

"Good. I told you we would be taken seriously. Wait until my parents see us. You just keep your arm around me."

"I don't think so. Some things I don't do around parents, and you have very nice parents. I don't want to anger them more than I have to. They don't like me to begin with. I'm still my father's son whether he ever sees me or not."

"Don't worry," she replied, "my family will be civil toward you. And me. This is, after all, a social event."

"Justin's another story. I saw the look on his face."

"Wait until this weekend is over. We will have a whirlwind courtship and then get engaged. Gabe, I don't know what I'd do without you."

"You keep that thought in your pretty head until we get home."

Why was he flirting with her, while common sense told him to back off? The lady was not his type and he didn't want to get seriously entangled with her. If only he could remember that each time he looked at her. Well, he'd better cling to wisdom like a lifeline when he kissed her tonight. At the mere thought, another heat wave swamped him.

If he had good sense, he wouldn't kiss her—tonight or ever again. But they had a deal. Besides, kisses he couldn't resist. Where he had to use willpower was ensuring they didn't go beyond kissing. He simply had to keep his wits about him.

He laughed to himself. He never would have thought Meg could do anything to make him lose all common sense.

Till now.

They stopped at the table with her parents and grandparents. Meg's dad came to his feet, as well as her grandfather who was the rancher, but her other grandfather did not.

Gabe offered his hand and Meg's father shook it, surprising him. "Hello, Mr. Aldridge, Mrs. Aldridge," he said, smiling at her mother.

Mason Aldridge also shook hands with Gabe, talking briefly to him about livestock and the need for rain.

When the old man sat down, Meg's father leaned in close and said in a harsh, low voice, so only Gabe could hear, "Do not hurt my daughter."

"Yes, sir," Gabe answered quietly. "I never have and I don't plan to. She's been my best friend since before we started school."

"You're a grown man now, not a kid, and she's a beautiful young woman. Don't hurt her."

"No, sir, I won't," he reiterated politely and turned to smile at Meg's mother, who was seated and ignoring him while talking to her mother, who sat beside her.

"We'll see you later," Meg said as she took Gabe's arm and pulled slightly. He didn't need any urging to walk away from her family.

"You get along with my grandfather."

"We're both ranchers. We have some of the same problems. But your dad threatened me. He told me not to hurt you."

"Did he really? I suppose it just never got through to them that they were hurting me by trying to push me into marrying a guy I don't love. By the way, do your brothers know about the fake engagement?"

"Yes, they do, and so do their wives. They accepted it as a simple favor I'm doing. Cade's amused that I would even agree to a fake engagement. And they're worried having a brief engagement may complicate my life."

She frowned. "I hadn't thought about afterward. There may be some women who'll be bothered about a previous engagement. Tell them it wasn't real. I'll be glad to tell anyone."

He smiled. "Don't worry. It won't matter, because marriage is not even remotely on my horizon."

She squeezed his arm lightly. "Well, I'm here if you need me. That's what friends are for."

He needed to remember that friendship when they got back to his house tonight and he was alone with her. He thought about her father's warning to not hurt her. He wasn't worried about her father, but he didn't want to hurt Meg. He glanced around at her, looking at the deep-vee neckline of her dress and how it clung to her lush curves and creamy skin. He was going to have to keep remembering she was his friend, not a lover.

The Callahan brothers stood as Meg and Gabe approached their table. She caught the look that passed between them when they realized who she was.

"Wow, Meg," Cade said, smiling at her, "you don't look like the kid who used to climb over our fence to play ball with us."

She laughed. "Thanks, Cade."

"You may remember Erin, Luke Dorsey's younger sister," Cade said, introducing his wife. "Erin, this is

Meg Aldridge, who was our Downly neighbor when Gabe and Meg were growing up."

"We do know each other, although we haven't seen each other in a long time," Meg said, smiling at Erin and remembering her big green eyes and red hair. Gabe touched her back to draw her attention. "Meg, you remember my older brother Blake, and this is his wife, Sierra."

She greeted the other brother and the beautiful brunette.

Gabe pulled out a chair for Meg and she sat at the table with the Callahans. In no time the men were sharing pictures of their babies on their phones. She saw pictures of Amelia, who had been adopted by Cade and Erin, and Sierra and Blake's baby girl, Emily. They seemed so happily married, she couldn't help wondering why Gabe was so opposed to settling down. Tonight wasn't a typical evening for Gabe and he probably wouldn't have attended if he hadn't been doing a favor for her. She knew he liked a wilder time than he was having at the staid country club.

She was grateful to Gabe for pouring on the charm, especially when she could see Justin sitting only a few tables away.

Gabe put his arm lightly across her shoulders and leaned closer. "I see one of my friends. Remember Marc Medina?"

"Yes, I do. I haven't seen him in a long time."

"He isn't going to recognize you. Let's go over and say hello."

Gabe stood and pulled out her chair and then took her hand in his as they wound through tables. Marc saw him coming and stepped away from his table to meet them. She looked at a handsome, broad-shouldered man with thick, wavy hair as black as Gabe's.

"Good to see you," he said to Gabe, shaking hands with him.

"Hey, Marc. Good to see you, too," Gabe said. "You remember Megan."

"Megan, I haven't seen you in a long time. You've grown up into a very beautiful woman," Marc said.

"Thank you."

"I've seen your landscaping around town. It's good. Do you have a card?"

She dug one out of her evening bag and handed it to him.

"Thanks."

"We've got to get back to the family," Gabe said. "We'll get lunch soon. I'll call you."

As they walked away, Gabe said, "Marc is doing well with his oil and gas business. I'm glad because he's a hardworking guy."

"A nice guy, too, as I recall."

Gabe pulled out her chair and they joined his family again.

With constant attention from Gabe, she couldn't keep from having a wonderful time. After the speeches ended and dinner finished, the band took over, playing soft ballads. She knew from other events that the music would change later in the evening when the older crowd disappeared.

Gabe sat with his arm on the back of her chair, turned slightly to face her. He leaned in close, and to anyone watching them he'd look as if he couldn't take his gaze from her.

"Justin hasn't taken his eyes off you," he whispered.

"If I take you out on that dance floor, he'll ask you to dance in a flash."

"I don't think so. I think he'd be afraid I'd say no and embarrass him." She looked up at Gabe, smiling at him. "If he's watching, I hope I look in love."

"Meg, darlin', if the way you look at me gets any hotter, I'll want to check us into that hotel across the road."

She wiggled with joy as her smile widened. "Oh, that makes my heart really flutter. I want to look so in love with you, no one will have a shred of doubt when we announce this engagement."

He wrapped his arm around her shoulders and pulled her close, nuzzling her neck. Gabe was everything she needed to pull this off. He was charming, fun and sexy, and she wondered how she would get through the month without falling in love with him. The more worrisome question for now was how would she get through the night without going to bed with him?

Five

She didn't want to, either, because as charming and sexy and handsome as Gabe was, he still wasn't her type. He was a wild man with a wild lifestyle like her younger brother had had, living life on the edge. And he wasn't into serious relationships, wasn't interested in commitment or marriage. She didn't want to fall in love and then have her heart broken when they said goodbye and went their separate ways.

And she certainly had no intention of getting casually involved with Gabe, either. So she needed to guard her heart—and tonight was the night to start doing her best to try.

Right now, though, wrapped in Gabe's arms, she was finding that difficult. They'd joined the others on the dance floor and hadn't missed one slow song all evening. She was resting her cheek on his shoulder when he leaned close to whisper in her ear.

"I think we've spent enough time at this shindig. Want to go?"

"I'm ready to go. I've done what I came to do," she said, turning. He was only inches away and she looked into the bluest eyes she had ever seen. Her heart drummed and she wanted his mouth on hers more than anything right then. But desire for Gabe's kisses scared her. His kisses could lead to seduction and an even bigger threat—him stealing her heart away.

Go home. Tell him good-night.

She should listen to that inner voice, thank him and then stay away from him. Instead, she was going home with him. How much willpower did she have? She couldn't even stop looking into his eyes right now.

She felt as if she had been caught in a spell and couldn't escape. How could Gabe have this kind of effect on her? It was Gabe—friend, chum, pal, buddy. Where had all this sexual appeal and steaming desire come from? Could she cope with it or did she need to call off this engagement?

She wasn't calling off the engagement. That she knew for sure. No, she'd just have to resist him. No matter what it took.

"I think tonight went well."

Gabe's comment was an understatement. In her opinion, it had gone as if she'd scripted it. Her parents had remained civil and even better was Justin's reaction.

"Thanks to you," she replied, looking at him as he drove them home, "it went even better than I had hoped. Justin certainly got the message, and so did my family. He wasn't happy, but he'll adjust and find someone who'll suit his folks just as much. My parents aren't their only friends with a daughter."

"Just because your parents are friends is no reason for the two of you to marry."

"Do I ever agree. I couldn't make any of them see that and then Justin's dad offered so many financial rewards that Justin absolutely wanted us to marry. Well, now I don't have to. You were perfect tonight. Everyone will believe us when we announce our engagement. Besides, I had a good time tonight," she said, sitting back and smiling happily at him.

"Thank you. So did I. It wasn't the stuffy, boring evening I thought it might be. Events like that at the country club I usually avoid. This one was fun, though, and I had the prettiest woman in the club for my date."

She smiled at him and patted his knee. "Thank you. We're alone and you don't have to say that."

"I mean it. You look stunning tonight. Believe me, if we weren't announcing this engagement, you would get calls, especially now that guys realize you're not locked into going out with Justin."

"I'm not interested in calls. I just want to be free and live my life my own way."

"You're on your way to your goal."

"Thanks to you."

"You can show me your gratitude when we get to my place," he said, teasing her.

She laughed. "Oh, I intend to—up to a point."

He flashed a smile at her and then focused on driving. She felt as if a mountain of worries had lifted off her shoulders. She regretted hurting her parents and Justin, but they would get over it and she couldn't spend a lifetime married to someone she didn't love. She glanced at Gabe and forgot Justin and the disagreement with her family. She'd had a wonderful evening with Gabe and his brothers and their wives. It was Gabe, though, who kept her heart racing. She was going home with him. She had told herself over and over as she spent the day getting ready for tonight that she should guard her heart and avoid falling in love with him—something she had never expected to have to worry this much about.

Gabe slowed the car and they entered a gated area and followed a tree-lined street with decorative lamp-posts as they wound toward his Dallas home. When it came into view, she felt surprised.

"It looks like a palace," she said, looking through a tall black wrought-iron fence at a sprawling mansion with lights shining in various windows on three floors. The well-landscaped yard held tall shade trees, leafy oaks and spreading maples. On the front lawn water glistened in a small pond with blooming lilies and in a lighted fountain with a silvery spray of water.

"Don't sound so shocked."

"I still think of you at your parents' home when we were kids."

"I haven't lived there since I left for college." Gabe drove to the back and parked beneath a carport, stepping out to go around and open her car door. "Come see my house and I'll show you your suite. If you'd like, tomorrow we can go to the ranch," he said as she stepped out to walk beside him.

He held open the door to a mudroom of sorts. The long, narrow room held rocking chairs, hat racks and coatracks on the wall, with a place for boots and shoes in a small alcove.

He took her arm. "Let's get something to drink. We can sit in the family room or go to the patio. It's a nice night."

"Sure, Gabe," she said. "But first, I want to thank you again for tonight and for what you're doing," she said, overwhelmed by having such a good friend who had come through for her and ended a huge worry in her life. She slipped her arms around him, hugged him tightly and then stood on tiptoe to kiss him.

After a startling moment that was no more than a heartbeat, his arms circled her waist and tightened, pulling her against him. His mouth pressed against hers, his tongue going deep, stroking hers as he held her close.

Her heart thudded and she tightened her arms around him. She had told herself that a few kisses out of gratitude would be acceptable and not dangerous to her heart. But now, with the first kiss, she stopped thinking about what she ought to do. Her focus was on the man holding her tightly. The man whose fingers wound in the curls of her long hair as he held her and kissed her.

And all her rules and promises to herself vanished like smoke on the wind. The only thing she wanted was to kiss him and never stop.

She ran her hand beneath Gabe's jacket to push it off. He shrugged out of it and it dropped to the floor. His elegant dress shirt was smooth to the touch, warm from his body heat. The studs in his shirt were sharp against her skin and she stepped back, reaching up to unfasten then. "These hurt," she whispered and looked up into vivid blue eyes that had darkened in passion. When she had the studs unfastened, she handed them to him. He dropped them into his pocket while she ran her hand across his chest.

"I'm not going to bed with you," she whispered, a reminder to herself as she was again caught and held by his startling blue eyes.

"Are you talking to me or to yourself?" he asked while he showered light kisses on her ear, her nape, brushing her lips with his. Her heart raced and his tantalizing light kisses fanned desire beyond anything she had ever experienced.

"I'm talking to both of us," she whispered. "Kisses of thanks for what you did tonight are the limit."

"You might have to remind me," he whispered and tightened his arms around her, settling his mouth on hers and kissing her passionately again.

Desire was a hot flame burning inside her. His touch burned away rational thought. All she could do was feel. She ran her hand beneath his unbuttoned shirt, feeling his smooth, muscled back, down to his narrow waist where she unfastened his cummerbund.

Leaning away she looked up at him and slid her arms around his neck. "You make me lose all caution and common sense."

"I hope so," he whispered and kissed away any answer she might have had.

She didn't feel his hands on her back, but was dimly aware as he pulled down the zipper to her dress.

She was crushed against him, holding him tightly while they kissed. Her heartbeat still raced. How long they kissed she didn't know. Finally, Gabe picked her up and carried her in his arms. She never once stopped kissing him to see where he was going; she didn't care. A moment later he sat down and placed her on his lap as he kissed and held her.

She felt his hands at her back, cooler air drifting over her back while he slid her zipper farther down to her waist and pushed her dress off her shoulders.

She caught the front of her dress in her fist, holding it to cover her breasts as she leaned away slightly to look at him. His heavy-lidded gaze met hers.

"Meg, where did all this fiery sex come from?" he whispered.

"Gabe, wait. You're going too fast and in seconds our relationship will change forever."

"It already has," he said in a thick, husky voice. "We can't ever go back to a next-door-neighbor, brother-and-sister relationship, even if we promise never to touch each other again. It won't ever be the same because now we know what we do to each other and it's so fantastic, I'm still in shock."

She placed her index finger lightly on his lips. "Stop. We may not be able to go back, but we don't have to go deeper into a sexual relationship. We're not suited—"

"Darlin', we are suited—in the best way possible," he said, kissing her just above her bare shoulder. "I almost don't know which is the most stunning—kissing you or looking at you."

She pulled her dress back in place and slipped off his lap. She straightened her dress and reached back to pull up her zipper. Standing, Gabe did it for her, tugging so slowly, trailing kisses above her zipper as he moved up to lift her hair and kiss her nape. "You're gorgeous."

"Thank you," she whispered, turning around to face him and stepping back. "I'm trying to use some sense and resist you. To think a minute. I'm not into casual affairs. That kind of covers the biggest difference between us. And then, should you get serious, I could never deal with your wild lifestyle."

"Whoa, darlin'. You're talking marriage and all we've done is share a few good-night kisses." He smiled at her. "I'll show you the house and we'll have a drink and sit and talk awhile and then you can go to bed all by yourself. How's that?"

"A good idea," she said, hoping her reminder about relationships really had stopped him and made him think about the differences between them. She fought the craving she felt to walk right back into his arms, kiss him and forget common sense, caution and her worries about the future.

"Gabe, I don't want to go from one problem to another."

"I know you don't," he said, looking intently at her, and she wondered what he really thought. "Okay, let's look at the house. So far we haven't gotten far beyond the back door.

"This back room leads into the hall with the main kitchen and an informal dining area," he said, leading the way and leaving space between them. Her gaze swept over him as he stopped in the center of the kitchen to tell her where to find things.

She didn't hear a word he said. His shirt was still open and pulled out of his trousers, the cummerbund tossed away. His chest was muscled, covered with a spread of dark curls, his stomach flat and muscled. She couldn't get her breath and she wasn't thinking straight.

She realized he had stopped talking and stood facing her, his eyes narrowed.

"I think you should show me where my room is and we should call it a night."

He closed the space between them in a few steps and wrapped his arms around her. "That's ridiculous, Meg. We can kiss and then stay friends. It's just kisses. Relax. You're blowing this all out of proportion." He took her arm lightly. "Come on, and I'll show you where your suite is, and we'll come back down here in a little while and sit and talk."

"You know, I should go to my room, close the door and not see you again tonight," she said.

He shook his head. "Nope. You wanted a fake engagement. We're getting into that and we need to do a little planning—unless you want to call all this off right now."

They stared at each other while her heart pounded. She shook her head. "No, I'm not calling anything off. We've come this far and I see freedom. Kissing you may be a problem, but it's nowhere near the problem of a lifetime with a man I don't love." She started walking down the hall. "You're right. We'll come back here and make some plans and then say good-night. You'll go your way and I'll go to my room alone. Okay?"

"Sounds like a plan. Come on. I'll show you to your suite."

He carried the bag and the carry-on she'd brought and they climbed a wide spiral staircase with a wrought-iron banister and oak steps. The staircase gave her a view of the front hall and the entryway with a huge crystal chandelier. Large contemporary paintings lined the walls along with mirrors and occasional potted palms and tropical greenery.

Upstairs, they turned for the east wing and shortly entered a room where Gabe switched on recessed lights. The room was decorated in white and taupe with charcoal accents. Contemporary steel-and-glass furniture had simple lines, and blended with the walls and white woodwork.

"This is beautiful, Gabe," she said, looking at the designs of the colored glass on the end tables.

He put her carry-on in a large walk-in closet and then set her bag on a luggage stand.

She stood in the center of the bedroom, looking at the king-size bed, the sleek chairs and sofas, glass tables and large contemporary paintings with bright strokes of red, green and blue.

More than her surroundings, she was aware of Gabe,

moving around, setting up her suitcase, opening doors onto a balcony. He turned to cross the room and come back to her. "Want some time to unpack and freshen up? Or are you ready to go have a drink and make our plans?"

"It's not too early."

He placed his hands on her shoulders and toyed with locks of her hair. "No, it's not. Let's just go sit and talk about where we go from here and what we do next."

Her heart raced as she gazed into his vivid blue eyes. "I know we need to make some decisions," she whispered. Once her gaze drifted to his mouth she couldn't speak. She inhaled deeply, trying to think, to focus on her problem when all she could really do was look at him and want to put her arms around him and kiss him.

"I think first we have to decide what we'll do about... this," she was finally able to say. "I can't get this close to you without wanting to kiss you. Gabe, that wasn't something I expected and I never factored it in. You were another brother, my childhood best friend, a fun guy, someone I trust completely. But then we kissed, and suddenly it isn't that simple anymore."

He ran his hands down her sides. "No, it isn't simple. I never expected any of this hot chemistry that has exploded between us. I keep asking you if you want to call off the engagement and you keep saying no you don't."

"I don't. We've already accomplished a lot. Everyone thinks I'm dating you. That stops Justin from that very public proposal. Hooray for that one because I would never accept his proposal and I shudder to think about turning him down in front of a crowd. I still think we should go ahead and get engaged this weekend. I've told Justin we're through, but getting engaged to you will send a message not only to him, but to his parents and my family. I can get engaged to you, Gabe. I can go out with you a couple of nights this week and then say goodbye. Is that too much for you?"

"Meg, I'll be happy to take you out every day and every night this week. I can spend the week just looking at you. You're gorgeous. But when this is over, I may want you to continue to go out with me."

She shook her head. "No, you won't. And I don't want to go out with you when this is over. Gabe, we're best friends, but it ends there. I can't deal with your lifestyle and you won't want to give it up. And I can't have a casual affair and you don't want a permanent relationship. I think that covers everything between us and the answer has to be we walk away from each other and forget we ever kissed."

She looked into fathomless blue eyes that held her in their depths and made her speech empty, meaningless words. She couldn't really say anything else while her heart pounded so violently.

He brushed her hair back and framed her face with his hands as he stepped closer and gazed down at her. She couldn't move away, couldn't protest.

"You want me to forget we kissed. Meg, if I live to be a hundred, I'll remember every kiss we've shared. We have a hot chemistry between us that sets me on fire each time I'm with you." All the time he talked, his voice dropped lower, became more husky. His gaze made her heart continue to pound. Desire was intense, a pull that she tried to resist, but it became more of an ordeal to resist each time she was with him.

"Gabe, how did this happen and where did common sense go?"

"I don't know how the hell it happened, but it's magnificent, breathtaking and too big to walk away from and ignore," he said, his voice lowering with each word as he leaned closer. She looked at his thick black hair that she wanted to tangle her fingers in. Her gaze moved to his mouth, his full, lower lip that she wanted to kiss.

A small voice continued to remind her that she did not want to fall in love. They had no future. She could really get hurt. She shouldn't kiss him.

And then there was her heart, beating with desire for him. How could she resist the most fantastic, sexiest kisses ever?

"Oh, Gabe, this is just dreadful," she whispered as he pulled her tightly against him and leaned forward to kiss her. His mouth was hard on hers, demanding, taking from her and then giving her a chance to kiss him in return.

Her world spun and she felt a dizzying plunge while at the same time, she wanted to hold him and be held by him, wanted his hard body against hers and his strong arms crushing her against him while he kissed her senseless.

Desire built as she fought the temptation to push away his shirt. Never had any other man made her respond the way Gabe did. How could this happen between them? They were buddies and had never been anything beyond buddies. Never before had there been this wild, insatiable attraction that threatened to consume her and turn her world upside down.

Pouring herself into her kiss, she clung tightly to him, aware of his strength, his arousal that pressed against her as they held each other. She let down her guard and kissed him passionately, lost in the moment and his kisses that melted all her resistance.

Gabe's hands slipped over her back, caressing her bottom and then moving to draw down the zipper to her dress and push it off her shoulders. His hands slipped to her waist and he shifted slightly as they cupped her breasts.

In seconds her bra was unfastened and pushed away and his warm hands caressed her, holding her while his thumbs lightly circled her nipples and made her gasp with pleasure as she clung to him.

"Gabe, we have to stop," she whispered, opening her eyes to look up at him. She didn't want to stop, but that small voice became more insistent, forcing her to think about her future and how she could be hurt.

While he still caressed her, he stepped back. "You're beautiful," he declared in a husky drawl. "Darlin', you're so beautiful."

She inhaled, holding his arms, closing her eyes and letting him kiss and caress her breasts for seconds before she shook her head. It was an effort to break away as she stepped back and caught his wrists. "Ah, Gabe. I can't do this. I'll fall in love with you. I never expected to want to kiss you or want you to kiss me. I didn't even think about us kissing."

She wiggled and shed her bra, pulling her dress up again. Gabe gasped for breath as much as she did.

"We should say good-night now."

He stood breathing hard while he stared at her seconds before he shook his head. "We need to talk. I'll sit out of reach and leave you alone as long as you want. Let's go get a cool drink, cookies, crackers and cheese, whatever you want. We won't kiss again tonight unless you want to. Come on. Let's go to the kitchen."

"I'll join you in the kitchen. I'm putting on my jeans and a T-shirt and maybe you'll see me more the way you always have."

"Okay. I'll meet you in the kitchen," he said, leaning

close and catching her chin between his thumb and fore-finger, "but, Meg, darlin', you could come out covered from head to toe in gunnysacks and I'll never again in this lifetime see you the way I did before we kissed."

"Try," she said, narrowing her eyes at him while her heartbeat still raced and she fought walking back into his arms and going to bed with him tonight.

He smiled. "See you downstairs. I'll go step into the walk-in freezer and see if I can cool down a little. I'll try to stop thinking about you changing clothes, unless you want me to stay and help with that zipper."

"No, I don't. Aren't you getting my message?" she snapped and then realized he had been teasing as he left laughing at getting her riled up over his suggestion. She crossed the room and closed the door because she didn't want him popping back in. She let out her breath. How was she going to live in his house, go out with him, continue to kiss him and avoid falling in love with him?

Six

Gabe went downstairs and wished his body would cool down. From the moment she had opened her door to greet him for the evening, he had been in shock over her looks, on fire with wanting her in his arms and wishing he could make love to her all night long.

Why hadn't he ever noticed her like this before? Her hair made a huge difference, but he should have been able to see beyond that. Makeup made a difference, too, but again, he should have seen her natural beauty and sexy appeal. He supposed he had known her so long, he never really looked at her. He did now and he didn't want to stop looking. Blonde or brunette, headband or long, flowing hair, makeup or none, he would always see her as a beautiful woman now. She took his breath away and he ached to hold her and kiss her and seduce her.

Of all the women he knew, why did it have to be Meg who set his heart pounding? She constantly reminded him they were not well suited. That was an understatement. In too many ways, she definitely wasn't the woman for him. Not the least of which was the fact that her whole family hated him on sight, equating him with his father and never giving him a chance to prove he was different.

At the same time, in some basic, essential ways, she was the most desirable woman he had ever known, and that's what really scared him.

"Aw, hell," he whispered to himself as he walked back to his kitchen. "Dammit, Meg. Why did you come back into my life like a cyclone ripping up my world?"

His little neighbor friend, dependable, sweet Meg whom he trusted with his deepest childhood secrets and disappointments, was the woman who suddenly made him weak in the knees, dazzled him with her looks, took his breath away when he saw her and set him on fire with longing to take her to bed.

She was a gorgeous woman with silky hair and enormous, thickly lashed brown eyes, a to-die-for body that could set him aflame with desire at just a glimpse. What would she be like in bed? He had a hard-on just thinking about it. How could she do this to him with just her appearance and a few kisses? The sexiest kisses of his entire life. Oh, if he had only known in high school. It was a good thing he hadn't. He couldn't lay a hand on her back then. Her dad and older brothers would have come after him. He wouldn't have been able to live with his conscience, either.

But now she was a grown woman, over twenty-one and making her own decisions. This whole scenario of her pulling him back into her life had been because she was making her own decisions. She liked to kiss as much as he did and she couldn't resist doing it, even if she didn't like his lifestyle and knew he would never be serious no matter how much they made love or how long they lived together.

Would he have to deal with his conscience if he seduced her? He thought it over, mulling over the past hours he had spent with her, and once again, he told himself she was a grown woman, making her own decisions about her life. If she went to bed with him, it would be because she wanted to make love. She was mature enough to make her choices—otherwise she wouldn't be asking him to carry off this fake engagement.

Did she want to make love? Well, she wasn't exactly saying no to him. And she'd kissed him into a frenzy. That was not the action of a woman who didn't want to make love.

He felt better about seduction, kisses and having Meg at his house. He even felt better about the fake engagement, which had worried him at first because he didn't like the deception and hadn't thought they could convince anyone they were engaged.

Her parents already didn't like him. What would they think if they saw him as a potential in-law? As a kid, when his dad and Meg's dad had worked together, he had enjoyed spending time with her family because they were very loving. He didn't have that at home and it had been an eye-opener to be with them.

Mostly, he hadn't thought she could convince anyone they were really engaged so quickly. That had been before tonight, when the spark of that kiss had suddenly ignited into a full flame with the magic of her makeover. She had looked gorgeous, sexy and sophisticated. Put that kiss together with her lifelong honesty and he thought she probably could carry off a fake engagement.

The seduction of Meg. He remembered her stepping close, throwing her leg across his and sitting astride his lap, facing him, challenging him with a kiss that was instant heat. Just thinking about that incident made his temperature climb.

The fact that Meg would be a challenge in bed and sexy still stunned him. He wondered if he'd ever get over the shock of going from seeing her as a child to viewing her as a desirable woman. A hot, appealing, breathtaking woman. A woman he hoped and dreamed of seducing and having hours with in bed. A fantasy come to life.

Right now, when she wasn't even with him and the house was quiet, he should be relaxed after a fun evening with the best-looking woman in the county and a delicious dinner with his family. He should be mellowed out, happy.

Instead, he was on fire with wanting her, aroused, breaking into a sweat while he tried to think how he could get her into his bed.

Or was that just a fantasy? What if she didn't want seduction and he had to do the honorable thing and stay the close friend he had always been?

He felt as if he was spinning himself in circles. She had sent his life spiraling into chaos. He couldn't even think straight anymore.

He groaned and went to the bar to get a beer when he heard her approaching. His pulse raced and eagerness gripped him. It was Meg, he reminded himself. Meg, his friend who trusted him, counted on him to come through for her in all sorts of ways that a best friend would.

She walked through the door and all his good intentions flamed into ashes as his gaze swept over her. He smiled at her and watched her cross the room toward him, remembering her with the black dress pushed to her waist, the lacy bra tossed aside and her soft, full breasts filling his hands.

She wore a bulky blue T-shirt, skintight jeans and leather moccasins. Her beautiful blond hair gave her glamour that she had never had before. The makeup she hadn't washed off just added to it, emphasizing her big, dark brown eyes. He was tempted to take her into his arms and kiss her right now.

"Wow, even dressed down you look good," he said, meaning every word. "I can't wait to take you out tomorrow night. I should have asked you out long before now."

She laughed and squeezed his hand. Locks of his dark hair fell on his forehead and she pushed them gently back off his face. "You're being ridiculous. You don't really want to take me out, but that's nice. You've had years to invite me out and you had no interest. We are not well suited and you know it."

"We're well suited enough to have a great time together. We've always had a good time together. Right now, let me get you something to drink and something to go with it. What would you like?"

"A glass of iced tea. But I'm not hungry, so I don't need anything to eat."

He stepped close. "I'd like to eat you up," he said, leaning forward to nuzzle her throat and kiss her ear. He grabbed her wrist and felt her racing pulse.

She pushed lightly against him. "Whoa, cowboy. Get my tea and pull yourself together. Remember, this is a pretend engagement and you don't have to pretend when we're alone."

"I'm not pretending," he said, gazing intently at her. "You're stunning, Meg," he said quietly. "I'm still in shock and I can't get used to the change."

"I'm still me and you've never wanted to kiss or hug or dance with me before this, so rein it in, my friend, because you and I aren't going anywhere together beyond this brief favor you're doing for me. Then it's adios and we'll probably go another year before we cross paths again. I'm not your type and you're not my type. Now, if you can comprehend all that, let's have a drink," she said, heading for his kitchen and his fridge.

He stood and watched the sway of her hips as she walked. He wanted to go after her, grab her around the waist and haul her back into his arms.

"Damn," he whispered. He needed to get her out of his hair and out of his life as soon as possible. She was right—they didn't have a future together and she wouldn't go to bed with him. She'd only keep him tied in knots in the meantime. His initial gut feeling of dread, when she first asked him for the fake engagement, had been on target. The lady was going to mess up his life for a little while and he needed to guard his heart. He had never before worried about falling in love with someone, but he worried now. He damn well didn't want to fall in love with her, but could he avoid it?

"Have a seat, Meg, and I'll get everything," he said, taking over getting drinks. She moved to the kitchen table, pulled out a chair and sat to watch him.

When he had drinks and crackers and slices of Muenster and sharp cheddar cheese ready, he sat across from her and sipped his cold beer.

"I've been thinking, Gabe. How about getting engaged tonight?"

He swallowed hard. "That's damn quick."

"Maybe, but we've known each other all our lives. We've gone out together. It's feasible. We can plan for a wedding far in the future. This is July. How about a spring wedding, like the first week of April, and a wonderful cruise for a honeymoon? That's so far away, so no one will do anything concrete right now. In the meantime, everyone will think we're in love because I'll be living with you."

"Until April?" he asked. If he had to live in the same house with her for months, he'd have to take her to bed. Either that or he'd surely go crazy.

"No, not until April." She gave him a sassy look, as if she wasn't sure whether he was teasing her or not. "We have a deal. One month and then you're off the hook." She sipped her iced tea. "I'm sure it won't take any time for Justin to find a new girlfriend, and I'll bet he does a better job of picking one out this time. Whoever she is, she'll have his parents' approval."

"What about your folks?"

"My folks have already given up, I'm sure. My mom understands now and she'll get the family in line. I've told Justin goodbye and— Actually, he told me goodbye. He said if I went out with you, we were through. Either way, I'm free," she said, waving her arms in the air and then smiling at him.

"Suppose he's burned and wants to back off from relationships and take his time, and doesn't even date?"

"No. He'll want to show everyone that losing me means nothing. That he can pick up and go on with his life. Which I hope he does. He won't hang around waiting for me to change my mind, either. He'll be angry and he'll want to show everyone that I didn't affect his life and he can get along fine without me."

"So you want to get engaged tonight," he said, wondering again how much more upheaval she would cause in his life. "Even when it's pretend, it's a big step that gives me sweaty palms."

"That's because we're not in love. When you're in love with someone, you won't feel that way."

"Thank you, for the reassuring engagement advice," he remarked and she stuck her tongue out at him, making him grin.

He thought for a moment. "They saw us tonight at the club. Tomorrow is Sunday and we can go to my church. If we go to yours, I don't think I would be welcome. Then—"

"Of course you'd be welcome at my church. Just not with my family."

"Okay. We'll go to your church and then let's go to the ranch and come back to Dallas Tuesday. We'll try to do something special then, and let's get engaged then instead of tonight. If you're going out with me and living in my house, you won't have to date Justin."

"True. I think that's a good idea. My family will definitely not like it when they discover I'm staying with you."

"Do I need to be on guard because of your dad and grandfathers?"

As she shook her head, she laughed. "What a thought. My grandfathers wouldn't do anything to you. My dad wouldn't, either."

"I don't agree, but we won't argue about it," he said. "If your dad does anything, it will be in the business world." And he was ready for it.

As he sat across the table from her and listened

to her make plans, he had to admit only half his attention was on what she was telling him. The other half—the lower half, to be exact—was studying her. She had changed into the plain clothes he had seen her wear hundreds of times before. And they had an entire table between them, so he was nowhere near her. None of that mattered. He still wanted to pick her up and sit with her on his lap and kiss her. He didn't care what she did about the engagement or when. He just wanted her in his arms.

Despite all their differences, he knew they'd be compatible in bed. But he could never marry someone who didn't like anything he did outside of the bedroom.

Marry?

What was he thinking? It was all pretend, he reminded himself. No one was getting married here!

He had to remember that.

He took a deep swig of his beer and tried focusing on what Meg was saying.

"Anyway, I'm so happy." She was practically wriggling with glee. "My folks won't push me to marry at all now. They certainly aren't going to want me walking down the aisle with you. Sorry." She shot him a sheepish look.

"I get it. It's okay. But if I were you, I wouldn't assume Justin is a done deal. The way you look now, he is not going to give up that easily."

As if to emphasize what he was saying, her phone buzzed. Her eyes widened in a startled look and then she pulled her phone from her pocket, looked at the caller ID and glanced in surprise at him. "It's Justin."

"Told you so." He stood up. "I'll leave you so you can talk in private. Good luck." Gabe picked up his beer and headed outside, closing the door behind him as he heard her quiet hello.

Gabe suspected Justin would put pressure on her to marry until they announced the engagement.

That would open up another can of worms, he realized. Her family would hate him more than ever and that was a sobering fact. He was unaccustomed to anyone actively disliking him, and he had respect for her parents and grandparents, and especially liked Mason Aldridge, her rancher grandparent. He wished she didn't have to let anyone know about the engagement except Justin, but that wouldn't ever fly. It had to be all her family, too, because they were the ones really worrying her, far more than Justin was. She would have been able to deal with Justin if all the parents had stayed out of it.

He heard the door and turned as she stepped outside and joined him.

"You're right. He wants to see me and talk. He was very persistent. He said he would drop by my office next Tuesday. How do you say no to that one?"

"I guess you don't. Want me to drop by at the same time?"

She laughed. "Indeed, I don't. You two don't need to get into it. I'm sure he doesn't like you."

"Enough about Justin. Want me to surprise you with an elaborate marriage proposal? Or do you just want to keep it simple? We go out and during the evening I give you a ring and then we go tell your parents."

"Let's keep it simple because it isn't real." She thought for a moment, then said, "The grandparents that live with my parents are going to Colorado to see my aunt, so after we tell my mom and dad I'll call both sets of grandparents."

"I may have a guilty conscience every time I see Mason Aldridge."

"No, you won't. You've got nothing to feel guilty about. You're coming to my rescue with this fake engagement."

Fake engagement. The words resonated in his head. He looked at her. "Is either one of us going to have trouble remembering this engagement isn't real?"

"What you're asking is, will I want the real thing before this is over. No, my friend, I will not. All I have to do is stroll out the door on your ranch and see those big rodeo bulls you raise and sell, and know that you ride them, too. Then see your motorcycle, remember your plane, look at your sports car that will do a hundred miles an hour in the first three seconds or some other ridiculous statistic, and I promise you, I will never want the real thing from you. Not for one teeny, tiny second. And I know you won't want it from me, because you don't want the real thing anytime with any person. Right?"

"You're on target there." He saluted her with his beer bottle. "Well, we know where we stand and what we're going to do. This has turned out to be a simple deal."

She clinked his bottle with her glass. "Oh, sure, except for one little surprise—when we kiss, we both lose all rational thought and want the other person in a way that is so fierce it's scary."

"We won't even think about that part of it. Keep your distance and try to be a little remote and untouchable. I can't believe I'm saying that to you."

"I can definitely be remote and untouchable. I'll get my old hairdo back and pack my bags and move home. You'll forget all about me, especially when I'm covered in dirt."

He doubted that.

"You know, I never did ask you about your business. I'm glad it's growing and you like it. Do you get out there and mow with the guys?"

She laughed. "No. I'm a landscape designer. I plan flower beds, how yards will look—what trees will be good and where they should be planted. I hire and keep up with everything, but mostly my job is planning." She looked out at his crystal-blue pool, with a waterfall and fountain at one end. "I have an interest in a pool business in Dallas, too. They do the pools in the yards I landscape. I'm surprised you didn't let me have a shot at doing yours, but that's okay. I haven't inquired about buying a bull from you."

He smiled at her. "Maybe I'll have you come do the yard over."

She looked around. "This yard doesn't need doing over. It's beautiful, Gabe. Your pool is gorgeous and this patio—with the furniture, the big-screen television, the fire pit and the outdoor rug—it's all perfect. When we arrived, I saw your beautiful shade trees. Your oaks are marvelous. And your two magnolia trees. They're big for how long you've lived here."

"Some of the biggest ones were already on the lot. I had the house that was here razed and this one built. It's more contemporary—lots more glass and plain lines."

"You have a beautiful home."

"Thanks. Maybe we should go inside. Seems kind of warm tonight."

He held the door for her and when she walked past him, he caught a whiff of her new exotic scent and looked at the sexy sway of her hips and desire tore at him. He wanted her in his arms. What was wrong with him? Only minutes ago he all but told her he would leave her alone. Once again his libido warred with his common sense. He wanted her but he knew he shouldn't touch her. He had to avoid seducing her or he would be doing this fake engagement for real, because of a guilty conscience. And, heaven forbid, he did not want to fall in love. That hadn't ever happened and he didn't think he ran much of a risk, but Meg had a way of complicating his peaceful life. He couldn't think of many disasters as big as falling in love with Meg. She'd tear his heart into little pieces. She didn't like any part of his life—his bulls, his motorcycle, his car, his planes, nothing except him. He had to keep reminding himself of that, so he'd keep his hands off her.

"I guess I'll turn in, now that we've made our plans," she said as they walked inside. "Tomorrow we're going to your ranch after church, right?"

"Yes. I'll take the small plane."

She spun around. "No way! I'm not flying in your small plane. I'll drive to your ranch."

"But it'll take so long to drive," he protested.

She stepped toward him. "Don't worry, I'll entertain you while you drive," she said, running her hands over his chest.

He shook his head and dragged her hands away. He couldn't risk having her touch him, not when he was about to explode. "Life is full of risks. You can't live in a bubble."

"There are some risks that are unnecessary and some that are definitely bigger than others. I don't have to fly to your ranch, therefore I'm not going to fly in your small plane." She tugged her hands from him and walked away.

The sashay of her behind was the last straw. He strode forward, grabbed her and spun her around. "The hell with this, Meg." He stepped closer, not a molecule of air between them. "Here's another wild risk in life. Live a little." And he kissed her.

Seven

Meg had had every intention of going straight to bed—alone. Till now. Once Gabe's lips touched hers, every intention to resist him disappeared, along with all her warnings to herself and her sense of caution. What was the harm? A few kisses would not bind her to him. It was ridiculous to worry over a few kisses with Gabe. The minute that thought came, it was followed by big doubts. How unforgettable would Gabe be?

When his lips parted and his tongue plundered hers, she wasn't capable of any more thought. Her body overrode her mind and she wrapped her arms around him, his kiss making her feel more desired than she'd ever dreamed possible.

Her heart raced and she couldn't get her breath. She only wanted to kiss him, hold him close and run her hands over his marvelous male body.

He held her tightly, his lean, muscled body solid

against her, his kiss sending her into a dizzying spiral. She thrust her hips against him. He leaned over her, kissing her and holding her while he caressed her with his other hand. His hand drifted over her nape, then down her back and beneath the shirt she wore. She had promised herself she wouldn't do this. She was putting her future, her heart at risk. She was taking the peace that she had finally achieved, turning right around and risking it all for Gabe's kisses. He could break her heart. If she made love with him, she would be in love with him, and that would lead to the worst kind of heartbreak because she had known him all her life and he was important in her life. Every second she touched and kissed him, she was wading deeper into a dangerous pool of heartbreak. She had never been emotionally invested in Justin. She was in Gabe. And that put her in danger.

Yet how badly she wanted his arms around her and his mouth on hers. Just a little longer, she told herself. How bad could it be? How could she lose her heart over kisses? Over just one night of love? Or was she simply fooling herself in order to shut out the sensible warnings of disaster?

Right now she couldn't answer that, not when her heart hammered with excitement, when desire burned hot through her fingertips that ran over his chest.

"You're a beautiful woman, darlin'. You can't imagine what you do to me," he whispered.

He kissed her again, stroking her sensuously with his tongue as he toyed with her breasts, his breath warm, his attention exciting. She ran her hands over his strong shoulders, wanting to pull him even closer, wanting him inside her.

She pulled back to drag in air. "You're pure temptation," she whispered. "You're taking me where I vowed I wouldn't go."

"I'll stop when you tell me to," he rasped out, his hands and tongue roaming over her. "Ah, you are so beautiful, so hot."

He tangled his fingers in her hair, tilting her face up so he could look into her eyes. She felt caught and held again by his blue eyes that mesmerized her and flashed so much blatant desire she couldn't get her breath.

Wrapping his arms around her, he pulled her tightly against him. He was on fire, his manhood thick and hard and ready to love.

This would be a commitment for her while it would be no such thing for Gabe. Was that what she wanted? If they made love tonight, she would feel a bond with him that he would never feel. Could she live with that? Was she moving closer to a big heartache? She was torn between wanting him and being sensible and keeping her distance.

She ran her fingers over his nape, aching to have him inside her, wishing to be one with him, desiring all of him. She wanted his loving all through the night and she knew he would give her that if she let him. But that tiny voice of caution would not remain silent. It kept calling out to her, begging her to be wary.

Gabe would never want anything long-term and she wouldn't want it even if he did. She couldn't deal with his wild ways, so why was she getting herself more entangled with him by the minute?

"Gabe, wait," she said, leaning away from him. "This is too fast and too far for me. I just can't take making love the casual way you do."

She placed her hand on his chest as she shook her head. "Besides that, suppose we have sex and it's the most fantastic sex ever, like our kissing is fantastic. Suppose sex between us is that way. How are you going to live with that?"

Gabe blew out a hot breath and she felt his arms loosen their hold on her. "Darlin', you sure know how to kill the moment. Holy hell."

"I have definitely and obviously not killed the moment for you," she said, glancing down at the hardness in his slacks. "We're going to be together for a while. I'm going to live at your house, maybe for the rest of the month. We have time. There is no need to jump into bed tonight. Let's stop and think. Suppose sex is the most spectacular thing ever between us—"

He groaned and placed his hands on his hips. "You can stop. We'll quit for now. C'mon. I'll see you upstairs and tomorrow will be another day, as someone famous said."

She frowned, staring at him. "You think about us, Gabe."

"As if I could think about anything else."

She faced him, taking him in. His hair, a tangle of dark waves, fell on his forehead. His broad shoulders made her draw a deep breath as her gaze ran across his well-muscled chest.

"Meg, my life was quiet and peaceful and uneventful until you came back into it. I'll tell you, in all my experience with women, you're unique."

"I find that a compliment."

"Take it how you will. You were a fun special friend when we were kids, but I never thought of you as unique. Tonight's a first in my life. I've never been asked to stop for the reason you gave me. The hell of it is—you make a degree of sense. Are you even listening to me?"

"Of course I am," she said, looking up at him.

"Sleep is shot to hell for the next few hours. I'm going to have an icy shower and come back here and drink a beer. If you want to join me, you're welcome to."

"I doubt if I'll sleep, either. I'll join you here in a little while," she said. She took one last long look, her gaze running to his toes and back up to find him watching her.

"You're incredibly sexy," she whispered. "I'm going while I still can."

"Thank you, I think, for the 'incredibly sexy' remark, although that parting shot isn't doing anything to cool me down."

"I'm gone," she called over her shoulder, hurrying out of the room before she walked back into his arms and into his bed for the night.

Gabe watched her go. Her fabulous blond hair swung with each step and it took an effort to keep from going after her.

He recalled all those initial feelings, days ago, when he had watched her come up his drive and then into his house and into his life again. Those feelings that said trouble was coming had been right. He had never known another woman like her, never been sexually involved with one. Right now, as much trouble as she was, he still wanted her. If she turned around and came right back and walked into his arms, he would take her to bed with him for the night, and for the week if she would let him. And then she would worry the hell out of him, even if she didn't say anything about what they were doing. Except she would say plenty.

She had him tied in knots and he hadn't even slept with her. And she was causing him sizable grief. In addition, her dad had threatened him, which was probably an empty threat, but her family definitely disliked him. After his dad and Meg's had split, Gabe learned later, when he was grown, his dad had pulled some sneaky dealings to buy out her father for way less than he should have been worth as a partner. Her father had tried to retaliate and hurt Dirkson's business, trying to outbid him on land deals and drilling rights, but it was like a fly buzzing around a bull. Dirkson Callahan hadn't been hurt, and it had left the Aldridges bitter and angry ever since.

Mason Aldridge, her rancher grandfather, was the least angry and did speak to Gabe, probably because they knew each other through cattle sales and rodeos and ranch activities. Gabe respected her grandfather and Mason seemed respectful of Gabe. Whatever happened, Gabe just didn't want to get into a business struggle or any other feud with her family, at least no more than they already had.

Her father had warned him, and Gabe had no intention of hurting Meg, but she was the earnest type who counted on certain things and would get hurt if she didn't get them. If he slept with her, would she expect him to marry her? She had to realize, given his reputation, that he certainly had no intention of walking down the aisle after taking her to bed. She should know that, since she had talked about it often.

Gabe gathered his things and went to his room. As he stripped off his clothes, his thoughts kept going back to the past hour with Meg. It was a crime how sexy she had turned out to be. He was on fire just thinking about her and he wanted her more than ever. He had a feeling a cold shower wouldn't do the trick tonight. It would take a soak in an icy lake to cool his body down.

Why, oh, why, did his little childhood chum set him ablaze just by entering the room? As absurd as it was, the sight of her had jolted him, because he had never for one split second expected her to arouse him so instantly.

And that silly argument of hers that sex between them might be too great? It had almost made him laugh, except the prospect had made him hard from wanting her. If it turned out to be the most fantastic sex ever, he would find that a welcome problem.

He scoffed to himself as he turned on the shower. All the way to cold.

The little girl next door...

Only she wasn't the little girl next door now. She was a stunning blonde who could blow him away. And she came with all kinds of trouble—her fear of planes, fast cars, rodeo riders, all the things he thought were great, fun or just downright convenient. She had a family who hated him. She wanted commitment and marriage if she shared her bed. It was a litany that was becoming far too familiar, but he had to keep reminding himself why he should view the lady as off-limits. Big-time off-limits. Meg would be nothing but trouble in his life if he seduced her. She already was a bushel of trouble. Why didn't that prospect cool him down?

Gabe groaned as he stepped into the shower, gritting his teeth at the cold and hoping it would freeze his libido. If only there were some spigot he could turn on to stop thinking about her and remembering how she looked and kissed—that's what he desperately needed.

He tried to think of something else to get her out of his thoughts. Another woman wouldn't do it. Business deals wouldn't, either. Meg trumped them all. Little Meg, who had him in knots and shivering in an icy shower, still unable to stop thinking about kissing her.

He had to get a grip because his thoughts were taking him to dangerous places. He started to think that it might not be the worst thing in his life if they made love and his conscience forced him into proposing to her. He expected to shudder at the thought, but not even that prospect stopped him from wanting her. And that scared him.

After a long shower, he pulled on a short-sleeved navy Western shirt and jeans. He took his time, but finally went downstairs and found her outside on his patio. He got a cold beer and joined her.

"Hi. Is it cool enough out here now?" he asked, his gaze drifting over her. She wore another loose-fitting black T-shirt and cutoffs that left her legs bare. It didn't matter what she wore, she looked great and he could remember exactly how she had looked naked from the waist up.

"It's cool enough, and it's so quiet out here. All I hear is the splashing water from the fountain, which is such a relaxing sound." She laid her head back against the seat back and stretched her long legs in front of her.

He couldn't help but think how perfect she looked sitting in his backyard. As if she belonged here.

"I'll miss you when this is over."

She turned to him, her face visible in the dim patio light. "No, you won't. We haven't hung out together for quite a few years. Not like we used to. After this is over, we'll go our separate ways again." She gave him a grin. "I'll read about you in Texas magazines or in the society pages."

He put his hands up. "Not me. I won't be in many society pages. My mom maybe, when she's here, which is seldom. My dad even less, and he keeps a low profile since he's gotten older."

"You expect me to believe you're a hermit? I know you too well, Gabe Callahan."

"Oh, I get around," he retorted, "but I tend to do my trolling out of the public eye." He shrugged. "Never had any complaints from the women I've dated."

She laughed and her whole face seemed to light up. "And I'm guessing that's a fair number of women, from what I've heard."

Gabe was not the type to kiss and tell. He simply shrugged and took a draft of beer.

She turned to him then, and sat up, suddenly serious. "Don't you ever want to get married, Gabe?"

"Sure, someday, but I'm young and I'm not ready now. I don't want to be tied down and I haven't found the right woman, anyway."

"I seriously doubt if she exists," she said and he grinned.

"Sure she does. I just don't know her yet. I could ask you the same question. Don't you ever want to get married?"

"Of course I do, but I want the right man and Justin definitely isn't him." She picked up her beer bottle. "But I think Justin has started to become history in my life, thanks to you. You're a real buddy and you came through for me in the best possible way."

"I can do even better if you'd let me," he said, his voice becoming husky.

"You have a one-track mind."

"If I do, it's because you're a good-looking, appealing woman who is fantastic to kiss." He stood up and picked her up, sitting back in his chair with her on his lap. "Maybe I do have a one-track mind where you're concerned," he said, running one hand lightly up her bare leg, his fingers slipping beneath her shorts slightly to caress her. He had limited access, but her soft, smooth inner thighs made him want to peel away the cutoffs. "I don't know how you expect me to think about other things when you dress like this. You're beautiful, Meg. You know what you do to me when we kiss. I can't stop wanting you or forget about that."

As he talked, he caressed her nape with his other hand, kissed her ear, brushed her lips with his and then paused to look at her. There was enough light that he could see her eyes were heavy lidded, her focus on his mouth. He leaned close to kiss her, pulling her tightly against him.

She wound her arms around his neck and kissed him in return, and he wanted her more than he had earlier. He picked her up and moved to a chaise longue and stretched out with her beside him, holding her close the whole time while he kissed her.

Lying beside her was an irresistible temptation. He tried to take time, to not push her, although at the moment she seemed as eager as he was. He ran his hand beneath her shirt, then shifted her slightly to unfasten the front catch to her lacy bra and pushed it away, pulling her shirt high to allow him to hold and caress her breasts.

She gasped with pleasure. "We weren't going to do this tonight," she whispered as she showered kisses on his jaw, his throat, his shoulder, unbuttoning his shirt and running her hand over his chest. In minutes she leaned away to look at him. "I need to catch my breath."

He nodded. He stood and took her hand. "Come on. We'll go inside."

"Inside and upstairs to our own suites," she added. "That's the safest plan. Tomorrow it's church and then the drive to your ranch."

"Whatever the lady wants," he said.

It wasn't what he wanted. Not by a long shot.

* * *

At the door to her suite, Meg turned and slipped her arms around his neck, leaning close to kiss him. Then she stepped back and opened her door. "This has been a wonderful evening, Gabe. Thank you."

He shook his head at her. "Darlin', you are a bundle of mixed signals. One minute you want to kiss me and the next minute you don't."

"Not so mixed. I want to kiss, but common sense takes over now and then."

He took a deep breath. "I don't recall you being this much trouble when we were kids."

"We had a simpler life when we were kids. You're a year older and could usually get your way or beat me in games so you didn't view me as trouble. I still don't see you as trouble." She glanced down at his hands, which were reaching out to pull her close. She grinned and said, "Well, maybe some trouble." She partially closed the door, needing that physical barrier between them.

"Still, Gabe, I'm so grateful to you for getting me out of the situation with my family and Justin. Remember," she said, "I'll do some big favor for you someday if you need me to help with a problem."

She smiled as she entered her suite, closing the door and letting out her breath. "If you only knew how much trouble you really are," she whispered.

She wanted to be in his arms, wanted his loving, wanted to be in his bed right now.

She decided to take her own advice and at least take tonight to think about her future and what she wanted to do. If she slept with Gabe—and supposing the sex was super—would she be able to walk away with her heart intact? Or would it be broken?

There would be no long-term relationship, no future

with Gabe, so she needed to come to a firm decision. Did she want to miss this chance to make love with him?

She wondered if she could sleep at all. Could Gabe sleep or was he going to lie awake and think about making love?

Sunday after church they got into Gabe's black sports car. He knew he would have to stay at the speed limit or lower or his passenger would be unhappy and let him know it.

She had come downstairs this morning, dressed in a tailored summer suit of pale-blue-and-white-striped cotton with a pale blue blouse and high-heeled blue sandals. Her hair was still in spiral curls and fell freely on both sides of her face, so she hadn't reverted to her old hairstyle. And even in the tailored clothes that covered her, she took his breath away.

They went to church together and sat far from her family, but she left Gabe to talk to them after the service was over. As he headed toward his car, he stopped to talk to friends while the church crowd thinned. Each time he glanced at Meg, she was talking to her mother, and both of them looked engrossed in their conversation.

He hoped she was getting across to her mother her feelings about Justin and he might escape this month-long fake engagement, but he suspected that was highly unlikely.

"Gabe, wait up," a man called, and he turned to see his friend Marc Medina so he stopped and smiled.

"Megan, I see you're with Gabe Callahan this morning," her mother said as Meg walked up. Her father was talking to a friend and farther away from them.

"Yes, I am. We went out together last night and today

he's taking me to see his ranch. Where are Lolo and Grandpa Harry?"

"They left for Colorado already. So Justin really is out of your life."

"Yes, he is. He never really was in my life as far as I was concerned."

Her mother frowned. "Megan, please think about what you're doing by going with Gabe Callahan. You know how the family feels about the Callahans."

"Mom, that is your generation. My generation has no problem with the younger Callahans. Gabe and I have been friends forever, as you know, and it's fun to be with him."

Her mother frowned as she stared at Meg. "I hope we didn't push you into doing something foolish."

"I assume you mean pushing me into going out with Gabe. We've been friends almost since we were toddlers. I like being with him," she said, glancing around to see Gabe standing in the shade of a tree, talking to a friend.

"Gabe is waiting. I'll talk to you later."

"Take care. I love you."

She hugged her mother. "I love you, too." She looked at her mother. "I know you mean well and want me to be happy."

"That's what's important."

"I better run," she said, turning to hurry across the lot to Gabe. He stood alone in the shade now, his arms folded as he waited. Her heart beat faster when she looked at him. He was dressed for church in a charcoal Western-style suit, his black boots and black Stetson. They had already planned to drive back to his house to change clothes and get some of her things before leaving for his ranch.

"Thank you for waiting so patiently," she said. "Wait until we're at your house. I'm going to give you a giant hug and jump up and down for joy. My mom finally gets it that I do not want to date Justin, much less marry him."

Gabe laughed. "Whoa, slow down. I got what you said, but you sound like Horace Grayson when he's auctioning cattle."

Feeling giddy, she laughed. "I'm just so happy. She finally understands."

Gabe held the car door open and she stepped forward to get in, but paused in front of him, with only inches between them.

"You handsome devil. You are the greatest friend ever and if we weren't on the church grounds, I'd hug you right now. You did it. See? Taking me out started opening the doors to my freedom. Hooray!"

She saw him glance around and then he ushered her into the car. "Get in before someone else comes over to talk and we never get out of here."

Smiling at him, she slid into the seat and he closed the door. She watched him walk around the car, something she enjoyed doing because he was so handsome in his Sunday outfit. He would be handsome out of his Sunday outfit, too, she was sure.

He sat behind the wheel, buckled his seat belt and started the car, driving slowly out of the lot.

Meg turned toward him as much as she could with a seat belt on. "I'm so happy, I can't sit still. I'm free. I owe it all to you. What a friend you are."

"You just keep those thoughts in your pretty head until we get to my house."

"I couldn't get rid of these thoughts right now if I tried. I feel as if I could fly out of this car."

"While you're on this high, is there any chance you'd like a real thrill and would let me fly you to the ranch?"

"Whoa, you know how to kill the moment, too, Gabe," she said. "No, I haven't changed my mind about flying in one of those little planes. I don't care how fancy or expensive it is. I don't like to fly in the big ones either, for that matter. I don't go anywhere so it isn't an issue. I'll drive to the ranch with or without you."

"I'll take you," he said, patting her leg. "I just gave it a shot. You're so exuberant, I thought I might get you in a plane."

"Sorry, not today." As euphoric as she was, noth-ing would get her in a plane.

"Want to get brunch now at someplace nice, or would you rather change, head for the ranch and eat a burger on the way?" Gabe asked as he drove. "Personally, I vote for the Sunday brunch at my favorite restaurant."

"I agree," she said. "And I'll try to control my grati-tude and my excitement."

"You can bottle up all that gratitude and excitement while we eat and then uncork it when we're in the pri-vacy of my house."

It was two hours later when they left the restaurant and he drove them to his Dallas home in a gated com-munity.

Turning to go through the big gate that opened au-tomatically for his car, he entered the subdivision. In minutes he went through another gate that surrounded his place. Finally, he slowed and stopped at the back of his house and went around to open her door. Before he could, she hopped out and kissed his cheek.

"Thanks a million, my friend. Don't forget my offer. I'm ready, willing and able to do something for you."

She instantly regretted her words when she saw the flare of desire in his blue eyes. She felt heat climb into her cheeks at her unwitting innuendo. Which was so unlike her. She'd never been embarrassed in front of Gabe.

"Besides going to bed, I mean," she clarified, smiling at him.

He laughed. "Meg, in some ways you haven't changed at all. At the same time, you have changed in the most delightful fashion possible. Darlin', I'm glad to be of help to you. Even though you've made a wreck out of me, I wouldn't have missed this week for the world."

"I'm so happy, I can't be still."

He reached out to draw her into his embrace, leaning close to kiss her, a possessive, demanding kiss that made her forget her resolution to avoid kisses and sex. Gabe held her close, kissing her into scalding desire.

She wanted more, so much more.

Did she want to keep saying no and maybe miss the most dazzling sex ever?

What they did to each other was amazing—she wanted to pursue that and make love with him because it had to be fabulous. But if it was that awesome, could she keep from giving him her heart, her love, along with her body? Could she make love with him and then just walk away, heart intact, the way he would?

That was the big question she faced and she didn't have an answer.

"Gabe, I'm still thinking about this," she whispered. "I can't resist kissing you but I'm not ready to go to bed with you. That's just the way I am. It'll be complicated if I make love with you."

"Will it ever, darlin'," he said, his gaze roaming over her.

"Let's go change. I'll get the rest of my things I want to take and we can leave for the ranch," she said.

Together they went upstairs and then parted, each to their suites.

She entered hers, closed the door and saw the vivid reflection of her eyes in the mirror. Could Gabe see what she detected so clearly there? Desire.

It was no secret that she wanted him. Whether she should act on it was the real issue.

If she refused to sleep with him and they parted, would she always feel she had missed something special? Would she regret not making love with him?

Someday she hoped she would fall in love and marry a man who was similar to her, who wanted what she wanted. Someone who led a regular life and didn't raise bulls and ride them, fly his own small plane, do all the wild things Gabe did. But for now…was she about to pass up something special that she would always remember?

Would she fall in love if she went to bed with him tonight at his ranch? She had to be able to answer no to that question or else say no to him. She'd have to lock her heart away and enjoy a physical time with him and then leave him the way he would leave her. No strings, no ties, no commitment, no love. Could she do that, especially when it was with her best friend and the sexiest man she knew? Or would she open herself up for heartbreak?

Eight

It was late afternoon when his ranch house came into view. She looked at the long, one-story stacked-stone house with rustic wood columns along the wraparound porch and a large porte cochere to the east of the building. She admired the landscaped, fenced-in front yard with berms of mature oak trees.

"You have a beautiful place," she said. "Great landscaping with your berms."

"I'm glad you like it." He parked in the shade beneath the porte cochere and walked around to hold the car door open for her. Desire kept her acutely aware of him and her gaze raked over his broad shoulders covered with a navy cotton shirt that was tucked into jeans and one of his wide, hand-tooled leather belts, complete with a big silver belt buckle she assumed he had won riding a bull or accomplishing some other rodeo achievement. Ironically, they had both changed into jeans and navy shirts, and they had laughed about dressing alike.

"Come in and let me show you around," he said when she stepped out of his car. He picked up her bag and retrieved her carry-on and as they walked in, she was aware of him beside her.

She entered into the kitchen, well equipped with state-of-the-art appliances and a tan-and-white decor. As they walked farther into the house, she glanced at rooms off the wide main hall, and finally he showed her to the suite where she would stay. It had a separate sitting room with a wall of glass and sliding glass doors that opened onto the back porch. A few steps led down to a wide patio with an outdoor carpet, cushioned chairs and sofas, tables, a fire pit, a large television and an outdoor kitchen. Beyond it was a curving swimming pool with a waterfall and two slides.

"This is beautiful, Gabe," she said as she looked outside. "You have everything the way you like it."

But when she turned around, the picturesque sight of his backyard paled in comparison to Gabe. He was hefting her bags onto a luggage stand, his shirt pulled across his broad shoulders and his biceps flexed. Memories of their kisses before they left Dallas were still vivid in her mind, and she felt desire once again flooding her.

"Do you—" He set down her bags and glanced at her, and whatever he was about to ask her died on his lips.

She no longer had to wonder, as she had back in Dallas hours ago, whether he could see the desire in her eyes. Clearly he did.

His gaze locked with hers as he strode across to her. He wrapped his arms around her and tilted her chin up. She looked into his eyes, the blue darkened by passion— eyes that mirrored the desire she felt.

"Ah, darlin'," he said as he leaned down to kiss her.

Letting go of her usual caution, doubts and worries, she clung to him as eagerness filled her. Making her decision, she expected she could live with it and hoped she had made the right choice.

His scalding kiss was possessive and passionate, making her feel as if she belonged in his arms. She experienced a bond of friendship with him that she didn't have with any other man she had ever known. Because of that and his kisses that set her ablaze with an incredibly intense longing, she wanted his loving, his hands and mouth on her, his body available for her to touch and kiss. Most of all, she wanted to pleasure him, to caress and kiss him. She longed to pour out some of what she felt for him, trying to convey how happy she was to have him in her life again, even if it would be brief.

"You're so good to me," she whispered, thinking he truly was her best friend and had stuck by her when she needed him, both as a child and now as an adult. Their kisses were stupendous. Were they so great because it was Gabe? Because friendship made it more intense? Or was it some other chemistry they conjured up when they were together? She didn't know. At the moment she only knew she wanted him, needed to draw him closer, keep him close. She longed to love him and his awesome male body that made her tremble with desire.

She was about to make a commitment when she knew there would be no commitment from him. But he would always be honest and up front with her. She had already decided to live with that and, hopefully, to walk away without leaving behind her heart. This time in his arms, in his bed, couldn't change her life unless she let it. She knew his feelings and understood them.

They were close, and this intimacy would be one more link in their chain of timeless friendship.

She stopped thinking about it. She was with Gabe and she wanted to make love with him.

Holding her, he leaned back slightly to look at her, a piercing look filled with unspoken questions. "You know what you want. This is a turnaround."

"Not really. We're friends. The closest of friends, which changes everything and makes intimacy something special. I can guard my heart as you will yours, and at the same time, that friendship will shine through and become special."

He drew her close to kiss her again, a slow, tantalizing kiss as his tongue thrust deep, stroked hers, touched the corners of her mouth and moved so lightly over her lower lip. All teasing strokes that built a physical need to kiss even more passionately.

She drew his head down and stood on tiptoe to kiss him, tangling her tongue with his, wanting to bind him to her for the next hour, to be as close as they could.

He raised his head slightly. His breath was ragged and his gaze was piercing. "You are unpredictable, unforgettable, special. I want this. Oh, baby, do I want this, but intimacy will change our friendship forever."

"I know."

His gaze faltered a mere second. "I'm not into commitment, Meg. Don't think you'll change me."

She smiled at him. "I'm not planning on changing you. I know I couldn't possibly. And you're not going to change me. See, you're being a friend right now. You know I don't casually make love and you're giving me a chance to stop and think twice. But, Gabe, I know what I'm doing."

He stared at her as if weighing what she'd said and

trying to come to a conclusion about how it would affect him. "I've never known a woman like you. I want you, darlin', even though you complicate the hell out of life." And with that he leaned down to kiss her and end their discussion.

While longing rocked her, she ran her hands over him. Her fingers worked swiftly to unbutton his shirt and push it away. As soon as she did, she tangled her fingers in a smattering of crisp chest curls while her other hand ran over his muscled shoulders. He was strong, fit, in peak condition, and his body was the perfect male specimen. She couldn't wait one more moment for the intimacy, the closeness that she'd resisted.

With a trembling hand she unbuckled his belt and pulled it free to drop it with a clatter. As she did, he pulled her shirt over her head, unclasped her bra and tossed them aside. His jeans went next, and he paused to yank them off, along with his boots and socks. Placing his hands lightly on her hips, he held her away to look at her. His gaze was a slow perusal that made her tingle as if his fingers caressed her. Swiftly, he unfastened her jeans and pushed them down, along with her panties. As she stepped out of them, he cupped her breasts in his warm hands, stroking their rosy tips with his thumbs and making her gasp with pleasure.

"You're beautiful, so beautiful," he whispered. "You don't know what you do to me."

Closing her eyes momentarily, she clung to his forearms as he caressed her and streaks of pleasure stirred her, making her want him more than ever. It seemed right, to be with him and kiss and caress him.

She pulled away his briefs to free his thick, hard shaft. She drew a deep breath as she looked at his body, a body that thrilled her and made her ache to touch him.

He picked her up and carried her into her bedroom to place her on the bed. He lay beside her, drawing her into his embrace, tangling his legs with hers while he kissed her—a deep, insistent kiss.

Stroking her hair away from her face, he paused to gaze intently at her. "You can't ever know how badly I've wanted to make love to you. You're a beautiful woman. You'll never know how much you excite me."

She kissed him and his fingers tangled in her hair while his arm held her against him. He was hard and she wanted to touch and explore his body. Right now, his kisses were sending her pulse racing and making her want him more than ever. He was important to her, part of her life, and now they would be closer than ever, sharing intimate moments that she hadn't expected to ever have happen. She had made love only a few times in her life, but never with anyone like him. She trembled with need and with wanting, more than she would have ever dreamed possible. She intended to seize the moment and make a memory that she would always have.

Shifting, he moved to caress her ankles, stroking, trailing his tongue slowly over her, kissing her as he moved up between her legs, running his tongue lightly on her inner thigh, making her writhe and want him more than ever. Her hands lightly drifted over his muscled thighs, higher over his hard butt and his narrow waist. His strong body was a marvel to her and she hoped to excite him as much as he excited her.

Arching her hips against him, she did what she could to give him more access, wanting to be touched more deeply.

Trailing kisses along her thigh, he moved higher while his fingers caressed her between her legs, stroking her, creating tension that built as she arched her back and thrust her hips against his hand.

Shifting her legs over his shoulders, he had access to her and ran his tongue over her. She gasped and cried out with pleasure, straining against him. "Gabe, please," she cried. All her focus was on wanting him inside her.

They shifted and she sat up, getting on her knees. When she looked into his eyes, her heart pounded. Eagerly, she wrapped her arms around him and kissed him passionately, pouring out her hunger for all of him. She trailed her hands over him and then leaned away to pull him down on the bed.

Trying to excite him as he had her, she lightly stroked him while running her tongue along his throat, across his chest, down over his belly and then along his thick rod. Holding his hard shaft, she kissed him while her other hand drifted between his legs, stroking him, toying so lightly with him and making him writhe beneath her touch. He gasped and tangled his fingers in her hair while letting her continue to pleasure him.

With another groan, he sat up to kiss her passionately, his hands cupping her breasts. He shifted, kissing her ear and whispering, "You don't know what you do to me. You're gorgeous, so incredibly sexy."

He leaned down to kiss first one breast and then the other, running his tongue over the taut peaks. One hand held her breast as the other hand went between her legs to stroke her.

She moaned with pleasure, trying to caress him in return. He paused to step off the bed and retrieve his jeans. Digging out a billfold, he returned to put on a condom.

Watching him, her heart raced. Exuding energy, he was every inch a strong, handsome, exciting man. She parted her legs, arching her back, eager for him as he came down to kiss her and press her back to the bed.

He entered her slowly, in control while he thrust in her and then almost withdrew. She gasped and cried out, pulling him closer as electrifying pleasure streaked through her. He filled her, still going slowly, building her excitement and desire. She gasped, wanting him, trying to pull his hips closer as he withdrew slightly again and was still, need making her desperate for him. She wrapped her long legs around him and pulled him closer while he again thrust slowly into her.

"Gabe, I want you inside me, all of you," she whispered, running her hands over him and raising her hips to meet him.

He thrust deeper, withdrawing slowly and then moving faster while she cried out and clung to him. In seconds he pumped faster, building her need.

She clung tightly to him, her legs locked around him as finally he let go of his control and pumped hard and fast. Her world was sensation and need that tore at her until she cried out with pleasure.

Release burst in a climax, her pounding heart shutting out other sounds as they still rocked wildly together, and then he shuddered with his own climax, taking her to another one. Pleasure spilled over her and she dug her hands into his buttocks as she moved with him.

Hot and damp, she gradually slowed while still gasping for breath. She held him tightly in her arms, her legs still clasped around him, both of them still united, and for this moment they were one.

Joy filled her as much as physical satisfaction. She embraced him tightly, still tingling and satiated. For this moment in time, she didn't want to let him go. Holding him pressed against her heart with their bodies joined, she wanted to keep him close for a while longer and not have to think beyond the moment.

Her breathing and her pounding heart were beginning to return to normal. Gabe turned his head to shower light kisses on her face and throat. While he did, she ran her fingers down his smooth back and over his buttocks, down on his muscled thighs, feeling the short curly hairs on his thighs against her palms.

Her hands came up again, traveling over him, and she tangled her fingers in his hair at the back of his head.

He rose up slightly to look into her eyes. "You were right. We're awesome together," he said solemnly. His usual joking and humor had disappeared as he looked at her intently.

"I keep catching you looking at me as if you have never seen me before in your life," she said softly.

"I wonder if I have. Your kisses blow me away. Making love is the best. I'm reeling in shock again. You did it with your first kiss. You stunned me again with your makeover. This is the third big surprise."

Smiling, she ran her fingers lightly along his jaw, feeling the short stubble. "It was fantastic. I don't quite have the experience you do to make comparisons, but sometimes you know something's special without having to compare it to anything else."

He turned on his side, holding her close so they faced each other. Their legs were entwined, their arms wrapped around each other.

She reached up to comb unruly locks of black hair off his forehead with her fingers. "It's crazy to think I just had the best sex of my life with my best friend in the whole wide world. I think my best friend should be female, but we won't tell anyone." She laughed and he did, too. "I know I'll always be able to count on you. You can count on me. If you need me, you let me know."

"I may need you again tonight," he said, grinding himself against her.

She smiled. "That wasn't what I was referring to."

"You know, I suspect when the dust settles, I'm going to discover that you've complicated my life beyond belief."

She shook her head. "I will do no such thing. Soon you'll say goodbye and you'll call and keep in touch."

"That might not happen quite as soon as you think."

"It'll happen when we can call off our fake engagement—which I think may be sooner than the end of the month. My mom got it. I'm sure Justin will be so furious that he'll stop pursuing me in spite of all his dad's offers. With that stupid old feud between our families, my parents will certainly be happy that I didn't marry you. They don't know how adorable you are." She tweaked his nose. "Back when we were little and you were at our house a lot, my mother and grandmother thought you were adorable, so I don't think they really dislike you as much as they dislike your dad."

"Frankly, I hope you're right. I really don't like to get blamed for things he's done."

Gabe pulled her close to hold her and she nestled against him.

"Tonight, I want you to stay right here with me," he said.

"It's where I want to be also," she said, smiling. "I'll stay tonight."

"I'm thinking," he mused aloud. "Maybe we shouldn't go back to Dallas until Wednesday."

"We should stick to our original plan. We go back

Tuesday and announce our engagement. I'll be staying at your house so it won't matter whether we're on the ranch or in Dallas, unless you have something pressing here."

"No, I don't. I just don't have as many interruptions here and I really don't want interruptions—or to share you with anyone."

"That's nice," she said, drawing her fingers over his shoulder and bicep, down along his arm. "You'll have to share me because I have a business to run," she pointed out. "We need to go out Tuesday night and that's when we'll get engaged and tell everyone. But when we go back to Dallas, I'll be staying at your house."

"So far, that's the best part of this plan," he said, winding long locks of blond curls around his fingers and letting them fall to pick them up again. His fingers lightly brushed her ear, every contact making her tingle.

"Later in the week or over the weekend, take a day so we can come back to the ranch. I want you to myself. You can get a day off because you own the business. Better still, take a couple of days off so we can be uninterrupted." He nuzzled her neck while he ran his fingers across her narrow waist then drifted lower, until she caught his hand and placed it at her waist again.

"Let me catch my breath," she said. She nestled against him, loving the feel of his arms around her, enjoying being with him, talking, touching and kissing each other. It was an idyll that would end when the fake engagement ended.

"This will be a big week in my life," she said. "It already is a big week because I'm here in bed with you. I think by the end of the week I'll be ready to take a day or two off. That's probably a good idea in a lot of ways."

"I think it's a fantastic idea, darlin'. A day we both need."

She smiled. "You don't *need* any such thing," she said. "It's a day we both want."

"Oh, I need you, Meg. You're special in my life," he said, his words warming her all over.

"How I wish that were true, Gabe, but I know better."

After a moment, during which time she continued stroking his back and winding her fingers in his hair, she said, "I've been thinking. I'm sorry that this is going to hurt my family, but they've pushed me into a corner trying to get me to marry someone I don't love."

"By this time next year you won't give any of that much thought, so don't worry too much about it now." He looked into her eyes, making her heart skip a beat, before he leaned closer to kiss her.

She wound her arms around his neck and kissed him back, their tongues stroking, hot and wet, each touch making her want to make love again. She held him tightly, enjoying being happy in his arms and refusing to think about the future. In minutes he rolled on his back and lifted her on top of him. She kissed him, sitting astride him.

As he fondled her breasts, making her need him again, she felt him harden beneath her. In minutes, each knowing when the other was ready, she rose up, then eased down on him. As he entered her, she closed her eyes and threw her head back, riding him as he bucked beneath her.

He thrust slowly, making her moan with pleasure as he fondled her breasts. She pumped with him, moving faster, tension and need building with her until she could not contain it.

When she climaxed, she cried out. Thrusting faster,

he reached his climax. Then, finally, she fell on top of him. She held him and turned her head to kiss him, feathery kisses along his shoulder, his neck and his jaw.

Exhausted but well sated, she was held against him. Their bodies were hot, damp from exertion. She smiled and toyed with the unruly locks of hair that fell on his forehead. "Do you ever run out of energy? I can't move. But I'm so happy."

"Darlin', you can't imagine how happy I am," he said, running his hand lightly over her bare back. "And if I have some extra energy, it's because I'm with you and you tease it out of me. You're beautiful. I want you here in my arms the rest of the day and night. Don't get out of bed."

She smiled. "Ridiculous man."

"I used to give you marbles or chocolate to bribe you to get you to do what I wanted. How can I bribe you to stay in this bed with me all day?"

"Promise me we can touch and feel and kiss all day," she answered in a sultry whisper while she ran her tongue over his ear.

He groaned, crushed her against his chest and kissed her hard. She wrapped her arms around him to kiss him in return.

Finally, she pushed against him, putting some space between them. He gave her a questioning look and she placed her hand on his jaw. "Hold it, cowboy. You're going to wear me to a frazzle and I think we missed some eating along the way."

"I'd like to eat you up," he whispered, kissing her throat.

"Whoa. Do you hear my stomach with a rebuttal? I would like to have dinner. We have been in this bed almost the whole time since we got here and my stomach is definitely hungry."

"Let me feel and see what I think," he said, rolling her over beside him so he could lightly rub her stomach.

When his hand dipped a little too low, she slipped out of bed and walked completely naked to the bathroom.

As she showered, she thought about Gabe. In a few days she would be engaged to him. And in a few days she would be telling her family. She dreaded it, because doing so would cause a firestorm of arguments.

She refused to let those fears bring her down, so she turned her thoughts to Gabe and their lovemaking that only made her want him more than ever. She was lost in memories of the past few hours. Because she was wrapped in euphoria from making love it was hard to know the extent of her feelings and how much they had shifted after becoming intimate with him. All she really did know was that she couldn't wait for tonight, when she got to share his bed and do it all again.

It was Tuesday when they returned to Dallas. Gabe drove and listened to Meg babbling about their plans. She was excited, bubbling with so much eagerness she could barely sit still. She'd called home and talked for almost an hour to her mother on Sunday, so her mother knew she'd been visiting Gabe's ranch and they were returning to Dallas today so she could go to work.

Filled with mixed feelings, Gabe thought about them as he drove. Early in the morning he had stirred while Meg was still asleep. He still wanted to look at her constantly because she was gorgeous. That wasn't all that'd had him staring at her while she slept. She was the most exciting woman to kiss and the most sensual and sexy in bed. Just thinking about it now could get him aroused and he took a deep breath, trying to focus on what she was saying and on watching the road as he drove.

He had a strange feeling that he might be getting in over his head. He hadn't ever had a woman in his life like her. She came into his life like a whirlwind and he suspected she might leave it the same way—with his life in a shambles when she was gone. He didn't want commitment and he couldn't commit to anything with her because they really weren't compatible when it came to lifestyles.

Frustrated when he hit some traffic, he wished he wasn't in the car. This long drive was ridiculous. She just needed to get on a plane and find out how easy it was to fly to Dallas from his ranch or to the ranch from Dallas, but she wouldn't fly.

She had turned his life inside out. He had never missed anyone after breaking up with them but he had mixed feelings about telling Meg goodbye at the end of the month. After these past few days he would miss her in his bed and in his life, but he would be glad to get his life back. And get back to ranching. He had taken her to see his prize bull yesterday. She had taken one quick look, shuddered and told him that was all she wanted to see of his livestock.

Despite that, for right now, he wanted every moment he could get with her and he wanted her in his bed and in his arms. She dazzled him in so many ways. She had certainly changed as she had grown up. She was so much more confident, self-sufficient, and she had a zest for life that amazed him. He couldn't imagine her family trying to push her into marriage, but he could understand Justin wanting to marry her.

Tonight Gabe wanted to do something special. It

wasn't a real engagement, and tonight wouldn't be a real proposal, but she deserved something special. Something that was just between them and had nothing to do with the goofy fake engagement. Something that told her it was great to be with her again even though he wasn't totally thrilled to admit that she excited him more than any other woman he had ever known.

Her looks still blew him away. She didn't seem to give them much thought, but that didn't change her beauty. He suspected at some point in time she would revert back to her grade school hairdo and drop the makeup. But he would be attracted to her no matter which way she dressed.

Because of their differences in lifestyles and outlooks, if she hadn't been desperate for his help, she never would have gone out with him. That might have been mutual because he wouldn't have asked her out, either. Funny how that worked out, he thought.

Soon they would part, but before they did, he wanted to make her happy. Starting with tonight.

She poked his thigh with her finger. "Are you listening to me?"

Amused, he grinned. "Sorry. I was thinking about this morning in bed and thinking about you. What were you telling me?"

"For just a few minutes, get your mind out of the bedroom."

"I'll try, but it isn't easy after some time in there with you."

She smiled and blew him a kiss, making him laugh.

"I was just reviewing the plan to announce our engagement this week," she told him.

"I want you to be absolutely sure that's still what you want because it will upset your folks."

"Stop worrying. I want the announcement."

He glanced at her and she smiled sweetly while nodding at him, making him laugh again.

Her car was at her house, so he dropped her there and got out to walk her to her door.

"You don't need to come with me," she said, stepping out of his car.

"Oh, yes, I do," he answered, taking her arm and inhaling her exotic new perfume.

She unlocked her back door and they stepped into her tiny entryway. He closed the door and turned to take her into his arms. Her brown eyes widened as she looked up in obvious surprise, which lasted one second before her arms wrapped around his waist and she gave in to his kiss.

She was soft, sweet, giving him the sexiest kisses of his life, and he wanted to carry her to bed now. He raised his head. "Go to work later."

Her eyes were heavy lidded and she tightened her arm around his waist and pulled him close again. His mouth covered hers and as he kissed her, he picked her up, carrying her to a bedroom.

It was three hours before he stood at her back door again. "I'll pick you up at seven and tonight you're staying at my house."

All she wore was a blue bath towel, which she pulled tight around her as she nodded.

"You look too good to leave," he said.

"You go. You're taking my whole day and I have to go to my office. Goodbye."

He wiped his brow and took one more long look at her. "If you drop that towel, I won't be able to leave."

"I'm not dropping it and you go now. The door will

lock behind you." She turned and left, stepping out of sight through a door into her kitchen.

He left and went to his car to drive to his house. He wanted her constantly. He expected that to wear off as it always did, but right now, he couldn't stop thinking about her and wanting to be with her.

At his house he fished out the fake ring she had given him and turned it in his hand. It was a beautiful ring and at a glance looked impressive and real. Yesterday he had phoned his florist and ordered flowers sent to her office so the flowers would be there when she arrived today. If Justin dropped into her office, he would see the flowers and probably find out who had sent them.

Gabe wanted to surprise her about tonight and had made reservations at an elegant steak house. On short notice he'd needed to call in some favors to get a reservation. The place had great steaks, the perfect ambience and there would be people they knew who would see them together—the essential requirement for Meg to consider the evening a success. He smiled and placed the ring back in the velvet box.

Soon Meg would be gone out of his life. He wasn't ready for that yet and hoped he could talk her into continuing to date for a while longer.

He suspected she would not. She was afraid of falling in love with the wrong guy and he assumed the minute this engagement was over, she would disappear out of his life.

If she did, he would have to live with that. Sooner or later he knew they would say goodbye, but he'd rather keep her around longer. She was incredible in bed—instantly responsive and eager, filled with energy, wanting him and trying to please him as much as he pleased her.

He left to go to his office, the tall building he shared with Cade in their commercial real estate business, but on the way he made a stop to get a present for her for the evening.

For the rest of the day he had the hardest time concentrating on work. All he could think about was Meg. He couldn't wait to get her to dinner, give her the ring and then get her back to the privacy of his house, where he wanted to make love to her all night long. Their time together was limited and he intended to make the most of it before they said goodbye.

At the end of the month or whenever they parted, would it bother him to tell her goodbye? It never had with anyone else, so maybe it wouldn't with Meg. Besides, she had a way of bouncing back into his life.

He put away his papers, closed up and left his office. While he couldn't wait to see her, this fake engagement was playing hell with his life. But it had given him Meg in his bed and that was definitely worth all the trouble she had caused him. How much more delight and trouble would tonight bring?

Nine

Meg heard her doorbell and rushed through her small house. She glanced in the mirror at herself again, looking at a red dress with a full skirt that came to her knees. Her sleeveless top had a vee neckline. She wore high-heeled red sandals and her hair fell loosely on either side of her face. Tonight she would get engaged to marry Gabe. The thought took her breath away even though she was totally aware it was a fake. After tonight she and Gabe would be bound together in the eyes of her family and the town. She wavered between excitement, even though it was fake, and worry that it would draw her closer to him, closer to falling in love if she wasn't already doing that. They were not suited for each other and neither one could change their lifestyle. She couldn't suddenly start flying and loving it, riding on his Harley—what a thought. She would be terrified. Gabe complicated her life in one way, but he had brought her freedom in another and he was a great guy. Whatever their future, tonight excited her and she couldn't wait.

She opened the door and drew a deep breath as she looked up at Gabe in his broad-brimmed black hat, his navy Western suit and tailor-made white shirt. He looked so handsome, she wanted to pull him inside, close the door, step into his arms and make love all night long.

Instead, she had to stick to the program they had agreed on for the evening. She smiled at him. "Hi, my handsome, irresistible cowboy," she said in a sultry voice.

"Oh, damn. I'm taking you to dinner when all I want to do is take you to bed."

Should she tell him she had the same thought? Should she tell him she wanted the same thing? His eyes were practically singeing her skin as they raked her over from head to toe.

His voice turned huskier when he said, "You know, darlin', we can skip dinner—"

She interrupted before he went any further. "No, we can't. We're going to stick to the script for tonight. We go out to eat where we can be seen and you propose. I accept and we have a fake engagement. We go see my parents and show them the ring. I call Justin and then we're free to do whatever you want, my strong cowboy."

"I'm not sure I can wait that long."

She laughed. "Yes, you can. Let's go get this show on the road. This is the night doors fly open and I walk out of Justin's life forever. We're both better off."

"I have to agree with that one. I'd hate to have to bribe someone to marry me." He pulled out his phone. "Stand still. I want one picture of you looking so beautiful, and then one with me." He took them quickly and put away his phone. "I'll pull those out on cold, empty nights and remember what fun I had with you."

"Oh, right. Like you have so many empty nights." She smiled at him, then locked up and started toward the car.

He took her arm and wrapped it around his. "Darlin', I'll be counting the minutes until I can get you in my arms and out of that gorgeous red dress."

"You really do have a one-track mind, don't you?" But she couldn't deny his words thrilled her.

He gave her a devilish smile as he held the car door open for her. "Don't you love it?"

"What I love is that bouquet you sent me. It was beautiful, gigantic. The flowers almost fill up my office. Roses, tulips, daisies, big white lilies, gladiola, baby's breath and freesias. And right in the middle of all the beautiful flowers was a new brown teddy bear," she said, laughing as he got in beside her. "That was the part that really got to me. That cute little bear. I'll thank you properly when we get home."

"Excellent. That's what I aimed for. That and to help get a message to Justin if he came to your office."

"They said he did drop by and he did see the bouquet. He left and never came back or called. I think he has the message and is acting on it. You darling man," she said, blowing him kisses.

He pretended to catch them and pull them close to his heart, his face taking on an exaggerated moue of passion while his eyebrows jumped.

She couldn't help but laugh.

"Gabe, you're still fun. I always thought you were amusing when we were kids. You still are. Handsome, too," she said. Actually, she'd go so far as to say he was the most handsome man she knew. As they pulled away from her street, she let her gaze run over his profile. Oh, yes, he was that. And she couldn't deny she wanted the evening to be over and to be home, his place or hers, and in his arms.

"I could say the same about you, Meg," he said. "I just had no idea the talents you would have when you grew up. I should have taken you out way before now."

"You wouldn't have had the same results, so don't fill yourself with regrets."

"It's those 'results' I'm looking forward to." As he slowed for a light, he shot her a smoldering glance that nearly set her on fire. "If not for your plan I would turn this car around and take you home and spend the evening the best way possible." He grabbed the gearshift.

She stilled his hand. "But you're not going to do that, because this is the most essential part of my plan."

Reluctantly, he kept the car in Drive and moved forward.

Minutes later they were pulling into the best restaurant in town.

"Here we are," Gabe said, turning onto a winding drive on broad, landscaped grounds. Ponds with fountains flanked the road, as well as tall oaks and willows.

Twinkling lights covered the red crepe myrtles at the entrance with the sun still above the horizon. A valet took the car and Meg entered on Gabe's arm.

It was dim inside, and she heard a violin playing in the background. The maître d' met them and led them to a table overlooking a sloping backyard of more tall trees, statues and fountains, with a creek running across the green grounds.

Candlelight flickered in the hurricane lamp on the table beside a crystal vase with four red and pink roses.

It was perfect. The place, the setting, the man. If she ever really did get engaged, this was the place she wanted it to happen.

For the first time, she felt a niggling pain in the area around her heart. *Remember, Meg, it's all pretend.*

"Give me your hand," he said, placing his hand on the gold linen tablecloth.

She forced a smile and looked up at him as she gave him her hand.

He tilted his head as he watched her. "Why the solemn look?"

"You're too observant for my own good, you know that?" Then again, nobody knew her as well as Gabe. She should have known she wouldn't be able to keep her feelings a secret from him. "It's nothing really. Just that…well, someday you're going to do this for real and she's going to be a lucky woman. You're a nice guy, Gabe."

"Thank you. But you sound as if you think it'll never happen for you. I promise you that someday a man will be asking to marry you for real. Darlin', you'll have so many great guys wanting to take you out the minute I get out of this picture. In less than a month you'll be having the time of your life." He smiled at her.

But she didn't smile back.

Gabe ordered champagne and when their waiter left, Gabe raised his crystal flute. "Here's to success in your endeavor that brought us back together for a very wonderful, unforgettable time."

"Thank you." She touched his flute with hers as she looked into his blue eyes in the flickering candlelight. Their glasses had a melodic ring when they touched.

Still watching him, sharing the moment, she sipped the bubbly, pale yellow champagne. A moment later she made a toast of her own. "Here's to you, Gabe Callahan, for being the cowboy to the lady's rescue, even though you didn't ride in on a white horse." As she sipped her champagne, once again she felt a squeeze to her heart. She had no future of any sort with Gabe. This had been a task to accomplish and he had nearly accomplished it, and they really were almost finished. The month would soon be over and they would go their separate ways. Gabe was great in so many ways, but he was definitely no more the man for her than she was the woman for him.

They touched glasses again and she took another sip as Gabe reached down and pulled a long black box out of his jacket pocket. It was tied with a blue silk bow. He placed it in the middle of the table.

"I know we have things we'll do tonight while we're here. This isn't one you had scheduled in. This one I planned." He swallowed and looked up at her. "This has been a special time, Meg. We've been the best of friends and together off and on through the years. Now we're not only friends, we're intimate, and that's a change to a deeper relationship that holds more importance. To make sure you'll remember the moment and know that it was important to me, here's a keepsake for you. When you wear that, think of me."

"But, Gabe, you sent flowers and another teddy bear. I don't need more presents."

He pushed the box closer to her. "Please."

Curious, she picked it up and untied the blue silk bow and opened the box. She gasped as she looked at the necklace resting on black velvet. Small diamonds formed the necklace, leading to a pendant that was a large sparkling diamond surrounded by alternating diamonds and emeralds.

She looked up at him. "Gabe, this is spectacular. It's beautiful."

"It's for you, and when we're home tonight I'll put it on you."

"I can't wait. I've never had anything like this. It's magnificent." She reached out and squeezed his hand. "Thank you."

"Whatever the future brings, Meg, we have a history that goes way back and you've been important in my life. You got me through some rough times. I wanted you to have something special."

"It's fabulous, Gabe. Thank you." She glanced down at the necklace and then back up to him. "I can't do much more than keep saying 'thank you' as long as we're in public here."

"You'll get your chance to thank me when we get back to my place. You can wait till then for me to put your necklace on you. Or you can come over here and sit on my lap and I'll fasten it for you."

Smiling, she shook her head. She didn't trust herself to sit on his lap right now. She gazed at him, taking in every inch of his beautiful face, thinking of how exciting he was, how good he was to her. Why did they have to be so opposite in lifestyles?

Their waiter came to take orders and as soon as he left, she turned to Gabe.

Raising her flute, she gazed into his blue eyes. "Here's a big thank-you to my very best friend for all my life." Smiling, she touched her flute to his and sipped her champagne as their waiter brought green salads on crystal plates.

The meal, like the place, was perfection. They both had rib eyes, sweet potatoes with pecans, and fluffy biscuits drizzled with honey.

It was after dinner as they sipped Irish coffee that Gabe got out another smaller box tied with a red satin ribbon.

"The time has come," he said after he glanced around the dining room. "You said you wanted a lot of people to see us so it gets back to Justin—well, watch this move. I'm betting this will blow up social media and Justin will see it within the hour."

She smiled, watching Gabe get up. As if on cue, the violin player strolled in their direction, playing a sweet ballad. He stopped several feet away from Gabe, who handed the box to her. As he did, she looked into his blue eyes and her heart pounded even though these actions were following a script she'd written.

Suddenly she saw this as a big moment, and one that made her feel as if her life were about to change, all because of the next few minutes.

"Open your present."

She smiled at the drama Gabe was adding to their plan. The quiet restaurant had grown even quieter and she realized they had an audience. He was right. Comments and pictures would fly on social media.

She untied the ribbon, glancing up at Gabe, whose blue eyes twinkled with mischief. She raised the lid, expecting to see the ring she had purchased. Instead a smaller black box was inside the bigger box. Unbuttoning his jacket, Gabe took that box as she looked up at him expectantly. He opened the box, tossed the lid on the table, removed the dazzling fake diamond she had selected herself and knelt on one knee in front of her to take her hand. She looked at his well-shaped hands as they held hers and she felt her heart seize.

The violin player stepped closer, still playing sweetly.

"Megan Louise Aldridge," Gabe said loudly enough

for his voice to carry, "will you make me, Gabriel Callahan, the luckiest man in the world? Will you marry me?"

She couldn't help it. For this one moment in time, she suddenly wished the diamond was real, this proposal was real. Gabe was her best friend. He was the most exciting lover possible. He was handsome and intelligent, caring and kind. For just an instant, she wished that his words were sincere and their lives would be joined forever. Wished she would be Mrs. Gabe Callahan. She saw it all playing out in front of her. The wedding, and a lifetime of happiness.

Then, just as quickly, the lovely images faded away.

She could never have a permanent relationship with Gabe. She could never live with a wild risk-taker, never love someone whose safety she would be in constant fear for.

Then she realized Gabe, as well as their audience, was waiting for her answer.

"Yes. Oh, yes, Gabe," she said, as he slipped the ring on her finger. He stood up, holding her wrist as she rose, and drew her to him to kiss her. Their audience clapped while the violin player broke into a snappy rendition of Mendelssohn's "Wedding March."

She barely heard it, because though the proposal hadn't been real, his kiss was. She held him as tightly as he held her and for a few seconds she forgot where she was or what was happening. All she knew was she was in Gabe's arms and he was kissing her as thoroughly as she was kissing him.

When she stepped back, she met his gaze. The spell was broken by the resounding applause and a couple of whistles. The violinist continued playing "Wedding March" as Gabe held her hand, and they bowed and smiled at the diners before sitting down again and letting quiet return to the restaurant.

"Gabe, let's go. You've already paid the waiter. I want to leave."

"You're not going to get to leave for a little while longer," he said. "Here come some people we know, and they probably want to congratulate us. Let's just hope everyone in the restaurant doesn't decide to wish us well."

"Oh, my gracious," she said, smiling as friends came to congratulate them.

The minute the last person left, Meg picked up her purse and present and the boxes. "Gabe, we have to get out of here. We've posed for pictures, and people took pictures of us when you proposed. There were probably people who even got videos of it. Our families will know about this. Justin will know before we can tell anyone."

"This worked out to be a little more of a response than I had envisioned in this quiet, staid, expensive restaurant. I'm ready, darlin'." He stood up, came around to pull out her chair. "They're probably all thinking we're going somewhere to make love. How I wish."

"Come on, let's go."

They walked out together and as soon as she was in the car, she called her mother. "Mom, can Gabe and I come by the house? I have some news."

Meg listened a moment. "We'll see you in about half an hour," she said, thinking about how long it would take. "See you then." She ended the call.

"They hadn't heard?" Gabe asked.

"No. My folks aren't on social media. Let's go tell them we're engaged."

"I hope your dad doesn't slug me."

"My father would never do any such thing."

Gabe smiled. "I really didn't think he would, but he is not going to like this and your mom isn't, either. And I hope it doesn't give your poor grandparents fainting spells when you call them."

"Stop being a pessimist."

Gabe shook his head. "I know one thing. Your folks won't hug me and say, 'Welcome to the family.'"

While Gabe watched traffic, he dreaded facing her folks and announcing they were engaged. Even though he'd agreed to this situation, it went against living an honest life. Meg's folks should never have tried to push her into a loveless marriage. She was too loving and full of life to settle for a guy who was marrying her solely to get a promotion in his dad's firm.

He heard her phone ring and glanced over at her as she checked the screen.

"Well, Justin must have seen a picture of us because this call is from him. I might as well talk to him about it now."

Gabe wondered if Justin had already heard about his proposal and was angry about what was happening, but he didn't care to hear her conversation.

"Seriously?" she gasped. "Seriously? You mean that?" She sounded so shocked Gabe glanced at her to see her staring at him wide-eyed with her mouth hanging open and her face pale.

Wondering if someone had died in Justin's family, Gabe signaled and once again got off the freeway and into a residential area where he parked.

"When did this happen?" she asked.

Now Gabe wished he had told her to put the call

on speaker. Something had happened to someone in Justin's family. Hopefully Justin was all right himself.

"I'm shocked. I wish you the very best. I really mean that. I hope you're so happy and that everything good comes your way."

Gabe stared at her, trying to guess what Justin was going to do that had her wishing him the best. His curiosity grew and he wondered what had happened and how it would affect her.

"Thank you, Justin. That's nice of you. Yes, we'll do that sometime. Tell your family hello and I'm thrilled for you, for all of you." She nodded as Justin must have been talking. "Sure. I'll see you then for sure. Congratulations. I'm so happy for both of you. Goodbye."

She turned to Gabe, but he wondered whether she saw him or not.

"I can't believe what he just told me," she said, sounding dazed. She focused on Gabe and he waited patiently. "Justin is engaged. He's getting married. He's engaged to Pamela Gatersen. They went together all their senior year in college and then went to different law schools. They just got back together and it was a whirlwind courtship and everything worked out perfectly. He sounded as if he had won the lottery. They'll have a Christmas wedding and travel around the world for a honeymoon."

Gabe knew of her. "Her dad owns Gatersen Equipment, which is a nationwide company—heavy-duty stuff, tractors, backhoes, trucks. Hon, she probably has way more money in her family than you do in yours and that seems to be highly important to Justin."

"I'm in shock. I didn't expect that. He sounded so happy to tell me."

"I imagine he is because you've given him grief.

He must have wished you well, though. I heard you thank him."

"He did. He said, 'Best wishes for a happy life with your cowboy,'" she said, smiling at Gabe.

"Think he heard about my proposal?"

She nodded. "Yes, he did. He has us to thank for getting him out of a loveless marriage."

She looked at Gabe. "This lets you off the hook, too. We don't have to announce our fake engagement now. You can have your life back, and peace and quiet."

"Don't be so hasty. We're going to see your folks. What about them?"

"Right. I'll call and tell Mom about Justin and say that was what I was going to tell her, but it isn't necessary to drop by. Let me call them now."

She made the call and as soon as she finished, she turned to him. "That was quick and easy, and Mom is happy for Justin, and for me since that was what I wanted. I'll talk to my dad next time I'm home."

Gabe took her hand in his, and he looked her deep in the eyes. "Come home with me tonight, Meg. Don't change tonight."

Before she could answer, Meg felt as if she'd been hit by a truck. Out of nowhere the thought entered her head. She couldn't believe she hadn't realized the problem right away.

"Oh, Gabe. What about your proposal in the restaurant?"

He shook his head. "Damn, that backfired, I guess. Justin's engaged and so am I."

"No, you're not. I'll just tell people we aren't getting married. I can tell my friends that my folks were pressuring me into a marriage and you did that to get me out of being pushed into one. It'll blow over with to-morrow's news. And your family already knows what the situation is. Mine might hear the rumors, but I'll tell them not to worry."

"True enough. So that's that, I guess." Gabe started up the car and pulled back onto the freeway.

"I think I owe Justin one for getting me back with you for a little while. It's been fun hanging out again, Meg."

She was deep in thought about this being her last night with him. Gabe had come back into her life and been all the great things he had been when they were kids, plus all the wonderful things he was now.

She twisted the big dazzling ring on her finger.

She smiled at him and placed her hand on his thigh, feeling his warmth through his trousers. Once again, she was struck by what a kind man Gabe had grown up to be.

She agreed to go to his house. Gabe was right. There was no reason to change that part of their plans.

Once he closed his front door behind her, he took her into his arms to kiss her.

"I want to put on my necklace," she told him when she stepped away.

"Sure," he said, pausing. "Get it out and I'll put it on you."

She opened the box to look at the dazzling necklace again. "Gabe, this is magnificent. I've never had anything like it. It's so beautiful."

"Good. I'm glad you like it." He picked it up and stepped behind her, scooping up her long locks to lift them out of the way. "Hold your hair up for me," he said. He bent to fasten the clasp and the safety and then he trailed kisses on her nape.

Gasping, she closed her eyes and stood for a moment, relishing his kisses before she dropped her hair and turned, putting her arms around Gabe's neck, standing on tiptoe and kissing him.

His strong arms banded her and held her tightly while he kissed her in return and made her heart pound. She could hardly believe this was the night she would tell him goodbye. After tonight Gabe would disappear out of her life again and she wouldn't see him, except for possibly some social events around Dallas. The knowledge hurt and she wondered how important he had become to her. Had she fallen in love with him? She didn't have to search deeply to know the answer was yes. And she was going to hurt badly when she told him goodbye.

Ten

Running her hands over Gabe's body, Meg wanted to kiss every inch of him. In her heart she was certain this was goodbye. There was no reason to stay now and every time they made love it bound her more closely to him and made him more important to her.

The longer she stayed, the more difficult it would be to leave. And maybe the more in love with him she would be.

Regardless, she wanted tonight with Gabe.

But what if he asked her to stay longer? Would she stay?

She couldn't. If she did, she would never want to leave him. Gabe had been her best friend as a child and growing up—he was still her best friend in too many ways.

Running her hands over him, she pushed away his jacket and let it fall. She twisted the buttons on his tailored white shirt free, taking out the gold cuff links he wore and dropping them in his trouser pocket while they continued to kiss.

She looked up at him. "I'm going to miss you."

"I'm not gone," he said. "Not yet." He tangled his fingers in her hair, tugged lightly to tilt her head back and then kissed her, his tongue stroking her lower lip, the corners of her mouth, before going deep with slow thrusts that made her hot, made her want him.

She unfastened his trousers to free him. Unbuckling his belt, she pushed away the trousers and briefs and he stepped out of them, yanking off his boots and socks.

He had already pulled down the zipper at the back of her dress and it fell around her ankles. He held her away from him while his gaze roamed over her and his hands followed.

"You're so incredibly beautiful. I want to look at you and touch you all night. I want you in my arms, your naked body against mine all night. I want everything, Meg. You'll never know how much I want you."

As he looked at her, she studied him, tingling at the sight of his strong, virile male body. He was fully aroused, ready to love. He was tan, fit, all hard muscles and flat planes. She knelt to caress him, running her hands between his legs along his inner thighs and taking his thick shaft in hand to stroke and run her tongue over him.

He tangled his fingers in her hair again, groaning quietly, his throbbing manhood dark and hard.

With a harsh cry, he slipped his hands beneath her arms to pull her slowly to her feet. She rubbed against him while his hands roamed over her and she showered kisses over him. Her hands traveled across his belly and down his legs, moving in feathery caresses all over him.

Finally, he picked her up and carried her to the nearest bedroom, tossing back covers and placing her on the bed, coming down to hold her close.

She loved him with abandon, kissing him and knowing it was the last time, memorizing how he looked and felt, and exciting him until he shook.

She did everything she could to pleasure him, to give him a night he would remember, lovemaking that would be important to him and intimacy that he couldn't forget. Her hands were everywhere over him, touching, stroking and teasing while she showered kisses on him, rubbing and caressing him and letting him do what he wanted to her.

With a groan, he stilled her hands and moved between her legs, pausing to put on a condom before he lowered himself and entered her in one thrust.

She locked her legs around him and held him while they kissed. They drew out their lovemaking, rising to a brink and falling back, then rising again until she could take no more. She gasped and clung to him, crying out when his control went and they climaxed together, hard and fast.

Exhausted and euphoric, they held each other. He stroked her lightly, his hand caressing her, moving over her. "You're marvelous, every inch of you," he whispered, showering light kisses on her temple, her cheek, her ear and her throat. He gently combed long strands of hair from her face with his fingers.

"Meg, I want you to stay. Stay this month."

While she felt a pang and longing enveloped her, she shook her head.

"I can't do that, Gabe. I'd be so in love I could never leave. The month would end and we would be right back where we are now."

"Stay this week then. That's not long and you won't fall in love in the few days left in the week."

She ran her hands over him. She lay pressed against him, her leg thrown over his while her hands continued to roam over him. She couldn't tell him that she was already in love with him. "No. You have your life and your things you like to do. I have my work that I need to get back to. I can't be casual about lovemaking. Physical love for me is still all tied up with my emotions and my heart."

"You always were sentimental. I guess that's why you still have that silly brown bear I gave you so long ago."

"I suppose." She turned on her side to face him. "I want you to know that this has been special, Gabe. You did a good job and saved the day for me. You gave me that beautiful necklace. You're the one who should get a present because you did just what I asked."

"This is my present, Meg, holding you in my arms, loving you all night, kissing you. Will you go to dinner with me next Friday?"

She looked down a moment while she twisted her fingers in his chest hair. Finally, she shook her head. "No, I don't think I should, because you'll want me to come back here and sleep with you and I'm not going to continue to do that."

"If you change your mind, call me," he said, looking solemn.

"I will. I haven't looked in the mirror at my beautiful necklace that I'm still wearing. I'm going to do that, then shower and get dressed and go home to Downly. We'll say goodbye."

"I'm going to miss you."

"No, you won't. You'll find a pretty lady who will be fun and you'll forget all about me."

She rolled over, wrapping the top sheet around her and stepping out of bed to go shower. "See you in a few minutes." She left, letting out her breath. She wanted to say yes to every question he asked her. She wanted to stay the rest of the month. She wanted to stay tonight. But anything more she did with him would bind her to him just that much more. She was in love with him. In the past it had been friendship and that had been all, but this time together had been different from the moment they first kissed. She wondered if she'd fallen in love with him right then.

She dressed in jeans, a red knit shirt and boots. When she stepped into the hall he was waiting. He crossed the hall to her and put his hands on her shoulders. "I don't want you to go. Meg, I want you to stay. At least stay tonight."

A knot formed in her throat and she took a deep breath. A longing to say yes tore at her and she hurt. "I can't stay with you. I'll fall in love, and that would just mean heartbreak because you won't want any kind of real commitment. Even if you did, I can't live with your lifestyle."

His jaw firmed and a cold look filled his eyes. "Dammit, Meg. I'm me. I love my life and doing the things I do. I make a lot of money raising and breeding and selling those rodeo bulls and my cattle. I fly often. I like fast cars. I live and enjoy life."

"Oh, Gabe," she cried, throwing her arms around his neck and crying, sobbing in his arms as he embraced her and held her close. When she could, she stopped and raised her head, telling him the words she never thought she'd speak to him.

"I'm probably already in love with you. But I know I don't love the way you live. I can't deal with it. I don't want to fall in love or be in love with someone who will be killed doing something wild and unnecessary like my brother was. It hurts too badly to lose someone you love, and you've been a part of my life since I was little. I couldn't bear it if something happened to you. And I don't want to be afraid every time you leave the house."

No matter how much she hurt and couldn't stop crying, she couldn't move in with him. She had to walk away, for all those reasons.

Looking grim, he wrapped his arms around her and held her while she clung to him and cried. When she finally managed to get control, she wiped her eyes and looked up at him. "I guess there isn't much else to say."

"I can't change completely, Meg. I'm me and I have to stay that way."

"I can't change either, Gabe."

"Is this our first fight?" he asked. She guessed he was trying to lighten the moment, but a muscle worked in his jaw and his blue eyes had darkened. While she knew he was hurt and angry, she couldn't move in with him. She hurt now, but it would be nothing compared to moving in with him and then having to say goodbye when she left—or when something terrible happened to him.

"It might be our first fight," she replied, but she couldn't smile because she hurt too badly. "We never fought as kids. You were always my best friend and I guess you still are."

"Good luck, Meg. I'll miss you more than you can possibly imagine."

"I'll have to get the rest of my things from your ranch. I'll do that soon, or you bring them to Dallas and I'll pick them up here." She looked up at him. "Thank you, Gabe, for my beautiful necklace. Thank you for everything you did."

"I told you, I wouldn't have missed this for the world. We've known each other forever, but in some ways, you're new in my life." He took her hand. "If you can change your mind, I'm here. Call me anytime, because you'll always be welcome back."

"Thank you, Gabe." She stood on tiptoe to kiss him and he held her tightly, leaning over her and kissing her until she was ready to head back to the bedroom with him. But she knew she had to go.

She hurt all over and was icy cold, shivering, hating every step she took away from him, but she couldn't change how she felt and neither could he.

He watched her drive away and with every bit of distance, she felt as if she was losing a chunk of her heart. She saw him in the rearview mirror as she went down his drive. He stood with his hands on his hips watching her go. She had fallen in love with him and she was leaving her heart behind. How long would it take to get over him? She wondered if she'd ever get over him because she felt as if he was the man she would love the rest of her life.

Tears filled her eyes and fell on her cheeks. She wanted to be in his arms, in his bed. She wanted his cheer and his laughter and his fun. She wanted his friendship that had always been so important to her.

It was over and she would just have to get over him someway. If she thought about all the wild things he did, maybe she wouldn't miss him so much.

She drove home, called the office to tell them she wouldn't be in and then threw herself on the bed, hugging both brown bears as she cried.

Gabe watched Meg drive away and he felt as if he was losing something important in his life. He liked women, had affairs, broke up, said goodbye, remained friends—all of that. But he hadn't ever hurt when he had said goodbye. Not once in his life. And he'd definitely never hurt like he did now.

It was ridiculous. How could she mean that much to him and make him want to be with her? Sometimes she was pure trouble. She didn't like his lifestyle. She was scared of his bulls, scared of his bull riding. She didn't like his fast car and she couldn't bear his motorcycle. Why in the world would he miss her?

She was his best friend in a lot of ways, but he had brothers, a half brother, other best friends. Meg had him in knots half the time. He had assumed she was bringing trouble to his doorstep the first day she showed up and he had been right. His life hadn't been the same since and it wasn't going to swing back to the peace and quiet he'd had before she arrived.

Could it be—

No, he couldn't be in love. He stared down his driveway. He could still see her driving away and it hurt to watch her go.

If she had captured his heart, what the hell would he do about it? He turned and walked back into his house that seemed silent and lifeless. He had never felt that way about his home, either. It was as if she had sailed into his life, turned it upside down, stolen his heart, melted him in bed and then driven right out of his life again, leaving him in shambles and feeling empty and lost.

"Dammit, Meg," he said, frowning. He was going to the ranch, would get her big bag and bring it back here for her to pick up. Maybe he would see her again when she picked it up. Maybe he could even get her to stay for a while.

That thought wasn't at all like him. What the hell had she done to him?

He refused to believe he could be in love with her. That would just be another disaster in his life caused by Meg. He didn't want to give up his way of life, his fun car, his planes. Speaking of his planes... He called to get one ready. Instead of driving to the ranch, he'd fly—and try to get her out of his system. He'd lived without her for years. Surely he could do so again.

"Oh, right," he said aloud. That was before they had kissed or gone to bed together. Her kisses were the most dazzling, bone-melting, instantly arousing kisses ever. And making love with her was the best.

Are you sure you're not in love with her?

"No!" he said emphatically. At least, he hoped to hell he wasn't. If he was in love—heaven forbid—she'd wreck his life. And she wouldn't ever marry him because of the way he lived. He'd managed to live his entire life and not once fall in love. His first time couldn't—wouldn't—be with Meg. That would be disastrous. Sort of. He thought again about kissing her and making love and in minutes he was hard and wanting her.

If this was love, then love was hell.

He nearly ripped off his clothes and changed, then closed up his house.

If he wanted Meg in his life permanently, he'd have to get rid of his bulls—a fine living there. He'd also have to ditch his planes—she didn't know he had two—also ditch his fast car and his Harley. If he married her, which was impossible, she probably wouldn't want him to go out in the rain or snow.

"Damn," he said aloud. It wasn't really living if you were scared of your own shadow. He knew her feelings were 90 percent because of losing her brother, but Hank wouldn't have wanted her to go through life scared of a lot of things.

Gabe got into his car to go to the airport and fly to his ranch. He was going to get her out of his life, out of his thoughts. He just couldn't be in love. Even if she accepted his lifestyle—which she never would—he didn't want to be tied down. That would mean the same woman for the rest of his life. He thought about Meg being with him all the time, in his bed every night, and he broke out in a sweat again.

He swore again as he got out his phone to call her, changed his mind and put it away. They had said goodbye and he was going to leave it that way.

He should have barricaded himself in his house the day he saw her coming up his drive to ask for his help.

Since he hadn't done that, he'd think about other women who could cure him of Meg. Mentally he ran through a list of beauties he'd been interested in. That lasted about thirty seconds before Meg returned to his thoughts. He remembered how she had looked when she had opened the door and he had faced a stunning blonde that he hadn't even recognized. He groaned, and wondered if she had changed his life irrevocably. He looked down at his speedometer and took his foot off the gas. He was going faster than even he thought his car should be driven.

He needed to get a grip and stop thinking about her. Even if he was in love, it couldn't be serious and she would fade into the background soon. She had to, because right now his life was hell without her.

Meg tried everything. She threw herself into her business, working harder and longer in order to be so exhausted she would sleep at night instead of lying awake thinking about Gabe. But that didn't work. She missed him. Without him, she felt a huge void in her life. She was beginning to think she wasn't ever going to get over him.

He had called and told her he had her bag at his Dallas home. But she had appointments and schedules to keep, customers who wanted landscaping plans, and she hadn't picked up the bag yet.

She was trying to forget him while at the same time she wanted to see him again. But she felt that when she went to get her bag it would be the last time she would see Gabe, and she couldn't face that.

She looked at the picture a friend had sent her, the one she'd shoved into a pile on her desk. It was a picture of Gabe in the restaurant on his knee, proposing to her.

The picture made her laugh, but it also made her long to be with him and remember all the fun they'd had together, plus the hot sex. Just thinking about that made her want his strong arms around her. She threw the photo into the desk drawer.

After he called twice about her bag, offering to bring it to her, she decided she should go get it. She made arrangements to take time from the office, called Gabe and finally set a time to pick it up on Wednesday. It had been a week since she had last seen him but it seemed as if it had been months.

Wednesday morning, she wound up his drive to his Dallas house and saw him waiting on the porch for her arrival. He was in a white shirt without a tie, charcoal slacks and his black boots. Her pulse sped up as he came out to meet her.

"Hi, come in. You don't have to grab your stuff and

go. Let's have coffee and you can tell me what's happening."

She wanted to decline the invitation, until she looked into his blue eyes and started tingling all over. Then she followed him inside.

"Nothing's happening, really," she said. "I've been busy with yards and pools, landscaping." She shrugged.

She wasn't sure how much he heard because his gaze was glued to her mouth. "I've missed you like hell," he said.

"I missed you, Gabe," she whispered, fighting the urge to throw her arms around him. He looked incredible with locks of his black hair falling on his forehead, a shadow of stubble on his jaw. The sight of him made her heart race.

"We wouldn't have any kind of future together, would we?"

His question hurt because it just emphasized their differences. She shook her head. "No, because I still can't take your lifestyle," she said, thinking about her brother's needless death, "and I know you can't give it up." They stared at each other in silence for a moment and she felt her heart break once again because there was no hope for a future together.

"Ah, Meg, come here," he said.

Her heart thudded while she walked into his arms eagerly and raised her face for his kiss. It felt like coming home.

It took a few moments before she realized her phone was buzzing in her pocket.

"Gabe, wait," she said. "My phone." She pulled it out and frowned. "It's my dad, and he doesn't call when I'm at work, which is where he thinks I am. I better take it."

She walked away and talked softly and in minutes

returned. "Gabe, I have to go right now. Last week my grandfather fell and he broke his arm and two ribs. The doctors in Colorado said he could travel. My parents want to bring him back here where all his doctors are. Dad and Mom are leaving to go get him as soon as they can get ready. I told them I'd go with them. Mom doesn't like highway driving and it's stormy all through western Kansas and into Colorado."

"Meg, let me fly all of you there. My plane is big enough to get him and bring him back here. Where in Colorado?"

"It's Colorado Springs. But we can't go in your plane."

"Yes, you can. It'll be easier on him and save at least a day of driving. All of you can go. My plane isn't little until you compare it with a Boeing 747."

"I can't do that, Gabe. I can't fly." Already she could feel her heart pounding, just at the thought.

He must have seen the fear in her eyes because he nodded. "You don't have to go. Your folks can come with me. Let me call the airport and get some information and get things ready."

She frowned, staring at him. She didn't want to fly and she didn't want to risk her family, either. On the other hand, Gabe was right. It would be easier on all of them.

In a few minutes, Gabe returned. "The weather is stormy, but it's okay to fly. The plane will be ready shortly. I'm flying and I have a copilot who works for me. He'll meet me at the airport. Call your folks and tell them I have a limo to take us to the airport. They won't object to flying with me, will they? If they do, let me talk to your dad."

"I'll call and you can talk to Dad." In minutes she

handed the phone to Gabe and walked away as he began to tell her father about his pilot qualifications. She stood by a window. It was sunny and a clear day without wind in Dallas. How far could they go before they hit stormy weather? She wound her fingers together and dreaded the flight, but made her decision. She wanted to go along.

Gabe turned to her and held out her phone. "Your folks are going. As soon as the limo gets here, I'll leave and pick them up." Gabe walked to her and placed his hands on her shoulders. "You don't have to go, Meg, but there's something you need to know. You're too vibrant to go through life being afraid. Life is full of risks, but some are bigger than others. You have to take some risks. You do when you go to work. You do when you fall in love." He dropped his hands and turned away. "I've got to get ready."

"Wait," she called out. "I'm coming."

She saw the smile he tried to hide before he went to pack his things.

A few minutes later she saw a black limo coming up his drive. They went outside and as soon as it stopped, the driver stepped out.

"Thanks, Gene, for getting here so quickly. Meg, this is our driver, Gene Gray. Gene, this is Miss Aldridge. She can give you her parents' address."

By the time they'd picked up her parents and made it to the airport, her heart was pounding so hard she thought it'd burst. But she felt remotely better when she saw the size of the plane.

"Gabe, this plane is a lot bigger than what Hank flew."

"I have two planes. This one is the bigger one. I have one like Hank's that I fly to the ranch."

She felt slightly better that she wasn't flying in a tin can. As Gabe took charge, she followed his directions and in no time she and her parents were on board, seated and comfortable in a plush lounge.

Gabe turned to her. "Okay?"

"So far." She even managed a small smile. "I have to tell you, you've impressed my dad."

"Good," he said. "Once we're up, the flight attendant will pass out drinks, pillows and magazines," he told her. "Just relax."

Meg buckled up as Gabe made his way to the cockpit. Minutes later she gripped the seat with white knuckles as the plane picked up speed going down the runway. She held her breath until they were finally airborne, lifting quickly, making a wide circle and heading north.

They had good weather until they were over Kansas. Gabe kept them posted at regular intervals and they were making good time when they flew into clouds. Cold fear gripped her and she couldn't relax. Her parents had fallen asleep and Meg wished she was able to do the same.

The flight became bumpy and she hated every jolt. She couldn't see out the window because of the thick gray clouds surrounding them and she couldn't imagine how Gabe could tell where he was flying, even with instruments and electronics and everything else he had. And how would they land?

Her mother woke up and looked at her, wide-eyed as she glanced outside. She looked at Meg's dad and then leaned toward Meg. "Are you all right?"

"I'm fine," Meg lied. She hated the flight and wanted it to be over and dreaded having to go back. They weren't flying back until the next day and she prayed the weather would be better then.

For the next hour, the plane hit more turbulence and she clutched the seat and closed her eyes. By the time the flight became smooth again, they were landing.

Gabe stood waiting as she stepped to the door behind her parents. He moved close to slip his arm around her waist. "How're you doing? You made it."

"Barely."

"But you did it. It might get easier." He smiled at her and squeezed her lightly.

He had a limo waiting for them that took them straight to Meg's aunt's house, where Gabe met her aunt and uncle and saw her grandmother again and spoke to her grandfather briefly. He was seated in a comfortable chair with his arm in a sling, the only obvious sign of his fall.

When Gabe got up to leave, Meg followed him outside and closed the door behind her. The air was cool even though it was summer, and she wrapped her arms around her middle. "Thank you for flying us here, Gabe."

"I was glad to. Tomorrow the weather should be good and the flight will be better."

She didn't want to say goodbye to him, but she knew he couldn't stay. "Well, I better go back in." She turned to open the door but he stopped her.

He pulled her to him, flush against him, and his body seemed to burn right through her. "Damn, it's good to be with you, even if it was just for that plane ride. I've missed you."

Her heart thudded and she held him tightly. "I've missed you, Gabe," she answered solemnly. She didn't want to miss him, didn't want to be so glad to have his arms around her. But she couldn't deny that was how she felt.

He leaned away to look at her and then he kissed her, and she kissed him in return, unable to resist him.

"I'll see you in the morning." She watched him get into the limo and it drove away before she went back in to join the family.

The next day the flight home was uneventful. The clouds were white puffs in a blue sky, the flight was smooth and her parents and grandparents were happily talking. She sat back in the plush, comfortable lounge and tried to relax.

Was she throwing away a lifetime of happiness because she was too scared to live and take some risks? She thought about Gabe at the controls. He hadn't been a wreck worrying about the weather yesterday. He was right about life being filled with risks. Would her fears cause her to miss out on a life with the man she loved?

Maybe she was focusing too much on dangers and not looking at what she would miss.

She loved Gabe with all her heart. Would his love be worth taking risks? Could she live with his wild ways if it meant also living with his love? He wasn't into commitment—could she accept that?

She couldn't answer her own questions, but she began to do a lot of thinking.

All her worries about this flight had been for nothing and it was far better than driving through blinding rain for days. Was she going through life with an unfounded anxiety about ordinary living? Not to mention some things that weren't so ordinary—like Gabe's rodeo bulls. She wondered if she was cutting herself out of what she really loved by being afraid to take some risks, and if she could find a way to live with Gabe's fearless ways.

After her parents and grandparents were home, she rode to Gabe's house in the limo. Her car was still at his house and she had to get her bag, as well.

As soon as they stepped inside his house and Gabe closed the door, he took her into his arms. "Ah, Meg, come here," he said.

Her heart thudded as she went into his arms eagerly and raised her face for his kiss, knowing exactly where this would lead.

Over two hours later, she shifted in bed as she lay in the crook of his arm.

He caressed her shoulder lightly. "Darlin', I've had time to think about us. I don't like life without you."

His words thrilled her and scared her.

"Gabe, I thought about us on the way back today and maybe you're right. Maybe my anxieties are cutting me out of what I want most. But that would be a huge change for me and I can't just flip a switch." She pulled back so she could see his face. "I can't suddenly say I don't care if you ride bulls or your Harley or fly your planes, but I do feel differently about it. Give me some time and let's both think about being together."

A smile broke out across his face. "Darlin', that's progress. Take all the time you need." His expression grew more somber. "But I hope it's not a lot of time. I really miss you."

"We need some space to think about what we mean to each other, Gabe."

"So does this mean moving in with me is out of the question?" he teased.

"Moving in with you would be a giant step for me. Besides, you aren't into a lasting commitment. If I lived with you, I'd fall in love more and more every day.

And then someday it would be over for you, and then what happens to me? I've got to think about dealing with that."

It didn't go unnoticed by her that he remained quiet. He merely held her closer, against the beating of his heart.

"Right now, Gabe, I need to get home. I had appointments I missed at work." She kissed him again and rolled away to step out of bed, go shower and dress.

Later, when she stood at his door after they kissed goodbye, she smiled at him. "Gabe, once again, you were the knight to my rescue. Thank you."

"You think about us and you call me, darlin'. But just remember that I really want you and I'm going to miss you more than I can tell you."

"And you do the same, Gabe."

She knew she should learn to live with and accept more risks in her life because some of her worries existed more in her imagination. But not all of them. There was no getting away from some of the risks he took. But there was another issue keeping them apart. Could she live with him, love him more than ever and then have him walk away sometime in the future?

If she moved in with him, she wanted it to be permanent and she knew he didn't. And if it wasn't permanent she worried that would eventually hurt her way more than telling him goodbye now. Did she want to risk a giant hurt for a month or two of living with him and then having him leave her? He always left the women in his life. Would she be fooling herself if she thought she would be different?

Eleven

Gabe spent the next week on his ranch doing the hardest physical work he could find. He had a call from his office in Dallas about a large business complex in Houston his company had for sale and complications because the buyers wanted possession within the next two months. He handed the call off to someone at the office. He had no desire to sit on the phone for hours.

At night he hated going home. The house was empty and his bed was empty. He missed Meg more each day instead of less. He caught himself at times during the day looking at her pictures that were on his phone. "I love you and I miss you," he said to the pictures.

As he worked putting up a new gate, he stopped, wiped his forehead and stared into space. Meg had said she would rethink her worries about his lifestyle and he had told her to call him, but so far he hadn't heard anything. His lifestyle was still between them and keeping Meg from moving in. Could he change anything, give up anything that might make her compromise? He picked up a board to saw it in two while he thought about the things he wanted to do the most, the things he enjoyed the most, the things she might consider the most dangerous.

And what about his lack of commitment? She worried about moving in and falling in love with no promise of permanence. She knew his reputation for never being serious. He'd dated scores of women, but he had never really been in love—until now. Yes, he could finally admit it. He loved Meg.

She had been part of his life forever but now it was different. He wanted more than a friend, and he wanted her more than ever. He was in love and there was no going back to the life he'd had before she showed up at his door. But something had to give. What could he concede? And would she meet him halfway?

He wanted her in his arms, in his bed, and he hadn't slept well since he'd told her goodbye. She'd said she'd missed him, but she had a way of bouncing back in life and going blithely on with what she was involved in and never letting anything really get her down. He thought he could do that, too, until he fell in love with her. For all he knew, she could be dating someone else. That thought sent a cold chill running down his spine.

"Damn, Meg," he said, tossing his tools in the back of his pickup and sliding behind the wheel. He intended to put an end to this right now.

Meg sat at her desk at home a little after ten o'clock at night. She stared at landscape plans for a large yard in an exclusive, gated residential area. She couldn't concentrate on her work. Her mind continually went back to Gabe. She stood up and walked to the kitchen to get another glass of water, lost in memories and thoughts of him.

She missed him. She couldn't concentrate. She didn't want to go out and she avoided going to visit her parents because she didn't want to answer questions and her mother worried because she thought Meg was losing weight.

She picked up the old brown bear on the kitchen counter. "I miss him," she whispered to the bear, its glass eyes staring back at her.

She got a text message, saw it was from Gabe and read swiftly:

I'm on your porch. I need to see you.

Shocked, she dropped the bear and ran toward the front door to yank it open. She couldn't believe it. Gabe stood in front of her and she threw herself into his arms, turning her face up to kiss him as he embraced her.

His arms were tight around her and while he kissed her hard he walked her backward inside where he kicked the door closed. Her heart thudded and joy and sorrow warred within her.

He held her away to look at her. "I've missed you too much. We have to do something. I've thought about what I can give up, to see what you can live with."

Startled, she stared at him as her heart started pounding and joy came rushing back. "You really did that? You'd do that for me?"

"Yes, I will because I don't want to live without you. I need you in my life. You're necessary now, darlin'. I'm hoping for a sort of compromise here."

"Good. 'Cause I've been doing some thinking of

my own. I'm up for a compromise, too. What can you give up?"

"Motorcycles. I've sold mine."

"Oh, my goodness," she said, shocked, and a thrill tickled her to her toes. "Seriously?"

"I'm serious, darlin'. I've never been more serious. Life is hell without you. I love you."

She smiled a huge smile. "You love me? The great love-is-not-for-me Gabe Callahan loves me?" She loved him, and she loved teasing him.

"Yes, darlin', I do." He swept her up in his arms again and gave her a kiss that proved it. Then he set her down and grinned down at her.

"Gabe, I love you with all my heart and I've been miserable without you."

He took her hands in his. "Then let's get through the official stuff so we can get to the good part." She laughed. "So what can you live with?"

"Well, I've been trying to think what I can live with. Believe it or not, your planes will head the list."

"That's good. I get to keep my planes. We're a step closer to getting together." He took off his hat and flicked it onto her sofa. "And I'll give up bull riding in rodeos."

"Oh, Gabe, really? That's enough. Well, maybe one more thing. Don't drive way, way over the speed limit."

"I can live with that. I promise."

Suddenly, she threw her arms around him. "You'd do all that for me? I love you so."

Laughing, he caught her and held her tightly as he leaned close to kiss her. Moments later she pushed away slightly to gaze up at him. "Gabe, I don't want to live in fear. You've shown me that. But there's still one more thing. I can't get so tied to you that I'd never want you to leave, not while you don't want a part of anything permanent."

"Don't decide what I want and what I don't want. Leave that to me." In one smooth motion he picked her off her feet and carried her to the bedroom. He set her on her feet again and looked down at her.

"There's no violin playing, no roses and no fancy setting, but this time I mean it." He went down on one knee in front of her and she thought her heart would burst from her chest when she saw the sincerity in his eyes. "Meg, will you marry me?"

With a screech of joy, she flung her arms around him and kissed him. She didn't need a violin to make this the most perfect proposal she could ever hear. All she needed was Gabe telling her this time it was for real.

He pulled back and gazed into her eyes. "I take it that's a yes?"

She threw her head back and spun around. "Oh, yes!" She vaulted into his arms.

"Wait a minute, Meg. I just realized I'm not doing this right. I should have called your dad and told him I want to marry you, but I was afraid it would cause real problems for us, and also that you might turn me down."

"It's not going to cause problems and I'm not turning you down. Maybe this will end the silly feud," she said, laughing and trying to stand on tiptoe to kiss him while she unbuttoned his shirt.

"Wait a minute, my hot lover." He reached into his pocket and brought out a box tied with a ribbon. "Darlin', I want to spend a lifetime telling you and showing you how much I love you. This is a token of that love."

Her hands were trembling when she took the box from him. She could hardly think straight, she was so dazzled that she would be spending the rest of her life with the man she loved and had always loved. She steadied herself enough to untie the ribbon and open the box. She gasped as she looked at a dazzling diamond solitaire on a band covered in smaller diamonds. "Gabe, this is beautiful. And it's a rock."

"Ten carats. I want the world to know you're my lady and I love you with all my heart. And darlin', I promise to be a better dad than the one I had."

He took the ring and held her hand, looking down at her. "Meg, I can't ever really show you how much I love you, but I want to spend a lifetime trying. You're my best friend, my world. I love you."

"I love you, Gabe. You're my best friend and always have been, and now you're my love," she said, gazing into his blue eyes.

He slipped the ring on her finger and then drew her to him to kiss her. She held him tightly, certain this cowboy had her heart completely and they had a future together that would be filled with joy, laughter and love.

* * * * *

MILLS & BOON®

Desire™

PASSIONATE AND DRAMATIC LOVE STORIES

A sneak peek at next month's titles...

In stores from 18th May 2017:

- **His Accidental Heir** – Joanne Rock
  and **Unbridled Billionaire** – Dani Wade

- **A Texas-Sized Secret** – Maureen Child
  and **Hollywood Baby Affair** – Anna DePalo

- **Claimed by the Rancher** – Jules Bennett
  and **Reunited...and Pregnant** – Joss Wood

Just can't wait?
Buy our books online before they hit the shops!
www.millsandboon.co.uk

Also available as eBooks.

MILLS & BOON®
are delighted to support
World Book Night

World Book Night is run by The Reading Agency and is a national celebration of reading and books which takes place on 23 April every year. To find out more visit worldbooknight.org.

www.millsandboon.co.uk

WB0517_2